Praise for
Restless in Carolina

"Tamara Leigh has done it again. *Restless in Carolina* will have you falling in love with its swoon-inducing romance, characters you won't want to leave behind, and message of hope and healing."

—JENNY B. JONES, four-time Carol Award winner and author
of *Save the Date* and *Just Between You and Me*

"Tamara Leigh is a master storyteller who weaves deep spiritual threads with quirky characters that I love. With *Restless in Carolina,* she returns to Pickwick, North Carolina, where Bridget has determined that happily ever afters don't exist and God isn't fair. Open the book and be swept into her journey, one filled with laughter, tears, and a large supporting cast that will make it seem like a return to a favorite vacation spot for readers of her other Pickwick books."

—CARA C. PUTMAN, author of *Stars in the Night*

"Wonderful wry humor, a plot that kept me glued, and delightful, unique characters—what more could a reader ask? Tamara Leigh has given us southern living with down-home charm and thoughtful insights all wrapped up in joy. Highly recommended!"

—GAYLE ROPER, author of *Shadows on the Sand*
and *A Rose Revealed*

"She's as southern as fried chicken, but Bridget Buchanan is no Scarlett O'Hara. She's spunky, quirky, and determined to save the world from environmental destruction—starting with her own family's estate. This southern gal loves faithfully, grieves deeply, and touches tender places in our hearts. A great story!"

—VIRGINIA SMITH, author of *Third Time's a Charm*
and the Sister-to-Sister Series

"Tamara Leigh creates another of her quirky heroines, Bridget Pickwick Buchanan, in *Restless in Carolina*. Bridget is sassy and unconventional, a green peg in a brown hole. She meets her match in J. C. Dirk. Don't miss an entertaining read about forgiving past wrongs and even the ones we love who make us crazy."

—LYN COTE, author of *Her Abundant Joy*

Restless
in
Carolina

Restless
in
Carolina

A Novel

Tamara Leigh

MULTNOMAH
BOOKS

RESTLESS IN CAROLINA
PUBLISHED BY MULTNOMAH BOOKS
12265 Oracle Boulevard, Suite 200
Colorado Springs, Colorado 80921

Scripture quotations or paraphrases are taken from the following versions: Holy Bible, New International Version®. NIV®. Copyright © 1973, 1978, 1984 by Biblica, Inc.™ Used by permission of Zondervan. All rights reserved worldwide. www.zondervan.com. New King James Version®. Copyright © 1982 by Thomas Nelson Inc. Used by permission. All rights reserved.

The characters and events in this book are fictional, and any resemblance to actual persons or events is coincidental.

ISBN: 978-1-60142-168-5
ISBN: 978-1-60142-361-0 (electronic)

Cover design: Kristopher K. Orr

Published in association with the literary agency of Alive Communications Inc., 7680 Goddard Street, Suite 200, Colorado Springs, CO 80920, www.alivecommunications.com.

Published in the United States by WaterBrook Multnomah, an imprint of the Crown Publishing Group, a division of Random House Inc., New York.

MULTNOMAH and its mountain colophon are registered trademarks of Random House Inc.

Library of Congress Cataloging-in-Publication Data
Leigh, Tamara.
    Restless in Carolina : a novel / Tamara Leigh. — 1st ed.
        p. cm. — (Southern discomfort series ; bk. 3)
    ISBN 978-1-60142-168-5 (alk. paper) — ISBN 978-1-60142-361-0 (electronic: alk. paper)
    1. Women environmentalists—Fiction. 2. North Carolina—Fiction. I. Title.
    PS3612.E3575R47 2011
    813'.6—dc22

                                        2011003735

Printed in the United States of America
2011—First Edition

10 9 8 7 6 5 4 3 2 1

*I dedicate this fourteenth book to my readers,
especially those who have supported me since my first book,*
Warrior Bride, *was published in 1994 and who stayed with me
through the transition from the secular to the inspirational market.*

*Thank you for believing in me and allowing me to weave
my faith journey through the characters who tumble
around in my head whispering, "Me next."*

*It has been an amazing eighteen years.
I couldn't have experienced them as fully without you.*

> *Your presence is eagerly anticipated*
> *at the wedding of*
> *Ms. Trinity Templeton to Mr. Bart Pickwick*
> *on Saturday, July 24, 10:00 a.m.*
> *at the Pickwick Mansion*
> *1001 Pickwick Pike*
> *Pickwick, North Carolina*
> *Reception to immediately follow*
> *Regrets Only*

Deep breath. "…and they lived…"

I can do this. It's not as if I didn't sense it coming. After all, I can smell an *H.E.A.* (Happily Ever After) a mile away—or, in this case, twenty-four pages glued between cardboard covers that feature the requisite princess surrounded by cute woodland creatures. And there are the words, right where I knew the cliché of an author would slap them, on the last page in the same font as those preceding them. Deceptively nondescript. Recklessly hopeful. Heartbreakingly false.

"Aunt Bridge," Birdie chirps, "finish it."

I look up from the once-upon-a-time crisp page that has been softened, creased, and stained by the obsessive readings in which her mother indulges her.

Eyes wide, cheeks flushed, my niece nods. "Say the magic words."

Magic?

More nodding, and is she quivering? Oh no, I refuse to be a party to this. I smile big, say, "The end," and close the book. "So, how about another piece of weddin' cake?"

"No!" She jumps off the footstool she earlier dubbed her "princess throne," snatches the book from my hand, and opens it to the back. "Wight here!"

I almost correct her initial *r*-turned-*w* but according to my sister, it's developmental and the sound is coming in fine on its own, just as her other *r*'s did.

Birdie jabs the *H, E,* and *A.* "It's not the end until you say the magic words."

And I thought this the lesser of two evils—entertaining my niece and nephew as opposed to standing around at the reception as the bride and groom are toasted by all the happy couples, among them, cousin Piper, soon to be wed to my friend Axel, and cousin Maggie, maybe soon to be engaged to her sculptor man, what's-his-name.

"Yeah," Birdie's twin, Miles, calls from where he's once more hanging upside down on the rolling ladder I've pulled him off twice. "You gotta say the magic words."

Outrageous! Even my dirt-between-the-toes, scab-ridden, snot-on-the-sleeve nephew is buying into the fantasy.

I spring from the armchair, cross the library, and unhook his ankles from the rung. "You keep doin' that and you'll bust your head wide open." I set him on his feet. "And your mama will—" No, Bonnie won't. "Well, she'll be tempted to give you a whoopin'."

Face bright with upside-down color, he glowers.

I'd glower back if I weren't so grateful for the distraction he provided. "All right, then." I slap at the ridiculously stiff skirt of the dress Maggie loaned me for my brother's wedding. "Let's rejoin the party—"

"You don't wanna say it." Miles sets his little legs wide apart. "Do ya?"

So much for my distraction.

"You don't like Birdie's stories 'cause they have happy endings. And you don't."

I clench my toes in the painfully snug high heels on loan from Piper.

"Yep." Miles punches his fists to his hips. "Even Mama says so."

My own sister? I shake my head, causing the blond dreads Maggie pulled away from my face with a headband to sweep my back. "That's not true."

"Then say it wight now!" Birdie demands.

I peer over my shoulder at where she stands like an angry tin soldier, an arm outthrust, the book extended.

"Admit it," Miles singsongs.

I snap around and catch my breath at the superior, knowing look on his *five*-year-old face. He's his father's son, all right, a miniature Professor Claude de Feuilles, child development expert.

"You're not happy." The professor in training, who looks anything but with his spiked hair, nods.

I know better than to bristle with two cranky, nap-deprived children, but that's what I'm doing. Feeling as if I'm watching myself from the other side of the room, I cross my arms over my chest. "I'll admit no such thing."

"That's 'cause you're afraid. Mama said so." Miles peers past me. "Didn't she, Birdie?"

Why is Bonnie discussing my personal life with her barely-out-of-diapers kids?

"Uh-huh. She said so."

Miles's smile is smug. "On the drive here, Mama told Daddy this day would be hard on you. That you wouldn't be happy for Uncle Bart 'cause you're not happy."

Not true! Not that I'm thrilled with our brother's choice of bride, but…come on! *Trinity Templeton?* Nice enough, but she isn't operating on a full charge, which wouldn't be so bad if Bart made up for the difference. Far from it, his past history with illegal stimulants having stripped him of a few billion brain cells.

"She said your heart is"—Miles scrunches his nose, as if assailed by a terrible odor—"constipated."

What?!

"That you need an M&M, and I don't think she meant the chocolate kind you eat. Probably one of those—"

"I am *not* constipated." *Pull back. Nice and easy.* I try to heed my inner voice but find myself leaning down and saying, "I'm realistic."

Birdie stomps the hardwood floor. "Say the magic words!"

"Nope." Miles shakes his head. "Constipated."

I shift my cramped jaw. "Re-al-is-tic."

"Con-sti-pa-ted."

Pull back, I tell you! He's five years old. "Just because I don't believe in fooling a naive little girl into thinkin' a prince is waiting for her at the other end of childhood and will save her from a fate worse than death and take her to his castle and they'll live…" I flap a hand. "…you know, doesn't mean there's anything wrong with me."

Isn't there? "It means I know better. There may be a prince, and he may have a castle, and they may be happy, but don't count on it lasting. Oh no. He'll get bored or caught up in work or start cheatin'—you know, decide to put that glass slipper on some other damsel's foot or kiss another sleeping beauty—or he'll just up and die like Easton—" *No, nothing at all wrong with you, Bridget Pickwick Buchanan, whose ugly widow's weeds are showing.*

"See!" Miles wags a finger.

Unfortunately, I do. And as I straighten, I hear sniffles.

"Now you done it!" Miles hustles past me. "Got Birdie upset."

Sure enough, she's staring at me with flooded eyes. "The prince dies? He dies and leaves the princess all alone?" The book falls from her hand, its meeting with the floor echoing around the library. Then she squeaks out a sob.

"No!" I spring forward, grimacing at the raspy sound the skirt makes as I attempt to reach Birdie before Miles.

He gets there first and puts an arm around her. A meltable moment, my mother would call it. *After* she gave me a dressing down. And I deserve one. My niece may be on the spoiled side and she may work my nerves, but I love her—even *like* her when that sweet streak of hers comes through.

"It's okay, Birdie," Miles soothes. "The prince doesn't die."

Yes, he does, but what possessed me to say so? And what if I've scarred her for life?

Miles pats her head onto his shoulder. "Aunt Bridge is just"—he gives me the evil eye—"constipated."

"Yes, Birdie." I drop to my knees. "I am. My heart, that is. Constipated. I'm so sorry."

She turns her head and, upper lip shiny with the stuff running out of her nose, says in a hiccupy voice, "The prince doesn't die?"

I grab the book from the floor and turn to the back. "Look. There they are, riding off into the sunset—er, to his castle. Happy. See, it says so." I tap the *H, E,* and *A.*

She sniffs hard, causing that stuff to whoosh up her nose and my gag reflex to go on alert. "Weally happy, Aunt Bridge?"

"Yes."

"Nope." Barely-there eyebrows bunching, she lifts her head from Miles's shoulder. "Not unless you say it."

Oh dear Go— No, He and I are not talking. Well, He may be talking, but I'm not listening.

"I think you'd better." Miles punctuates his advice with a sharp nod.

"Okay." I look down at the page. "…and they lived…" *It's just a fairy tale—highly inflated, overstated fiction for tykes.* "…they lived happily…ever…after."

Birdie blinks in slow motion. "Happily…ever…after. That's a nice way to say it, like you wanna hold on to it for always."

Or unstick it from the roof of your mouth. "The end." I close the book, and it's all I can do not to toss it over my shoulder. "Here you go."

She clasps it to her chest. "Happily…ever…after."

Peachy. But I'll take her dreamy murmuring over tears any day. Goodness, I can't believe I made her cry. I stand and pat the skirt back down into its stand-alone shape. "More cake?"

"Yay!" Miles charges past me.

Next time— No, there won't be a next time. I'm done with Little Golden Books.

Birdie hurries to catch up with her brother. "I want a piece of chocolate cake."

I want to go home. And curl up in my hammock. And listen for the hot air to stir up a breeze and creak the leaves. And try not to think about my lost happily ever after. I set my shoulders and thoughts against memories and check my watch. I've been in this dress and these shoes for four hours. It's time.

Outside the library, I pause at the grand staircase, step out of the heels, and try to flex my toes. They're numb. I declare, if I have to have anything amputated, someone will hear about it. I retrieve the shoes and hobble into the hallway, through the kitchen, and outside into a bright day abuzz with wedding revelry.

No matter the season, the beauty of Uncle Obe's garden always gets to me, especially now that it and the entire Pickwick estate will be passing out of Pickwick hands. For months I've about killed myself trying to find a way around the sale that will provide restitution to those our family has wronged as well as something of an inheritance to kin, but everywhere I turn, I find walls.

"Hey, babies," my sister's voice rings out, "did you have fun with Aunt Bridge?"

I halt and look toward the linen-covered table, where a large three-tiered wedding cake was the centerpiece earlier. Only one tier remains, and it's had its share of knifings.

"Yeah, it was okay." Miles holds out a plate for his mother to fill. "Until she made Birdie cry."

My little sister's gasp shoots around those standing in the twenty feet between us. "What happened?"

"Aunt Bridge didn't want to finish the book. Did she, Birdie?"

Hugging it to her, she shakes her head.

"Well," Bonnie slides a piece of cake onto each of their plates, "maybe she's tired."

"Nuh-uh." Miles leans his face into the cake, takes a bite, and with crumbs spilling and frosting flecking, says, "She told us the prince gave the glass slipper to another girl and kissed Sleeping Beauty and then died."

"Oh." Bonnie's lids flutter. "Huh." Sunlight glints off the knife in her hand as she meets my gaze. "Well." She forces a smile. "Hmm." Back to her daughter. "We know that's not true, don't we, Roberta baby?"

Birdie bounces her head. "They lived happily…ever…after."

Time to go. But as much as I long to run, I'm civilized, despite rumors to the contrary. I search out my brother where he stands with his bride, Trinity, my mother and father, and Uncle Obe in the gazebo built for the reception. A quick congratulations and I'm out of here.

"Bridget!"

I hurry past Maggie's brother and his latest wife, around Uncle Obe's attorney, between—

"Don't think I don't know you can hear me, Bridget."

And so can everyone else. I swing around. "Bonbon!"

Bonnie rushes the last few feet. "I know we're mostly family here, but I'll do you the kindness of talking to you in private." She points to the mansion.

I don't care to accompany her, but neither do I want to throw a shadow over Bart's special day. And going by the eyes turning our way, it's fast approaching. "Of course." I set off ahead of her, raise my eyebrows at Maggie when she turns a worried face to me, and give Piper a shrug.

In the kitchen, I cross to the pantry and raise my hands in surrender. "I didn't mean to say what I did. I certainly didn't mean to make Birdie cry."

Bonnie steps near, causing my hackles to rise. I don't like sharing my personal space, even with my own sister. My *hotheaded* sister. And then she goes and puts a finger in my face, and I have the urge to bite it. But I won't. That would end badly.

"I trust you with my most precious possessions," Mama Bear growls, "and what do you do? Try to steal my babies' sweetness and innocence with that 'life is dark' outlook of yours."

"I'm sorry. I'm just on edge, what with tryin' to find a buyer for the estate who won't turn it into a crowded development or a nasty theme park. And now Uncle Obe has listed it, and the real estate agents are swarmin'. It's too much, Bonbon."

She narrows her lids. "Don't you Bonbon me!"

Though she's five foot two, one hundred ten pounds to my five foot six, one hundred twenty pounds, I know she could take me down if I riled her enough to forget we're grown women. But that's not the reason I pull back on my emotions. I do it because I'm the one who lost control in front of her twins. I clear my throat. "I didn't mean to—"

"Yes, you did!" The finger again. "You can't stand for anybody to be happy if you aren't happy."

Ignore the finger. "That's not true." My throat strains from the effort to keep my voice level. "I—"

"Woe is me. My husband's dead, and I refuse to get over it. Even though he's *four* years gone!"

I suck breath. *Oh, God. I mean, no! I'm not talking to You. Of course,*

I could use a little self-control if You've got some lying around. But that doesn't mean I'm talking to You.

"Have mercy on us, Bridget, 'cause you know what? Grief is contagious. And I don't want my babies catchin' it."

A chill goes through me. I never thought of grief as contagious, but I suppose it could be.

"So stop casting your widowhood like a net, catching others in it and saying stuff like that just because Easton is dead."

Just because? I feel warm again. "Maybe…" My voice sounds all wet and boogered up with that stuff that boogered Birdie's nose. "Maybe I said it because my *constipated* heart needs an M&M."

Bonnie startles so hard I find myself checking the whereabouts of my hands to be certain I didn't slap her. Not that I would, although she might slap me.

"Oh." She steps back and gives a nervous laugh. "They told you I said that?"

Having regained some of my personal space, my shoulders unbind. "Out of the mouths of babes."

"Uh, yeah. I didn't realize they were listenin'. They had their earphones in and were singing along with their iPods." She frowns. "Or so I thought."

I pull a hand down my face. It's a good thing I never took to makeup. "It's all right. I know you didn't mean it to hurt me."

She raises her hands palms up. "I needed to talk it out with Claude. You know how I worry about you."

Not really, but we live a ways from each other, averaging two visits a year when she and her family drive through on their way to elsewhere.

However, that pattern will be broken when my sister and her husband leave the twins with their grandparents for eight weeks while they're in the Ukraine to study the development of children awaiting adoption. My mother will have her hands full, but I'll help however I can.

"I really am sorry for what I said to Birdie and Miles. It won't happen again."

Once more, Bonnie invades my space, and this time I'm the one who startles when she lays a hand on my cheek. "Oh, Bridget, how are you going to keep that promise when you're still wrapped up in all those widow's weeds?"

Don't pull back. It's your sister, not a "widow sniffer" trying to get a hook into the lonely little widow. Pressing my dry lips, I long for my Burt's Bees lip balm. "I've accepted my loss. It's just taking me longer than some to adjust. But I am adjustin'."

Her eyes snap to slits. "Really?"

"Yes."

"No, if you were adjusting, you wouldn't still be clinging to your wedding ring."

I catch my breath. "There's nothing wrong with wearing it."

"Yes, there is." She grabs my hand and lifts it before my face. "It's time. *Past* time. You have to let him go."

I do *not* like this. "I have. I accept he's gone—"

"No, not *gone*. That implies he can come back. He's dead. And you have to call it what it is and get on with your life. Not yours and Easton's life. *Your* life."

I pull my hand free. "I'm getting there."

"Well, at this rate, you'll be in your own grave before you arrive."

My own grave… I feel cold. At thirty-three, if I live to see my body stoop and shrivel, that will be a very long time. Like one big unending yawn.

Bonnie tilts her chin forward. "That makes me plain sad, so take off the ring."

Now? That's asking too much. "I will when—"

"Take it off."

"But—"

"You made my little girl cry!"

I did. And though I don't care to look too deeply into myself, here I am, still holding tight to my interrupted life with Easton.

"Give me your hand."

I don't want to, and yet I raise my arm.

With surprising gentleness, Bonnie cups my fingers in hers. "It's for the best. I promise."

I hold my breath, and she tugs. And tugs. Then wrenches.

"Ow!" I try to pull free, but she sets her jaw and lifts her foot, as if to brace it against me for leverage.

"Stop it!" As I push her away, the ring comes free.

"Got it!"

Staring at it between her thumb and forefinger, I feel the air go out of me. How long before my deflated self pools on the floor? It doesn't happen. I miss the constriction around my finger, and I may be a bit numb, but that's it. Am I in shock?

"You okay, Bridge?"

"I think so."

She presses the ring into my palm. "Put that in a good place where you won't be looking at it every day."

I close my fingers around it. How's that for a good place?

She smoothes her blouse. "Now let's go outside so everyone will see I didn't yank out those ugly dreadlocks of yours."

"They aren't ugly."

"They aren't beautiful. Just"—she waves at my head—"more widow's weeds."

She's not the first to call them that, seeing as Easton had dreads and always wanted me to try them. Unfortunately, God didn't give him a chance to see how well I wear them. No, God had other plans for my man, and they didn't include me. If ever there was a reason not to talk to Him or His Son, there it is.

"Those are next," Bonnie says.

"What?"

"The dreads have to go."

I want to argue, but I don't have the energy. Besides, maybe she's right. Since that night on the mansion's roof months ago when a dread caught in the telescope and I had to cut it free, I've considered returning to my formerly undreaded locks that once fell soft and fluid down my back.

"Bridget?" She worries her bottom lip. "I know you have a business to run, but when Miles and Birdie come to stay in September, you will help Mama, won't you?"

"Of course."

Her gaze intensifies. "I mean really help—take them off her hands overnight and some weekends."

Overnight? Weekends? Visits to the park, nature walks, and occasional lunches out are what I had in mind. Though Maggie's daughter, Devyn, sometimes sleeps over, she's the only one I've allowed to do so since I lost Easton. And she either shares the bed in the guest room with me or crashes on the couch. There's no way Birdie, Miles, and I will fit into the guest room's full-size bed. ·

"It's going to be a long eight weeks for"—Bonnie's voice cracks—"everyone."

I can't remember the last time I saw her so sorrowful. Was she ever? I have a sudden impulse to give her a hug, but she's not a hugger, and since Easton's death, I've related to this side of her.

"So?" She prompts.

She's not asking much. And it's not as if she even knows what she's asking. Or does she? Keeping Birdie and Miles overnight fits nicely with her demand that I remove my wedding ring. *Which is only a problem if you plan to live the rest of your life in mourning and persist in making little girls cry.*

"Bridget!"

Out of my mouth pops, "I'd be happy to keep them overnight."

Bonnie's body eases. "Thank you."

I can handle it—once I get used to my bare left hand. And it is six weeks before my niece and nephew return to Pickwick. Surely between now and then I can…well, reset my life.

"Eight weeks didn't seem long when we started planning the study a year ago, but now…" Bonnie sniffs, only to snort. "My period must be coming. We won't be gone that long, for goodness' sake! And this *is* our last opportunity to conduct a full-fledged study abroad before the children start school."

Is the study the reason Miles and Birdie aren't enrolled in school this year? The newly minted five-year-olds certainly seem bright enough to start kindergarten.

Bonnie points a finger at me. "No more tales of heroes dying."

"I won't make that mistake again."

"Good. Let's get back to the party."

Over the next two hours, I stand on the sidelines, watching happily married couples as my finger silently mourns the loss of its constant companion. Time and again, I touch it through the dress's crisscrossed top where I slipped the ring into my bra. I know it's just a symbol of the love Easton and I shared, but on *my* wedding day, I'd believed I would wear it to the grave after years and years with the man I loved. I didn't even come close. And as I watch Trinity with her Bart, Piper with her Axel, and Bonnie with her Claude, I force myself to put a name to what earlier made me retreat inside the big house.

Envy.

An ache opens at my center and radiates out to the ends. I want what they have—one another. All I have is "one." My "another" is gone, and every time I think about opening my eyes to other men, I'm set upon by guilt and uncertainty. After all, it may have been four years, but Easton wasn't a coffeepot that needs replacing every so often. He was my love. How could I ever have another? And yet…

My cousin Maggie puts her head on the shoulder of what's-his-name. I frown. What *is* his name? Since it looks like he plans on being a major part of her life, I ought to make more of an effort to—Reece! That's his name. Reece, who runs his fingers through her red curls, tilts her chin up, and kisses her.

My hand goes to my ring, but the feel of it does little to ease my longing for a shoulder on which to lay my head…a mouth to make mine flush…a heart to make mine jump…

2

S he did not do that. Oh yes, she did—chucked her gum out the window, which landed on my windshield, after she crossed a double yellow line into the oncoming lane and flew past me, after she honked at my unavoidable deceleration up a particularly steep rise on Pickwick Pike. If that doesn't beat all, according to her magnetic door sign, she's a real estate agent.

Let it go, Bridget.

"I know," I mutter, doing my best to reduce the gum in the corner of my windshield to a blur, "but…" It's been one of those days, and so near a total loss I don't see how anything I do can make it much worse.

Bringing the gum back into focus, I put the pedal to the metal, causing Buchanan's Nursery truck to lurch and growl. Fortunately, with a bit of prodding and flattery—and now that I'm on the other side of the incline—I can always count on my trusty Ford to pick up speed. "You can do it. You're strong. And not bad lookin' either." Beauty is in the eye of the beholder.

Before long I'm riding the bumper of the sporty little Cadillac, honking and blinking my lights and motioning for the litterbug to pull over. But she pays me no mind, just keeps yakking at her passenger—probably a client, and it looks to be a man.

Time to take it to the next level. *Far better you get home to Reggie and let this day wash itself away.*

As the pike curves to the right, the sinking sunlight zings off the roof of the car ahead, nearly blinding me, but I flip my sunglasses on and I'm good to go. Gaining momentum, I swerve into the opposite lane that is empty as far as the eye can see and roar past the Caddy. I'm not rash, so I give the woman plenty of warning, gradually decelerating as I straddle the two lanes so she can't get around me on the narrow road. When I stop, she has no choice but to brake or mess up that shiny grille of hers.

I push open the moan-and-groan door, swing my legs out, and drop to the asphalt, only to remember I'm barefoot—and still wearing Maggie's dress that poufs up around me like an open umbrella. I whack it down as I approach the car.

When I'm twenty feet out, the driver's door swings open, and the woman says, "Gracious no, it's just one of those good ol' girls I told you about. I can handle her."

Oh yeah?

"Besides, I know how important it is we maintain your anonymity."

Obviously, someone full up on himself. As the asphalt heats my feet, almost making me wish for Piper's pointy shoes, I attempt to make out the man on the other side of the windshield. However, he's mostly in shadow.

The woman, jacked up on three-inch heels, steps from the car, closes the door with a swat, and saunters forward to meet me at her front fender. She cants her glossy head to the side, revealing a talkie thing in her ear. "What is your problem?"

Man, the asphalt is hot! I pull off my sunglasses, the better for her to read my eyes. "That would be the gum you tossed out the window a ways back. It's called litterin'. And it's illegal."

Her copper-colored lips part as she stares at me. "All this because of a little piece of gum?"

"That and your reckless driving."

Shifting her gaze past me to my truck, she drawls, "Right, and there's nothing at all reckless about parking in the middle of a two-way road, hmm?"

I open my mouth to tell her there's good line of sight in both directions, that I'm not the one who crossed a double yellow line, and Pickwick Pike is rarely traveled since the new highway exit went in, but she does have something of a point. So I close my mouth and raise my eyebrows.

She plants her manicured hands on her hips. "Look, I have a very important client in the car, and people like you, putting on displays like this, make people like him think Pickwick is uncivilized and unfit to live in."

"I'm okay with that."

She looks me up and down. "Well, of course you are, darlin'."

My imagination momentarily transports me out of my body, and I see myself as I appear before this professional woman and her client—barefoot, wearing a fancy dress a bit too long, a bit too wide, and way too stiff, no makeup, and dreads hanging down my back. And mustn't forget the backdrop of my battered Ford. Oh, to be in a pair of jeans, not too long, not too wide, and soft as peach fuzz. And my Crocs. If I don't get off this asphalt soon, I'm gonna be blistered.

The woman checks her watch. "I need to get back to Asheville."

I shift my weight to my right foot to give my left a break. "Just as soon as you take care of the gum."

With a chicken bob of her head, she says, "You expect me to go back and scrape it off the road?"

"You're in luck. It's stuck to my windshield." I hitch a thumb over my shoulder.

She rolls her eyes. "Honestly!"

"I have all day." I fold my arms over my chest.

She peers beyond me, as if to calculate the likelihood of squeezing past my truck without scraping the guardrail on one side and the chiseled-out mountain on the other. Of course, if she waits long enough, eventually a car will come down the pike and I'll be forced to move out of the way.

She huffs. "Fine."

As I start to follow her to my truck, I glance through the Caddy's windshield and catch sight of reflective sunglasses. And a wedge of white teeth.

Yes, this is a peculiar situation, and I might find humor in it if my feet weren't blistering, two five-year-olds hadn't manipulated me into saying *H.E.A.,* and my wedding band wasn't burning a hole in my bra.

I hurry after the woman. "You know, if your gum hadn't landed there, it could have become a deathtrap for some critter that got it caught in its craw."

"Uh-huh." She reaches to my windshield only to snatch her hand back, whip around, and splay that same hand in my approaching face. "Oh. My. Word. Hold it!"

I do, ensuring her white-tipped fingernails don't come within a foot of my face. "What?"

"I know you."

I look closer at her. "No, you don't." Unless she knows *of* me, what with me being a scandalous Pickwick, more specifically, she of The

Great Crop Circle Hoax that gained worldwide attention years ago before I exposed my creation for what it was.

With a satisfied smile, she drops her hand. "You're Bridget
Pickwick—"

Buchanan.

"—tree-huggin', animal-lovin' prankster."

"Your point?"

"Cotillion."

Oh. That. "Yes, that was me."

"And your skunk—was it Stripe?"

I'm surprised she knows his name. But then it was in the Asheville
newspaper, along with the headline: "Pickwicks Raise a Stink at Cotillion."
More accurately, Bridget Pickwick, who foiled her mother's attempts to
transform her into a Southern lady by loosing her skunk on the ballroom.

I reconsider my once-fellow debutante—her wide mouth, narrow
nose, and heavily lashed eyes. "I suppose you were there."

"I was. Sprained my big toe and tore my new dress in the stampede."

"Sorry about that. He was deskunked, you know."

"Found that out after the fact." She narrows her lids. "You haven't
changed much, have you?"

Not a compliment. "Thankfully, no." I point at the windshield. "Do
you mind?"

She gives a throaty laugh. "If you ask me, we're more than even."

But— Oh, all right! "Even we are."

She sidesteps. "Thank you for the lesson in environmental stewardship. I can't tell you how it's impacted me." She walks past. "Oh, here's
a little something for you."

When I turn, she's holding out a business card. "Wesley Trousdale, Premier Real Estate Agent." Her smile turns sly. "I have a feelin' we'll meet again soon."

The Pickwick estate. That's probably why she's here all the way from Asheville. The day just gets heavier. "Not likely." Still, I take the card.

As she sways back to her car, I peel the gum from my windshield and climb into my truck. After wrapping the sticky offender in an old paper napkin, I press the accelerator with a foot destined for blisters and pull into the right lane. Not unexpectedly, Wesley Trousdale draws alongside. As she accelerates past, I glimpse the sunglassed face of her anonymous client.

"No, you are not getting your hands on my family's estate," I mutter. Though how in the world I'm going to stop him, I haven't the foggiest.

Ten minutes later, I halt at the end of my long driveway and lower my forehead to the steering wheel. What a day—my brother married to a female version of himself, that whole *H.E.A.* business, the argument with Bonnie, happy couples all around...

I tug a dread—a comfort, especially when I'm missing Easton—then dig my wedding ring out of my bra and stare at its out-of-place shape between my thumb and forefinger. How's Bonnie to know? I start to slide it on, but the pale circle at the base of my finger that contrasts with the tanned length above and below makes me hesitate. It's as if I'm wearing an invisible ring and, actually, I can still feel it there.

Goose bumps rising, I turn the simple band around, reading the words inscribed on the inside: You and me. Forever.

"About as make-believe as *H.E.A.*" However, once more I position the ring to slide it on. *Don't do it. Bonnie's right. When you make little girls cry, it's time to say good-bye. Time to stopper the big yawn between now and the grave and get on with your life. Your life, Bridget. Easton is dead. Dead.*

I try to say the four-letter word, but I can only mouth it. Yes, Easton is. Not just gone, as Bonnie pointed out. He's… Yes, he is.

In the next instant, anger stomps me up one side and down the other. What is my problem? "Easton is dead. D-E-A-D." I curl my fingers around the ring. "And I can say…"

A mental door behind which I haven't looked in a long while creaks open, and I see Easton on our wedding day. It's the first dance. A slow dance. He's so near I can feel the beat of his heart. "And they lived," he lowers his forehead to mine, "happily ever after."

I swallow hard. "No, they didn't." But I can say it. "Happily…" I draw a breath. "…ever after."

Now all I have to do is figure out how to live happily after ever after.

3

The magazine made me do it. More specifically, the man on the cover—J. C. Dirk, whose Florida oceanfront condos have set the new standard for environmentally conscious developments. Forget that he hasn't returned my phone calls and his assistant has become testy. I'm not going away. In fact, since he's so busy, I'm going to him. Just as soon as I've done what I came here to do.

"Ow!" I come up out of the chair only to be pushed back down.

"It's your own fault." Georgia of Sisters' Day Spa, with whom I attended kindergarten through twelfth grade, pulls her hand from my shoulder and frowns at me over the top of her hip, thick-framed glasses. "What'd you expect? They'd come out pretty as you please?" She returns her attention to the dread she's attempting to unravel with a steel-toothed comb. "No ma'am, you don't traipse around in gnarly hair for years and get off that easy." Georgia never much liked me.

"Don't be givin' her a hard time, Georgie." That's older sister Savannah—yes, Savannah and Georgia, whose mother never got over her homesickness when she married into Pickwick, North Carolina.

Savannah, with hands infinitely gentler and personal style finitely more laid back (she wears contacts), continues. "She's here, isn't she? I'd say she's seen the error of her ways."

I've seen no such thing. It's time, is all. Under cover of the itchy cape, I rub the ring suspended from a chain around my neck. Unfortunately, the quest for J. C. Dirk has pushed up the timetable. The only reason I haven't suffered much backlash from wearing dreads all these years is because I own and work a nursery, but if I'm going to gain an audience with the environmentally conscious developer, I have to fit into his world. And according to the article in the magazine I stumbled on two weeks ago, my dreadlocks are not a normal part of his uppity world.

"Isn't that right, Bridget?" Savannah leans to the side to meet my gaze in the beauty station's mirror.

As much as I'd like to challenge the "error of my ways," the sisters have personal experience with them, even though my erroneous ways predate today by more than a dozen years. Too, I am at their mercy. And they came in after hours so this could be done without gossips looking on.

I clear my throat. "I've certainly made mistakes in my life"—such as believing in happily ever after—"but I'm headin' in the right direction."

" 'Course you are." Savannah pats my shoulder before once more ducking out of sight to work on the dreads at the back of my head.

"Goodness!" Georgia jerks the comb through a conditioner-drenched dread.

"Ow! Oh, ow!" I'm up out of the chair again. And down.

"I can't do this if you don't hold still," Georgia snaps.

Savannah gives my watery-eyed reflection a sympathetic smile. "I know it hurts, but we're doin' our best. How about an aspirin?"

"Do you buy them in bulk?"

She laughs, causing her rolled bangs to bounce. "Who woulda thought you had a sense of humor? See, Georgie, she's not so bad."

Georgia thinks I'm *bad*? I'm not surprised, what with her behavior, but it's unfair to continue to hold The Great Crop Circle Hoax against me. And it's not as if her daddy didn't more than make up for the loss of the crop I laid down by charging admission to the thousands who flocked to Pickwick to get a look at what experts deemed "genuine." Of course, maybe she simply doesn't like me because I'm a Pickwick. Or she could be an anti-environmentalist. Or an animal hater. Is it the dreads? All of the above?

"Not so bad," Georgia mutters, wiggling the comb and making no attempt to keep the strain from the roots. "*That's* subjective."

"Here"—Savannah thrusts a bottle at her—"try detangler."

"But her hair's already knee-deep in conditioner."

"I know, but I've taken out nearly two inches for every inch you've undone."

Georgia sprays the end of the dread until it drips. "I don't see why you don't just whack it all off, Bridget. Short hairstyles are in."

I thought it would come to that, which is why I stopped working the new growth into dreads following Bart and Trinity's wedding—to give me a couple inches to fashion into something presentable—but then I ran into Savannah two days ago. Though we rarely exchange more than nods, she stopped me as I was coming out of the Pickwick Arms Hotel next door and told me God had put me on her heart. I started to lug my watering can and tool bag past, but she said that when I was ready to do something about my dreads, she thought she could save most of my hair.

Her timing gave me chills, but I passed it off as Savannah simply being observant—until I realized it had been less than three weeks since I'd stopped working my dreads and the change was barely apparent.

Coincidence, then. With no intention of enlisting her services, I hurried off. Now here I am.

"That is better." Georgia wiggles the comb through another inch of dread. "Still, I'll probably end up with arthritis." She peers at me. "If we cut off a bit more—say, six inches—you could still manage a shoulder-length do."

It's tempting, since Savannah's New York stylist friend estimated that with the two of them working together, the "takedown" would require five hours to undo the four years invested in my dreads. But the change would be huge, and I'd prefer to ease into this.

"Don't cut any more than you have to."

Georgia grunts. "Afraid you'll lose your strength like Samson?"

Old Testament Samson. In my opinion, that man deserved what Donna or Delia or whatever-her-name-was did to him. Some leader he turned out to be. "I like it long."

She sighs, and I wrinkle my nose at the scent of something peppery on her breath. "At this rate, we won't be done before midnight. Mark my words, Savannah."

"Nah, we'll have it out by ten. Providin' you stop giving Bridget a hard time."

"And she stops jumpin' outta the chair."

This time Savannah sighs. "Just keep that detangler going, Georgie."

"Time?" Savannah calls.

"Nine fifty-five," Georgia says from somewhere to my left. "You gonna make it?"

"Almost there."

More spraying, more tugging, and my head is one big ache despite the three aspirin I took. Staring at my lap where my head hangs forward, I notice I'm no longer looking through a blur of tears. Dehydration?

"Time?"

"Nine fifty-seven."

Savannah's breath comes in puffs on my neck, as if her adrenaline is chugging full speed. "And it's done!" Cool air rushes in where her breath was. "*You* mark *my* words, Georgie! By ten, I said, and so it is—and without your help this last quarter hour."

"Yeah, but it looks like a tornado went through her hair."

Does she think I'm sleeping? No, it's just Georgia, who hasn't stopped grumbling about the "dread-ful" arthritis for which I'll be responsible when it's diagnosed twenty years from now.

"That's to be expected, but the worst is over." Savannah lays a hand on my shoulder. "Are you ready?"

No, but I want out of this chair, out of this salon, and into the hammock awaiting me at home. I lift my head. However, once my chin is level, I can't raise my eyes. It's hard to believe that the wiry mess of unraveling hair I last glimpsed two hours ago can be anything but, especially considering the amount of hair Georgia has been sweeping up since she chucked the comb and said she couldn't do any more. A small rug could be fashioned from all those blond strands. Though Savannah warned there would be a lot, since what I would normally shed had been locked into the dread, I won't be surprised if I'm a candidate for a "sweep over."

"Come on, darlin', it's not so bad."

Drawing a breath that shames me with all its shuddering, I raise my lids. "Oh. Oh. Oh." My hair kinks and juts despite the month's supply of conditioner and detangler weighting it. Worse than looking downright scary, I don't look like me. I don't look like Easton's wife. *Actually, it's his* widow *you don't look like.*

"Don't fret," Savannah says. "Once we get you 'pooed, rinsed, and blown out—"

"Oh no, you don't." Georgia hustles forward, broom in hand. "We're done. If she wants a proper stylin', she can come back tomorrow during regular business hours."

Savannah frowns. "You let me be the judge of that."

I pull the cape's Velcro fastener. "No, Georgia's right. You've both gone above and beyond, and it's late. I'll come back tomorrow." Providing I can bring myself to go out in public. The thought of all the attention my dread shedding is bound to attract nearly makes me groan.

"You sure?" Savannah comes alongside, her plump figure a bit bent from the nonstop hours, her flushed hands dripping from her wrists.

"I'm sure." I sweep off the cape, causing a mess of hair to empty from the nylon folds. "Oh, sorry."

Grumbling, Georgia takes up her broom again.

As I step out of the chair, I groan at the straightening of my body, the numbness of my backside, and the pressure on a bladder that should have been emptied an hour ago.

"Five hours is a long time." Savannah pats my back as I reach for my fanny pack on the counter below the mirror.

"I'd best use your bathroom." When I emerge, I pull my cell phone from the pack. Earlier I'd turned it off, seeing as I can't stand being at the mercy of others' whims. It might be fine for some, who I can only imagine are mighty lonely to allow their privacy to be violated at all hours, but it's not for me.

As I cross the salon, I turn on the phone to see if Maggie's daughter, Devyn, responded to my invitation to spend the night this Friday. The screen shows I missed two calls, one from Maggie, the other from Piper, ten minutes ago.

I halt. This late at night, Piper might be calling about Uncle Obe's dementia that has crept closer since its diagnosis a year and a half ago. What if—?

It's the "what is" that matters. Still, I hold my breath as I access my messages.

Devyn would love to spend the night. "Good," I murmur.

Next up is Piper's message. "Uncle Obe is missing. I ought to have heard the bell on the door, but I was sitting in the garden with Axel, so…" Her voice breaks. "I shouldn't have left him alone in the house, but he was in bed asleep. Anyway, he's on foot and can't have gone far. Axel and I are scoutin' the property, and if we don't find him soon, we'll call the police. I was hoping you might drive down this way in case he took to Pickwick Pike. Not that I think he would, but…call me."

"Something wrong?" Savannah asks as I snap my phone closed.

"You know them Pickwicks," Georgia mutters from where she's urging a hill of hair into a dustpan. "There's always something wrong."

That's an exaggeration—mostly. "I need to get going. Mind if I square up with you tomorrow when you wrestle this mess into something presentable?"

Though worry remains on Savannah's brow, she says, "Sure. Same time?"

Since three employees are scheduled to work the nursery tomorrow, I think I can manage to stay out of sight until then. "Same time. See you tomorrow."

"Not me. I'm done."

Georgia will get no argument from me.

"You be blessed, you hear?" Savannah calls as I push through the front door.

One foot on the sidewalk, I hesitate over those words that ought to roll off me like water off a duck's back. Exactly how does one go about being blessed? *By recognizing a blessing when it's staring you in the face.*

I turn and look from sister to sister. "Thank you, Savannah... Georgia. It was kind of you to stay after hours."

Savannah breaks into a smile. "Our pleasure."

Georgia shrugs.

Shortly, I leave the town square behind, point myself toward Pickwick Pike, and make a call to Piper, who's on the verge of calling the police.

4

I don't expect to find my uncle on the pike, certain like Piper that he's somewhere on the property. Thus, when I catch sight of a white-haired, orange-robed figure walking slowly alongside the road, heading in the direction I'm coming from, it takes a moment to react. Then I'm whipping a U-turn and fumbling for my phone as my headlights illuminate his backside and the slight limp that is back despite last year's knee replacement.

"He's walking down the pike," I say. As Piper starts thanking the Lord, I talk over her. "I'll bring him home." More Lord thanking. I snap the phone closed.

"Uncle Obe," I call as I step from the truck.

He turns and shields his eyes against the glare of headlights. "Who's there?"

"Bridget." I jog toward him.

"Bridget?"

I hurt for the question in his voice. It's not the kind rooted in disbelief, but the "Bridget who?" kind. "Your niece, Bridget." I halt before him.

"My niece. Niece?"

I put an arm around his shoulder, and frustration runs through me at how feeble this six-foot-three man feels alongside my five-foot-six frame. There's about as much justice in that as there is in making a happily married young woman a widow. And Piper wants to praise the Lord.

As I urge Uncle Obe toward my truck, he says, "You don't look like Bridget."

"I ditched the dreads."

"The what?"

"I changed my hairstyle."

He squints at me. "You don't wear it in a b-braid anymore?"

What year is he in? I haven't worn a braid since long before I went into dreads. "It's been awhile."

"What's this?" he says when I pull open the passenger door.

"My truck."

"Yours?" Out from the headlights, there isn't enough light to see his frown, but it's in his voice.

"Yep." I pat his back. "I'll give you a ride home."

He chuckles. "You're funnin' me. Now, come on, where's that bicycle of yours?"

He's certainly not stuck in any of my high school years. Maybe not even middle school. *See, God? You let stuff like this happen to good people and expect me to love on You. What do You take me for?*

"Why, I don't know the last time I rode in a truck." Uncle Obe runs a hand over the worn seat. "She's an old one."

"But a goodie. Even gets decent mileage, all things considered."

"Ford?"

"That's right."

He lets me help him into the cab, doesn't appear the least surprised when his bicycle-riding niece climbs into the driver's seat, and sighs as I swing the truck around. "I like ridin' up high."

"Me too."

Though he doesn't speak again until I pull the truck through the estate's gated entrance, the air thickens with his anxious thoughts, and I guess he's back from whatever beckoned him onto the pike.

"I'm afraid, Bridget."

Did You hear that up there? A grown man afraid. And he still believes in You. And why am I talking to You anyway?

As I negotiate the brightly lit driveway that winds upward to the mansion, I look at Uncle Obe. "No reason to be afraid. I'm here."

"That's the problem." He rests his head against the window. "I don't rightly know how I got here with you. One minute I'm in bed, the next…"

I try not to reach to him, not because of the issues I have with personal space, but because a show of sympathy can upset him when he's in this state. Still, I put my hand on his arm.

"It will be too late," he says. "If ever."

As the incline increases near the top of the driveway, I give the Ford more gas. "What, Uncle Obe?"

"My little ones."

Antonio and Daisy. But his children aren't little. They're in their early thirties like me. "You'll hear from them soon," I say, although I have no business doing so. After all, they've been estranged for thirty years. If my father had chosen an inheritance over me, could I forgive him? True, they were young when their mother wearied of waiting for Uncle Obe's father to pass away so they could be a family, but it has to hurt that he placed money before them, especially if they're unaware of his sacrifice— that most of his wealth was drained off to keep his three brothers, my father included, out of financial trouble when they were cut from my grandfather's will for scandalous behavior.

"I don't know," Uncle Obe says as I brake in front of the mansion where Piper and her fiancé, Axel, await us on the steps. "It's been months since I sent them that l-letter. Maybe they wrote me off."

Times like these, it would be merciful if the dementia had him fully in its grip so he wouldn't know any better. But the disease is cruel, preferring to play with its food while it slowly eats him alive.

I open my door. "No, I don't believe they've written you off. You'll hear from them."

Too bad saying it doesn't make it so. Of course, my mother would disagree. She leans toward the "speak into existence"—say it again and again and it will happen—philosophy of life. With the caveat of prayer, of course. Unfortunately, her speaking into existence doesn't have a very good track record, especially where my father is concerned.

As I come around the truck, Axel opens the passenger door and reaches in to assist my uncle. "Did you have a nice walk, Obe?" he asks as if it were an intentional late-night outing.

"I'd have to remember it for it to have been nice," my uncle grumbles.

Axel looks at me. Midshrug, he widens his eyes. Before I can translate his reaction, Piper gasps, staring at me from the bottom step, a hand over her mouth.

The hair. I don't know how I forgot, especially since my head hurts all over.

As Axel recovers sufficiently to lead Uncle Obe up the steps, I lean against the front fender and wait for Piper. Like me, she's also cautious about setting off our uncle with a show of concern. She tells him she'll be in to fix him some tea, then crosses to me and looks up from her three-inch deficit. Not that I'm tall. She's just short, and shorter yet considering my thick-soled Crocs.

Her eyes pick at my hair in the light cast by the numerous bulbs that shine up the face of the mansion. And it annoys me, but as I'm about to say so, she shakes her head. "I'm wonderin' "—for once, she doesn't wince at the return of her drawl—"what happened to my dreadlocked Barbie-doll cousin."

Despite the circumstances that brought me here tonight, I feel a smile. Though she and I clashed when she first returned to Pickwick after trading in our hometown for Los Angeles twelve years ago—chalk it up to the pickled corn incident—I've gotten to like her. For the most part.

I smooth a hand over my hair and grimace at the oiliness of the conditioner. "I had myself undreaded. Came straight from the beauty shop to find Uncle Obe."

She glances over her shoulder at where our slump-shouldered uncle is entering the mansion. "Thank you, Bridget. Lord knows what would have—"

"Yeah, well, he's home safe and sound." I push off the fender. "Which is where I ought to be."

"I need help," she says with unexpected force.

"With?"

"Uncle Obe. I won't put him in a memory-care unit, but I have to do something."

"I thought you hired someone."

She nods. "Ida Newbottom."

That's right—ex-champion hog wrestler turned nurse, now retired.

"She's odd, but does a good job. The problem is, she can't give me more than twenty hours a week now that she has a new grandson."

Although Piper sold her partnership in a prestigious PR firm in L.A. to move back home, she does consulting work that takes her out of town several times a month. Fortunately, Axel lives in a cottage on the property and can spend nights with Uncle Obe when needed, but during the day Axel is maintaining the estate grounds in his capacity as gardener or running his landscaping business. That puts Piper in a bind.

"This time of year, I'm puttin' in lots of hours at the nursery, but I'll help however I can. And if you and Axel want a night out, I'll stay with Uncle Obe."

"I can't tell you how much I appreciate the offer."

Enough to hug me, I'm afraid. I sense it. "It's not as if I have anyone to go home to." No sooner does my attempt to lighten the mood exit my mouth than it stings me. I can't believe I said that. "Other than Reggie, that is." I slide past her. "Call me anytime."

As I start to climb in the truck, she says, "I will, but only until I find someone who can give me forty hours a week—a live-in, though it's bound to be expensive."

Whatever it takes to keep Uncle Obe in his home, even if only for a while longer.

"Good night."

"Bridget?"

I peer across the hood. "Yes?"

"Your hair—does it have something to do with that J. C. Dirk you asked about?"

In her line of work, I thought she might have a connection to him that would get my foot in his door, so I showed her the magazine article. After noting he looked like Simon Baker, an actor who plays a body language expert on one of the few shows Piper tunes into—something "mental" or other—she said she'd only heard of J. C. Dirk. However, she agreed that if the Pickwick estate were to fall into the hands of a developer, he looked to have decent enough hands. I told her that even if I had to storm his office, I would get in to see him.

"I needed a change, but the timing is good."

"Then you are going after him."

"I fly to Atlanta on Monday." I lift my gaze to the impressive Pickwick mansion that, when my great-granddaddy built it more than a century ago, was his attempt to put him on par with George Vanderbilt and his Asheville castle. "I have to try, Piper."

"Maybe I can help."

"How?"

"I *am* a PR specialist."

I narrow my lids. "Are you trying to tell me something?"

"Only that I'm familiar with the world you're steppin' into, and just as dreads don't exactly fit there, neither do jeans or dirt under the nails."

A firefly flits by, its little green bulb flicking on and off. I gently scoop the slow-moving creature into my palm. "What's your definition of help?"

"The right clothes, the right body language, the right words."

I could be offended, but it would only further prove how contrary I can be. I open my fingers and the firefly glows green against my skin before it lifts off and rejoins the night. It makes me smile. "You forget that I attended cotillion."

Piper laughs. "Only the one time. Banned for life, I believe."

"All because of a little old skunk."

"Okay, admit it. You need me."

I sigh. "Let me think on it. Good night." As I slide into the cab, she hurries up the steps to Uncle Obe and Axel. And I head home to no one. Well, there is Reggie.

"Hey, you," I coax. "It's me. Come on out."

In the darkness I strain to hear a response, but the only sounds are those of the night beyond the screened-in porch—insistent cicadas, cacophonous crickets, and the murmur and whisper of things high in the trees and low in the grass.

"I could use a little company."

Still nothing.

"You don't know what you're missing." I lower a leg over the side of the hammock and push off the planks. "Nice." And it is, the cooling air stirred by the hammock's sway—far better than my stuffy house that requires an enormous waste of energy to be anywhere near as comfortable in a short amount of time. In fact, though I only meant to hang out here until the windows I threw open cooled off the inside, maybe I'll sleep out tonight. *If* I can get to sleep. Some nights I'm so restless it's nearly impossible.

"Come on, Reggie." I run fingers over the damp hair that took three shampoos to remove the conditioner, as well as built-up residue despite years of conscientious grooming. "Same old me." I make kissing noises.

The screen door between the house and porch squeaks, and I hear the patter of feet. A moment later, a cool nose touches my ankle where it dangles over the side.

More pattering, and when I reach down, soft fur grazes my fingers. I stroke the little body and, once it relaxes, scoop it from the porch and settle it against my side. It's too dark to see much, but a bit of light reflects off Reggie's beady eyes.

"I didn't mean to frighten you, sweetums." My nearly tailless opossum rarely moves as fast as she did when I let myself into the house an hour ago. After a frozen moment, she shot under the sofa and refused to come out. "And I'm sorry for being so late in gettin' home."

As she works a place for herself, I swing my leg into the hammock.

"My hair will look better in the light of day. I promise." A promise J. C. Dirk is going to help me keep. Though I may not fit into his world, Savannah will bring me one step closer. But as for the rest of the way…

Maybe I should let Piper make me into someone like her. Imagining myself recast in her image, I reach to tug a dread. All gone, nothing but fine strands that slide through my fingers. "Okay, Piper. Do with me what you dare."

5

Monday, August 16

Piper dared big, from my hairline where the pore-clogging makeup starts to the fitted jacket and skirt to the tips of my toes that are stuffed into high heels that have no business on my formerly calloused feet. Yes, formerly. Over the past few days, I've been pumiced, scraped, and plucked nearly raw.

I frown at the woman reflected in the back wall of the elevator. She may look put together, especially holding Piper's expensive briefcase, but she's a fake. However, if she gets me an audience with J. C. Dirk, I'll suffer her. And if she doesn't… On the upside, I'll be back in jeans. On the downside, I'll have to figure out something else.

As I continue my solitary ascent, I perform a quick check of my hair on which Savannah worked her magic such that it angles down from my cheekbones, brushes my shoulders, and capes my upper back. It's more feminine than I aimed for, but Piper assured me the style went well with the professional attire, softening the look enough to decrease the chance of being thrown out on my rear. In other words, it might help if Dirk finds my looks even more appealing than my proposal.

Hmm. I already don't like him. But if I can put the ball in play, he'll never know that beneath the makeup, clothes, walk, and talk is a formerly dreadlocked nursery owner more inclined to dirt under the nails than the acrylic tips that make my nail beds ache something terrible. Once I'm on the plane home, they're coming off.

As the elevator slows, I set my shoulders back per Piper's crash course in exuding confidence in the world I'm about to enter. "You can do this," I mutter. "Now get in there and do it."

Hoping "speaking into existence" works better for me than my mother, I step into the lobby of Dirk Developers Inc. It's all gleaming wood, faintly green glass, and cows. That's right. As environmentally friendly as J. C. Dirk is said to be, he likes his leather, as evidenced by the plush chairs and sofas that congregate in the waiting room.

Noting the other occupants who likely have appointments, I approach the receptionist's desk. And once more my feet beg to be free of the heels Piper assured me were worth the fifty dollars I plunked down so I wouldn't have to borrow her too-small shoes again. While I probably should have broken them in, I have a nursery to run, and heels are not compatible with fertilizer and the like. Too, the last thing I need is to draw more gawking and gossiping than what's come my way since I undid my dreads.

"May I help you?" a well-rounded young woman asks as I near the reception desk. *Zaftig,* my new sister-in-law, Trinity, would call her as she referred to my mother not long ago, rousing Daddy's ire, though Trinity thought the "pleasingly plump" label was flattering. She still has a lot to learn about my family.

I set the briefcase on the counter. "I'm here to see Mr. Dirk."

She glances at her computer screen. "The eleven o'clock meeting?"

"No." Ugh, that could have been my in. "But he'll want to see me."

"Then you"—her pretty smile falters—"don't have an appointment?"

Not for want of trying. "I don't, but if you tell him Bridget Buchanan is here to discuss an investment opportunity, I'm sure he'll make time for me."

"I'm sorry, Miss Buchanan—"

"Mrs."

Her gaze flicks to my barren left hand atop the briefcase, and I feel the pale band of skin that is the only visible symbol of my marriage. "Er, Mrs. Buchanan."

Great. Not only was I short with Dirk Developers' first line of defense but she's correct in assuming I'm husbandless. Old habits, even good ones, are hard to break.

"I'm afraid that Mr. Dirk is about to go into a meeting."

"The eleven o'clock."

"Yes."

"That's twenty minutes out. More than I need." I nod at the multiline phone, causing my hair to shift across my brow so lightly I nearly mistake it for a cobweb as I've done repeatedly since my change of hairstyle. I clasp my hands to keep from swiping at my face. "Would you let him know I'm here?"

"I'm sorry, but his schedule is full."

Don't burn bridges. Piper's final piece of advice swoops down on me. "Well then, I could be in for a mighty long wait." Hopefully not so long that I miss my return flight.

I cross to the waiting area and lower onto a cow that, in another life, was hardly as plush or pleasantly scented. As I settle in, I hear the receptionist on the phone. Though she's discreet, I catch my name. I only hope she's not going through Dirk's cranky assistant—probably a futile hope, but maybe the woman is out of the office.

"Mrs. Buchanan?" the receptionist calls.

I stand. "Yes?"

"Mr. Dirk's assistant has confirmed that he's unable to fit you in. She said for you to call her and she'll be more than happy to set up an appointment."

I struggle against the urge to burn a bridge. This young woman is only the messenger.

I return to the desk. "I've been tryin' for weeks to do just that, but Ms. Wiley has been far from happy to pencil me in. That's why I'm here—all the way from North Carolina."

She rolls her lips inward.

"So please tell her I'm not goin' anywhere until Mr. Dirk gives me ten minutes." When I turn back to the cow, the framed photos around the waiting room catch my eye.

Hearing the receptionist on the phone again, I step to the first photo. It's an aerial of a sprawling ski lodge in Aspen, Colorado—doubtless one of the Dirk developments. And since the magazine article that brought J. C. Dirk to my attention mentioned his love of the outdoors, he's probably enjoyed the fruits of that labor. As I continue around the room, mostly admiring but sometimes cringing over the height, breadth, and amount of glass and metal used in the buildings, the elevator hatches more visitors.

I look from a family-themed wilderness resort to the three men and two women who exit.

"I'll let Ms. Wiley know you're here." The receptionist glances at me and back to the new arrivals, then comes out from behind her desk and steps toward them with a soft tinkle from her coin belt. "Actually, why don't I take you back?"

Afraid I'll make a scene in front of Dirk's VIPs?

She holds open a door and leads them down a glass-fronted corridor and out of sight. No sooner do I return to the photos than movement pulls my gaze back to the corridor. A very front-loaded woman peers into the waiting room. Ms. Wiley?

Her frown momentarily settles on me, and I give a wave that makes her stiffen and waddle in the direction the VIPs went. Definitely Ms. Wiley.

Continuing to move around the walls, I keep a peripheral eye on the corridor. Shortly, the receptionist returns to her desk. Since she surely has the task of keeping an eye on me, leastwise until someone escorts me off the premises, I feel for her.

The next photo shows the environmentally friendly oceanside condos featured in the magazine that first brought J. C. Dirk to my attention. Again, I'm struck by how beautiful they are—low to the ground, generously spaced, and constructed of easily renewable natural materials that enable them to blend with the environment. If there had to be a development, at least it's conscientious. That's why I need J. C. Dirk.

As I cross to the next photo, I catch sight of a fast-moving object in the corridor—a man, and Ms. Wiley is hurrying alongside him despite her baby bulk. He's not tall, leastwise not compared to Easton, whose lanky six-foot-six frame is the standard by which I measure all men. In fact, this man, who is definitely the one who graced the magazine cover, would be lucky to top me by an inch were I standing beside him in heels that boost me from five foot six to five foot eight. But what J. C. Dirk lacks in height, he makes up for in breadth. Even outfitted in a business suit, it's evident he's buff. And he's about to go from sight.

I glance at the door. Can I make it into the corridor ahead of the receptionist? I can, but Piper would see it as an act of aggression that could blow my chance of a face to face. I look back at J.C. and nearly startle when I see he's stopped on the other side of the glass wall. He's staring at me, and Ms. Wiley is nodding in my direction.

I stand taller, resisting the temptation to open my hands to prove I'm unarmed.

Eyes narrowing beneath a thatch of light brown hair, he returns his attention to his assistant. Whatever she's relating about the woman who has badgered her with calls, it can't be flattering.

J. C. Dirk looks sideways at me, and his mouth curves. Though I resent being sized up, there's consolation in knowing Bridget Buchanan, nursery owner turned attractive, smartly professional woman, has passed Go. He'll see me now.

He nods at Ms. Wiley, checks his watch, and continues along the corridor.

No! I did not suffer this getup to have him walk away. I don't care to attract the eligible bachelor, but a slightly closer look would have been all right if it allowed me to present my proposal.

I reach for a dread, but the blond hair slides through my fingers, reminding me of what I gave up for J. C. Dirk before I was truly ready. And that makes me plain mad.

Feeling the receptionist's gaze, I turn back to the photo. Five minutes later, the elevator pings and a man and two women exit.

I return to my chair as the women are directed to the waiting area with the promise that a Mr. Strom will be with them soon. Next, the receptionist addresses the man. "The meeting has just started. Let me take you back."

I stick my nose in a magazine in hopes of appearing oblivious to the door that is opening to me. A moment later, the receptionist leads the man away. Once they're out of sight, I grab the briefcase and hurry to the door.

My trek down the corridor is uneventful, but the next corridor is lined with offices. "Act like you belong," I mutter as I scan the plaques that identify the occupants of each office. Most of those whose doors are open don't glance up, but the ones who do are given a smile I wish I felt.

As I approach the next corridor, I hear the tinkle of what can only be the coin belt. Deciding on the plaque that reads Lunchroom, I push open the door. Thankfully, the room is empty. When the tinkle fades, I return to the corridor. Rounding the next corner, I see J. C. Dirk behind a bank of windows in a fancy conference room that boasts a view of the murky Atlanta skyline. Not my kind of view. I'll take clear and Carolina green any day.

The man I'm here to see is at the head of a table that seats his visitors and Ms. Wiley, who has her back to me. He's expressive, hands gesturing, lightly stubbled face shifting from serious to excited to something that makes him smile and laugh.

I have the feeling I'm staring at a fountain of energy that the magazine article hinted at with phrases like *go-getter* and *adventurous,* but I can handle him. Though I'd prefer to locate his office and wait there, I risk being intercepted and forcibly removed. Thus, I'll have to interrupt his meeting. The end will likely be the same, but at least I'll get my face-to-face, even if only thirty seconds' worth.

"May I help you?"

I jump at the appearance of a slender, spectacled man at my elbow. "Just headin' into the meeting." I cover my surprise with a smile.

He frowns, causing a crescent-shaped scar above his right eyebrow to pucker. "J.C.'s meeting?"

"That's right." I check my nonexistent watch—nonexistent because Piper insisted my Velcro-banded water-resistant watch didn't go with the outfit. "Looks like I'm runnin' late." I step forward with such haste my right ankle nearly goes out from under me. I hate heels.

"Since I'm going your way"—he touches my arm—"we can go in together."

Well, open me a jar of peaches and call me a pie. Is this my lucky day or what? "Certainly." As he opens the door, the voices within trail off and all eyes turn to me, most heavily those of J. C. Dirk—a brighter green than they appeared on the magazine cover; however, they quickly transition from enthusiasm to questioning to annoyance.

"Ms. Buchanan!" his assistant exclaims from the far end of the table.

I don't correct the flubbed "Mrs." Progress.

She rises from the chair. "This is a closed meeting." She glances at the four men and two women around the table that could accommodate a dozen more, then frowns at my escort whose confusion I feel. "I have to ask you to—"

"Make an appointment. I know, but that hasn't worked. So here I am." As my escort lowers into a chair, I shift my regard to J. C. Dirk. "I understand you're a busy man, but all I need is ten minutes."

He picks up a pen between both hands and twists it back and forth, as if to give his energy an outlet.

Come on, I'm out of the bridge-burning business. All gussied up. Wearing heels, a skirt that seriously constricts my stride, and a jacket that has nothing on denim. Say yes.

Nothing. I look to his visitors. "I apologize for interruptin' your important meeting, but I need to discuss something with Mr. Dirk that can't wait. Do you mind?"

"I'll call security." Ms. Wiley picks up the phone. And her employer doesn't stop her.

Fortunately, I already don't like the man. Unfortunately, my chance of preserving something of my family's estate is going bye-bye.

I set the briefcase on the end of the table opposite J. C. Dirk. "You're looking for a new challenge." According to the article. "And I have just the one for you." I press the briefcase's latches, but they resist.

"Security," Ms. Wiley says, "would you send an officer to Dirk Developers? We have an intruder in our conference room."

I suppose I am an intruder, though she makes it sound as if I'm armed. What's with these latches? I wiggle them. It's as if they're—

They are. From the inside pocket of my jacket, I dig out the key. Piper told me to carry it in my wallet, but since she barred me from wearing a fanny pack and I saw no reason to tote a purse when there was plenty of room in the briefcase for my wallet, I kept it close.

I hold it up for all to see—J.C., who raises a very visible eyebrow and rolls the pen faster, Ms. Wiley, who returns the handset to the cradle, and their visitors, who settle back with strained patience.

I spring the lid and grab the portfolio Piper helped me put together. "The Pickwick Estate, over five hundred prime acres located in picturesque Pickwick, North Carolina." I open the portfolio to a highlighted map and turn it face out. "Less than an hour's drive east of the famed Biltmore Estate." I trace the highway between Asheville and Pickwick with an acrylic-tipped fingernail, then glance at J.C. to see if he's still with me. He is.

"Easy in, easy out, by car or plane. An investment opportunity for an eco-friendly development, ideally along the lines of the Biltmore Estate, offering tours of the mansion and gardens. Perhaps an on-site hotel but modest so it doesn't overshadow or *impinge*"—fancy word courtesy of vocabulary-conscious Maggie—"on the natural environment. For instance, your award-winning oceanside development, Mr. Dirk."

He stops twisting the pen. A good sign?

"Correct me if I'm wrong"—the drawl of the South peeks above the surface of his voice—"but there's good hunting in those parts."

I stiffen. "Yes, and plenty. No need to add to it." I clear my throat. "Nature walks, bicycling, canoeing, and horseback riding are more the speed of the development I'm talkin' about."

He leans back. And smiles lightly.

Did he just push my buttons? It would seem so. Had I stamped *tree hugger* on my forehead, it would have been seriously redundant.

"Your concern for the environment is admirable, Ms. Buchanan, but should I decide to be interested in the"—his gaze grazes the portfolio—"Pickwick estate, why would I go through you and not another real estate agent?"

"Another…?" Is this the reason for the brush-off? Ms. Wiley's assumption that a real estate agent was behind my calls? Although I didn't say anything to that effect, it's a valid assumption considering the business Dirk Developers is in.

Relief flows through me like a cool-water dip on a Carolina summer day. "I'm not a real estate agent."

J. C. Dirk tilts his head to the side. "Then what are you, Ms. Buchanan?"

"I'm Bridget *Pickwick* Buchanan."

He startles. Well, his eyes—a momentary widening I might have missed were I not so intent on him. Then those eyes dip to my barren left hand, sweep back up, and shift left and right of my face.

What? I gave myself a good ironing with the straightener I bought to counter my hair's stubborn memory. Of course, considering he's looking at me the way a lot of folks looked at me after I came undreaded, maybe the Atlanta humidity did me in.

He shoots my escort a look that makes the man shake his head, as if to deny all knowledge of me. "So you're a Pickwick."

He says it with a derogatory tone, but that's nothing new. Despite our family's fall from prominence long ago, the name still draws attention, especially in association with scandal.

"I am."

His lips twitch. "*Mrs.* Bridget Pickwick Buchanan."

Though tempted to burn this bridge, I can't. "Yes, widowed." Then to dispel any notion my qualifier is a hint I'm open to achieving my end on a more personal level, I add, "Most unfortunately."

Behind me the door opens, and when I look around, I see a security guard enter, followed by the wide-eyed receptionist. *God, I'm still not talking to You, but if You care more for Your earth than You ever cared for Easton or me, You might want to give this situation a look-see.*

"I'm sorry, Mr. Dirk," the receptionist says. "I didn't realize she slipped in."

"You'll have to come with me, ma'am." The security guard halts alongside me and places a hand on his holstered pistol.

The gesture would be funny if not for the alternative—manhandling, which he's wise not to try. I may be on my best behavior, but I could forget myself were he to overstep my bounds.

I swallow my pride. "Please, Mr. Dirk. All I ask is for ten minutes."

"Mr. Dirk?" the security guard says.

The object of my *affliction* resumes his pen twisting. "Mrs. *Pickwick* Buchanan is welcome to stay"—his voice picks up speed and the drawl ceases to be—"providing she waits in my office while I conduct my meeting."

I catch my breath. "I'll wait."

He looks at his assistant. "Ms. Wiley, would you show Mrs. Buchanan to my office?"

Her jaw tightens. "Certainly."

As she steps toward me, I stuff the portfolio in the briefcase.

The security guard and receptionist follow us from the conference room, and we don't part ways until we pass through the glass-fronted corridor and Ms. Wiley leads me past the door that leads into the reception area.

"Here we are," she says after two more turns find us standing in a large, sparsely furnished office, also with a view of the murky Atlanta skyline. "If you'll take a seat, Mr. Dirk will be with you as soon as possible." She turns, pauses, and looks back. "Can I send in some coffee? It's likely to be a long wait."

"I'm not much of a coffee drinker."

She gestures across the room. "There's bottled water in the refrigerator."

Bottled—all that unrecycled plastic clogging up landfills. Exactly how "green" is Dirk Developers? "I'll pass."

She departs, leaving the door wide open. The better to keep an eye on me?

I consider the chairs in front of the desk near the windows but make myself comfortable at the nearby oasis where two sofas face each other across a marble-topped table. Setting the briefcase on the latter, I start to lower into one of the fabric-covered sofas, but more comfort is in order. I step out of the heels. And why not? I made it past Go by doing what Piper would have advised against. Surely, I can make it the rest of the way without causing my feet further hardship.

I remove the jacket and toss it on the back of the sofa. As I settle into the overstuffed cushions, I free the blouse's top button and would free the next if not that it would reveal the ring around my neck. That's personal.

I drop my head back and groan with gratitude. I don't like airports or planes or traffic or smog so thick it fills the air with cancer. I don't like honking horns or high rises or people too important to be seen. I like my corner of Pickwick. Sometimes it's dirty, but it's with good old-fashioned dirt that can be washed off and returned to the earth without doing harm. So here I am, in the middle of all I don't like, to keep Pickwick the way I like it as much as possible. Now if my luck holds—

Or was it luck? I imagine the sky beyond the ceiling. *Was it You? If so, thanks. Not that You would do it for me, but that's fine since we want the same thing.*

I close my eyes, slowly exhale, and float back to four o'clock, when my alarm dragged me out of hard-won sleep so I could get to Asheville and on the plane that would take me through Charlotte before dumping me in this nature-forsaken place. Back to the scent of darkness and warm air. Back to the embrace of the hammock that is as close as I come to a man's arms.

6

Something jangles like loose change.

"Mrs. Buchanan?"

Nice voice. Not much of the South to recommend it, but nice.

More jangling. "Mrs. Buchanan?"

I open my eyes, and the man takes shape where he stands over me—hands in pockets, the right one doing the pocket jangling. Higher up, there's a decent stretch of shoulders beneath a creased white shirt; higher yet, a lopsided slice of a smile; highest of all, sparkling green eyes beneath an expanse of forehead.

Placing myself in Atlanta, in the office of J. C. Dirk—on his sofa, no less—I straighten from my slump, swipe at my bangs, and yank at my skirt that has inched above my knees. Was he peeking at my legs?

"I'm sorry to keep you waiting." He pulls his hands from his pockets. "The meeting lasted longer than expected."

Returning my gaze to him, I strain my neck as well as my pride. As I don't care to be looked down on, I spring upright—poor planning on my part, since it brings me within inches of him, bad form on his part, since he simply stands there. So I'm the one who sidesteps, taking with me a breath of cologne. I don't like the stuff. It makes my nose and throat itch. Give me a man who smells like hard work and salt any day. That's how Easton smelled, soap as close to unnatural as he came.

I smooth my skirt with one hand and reach for my jacket with the other. "I didn't mean to doze off."

"Long day?"

"Very." I thrust my arms into the jacket.

"Then it's a good thing it's almost over."

There's my ten-minute cue. I grab the briefcase from the table. "Let's get started."

"I'm all yours."

Sensations of an unwelcome sort brush my emotions. Not that his voice sounds like Easton's, but the words are my husband's. Well, *were*. Now they belong to another man, even if it is in a different context.

I clear my throat. "Here? Or would your desk be better?"

"Actually, I'd prefer that we discuss your proposal over dinner."

Is that an invitation? I'll bet he *was* looking at my legs. And though I may not have the Pickwick red hair, thanks to my naturally blond mother, that doesn't mean I don't have the temperament. *Do you or don't you want this to work?*

I press a smile into place. "Unfortunately, by the time dinner rolls around, I'll be on a plane, so we'll have to do this here." I move to the opposite side of the table and bend to the briefcase.

"You must have been asleep for some time, Mrs. Buchanan. It's almost five."

"What?" I look to the windows, but they're tinted. And my nonexistent watch isn't talking. "Are you yankin' my chain?" I know it sounds boorish the moment the words exit my mouth, but I don't have time to think of a prettier way to phrase it.

He reaches across the table, the stretch causing his cuff to retract and reveal a watch with several small dials.

I grab his thick, golden-haired wrist and lift it near my face. Sure enough, the middle dial confirms that when he earlier said the day was almost over, it had nothing to do with my ten-minute proposal. "I'm gonna miss my plane!"

"Then you really are leaving tonight?"

I flick my eyes back to his face, and something catches in me as I get my first up-close look at him. I knew from the magazine he was attractive—in an odd way, what with his broad forehead, rather thick eyebrows, slightly downturned eyes, and thin-lipped mouth—but I didn't expect my insides to go catching on anything. Of course, maybe it's because he does rather look like that actor Simon Baker. Not that I've seen his show, but I did Google him after Piper mentioned the resemblance.

As a frown rises on J.C.'s brow, I replay his question. "Er, yes, my flight is at six thirty, and— Goodness! Reggie!"

"Who?"

"Reggie doesn't like to sleep alone."

His lids narrow. "Your boyfriend?"

"No, my po—" Oops. "My friend. But if I leave now, I might make my plane since I don't have baggage to check."

"You flew in this morning?" He tips his head to the side. "Just to see me?"

I narrowly avoid rolling my eyes. "Surely I made that clear, Mr. Dirk. I'm not merely passin' through. What I want to talk to you about is important." Meaning I'm going to have to do a bit more begging. "So important that I would be beholden if you would accompany me to the airport so we can discuss my proposal durin' the drive."

"All right." He concedes more easily than expected. "I'll call for a driver."

"Thank you."

He looks down his outstretched arm. "Of course, it would be easier done if I had my hand back."

Why am I still holding on to him? I release him so fast you'd think I had hold of a viper.

He shakes his sleeve down and turns, but not before I glimpse a grin. And that gets my back up.

Put those matches away! Fine, but if he turns up his nose at my proposal…well, I'm bound to say something which Piper won't approve of. But it's not as if I'll see his miserable self again.

"Five o'clock traffic," J. C. Dirk says as the driver of the cow-appointed (leather again) luxury car maneuvers through the downtown traffic on our trek toward the freeway.

Despite the strong possibility I'll miss my plane, I settle down to business. "As I said earlier, the Pickwick estate consists of more than five hundred prime acres." I open the portfolio to the map and set it on the seat between us.

He continues to stare out the window, right leg crossed over left, foot bouncing with that corridor-running, pen-rolling, key-jangling energy. But then he suddenly angles toward me. "Why prime?"

I flip to the data sheet the chamber of commerce compiled to promote the town of Pickwick that has undergone revitalization since the new highway exit provided easier access. "It's all there." I pat the page. "A diverse population base, a variety of established and thriving businesses, new single-family developments located less than an hour's drive from the Biltmore Estate—"

His cell phone rings, and he pulls it out. "Excuse me."

Be calm. Telling him off will get you nowhere.

After a minute of mostly monosyllabic conversation on this side of the phone, he returns his cell to his pocket. "May I?" He nods at the portfolio. "I'm more visual than auditory." He starts flipping through the carefully constructed pages, as if flipping through an advertisement-heavy magazine.

If that's all the notice he's going to give my presentation, this is a waste of time.

"There appears to be a lot of woodland." He considers the topo-graphic map.

I lean closer. "Natural and unspoiled. When my great-granddaddy set up his textile business and founded the town, he decided to build a grand residence on a scale that would grant him entrance to the society inhabited by the Vanderbilts. So he bought up everything he could in this area outside of town. As you'll see in the photos on the next page, the Pickwick mansion is somethin' to behold." Unfortunately for my an-cestor, though the textile business made him wealthy, it wasn't enough to grant him elbow-rubbing status with the Vanderbilts.

I reach past J.C. to turn the page. However, he stretches a thumb across the map and touches a large rectangular piece that Uncle Obe marked. "Why is this acreage outlined?"

Discomfort triggers an itch I long to scratch. But why am *I* feeling discomfort? Although it's rumored the Calhouns were swindled out of that piece of land in a poker game rigged by my great-granddaddy, I had nothing to do with it. Besides, once the estate is liquidated, Uncle Obe intends to make restitution to the descendants of that family who long ago left Pickwick—another of his quests to right our family wrongs. In this instance, an expensive wrong *and* the reason he'll likely be forced to vacate his beloved residence before the dementia settles in deep enough to make the matter a nonissue.

"Mrs. Buchanan?"

When my pale green eyes meet their bright green counterparts, I realize how near our heads are and that his cologne is tickling my nose. And I'm the one responsible, as evidenced by my reach to turn the page that has left my hand suspended above the portfolio, I snatch my arm back and swipe at the hair on my brow.

"I'm not sure why my uncle outlined those middle hundred acres…" Likely a reminder to make restitution, but no need to speculate. "Though that acreage was acquired later than the surrounding areas, it is part of the estate in which I'm proposin' you invest your eco-friendly self."

"So these hundred acres were a holdout."

"If you mean the owner held out on selling to my great-granddaddy, that is my understandin'."

"But he finally gave in for the right price?"

There's that itch again. I agree with my uncle that our family wrongs should be righted, but it can be embarrassing. "You could say that. Now let me show you the photos—"

"What about the quarry?" He points to the center of the Calhoun acreage.

I peer at the tiny lettering that, to my surprise, records that ugly bit of history when the dirt-poor Calhouns put food on their table and clothes on their backs by the grace of my great-granddaddy's desire to construct his mansion out of North Carolina stone. According to yet more rumors, he promised to set the land right once he took what he needed. However, after the mansion was completed, he continued to pay the Calhouns a pittance for the privilege of gouging out their land and selling the stone elsewhere—making the land so undesirable that only he, possessing extensive acreage on either side, was interested in buying it. Or winning it, as it were. Possibly stealing it.

I sigh over the injustice, not only to the Calhouns, but the land. "If you're asking if the quarry is active, it isn't. Not for years and years."

"Just an eyesore." Beneath the surface of his voice is resentment that makes me warm to this environmentally concerned citizen.

"Yes, but it could be put right."

He gives a slow nod. "And this acreage on the edge of town?" He taps a smaller outline at the northernmost boundary of the Pickwick estate.

So much for warming toward him. "Those thirty acres are spoken for." As in *mine*, Uncle Obe having set it aside as my inheritance so I can expand my nursery to include organic gardening.

"That's a choice piece of real estate. Commercial acreage…road frontage…"

"Not for sale." Once more finding my hand stuck above the port-folio, I bypass his grip and turn the page. "As you see, the mansion is spectacular and the grounds—"

"Lovely." He passes the portfolio to me, settles back, and studies my face. "I have to ask what every informed buyer wants to know. Why is the seller selling?"

Piper warned me to expect the question. "As you've probably guessed, money is an issue; however, not such an issue that the Pickwick estate will necessarily go to the one who offers the most."

His face relaxes into a faint smile, but his foot starts bouncing again. "That's an enviable position to be in—to be able to pick your buyer based on factors other than money."

I nearly smile at his suddenly accelerated speech that makes me imagine his words running roughshod over one another in their haste to exit his mouth. "It is an enviable position." One I'm trying hard to keep hold of.

"And the determining factor is that the developer is eco-friendly."

I nod and, once more, swipe at my hair. "That's right, keeping the property in as natural a state as possible."

"You think I'm the one to do that?"

"That's why I sought you out, Mr. Dirk."

"Call me J.C."

Grateful I didn't burn the J. C. Dirk bridge, I smile. "Thank you. Call me Bridget."

He shifts his gaze to my mouth, considers it longer than he ought to, then puts out a hand. "May I keep the portfolio?"

I pass it to him, and though our fingers don't touch, something quavers between the covers and pages. However, I'm too newly determined to shed my widow's weeds to take it seriously, especially where this man is concerned. This is business, after all.

He drops the portfolio in the case at his feet, then looks out the window at the cars his driver is doing his utmost to pass.

Relaxing a little, I retrieve the briefcase that contains all I need to get me out of Atlanta if I can just make it to the airport. I pop the latches, and that's when I hear a crack and feel a sting at the tip of my index finger. I stare at the flesh-tinted nail revealed by the parting of ways. "Thank goodness!" One down, nine to go.

"Thank goodness?"

Warmth spreads to my face as J.C. picks the fingernail from his pant leg and extends it. "I would expect the breakage of one of these to be more an occasion for gnashing of teeth, not giving thanks."

I snatch the vile acrylic tip from him, and when our fingers actually touch, I'm thankful there's only a little of that quavering going on. "What I mean is, thank goodness I'll be home soon so I can have it repaired." Downright lie, especially considering the rest will surely be off before I touch down in Asheville, but if he's going to take my proposal seriously, I have an image to maintain.

"You might want to get that fixed too." He jerks his chin toward my head.

"What?"

"Your hair seems to bother you a lot."

Did I swat at it again? "I just need to get used to it."

"New hairstyle, then."

Though it isn't a question, I consider answering it with another lie. But it's not as if I don't have the best excuse in the world. I wrinkle my nose, imitating my cousin Maggie, who is practically tattooed with feminine wiles. "You know us women, one day this, the next day that."

This time his smile has teeth, as if he's given himself permission to enjoy the moment. "Pity."

"What do you mean?"

"Call it ego, but I thought maybe the hair, nails, and flattering outfit were aimed at getting me to take notice of you as a woman."

How dare he—? *Read the situation right? Come on, Bridget. If this leads to what is best for the town of Pickwick, the cost is minor.*

"The end result being I take notice of your proposal."

Bull's-eye. Still, pride begs me to differ, common sense to do so civilly. "You're right. Best we chalk it up to your ego."

He chuckles, props an elbow between window and door frame, and turns his attention to the traffic outside.

When the driver pulls the car to the curb for departures, I lean forward to peer at the dashboard clock. It's possible I'll make my flight. Gripping the briefcase, I turn to J.C., but he's already outside. A moment later, he opens my door and reaches in.

I hesitate to accept his gentlemanly gesture for fear I'll regret it and, sure enough, sensation runs up my arm when my fingers make contact with his palm. And keeps on running as I rise before him and his eyes fasten on my face with an intensity that makes my insides catch again. However, in the next instant, he frowns and releases me.

I take a step back. "Thank you for the ride."

"You're welcome." He pushes his hands in his pockets and, once again, starts jangling.

"I'd better go." I step past him but look over my shoulder. "You will give the Pickwick estate serious consideration, won't you?"

"Sure."

Sure? That sounds like someone who's been asked to hold another person's place in line. "My cousin's card is in the front of the portfolio. If you have any questions, Piper will be happy to talk to you."

His lids narrow. "I was under the impression that should there be further contact, it would be between you and me."

I turn to him. "Piper is the one handling the liquidation of our uncle's estate. I'm just the messenger."

His mouth turns upward. "I doubt that."

I start to argue, but not with my plane about to depart. And considering I initiated this, he's right. "Well, I suppose—"

"Should I decide Pickwick warrants further interest, we will speak again, Bridget, messenger or not."

This time I'm the one who says, quite simply, "Sure," then I'm hurrying toward the glass doors and feeling J.C.'s gaze all the way. I'm nearly knocked sideways by the mammoth of a man who cuts in front of me. Ruder yet, he tosses a fast-food bag at the trash can near the doors. It misses, spilling its mustard- and ketchup-smeared contents across the sidewalk.

"Hey!" I start to chase after him but remember J.C. While I long to confront the litterbug, it would likely result in a nasty scene sure to dispel any belief in my credibility. Still, I can't leave the mess. I scoop up the bag and wrappers, shove them in the trash can, and with red- and orange-streaked fingers, enter the building. Safely out of sight of J.C., I scan the ticket lines, but the mammoth has disappeared. He has no idea how lucky he is.

Now if I may be so lucky to make my flight. And forget whatever it was that passed between J. C. Dirk and me.

7

> On behalf of the Pickwick family,
> it is an honor to extend an invitation to you
> to attend the dedication ceremony of
> **The Master Weaver**
> created by sculptor Reece Thorpe
> and commissioned by Obadiah Pickwick.
> This event will be held at the
> Pickwick Town Square
> on Saturday, September 18 at 2:00 p.m.
> Cordially yours,
> Magdalene Pickwick

Saturday, September 18

The vultures are circling, and not a word from J. C. Dirk. The dog! As Uncle Obe, looking more present than he has in weeks, consents to a photographer's request for another picture, I scan the dispersing crowd to count the real estate agents who attended the unveiling of our town square's new statue. Six vultures in all—that I know of—and that gum-slinging Wesley woman is one of them.

"A kettle of vultures," my daddy would call them had he attended the dedication ceremony. Though he had three weeks' notice, he couldn't see his way to reschedule his trapshooting date. After all, he reasoned, it's just a statue; money foolishly spent to ease his brother's conscience for having dumped the original statue of Great-Granddaddy Pickwick in the lake during a secretly rebellious phase.

As for Mama, she's not here either, but she has a good reason not to venture out on this balmy end-of-summer day. When I stopped by the house to pick her up, along with Miles and Birdie, who kicked off their eight-week stay in Pickwick two weeks ago, Mama said she'd sent her grandchildren ahead with Bart and his new wife, who agreed to keep the children overnight while Mama recovers from whatever bug has hold of her. Guessing the "bug" to be more a matter of keeping her busy grandchildren, I resolved to make good my promise to Bonnie to relieve Mama.

Though Bart and Trinity also seem willing to help, I worry about their ability to keep control of those two. Of course, from where I stand back from the crowd, they appear to be doing a good job.

Peering past them, I consider the creation of Maggie's beau that rises from a great granite block against the backdrop of the church across the street. The immense bronze sculpture shows a master weaver at his loom, a commemoration of the textile industry upon which the foundation of the town of Pickwick was laid. A foundation that, despite cracks and uneven settling over nearly a century, held firm until my daddy demolished it with his mismanagement. So say most Pickwickians, and though I love my socially and financially challenged father, no one will get an argument from me.

Now on the matter of the Pickwick estate… I declare, if I ever see

J. C. Dirk again, no fancy briefcase or high heels or binding skirt will keep me from letting him know what I think of his refusal to return the calls I've made since our meeting last month. Why, I—

"Long time no see," a familiar voice warms my ear.

What is *he* doing here? I look around at the man who is standing far too near. His toothy smile might make many a girl curl her toes, but not me. I've had just about enough of it.

As I turn to fully face him, I say, "Boone," measuring out all the little sounds that make up the name of my most persistent widow sniffer.

His gaze sweeps me head to toe. "You sure look pretty today. I don't think I've ever seen you outta your jeans—" His eyes widen. "I mean, wearin' anything *other* than jeans. A-and a top, of course."

Though tempted to say something that will make him tuck tail and run, I don't. His unwanted attention may frustrate me, but he's a decent man, and I'm working hard on keeping my wayward tongue from its arsonist tendencies.

I glance down the off-white dress that was over Maggie's arm when she appeared on my doorstep this morning. I suppose it isn't bad, what with the absence of ruffles and floaty material. Also, its skirt isn't any of that fitted stuff that restricts my stride. If I have to wear a dress, I could do worse.

"That dress does you good." Boone's color is almost back to normal.

"Thank you. It's on loan from Maggie. Of course"—I smile—"I doubt she expected me to accessorize with a fanny pack."

"Or the critter in there."

Especially the critter. I ease back the zippered flap to reveal my sleeping opossum. "I didn't set out to bring Reggie, but she worked herself into a state as I was leavin'. Seeing as I haven't gotten her out much lately, I gave in."

Though Boone can see her just fine, he leans in, and when he returns his gaze to me, he shows no sign of relinquishing my personal space. "Is that why you're hangin' back here rather than joining your family?"

I lower the flap. "I thought it best, but now that the hoopla is past"—including a hair-raising moment when Birdie threw a tantrum that Trinity quickly got under control—"I'd better put in an appearance. Bye, Boone."

"You know, if you took me up on my offers of dinner, there'd be more occasions to dress up."

Why does he persist? Twice a week I stop at the Pickwick Arms to tend their live plants, Boone asks me out, and I turn him down—twice a week, every week since he was hired three years ago to manage the newly renovated hotel.

"Have I told you how much I like your new hairstyle?"

Twice a week, every week since I came undreaded. "Yes, thank you." I look to the other members of my family who have gathered near Uncle Obe and the sculptor, Reece Thorpe. "Well, I'd better—"

"And that I think it's healthy you finally took off your weddin' ring?"

Twice a week, every week since I strung it around my neck. I glance down at my ring finger and am relieved by the pale circle of flesh that remains, though only because I started wearing a bandage while working outdoors so it won't tan.

"I'll see you again soon, Boone." I hurry across the town square park toward the Pickwicks.

Maggie's thirteen-year-old daughter sees me coming and breaks from the group. "You made it!" A few moments later, she gives me a side hug to avoid crushing Reggie, and I don't protest her invasion of my personal space.

Although she's my second cousin, I've always felt more of an aunt to her than I do to the rarely seen Miles and Birdie, both of whom are asleep on Trinity's and Bart's shoulders respectively.

Returning Devyn's hug, I momentarily close my eyes and sink into the rare feeling of being held and loved.

"You should have seen the ceremony!" She gazes up at me from behind thick lenses, and I feel a ripple of movement at my waist. Reggie is awake.

"I did." I release Devyn. "The whole thing."

"Really?"

"From back there." I nod over my shoulder at the massive magnolia tree.

"Why didn't you come sit with—?" She rolls her eyes. "Oh, I know you."

Yes, she does. "Reggie was also a consideration, what with all the media."

She lifts the fanny pack's flap. "Hey, Reg."

My opossum sticks out her pink nose, snuffles at Devyn's hand, and resettles.

I loop an arm through Devyn's and draw her toward the others. "Uncle Obe did a wonderful job."

"He did, though considering the way he was yesterday—all mixed up and lost—we were worried he might not be up to the dedication. But Mom and I prayed last night, and he was more himself today." She glances at me. "See, prayer works."

So does coincidence. Not that I'm ungrateful my uncle was able to beat back his advancing dementia to present the magnificent work of art to the citizens of Pickwick. It's just that I don't see why God would bother Himself over a little speech when He doesn't bother Himself over rampant injustice, the suffering of innocents, the lives of those too young to be cut short…

Oh, Easton, I need to let you go. I touch the ring beneath the dress. *But not yet.*

"How are things going with your mom and her beau?" Entirely rhetorical, as evidenced by their joined hands where they stand before the statue.

"Mr. Reece is the one"—Devyn allows the change of topic—"but Mom says there's no reason to rush things, and much as I'd like to have a father full time, I know she's right. And Gram says it's best too."

She's not talking about Maggie's uppity mother, Adele, who went to Mexico for a month to visit her estranged husband and decided to stay "awhile longer." She's talking about her newly discovered grandmother, Corinne Elliot. At the end of my cousin's recent DNA quest to discover which of her high school beaus fathered her daughter, it wasn't Reece who was standing but Corinne's son. And yet to my surprise, Reece *is* still standing. By Maggie. Had I never known love myself, I wouldn't believe what those two have, but there it is. Thankfully, Devyn is a part of it. And a good thing, or Reece and I would have words.

As we reach the others, I murmur, "To be continued."

"When I spend the night."

"Sounds good." I release her.

Maggie's gaze falls on me first, and she pulls a face at the sight of my fanny pack around her raw-silk dress. She'll get over it. Now Piper…

She also pulls a face, but more of the "you've got to be kidding me" kind. I'm tempted to lift the flap, but she wouldn't see the humor in it—that whole pickled corn incident. How was I to know Reggie would investigate the meal Piper abandoned to take a phone call in the middle of our supper?

No, I shouldn't have left Reggie unattended, but Piper shouldn't have frightened her into playing possum—well, *trying* to play possum. Reggie's wiring is a bit messed up, probably from the hit-and-run that killed her mother and siblings and left her nearly tailless.

"I told you Bridget would be here." Bart shifts a softly snoring Birdie on his shoulder.

With a hand circling Miles's back, Trinity bobs her head. "You were right."

Suddenly I have an image of them with their own children, and it isn't as worrisome as it was months ago. Maybe they will be good at parenting.

I cross to Uncle Obe and kiss his whiskery cheek. "That was a nice dedication. And this is certainly an improvement over that statue of Great-Granddaddy."

He gives a small smile. "This statue better serves our town."

I let my gaze climb over the curves and hollows and feel heat radiate from the bronze, evidencing the sunlight absorbed by the big hunk of metal. Good old solar energy. "It really is amazin'."

"Did you see the…sign, er, plaque?"

"No."

"Come 'round here." He leads me to the other side that faces the church.

I catch sight of that Wesley woman where she stands alongside her Caddy, fluttering her hand at someone, and I glare at her back.

"Here." Uncle Obe gestures at the engraved plaque set in the granite base.

I bend, causing my hair to fall forward. Pushing it behind my ears, I hunker down.

The Master Weaver
by Reece Thorpe

In commemoration of the textile industry
and the dedicated men and women
who wove life into the town of Pickwick

Psalm 139:13–16

Had to throw God into the mix. But it's Uncle Obe's right, seeing as he footed the bill. Shading my eyes, I peer up at him. "Very nice, but how does this statue of a textile worker—"

"This here's the master weaver."

I nod. "How does it tie in with the Bible reference?"

"You don't know those v-verses?"

He's forgotten whom he's talking to. "'Fraid not." Leastwise, not by their numbers, though to admit it would give him too much hope, and I don't want to disappoint him.

"Psalm 139:13–16." He looks heavenward. "'For you created my inmost being; you knit me together in my mother's womb. I praise you because I am fearfully and wonderfully made; your works are wonderful, I know that full well.' "

How does he recite verses without stumbling, as if memory is not an issue?

" 'My frame was not hidden from you when I was made in the secret place. When I was woven—' " Down comes his chin. "Woven...weave... weaver. See?"

I nod, still trying to figure out how the words are flowing like a river.

" 'When I was woven together in the depths of the earth, your eyes saw my unformed body.' "

Struck by a feeling of being watched, I glance over my shoulder, but the real estate agent and her car are gone, and no one appears to be looking my way.

" 'All the days ordained for me were written in your book before one of them came to be.' " Uncle Obe looks at me again. "Appropriate, hmm? And beautiful."

Under the circumstances, I beg to differ on the beautiful part, since God's Word admits to ordaining that my uncle's last days be fraught with early onset dementia, causing him to teeter toward childlike dependence. Why, he can't even shave himself anymore, that task falling to Piper—when he allows it, which he didn't today.

I straighten, and though he lifts his eyebrows to remind me he's waiting on my agreement about the verses, I say, "So this statue is not only in commemoration of the textile workers, but of God."

He frowns, and I'm slapped with guilt at the confusion caused by the turn in the conversation. "You can't honor one without the other. But see, I only referenced the..." He taps the plaque. "...verse in case someone decides to be offended by God's Word and tries to have it removed."

It's hard to believe he compromised the expression of his beliefs, especially considering how important they have become to him these past few years.

"Of course, it has the added…you know, good thing—"

Benefit.

"—of piquin' a body's curiosity and making him turn to the Bible or…" He nods over his shoulder. "…the rather convenient church across the street." He chuckles, a warm sound I could wrap myself in for how scarce it's become.

Once more bothered by the feeling of being watched, I start to glance over my shoulder, but Uncle Obe says, "Can't say I don't still have a few brain cells wigglin' around up here."

"You're a sly one."

"Don't tell my mother."

I catch my breath. Is he doing a bit of that back-in-time traveling that seems to be happening more frequently?

"Something wrong?"

"No!" I sweep a hand toward the statue. "I'm just impressed by all you've done. And I'm proud of you. We all are."

His smile comes out again, only to turn down. "Not all. They didn't come."

His estranged son and daughter.

"Piper sent invitations, but…nothing."

I long to tell him he'll hear from them soon, but I can't keep feeding into his hope.

"My prayers aren't being answered, Bridget."

Welcome to the club— *Oh, stop your woe is me-ing! This is about Uncle Obe and his last wish. A dying wish.*

"I'm startin' to think I might never see them again."

Maybe that wouldn't be such a bad thing since they appear unwilling to forgive.

"Bridget?" He lays a hand on my shoulder.

"Yes?"

"I know it's not your…thing…but would you pray for me?"

It's more than "not my thing." It's not *me*, Easton Buchanan's widow. Unfortunately, the only way out is to hurt Uncle Obe. Or fake it. I give his hand a squeeze. "All right, but I warn you, it's been a long time."

His face lightens. "Too long."

Is he using his dementia to his advantage again? Regardless, his need is real. "Okay. I think we bow our heads, right?"

My attempt at funny bounces off him. "You can. I'm gonna look up."

Not a bad idea, especially if it keeps onlookers from getting the wrong idea about the state of my faith. Give them an inch, and they'll be walking the quarter mile up my driveway to talk me into church. *Er, in case You get any ideas, God, this doesn't change a thing. This time, I really am just the messenger.*

Focusing on the blue overhead, I say softly, "God, You know my uncle's heart and the hearts of his children. I pray You will give them peace and restore them to one another." *Of course, knowing You, that's asking a lot.* "Amen." I pull my hand from Uncle Obe's.

He drops his hand from my shoulder. "That was sh-short, kind of sweet."

"My specialty. Now let's rejoin the others."

He steps ahead of me. As I follow him around the statue, I once again have the feeling of being watched and look over my shoulder. That's when I see him where he sits on a bench in front of the church. He's here. In Pickwick. The dog!

8

Here's my chance to tell J. C. Dirk what I think of his big-city manners, his superior attitude, his—

Whoa! Bad manners aside, this could be good. What else would he be doing here if not to take me up on my proposal? Or at least consider it more fully? This means I'll have to hold on to that piece of mind I was going to give him.

Though I can't see his eyes behind the sunglasses, I know from his closed-lipped smile to the palm-out hand he raises in acknowledgment that he's looking at me.

Suddenly grateful for Maggie dressing me—not that I would have worn *ratty* jeans to the dedication—I turn toward him. And feel a wiggle at my middle. Reggie. In a fanny pack around a silk dress.

I hold up a finger, turn, and loosen the pack's clasp as I hurry around the statue. Piper is the only one of the family who remains, and a look around reveals the others are heading across the park.

"Axel went to get the Jeep so Uncle Obe won't have far to walk." Piper hooks her straight red hair out of her eyes.

"Good." I extend the fanny pack, out of which Reggie has stuck her pink nose. "I'm sorry about this, and I know you'd rather not, but he's here."

"What?" She shakes her head and peers past me. "Where—?"

"J. C. Dirk. The developer. Here." I snatch up her hand and push the pack into it.

"Oh no!" As she thrusts it back at me, my opossum's head emerges; however, when my critter gets a gander at who's holding her, she goes back under.

"I won't be long." I head opposite. "Be gentle."

"I…but…this…" As I turn the corner of the statue, Piper says sharply, "Where's Uncle Obe?"

That stops me. Surely he's here, having come around the statue ahead of me. However, when I scan the area, there's no sign of him. But I was only momentarily distracted by J.C. Or maybe not…

"He was just in front of me."

The concern on Piper's face doubles. "He's wandered off again."

On my watch. But he can't have gone far. He has to be near. I look across the street to where J.C. sits, but my uncle is not among those strolling the sidewalk in front of Church on the Square, the boutique, or the ice creamery. I turn to the west side of the square. Not in front of the gift shop, Maggie's auction house, or the coffee—

Back up! That's him going into Copper's Beanery and Lending Library. "I see him!" I show Maggie's dress no mercy as I cut diagonally across the park. Fortunately, the shoes are flats. Not so fortunately, I'll bet my little scene doesn't escape J.C. But at least he won't witness my opossum-toting side.

I enter Mr. Copper's shop and am assailed by the scent of ground coffee beans. Though the place is a local favorite, especially since the recent opening of a chain coffee shop forced him to renovate and add the lending library, today it's busier than usual owing to the dedication.

I stand on tiptoe and spot my uncle in the back corner. All the tables are occupied, but he stands in the middle of the area frowning from one table to the next.

"Uncle Obe!" I call but am drowned out by the buzz of customers and the hiss, grind, and roar of the monstrous espresso machine. Squeezing past those in line, I slowly advance across the shop. As I near, a woman with dark auburn hair, who appears to be about my age, rises from a two-person table. She says something to my uncle and gestures for him to join her.

He stares at her for a long, socially inappropriate moment before nodding.

I'm grateful for her compassion, though it's almost unnecessary. No sooner are they seated than I reach them. I claim my uncle with a peck on the cheek. "I'm sorry we were separated, Uncle Obe."

"Were we?"

"Just for a moment." I look at the woman. "Thank you for offering my uncle a seat. It's been a long day, and he's tired."

Her smile is tentative, gaze faulty. Still, she's pretty in a Catherine Zeta-Jones way. Of course, that's an understatement, since anyone in a Catherine Zeta-Jones way is beyond pretty.

"I imagine he is." There isn't an ounce of the South in her voice. "I attended the d-d-"—cheeks coloring, she swallows—"I attended the dedica-cation."

Either she's terribly shy or it's me. Though I'm used to bringing out the nervous in people (that Wesley woman was an exception), it doesn't happen as frequently since the shedding of the dreads. Too, today I'm dressed "civilly." Terribly shy, then.

"It"—her smile is apologetic—"ran a bit long."

Not my uncle's fault. That honor goes to our yackety mayor. "Well, I'm glad you could attend. It was a special day for our family."

Her gaze becomes more certain, and I wonder if the glimmer in her eyes is silent laughter. "The Pickwicks."

Our reputation for dysfunction precedes us again. "That's right." I touch my uncle's arm. "Time to head home, Uncle Obe. Piper's waiting."

"Oh, Piper," the woman says. "I have an appointment with her—your cousin, I believe—on Monday."

I look more closely at her. "For?"

She glances at Uncle Obe, presses her lips together, and raises her dark, thinly shaped eyebrows.

Oh. *That.* I forgot Piper is seeking a live-in caregiver. Maybe compassion wasn't what made this woman rescue Uncle Obe. Maybe she wanted to see what she was getting herself into.

She stands and sticks out a hand. "M-Mary Folsom."

Hopefully her caregiving skills are more certain than her speech. Uncle Obe may be the best in the line of Pickwick men, but when his streak of stubborn meets the disease of dementia, he's difficult to handle.

I shake Mary's hand and am surprised by her firm grip. "Bridget Buchanan."

As we part hands, her eyes shift to my ring finger, and my heart goes bump. What if she thinks I'm divorced? That Easton left me? *Since when do you care what people think?*

Since I took off my ring. It wasn't hard to go from being Bridget Pickwick to Bridget Buchanan, wife of Easton. Hard was going from wife to widow, and now widow without a ring that might make some think I've shed my husband and his memory as easily as my dreads. That fear visits me when someone who doesn't know about Easton glances at my left hand, and I long to pull the ring from my shirt and say, "See, not divorced! Happily married. Unhappily widowed." But I don't. And I won't. If Mary Folsom is hired, she'll learn more about our family than she cares to.

"It was nice m-meeting you," she says.

Maybe that's not shyness but a stutter. "And you, Mary." I turn again and cup Uncle Obe's elbow to urge him to his feet.

Frowning at the woman, he says, "It was good to meet you, Marie."

She appears taken aback, but while I expect her to correct him to "Mary," her slightly gaped mouth turns into a smile. "I hope to see you again, Mr. Pickwick."

"That would be n-nice."

They share a speech impediment, though his is dementia based. I give Mary a parting smile and step aside to allow my uncle to precede me across the coffee shop. It takes some zigging and zagging to get past the press of customers, but finally we exit onto the sidewalk.

"Pretty woman," Uncle Obe says.

"She is." I peer across the square at the church where J.C.—

He's gone, and I'm part disappointment that I missed an opportunity to connect, part relief that I won't have to hide Reggie after all.

"Over here, Bridget!"

Piper stands in front of the old theater Maggie recently purchased from the Pickwick estate to serve as her auction house. On the other side of her is the Jeep that Axel has pulled to the curb. Her face is anxious, and for good reason.

J.C. is with her.

As I stare at them, he looks up from where Reggie's head peeks above the fanny pack Piper gingerly holds before her. His eyes no longer hidden by sunglasses, he smiles. He knows, and all because I had to chase after Uncle Obe. Which is my fault—and J.C.'s! What does he think he's doing, showing up here after weeks of silence and without a word of warning? Come to think of it, this whole thing is more his fault than mine. Maybe I will give him a piece of my mind.

Don't go burning bridges that may still be passable.

I force a smile for J.C., who shifts his gaze to Uncle Obe and frowns. Doubtless, he's drawn a connection between my flight across the park and the man at my side. For fear he'll identify Uncle Obe's affliction and use it to his advantage in acquiring the property, I determine to avoid introductions.

"Piper and Axel are over there, Uncle Obe." I ease him to the right.

"My godson," he says as Axel exits the driver's side. "Goodness, that boy's gotten big."

Oh dear.

Leaning into me, Uncle Obe allows me to guide him down the sidewalk, which makes me sad. I wish he would grumble and shake me off. But not today. Maybe not ever again.

No, it's just been a long day. Tomorrow he'll be more himself. I hope. *Okay, Lord, I give in, but don't think this means we're good. Here goes: Please don't let my hope be in vain.*

As Uncle Obe and I continue forward, Axel moves toward us with a slight hitch that draws one's eye to his prosthetic leg, a mechanical marvel he is unashamed of. Rightly so.

As sometimes happens, the smile in the middle of his goatee makes me regret I wasn't ready to reset my life when he came to Pickwick several years ago. He's a good man, but he and Piper are a better fit than he and I would have been, especially taking into account his faith. How does one go from being a lukewarm Christian to embracing God *after* He allows friendly fire to mince one's life?

"May I?" J.C. says.

Returning my gaze to him, I catch Piper's eager nod a moment before she lets J.C. lift Reggie out of the fanny pack. I suppress a cry of dismay.

"Don't take it personal." Axel appears before Uncle Obe and me, then nods over his shoulder, allowing a glimpse of his sandy-colored ponytail. "Piper's just not much of an animal person."

"Then I hope you're not planning on having rug rats." Of course, I know they are. I'm just out of sorts. This is not how my day was meant to shake out. Home is where I ought to be heading, a tomato and mayo sandwich on my mind—*not* J. C. Dirk.

I relinquish Uncle Obe into Axel's care and step past them. Piper watches my approach. Face guilty as all-get-out, she gives a helpless shrug.

Helpless, my foot, the pickled corn addict! Still, I manage to pop a pleasant expression in place for the benefit of the man who appears at ease holding a wild animal. It helps that Reggie also seems at ease, sniffing at his shirt that probably cost what I spend seasonally on jeans.

Putting on the brakes two feet from J.C. and Piper, I squash the impulse to snatch my baby back. "Mr. Dirk, what a surprise—"

"J.C." His green eyes are intent. "We did make it to a first-name

basis the last time we met, *Bridget*." His smile seems to come easily, as if
a natural by-product of all that laughing he's doing at my expense.

"Did we?" My voice rises. "Why, that was so long ago, I hardly recall." *And you are in no position to scold. Play nice!*

He nods. "Longer than anticipated, but I'm here now. And holding
an opossum, no less. Interesting choice of pet."

He's thinking *redneck*. Unfortunately, with embarrassment rising up
my neck, the word fits—colorwise. "Reggie is one of my rescues." *Did
you just deny her? Why, all that's missing is a rooster's crow.* No, what's missing is a filter. I don't know what the Bible is doing in my head. Was it
the prayer Uncle Obe forced on me? The little prayer *I* slipped in?

"Reggie?" J.C. glances down. "So *this* is the friend that doesn't like
to sleep alone."

It takes me a moment to decipher that, but then I recall standing in
his office and voicing my concern that Reggie would have to sleep alone
if I missed my plane. J.C. assumed I was talking about a man. Now he
knows better, and there goes a piece of the image I suffered for.

Resigned to whatever he thinks of me, I say, "Yes, Reggie," and step
forward. She looks around, and although I expect her to scramble for me,
she stares at me as if with accusation. Why do I have this feeling she
knows I denied her?

J.C. hands her over, and our fingers touch in passing. On the outside, I bear up, but on the inside, something wrong is going on. *Get
behind me, Sa—!* Ah! The Bible again, much of it learned through everyday conversation with Easton who, for all his unwillingness to conform
to how a Christian ought to look and behave, believed as I've never
known anyone to believe. And look where that got him.

No, I won't. I have too much going on to top it with regret and bitterness I'm doing my best to get past.

"It's been a long while since I had contact with an opossum," J.C. says as I settle Reggie against my chest, "but I know tails are standard equipment."

Making fun of Reggie's affliction, is he? "I'm surprised you've had any contact with opossums."

A muscle moves in his jaw. "You assume I'm a big-city boy."

Boy nothing! "Aren't you?"

"For the most part." He sweeps his gaze around the town square. "But this setting isn't entirely unfamiliar to me."

Then he's lived in a small town? The pace must have driven him crazy.

"Excuse me." Piper holds out the fanny pack. "But I need to get going. Axel and Uncle Obe are waiting."

I forgot about her—rude. Hooking the pack over my arm, I smile at my cousin. "I assume the two of you introduced yourselves."

"We did, and I told Mr. Dirk I'd be happy to discuss his interest in the Pickwick estate."

Meaning I can slip into the background, holey jeans and all.

J.C. extends a hand to my cousin. "I look forward to meeting with you and your uncle." They shake. "And, of course, Bridget."

There's no *of course* about it. Not only does this man disturb me like I'm not ready to be disturbed, but this time of year is about my busiest, what with running the nursery and constructing crop mazes for farms in the area that depend on the extra income generated by harvest festivals. "Actually, my part in bringing together the two parties is done, so I'll let you and Piper hash it out."

J.C. frowns. "I believe I made it clear that should I pursue an interest in the Pickwick property, your continued involvement would be required."

That gets my back up. Yes, he said that if he decided to look into my family's property, he and I would speak again, but we've spoken.

"And you did lead me to believe you have a special interest in the land being developed in an environmentally responsible manner."

Still, I want to argue with him. But I also want something good to come of the sale of the family estate, and seeing as he's the closest we have to a "taker," I have to be on my best behavior—what's left of it.

Stroking Reggie, I look at Piper. "I'll see you at the meetin'."

She nods and steps toward the Jeep. Momentarily, it pulls from the curb.

"Your uncle," J.C. stares after the vehicle, "is he all right?"

His inquiry sounds genuine. Even so, considering his reason for visiting Pickwick, it's best to leave him in the dark for as long as possible. "He's tired." Not a lie. "It's been a big day."

"Yes." J.C. returns his gaze to me. "The statue is a nice addition to the park—his gift to the town of Pickwick, I understand."

Did he see the unveiling? "That's right."

The space between his eyebrows creases, then clears. "So, tomorrow morning. Nine o'clock. While it's still cool. Will that work for you to show me the property?"

Of course he wants to see it. But I'll be laying out a design for a corn maze. And isn't showing property the job of a vulture—er, real estate agent? "I'm sure the agent—"

His cell phone rings, and after an "Excuse me," he leaves me hanging. Fortunately, his noncommittal responses to his caller span less than a minute.

As he lowers the cell, I clear my throat. "As I was sayin', I'm sure the agent who has the listing will be happy to take you over the property."

"I prefer to be shown by someone who knows it well. My guess is that's you."

I grab at the nearest excuse. "You do realize tomorrow is Sunday. And in these parts, it's a day of worship and rest." His offices *are* in the South.

"I hadn't considered that. I apologize. So why don't I join you for the service? Afterward, we can look over the property."

Me in church? Bridget Buchanan whose last walk down the aisle was on legs that barely carried her to the casket—

"Ow!" I snatch my finger from Reggie's mouth. She bit me! Of course, I am about squeezing the life out of her. "Reggie," I gently rebuke, "not nice."

"I suppose that's why people shouldn't keep wild animals."

He supposes wrong—in Reggie's case. She needs me. I smooth her tense back. "She's just out of sorts what with all the handling." *No thanks to you.*

"Should you have a doctor look at that?" He eyes my hand.

"Reggie is perfectly healthy. Nothin' to worry about."

He nods. "I see you decided to do away with the fake nails."

My throat clenches as I remember the ride to the airport when I said I was grateful I'd be home soon so I could have my nail repaired. So there goes another piece of my image. Not that my fingernails look bad—I *did* clean under them.

"My nails needed a break from the nasty chemicals."

"And your face?" He leans into my personal space. "You have freckles that you didn't have in Atlanta."

Makeup had concealed the light sprinkling. Yet another chink in my image. "I'm lettin' my skin breathe."

With a cheeky smile, he takes a step back. "So, which church do you attend?"

Not a one. And had I considered J. C. Dirk in the context of church, I believe I would have applied "not a one" to him. I don't like it when people surprise me. I wave a hand. "Don't let my Sunday habit inconvenience you. We can meet up afterward."

He tilts his head to the side, causing the afternoon sun to turn the tips of his light brown hair blond. "No inconvenience. I like a good service, especially as I too often allow work to keep me from regular attendance."

My attempt to keep my Sunday out of his greedy hands has backfired. "All right." Honestly! What else can I say? *How about "I don't attend"?* And damage my image further? Make him think I'm not only a redneck but a heathen? Cause him to reconsider doing business with a Pickwick?

"I didn't realize I was asking such a difficult question." His eyes glint.

"Sorry, I'm just…" I touch my forehead. "Long day."

"I understand. Where should we meet tomorrow?"

Feeling the call of Church on the Square, I peer past him. It was *our* church.

"Convenient." J.C. follows my gaze. "I'm staying at the Pickwick Arms."

Great. Not only is he zeroing in on my ex-church, but he's parking himself at a business on my plant-care rounds. And why is he staying at that old hotel? It's had a face-lift, but surely the new all-suites hotel is more the speed of a technology-savvy, concierge-dependent businessman.

"It's all of a thirty-second walk," he adds.

More like a minute, but with that energy of his...

"I saw the church has an early service at eight thirty. Let's meet in the lobby at eight twenty."

Just like that? As if it's a given?

I jump at the rumbling hiss that rises from my chest like a teakettle before it sets to whistling. It's Reggie, the surprise being that I rarely hear the sound from her. Fortunately, this time my squeezing doesn't earn me a bite. Easing my hold, I look up to find J.C. watching me with raised eyebrows.

"Am I ruffling your feathers, Bridget?"

"No, I—" Oh, forget it! "Yes, you are."

He considers me, giving rise to the hope he'll back off and leave me to my Sunday. "I apologize."

Then we understand each other.

"However, I do need to see the property. And I'd like you to show it to me."

Well, *I* understand *him*, a man who is accustomed to getting his way.

"I'm weighing a few projects to determine which best fits the needs of my investors." He jangles the contents of his pockets. "So before I return to Atlanta Monday night, I need to evaluate the property's potential."

My nerves teeter. Regardless that his development of the Pickwick estate would be environmentally conscious, I'm realistically aware it would have to be a moneymaker, but *potential* sounds exceedingly *commercial*.

"Tomorrow it is." J.C. reaches to me.

I startle, but it's Reggie's feathers—er, *fur*—he ruffles. And she doesn't bite *him*. "See ya around, Reg."

I watch him all the way to his hotel across the square, not because I like his backside or anything carnal like that but to be certain he doesn't see me heading for my truck. I'm not ashamed. It's just that I've lost enough of the image created for him.

9

Sunday, September 19

N ot going in. Can't. Not won't—can't. Not yet.

How's that for "speaking into *non*existence"? Uncurling my fingers from the door handle of the Jeep I borrowed from Axel, I look from Church on the Square to the dashboard clock. Eight twenty, and I'm not where I should be. I'll just have to say something came up. J.C. doesn't have to know the "something" was memories. He wants to see the Pickwick estate, fine. He wants me to walk down that aisle and sit beside him in a pew, not fine.

At 8:25, he exits the Pickwick Arms and strides down the sidewalk to join those heading for church. I slip down in the seat. "Late, hmm?" And here I assumed he was waiting inside. But then I can't see him hostage to anyone's timetable. Meaning, he's not going to like my no-show, but what can I do? I can't. Not yet. All I can do is wait for him to get his "God fix" and hope the interest of the single women in church appeal to his ego enough to render my absence unnoticeable. And our Pickwick-ettes are sure to take a shine to him, what with his fine face, expensive attire, and absent wedding band.

I glance at my ring finger that less and less misses the weight of *my* wedding band. It felt so light at first.

When J.C. enters the church, I return to a full upright position and shift my thoughts to how to pass the next hour. I consider the hotel that is on tomorrow's plant-care route. Had I brought my "stuff," I could take care of business today, but I'm empty-handed. And overdressed.

I peer at the white blouse and black slacks I pulled from the back of my closet—not the best attire in which to explore the Pickwick property, but I dressed according to the belief I could walk into church. Of course, it could be worse. I could have worn another of Maggie's dresses that she offered when I tried to talk her into accompanying me today. Unfortunately, since she and Reece are taking Devyn horseback riding at the Biltmore Estate in Asheville after church, it'll just be J.C. and me.

I tune in to the *Carolina Gardening Spot* radio show, not only to have something to show for my time, but to drown out any hymn singing that might sneak out the cracks in that old building.

I try to appear casual-like, though not five minutes ago I was thanking my stars I'd roused from my doze before church let out. Had I not, I might have missed J.C.—or been caught sleeping behind the wheel.

As he strides toward me, I straighten from where I leaned against the Jeep's fender moments before the church doors were propped open.

Holding me with his half-hooded gaze, he halts. "I've been stood up before—"

And he admits it?

"—but never after being invited to someone's church."

He *wasn't* invited! *Play nice, Bridget.* "I apologize." I relax into my Southern lilt, the better to defuse the situation (when I need to tap into my inner belle, I can). "There are just some days when a body can't get going. But here I am, and your carriage awaits."

His eyes shift to the vehicle behind me, and he frowns.

Does he consider it beneath him, this man accustomed to having a driver? Huh! Wonder how much deeper that frown would go had I picked him up in my truck.

"Borrowed?" he asks.

Is that what the frown is about? That he recognizes the Jeep as the one Axel picked up Uncle Obe in yesterday? "It is." I turn and give the hood a pat. "Great for all terrain. So jump in and we'll—"

"You might want to dust off your backside."

I jerk my head around.

Smiling up one side of his mouth, he looks at said backside. "I'd offer to, but my attempt to set you right might see *my* backside dusted."

I twist myself out of shape to confirm the presence of dirt that transferred from the Jeep's fender to my black slacks. Lovely. I slap at my rear. "It's good to know you have common sense, J.C."

Ten minutes later, we're cruising down Pickwick Pike. With the only sounds those of the road beneath the tires and the air flapping at the canvas top, I'm grateful for J.C.'s interest in the passing scenery that saves me from conversing.

"Good message today," he says.

Grateful too soon.

"All about being yourself."

If not for *him,* I could be myself. Could be wearing 501s instead of fancy slacks. Could be going about my day without a growing awareness of the man beside me.

"Something a lot of people struggle with. What about you?"

I catch my reflection in his sunglasses. "I'm Bridget Buchanan. What you see is what you get." Ninety-nine times out of a hundred. This just happens to be the *one* time.

"Is that right?" He angles toward me. "I wouldn't have guessed that."

No? Of course, toting Reggie around in a fanny pack was a pretty big giveaway. And I am missing my claws. However, to counter those losses, I did apply a thin layer of makeup this morning.

Peripherally, I catch the tilt of J.C.'s head. Disturbingly, I feel the rove of his eyes. "Often when people want something from someone," he says, "they put their best face forward."

And I let it be known I want something from him. "We all do that, don't we?" *So don't think you're immune, J. C. Dirk! I'll bet there's another side of you not open to viewing.*

"True, that's one of my shortcomings—not being a 'what you see is what you get' person."

Something in his tone makes me glance his way.

"You've been warned," he says, then directs his attention out the window.

What does that mean? Something to do with the Pickwick estate? But he wouldn't come all this way if he didn't have a genuine interest in the property. He's a businessman. He doesn't have time—

Could be a widow sniffer.

Not likely. I've had my share of male attention, even when I was dreaded, but this man has plenty of access to pretty women. Guess I'll have to keep my eye on Mr. What-you-see-is-*not*-what-you-get.

"I appreciate the warnin'," I drawl, slowing the Jeep as one of several entrances to the Pickwick estate comes into view. Farther up the road is the gated entrance, complete with a long aggregate driveway that ends at the mansion set regally atop a hill, but I'll save that for when Piper, Axel, and Uncle Obe return from their brunch-after-church outing.

I cross the opposite lane, bump to a halt in the scrabbly grass before a rusted access gate, and reach for the door handle.

"I'll get it." J.C. jumps out, unwinds the chain wrapped around the adjoining fence post, and walks the gate inward. "Should I close it?" he calls as I drive through.

"No, it's years since any livestock was kept here."

The Jeep jostles us as we traverse the overgrown dirt road. During the next hour and a half, I talk and point and J.C. listens as we cross the land that Easton presented as the work of God when we first dated—groves of trees, the leafy limbs of which are moved by what he called the sweet breath of God; gently rolling hills he named the bosom of God; wide open meadows he claimed to be the lap of God; vegetated stone ravines, out of which no grass ought to poke through, proof of the tenacity of God's love; streams and rivers ever flowing to slake the thirst he likened to the Word of God; and traces and sightings of wildlife, the immense variety of which he was certain only God could have formed.

Try though I do to keep Easton's poetry out of my head, his lyrical words and reverent voice rush to the surface of my emotions as if to gasp for breath after having been under a long time.

I turn the Jeep onto the service road we've mostly stuck to throughout the drive. "That ought to give you a good idea of the property's potential. Let's head up to the big house, and you and Piper can sit down and talk."

"Let's not."

Then he's decided to pass on the property? "Why?" I hate the creak in my voice.

He looks around, and I try to see past the distorted image of myself in his lenses. "You've shown me the best the estate has to offer. I'd like to see the worst. The quarry."

That torn and desecrated acreage that sits in the middle of the property like a scar at the center of a gorgeous woman's face. I hoped he wouldn't bother himself over it considering how beautiful the rest of the property is. "We can take a look, but—"

His phone goes off and he answers it. I declare, if I didn't care so much about the land, I'd work him up one side and down the other. This call is also indecipherable, and I decide to flick him a little guilt when he hangs up.

"As I was sayin' *before* you took a call in the middle of my sayin'"—I give him a narrow-eyed look—"since it's so warm and I'm sure you'd like some refreshment, it would be better for us to come back later." The quarry doesn't look near as bad at twilight.

"I'd prefer to see it now with the sun overhead."

Of course he would.

"And I apologize for taking the call. It was important."

I draw a deep breath. "The quarry it is."

We head down a different service road at a speed that churns the dirt beneath the grass and weeds and causes dust to float through the open windows. And not a word of complaint from J.C., though his slacks are as formerly black as mine.

I navigate a half-dozen hills, the lushness of which does nothing to prepare a body for what lies ahead. And then, suddenly, it's there, and I feel embarrassment—an increasingly familiar emotion when I'm around him—as I pull into what should be a scenic lookout point. But there's nothing scenic about that long, deep gouge in the earth below us.

Though vegetation has reclaimed large portions of the quarry in the century since the land was mined, it will take several hundred more years before it begins to look like anything other than earth carved out by man and left to fend for itself—unless man gives it a hand. Maybe that hand will be J.C.'s.

Face taut, he peers down into the mess made by my great-grandfather.

"As you can see," I venture, "nature is reclaiming it, but it's slow."

"Too slow."

"Yes, but with a little help—"

"A little?" He looks around. "There is nothing little about this, Bridget Pickwick."

"Buchanan is the name."

He shifts his jaw. "If your family's estate is to be turned into income-producing property, the quarry has to be reclaimed. And it will be a major undertakin'."

The rebuke, sounding more personal than it has a right to—as if *I* had something to do with this—is softened by the drawl that slipped the *g* off his last word.

"Yes," I say, "and I know it won't be cheap."

He opens the door and steps out.

Guessing he doesn't need me tagging along, I cut the engine and sit tight as he walks to the front of the Jeep. While he stares out across the gouged-out earth, his cell phone rings but he doesn't answer.

Dare I believe that had anything to do with my rebuke?

When he sets off along the rim, I lean back in the seat to watch his progress. Unfortunately, it's hampered by frequent stops and minutes spent surveying the quarry from different angles. The minutes tick by, then quarter hours. And though I'm tempted to start the engine to air condition my perspiring body, I resist the waste of energy. It's not as if I'm going to die in this heat—maybe pit out my clothes, but I can wash them. However, ten minutes later I escape the sunlight, abandoning the Jeep to stand beneath a nearby tree.

From time to time, J.C. goes from sight, and each time he reappears, he's more distant. It soon becomes apparent he intends to walk the quarry's perimeter. If that isn't a good sign he hasn't written off the estate, I'd be real annoyed.

When he finally approaches the Jeep from the opposite direction, I've given up on my denimless outfit and plunked down at the base of the tree.

I feel J.C.'s gaze through his sunglasses, but he halts before the Jeep and pushes his hands in his pockets to consider the quarry. I leave him to it, since for a man who moves in fast motion he seems to be making up for it now.

Finally, he peers over his shoulder. "It must have been beautiful before they cut it up."

"I imagine so."

"Tell me about that." He points to the right.

I stand and slap at my backside as I cross to his side. "What?"

"There."

I lean near to follow his finger out past the quarry to a distant cleft in the land made not by man, but nature. Barely visible are the remains of a cabin I haven't seen up close in ages.

I wrinkle my nose at the scent of J.C.'s cologne, though it doesn't smell as powerful as it did before, and pull back. "That's the old homestead of the Calhouns, who owned this portion of the estate before my great-granddaddy."

He lowers his arm. "Are they still around?"

"No." And hard to track down, according to Piper. "Long gone." Not that a remnant of the family didn't linger, but eventually the last of them left Pickwick. Apparently, when I started grade school, there were some Calhoun kids in the grades ahead of me. I don't remember them, but that's probably because they left Pickwick shortly thereafter. *White trash,* some called them, according to Uncle Obe, who related it with disapproval.

With a jangle of his pockets, J.C. says, "The deed for this land is in your family's name?"

"Uncle Obe's, but it's proper and legal."

He turns toward the Jeep. "If you're ready, I'd like to see the mansion."

If *I'm* ready? "Forgive me for keepin' you waiting." I know I shouldn't nip at him, but I'm stretched thin.

J.C. pauses at the passenger door, and one side of his mouth curves higher than the other. "Sorry, that came out wrong."

I raise my eyebrows and climb into the driver's seat.

Though it would take less time to reach the mansion by continuing on the service road, I return to Pickwick Pike to afford J.C. a better impression of our family home via the gated entry and the driveway that ends atop the hill where the big house perches in all its old glory.

"So this is where some of the stone taken from the quarry ended up," J.C. says as we near the mansion.

Being a Pickwick by birth, an environmentalist by heart, I'm guilted at knowing the earth was ripped open so its beauty could serve my great-grandfather's aspirations. "That's right." I make a sharp turn to pull into the front parking area. "Let's go inside."

The mansion shows well—far better than it did before Piper came home. Although there is still plenty to do, the efforts of my PR-consultant-turned-HGTV-viewing cousin are visible upon our entrance.

Piper leads us down the hallway toward the grand staircase. "We're in the library." She pauses at the arched doorway.

As J.C. steps inside, Uncle Obe raises his head from where he sits on a worn sofa perpendicular to a wall of floor-to-ceiling bookshelves. "Who's this?" He squints at J.C. from beneath a gathering of eyebrows.

Piper hurries forward. "It's Mr. Dirk, Uncle Obe. You met him in church today."

He did? I shift my gaze to J.C., who has gone to stand to the right of my uncle.

"Remember?" Piper prompts. "I told you he'd be dropping by to discuss the purchase of the estate so you can continue your good works."

Uncle Obe's face slumps. "I was hopin' it was Antonio."

My heart squeezes. *First,* his son would have to respond to his repentant father's letter, and it seems that neither he nor his sister are willing. Again, I wish his early onset dementia would release him from his regrets.

As I halt beside J.C., he leans forward and extends a hand. "It's good to see you again, Mr. Pickwick."

Uncle Obe places a bony hand in J.C.'s. "And you, Mr.…."

"Call me J.C."

As they part, Uncle Obe looks closer at the other man. "The only J.C. I know is Jesus Christ. What does your J.C. stand for?"

With a faint smile, J.C. says, "If I told you, I'd be back where I started when I made the shift away from my given name. Suffice it to say, I have a good reason to favor my initials."

"An embarrassin' family name?" Uncle Obe chuckles, unaware of J.C.'s suddenly stiff stance. "Try livin' with *Obadiah*." In the next instant, his smile goes belly up. "Not to mention *Pickwick*."

The awkward silence that follows is broken by J.C. "Bridget has shown me around the property. It has good potential, but it's not without its problems, foremost among them the quarry—"

Uncle Obe makes a wide sweep with a hand. "It's been a long day, seein' as I was up early to walk with God in my garden. I'm not up to this…er, talk." He pushes to standing. "Piper here knows what's what and has authority to act on my behalf."

J.C.'s brow furrows in what seems like concern. "Certainly, sir."

Uncle Obe reaches to me. "Would you see me to my room?"

His lack of effort to play down his infirmity makes me hesitate. "I'd be happy to." More than happy if it removes me from the business side of preserving the Pickwick estate.

I settle his hand in the crook of my arm. With a glance at Piper, who is nibbling at her lip, I guide my uncle from the library. We cross to the corridor that leads past the kitchen, then enter the living quarters that belonged to the cook during the mansion's heyday. Though Uncle Obe was forced to move downstairs following his knee surgery over a year ago, he has yet to return to his upstairs bedroom. Piper says it's a good thing considering his wandering, and he seems content with the arrangement, since it affords him one of the best views of his backyard garden.

"All better now?" Uncle Obe eases onto the mattress edge.

"Better?"

"I know you don't care to be in that meetin' any more than I do." As I open my mouth to object, he shakes his head. "It's right what I'm doin' selling the…" His eyes flit left and right. "I can't think of the w-word. Can't even think of another word to use."

I sink down beside him and lay a hand over his hands. "I believe *estate* is what you're looking for."

"Yes. Estate."

"And you said that selling it is the right thing to do, but…?"

"It doesn't make it hurt any less." He half smiles. "Actually it lessens the blow knowin' I'm doing the right thing, but it still hurts. And I know you, of all my k-kin, understand my ache at losin' our family home." He stares at my hand on his. "Times like these, it might be better if this thing I got would…get on with it."

I catch my breath.

He looks around, eyes watery. "You think that's wrong? For me to want to use this disease as poorly as it's usin' me?"

"No, I…" *Was thinking the same thing.*

He pulls a hand from beneath mine and sets it atop my fingers. "Don't tell me that, along with that mess of"—he looks left and right of my face—"hair you got rid of, you also did away with your refreshin' ability to speak in truth."

"Refreshing? There are plenty of people who would say otherwise. I can't tell you the number of bridges I've burned speakin' in truth."

He grunts. "Some people take themselves too seriously. As for my b-bridge, if you burn it, chances are I'll forget and it'll be good as new come mornin'. So is my thinking wrong?"

I stare into the pale, lined face of this beloved man who became beloved too late in my life, absorbed as I was in my causes and my marriage. Not that he's all that old—sixty-two or three—but he's aged so rapidly these last few years, he could be in his seventies.

He raises his eyebrows, and I have to be truthful. "I understand your thinkin'. Ashamed as I am to admit it, I've thought it too—that it might be better were you unaware of all this change. But I don't want you to go someplace in your mind where you can't be reached." My voice breaks. "You're the last great Pickwick. Maybe the only great Pickwick. And I don't like to see you hurtin'."

He regards me a long time, then lowers his chin to his chest. "Thank you. I should get some rest now."

Bridge still standing, I rise and hover as he lifts his legs onto the mattress. "Would you toss that over me?" He points to the throw at the foot of the bed. "I have a chill."

On an eighty-five-degree day. I spread the throw over him. Despite its many years—from the day his mother finished crocheting it to this—it's still vibrantly blue and green.

I look to my uncle to ask if he needs anything, but his lids are lowered. "Rest well," I murmur.

Though I know I should return to the library for the discussion between J.C. and Piper, I need air. And pretty things around me. All of which can be found in Uncle Obe's garden.

10

I was just thinking I might have to beg a ride back to town."

His voice striking me square in the back, I look around at where J.C. stands over me. Caught. On my hands and knees in my *very* formerly black slacks. I only meant to pull the most aggressive weeds from the flowerbeds, but I couldn't stop myself. And now I'm at J.C.'s feet, my image further tarnished.

Brushing myself off, I rise. "Leave it to me to get caught up in gardenin'. I do enjoy the outdoors."

"I can see that." His green eyes travel over me, a bit too slow for comfort. "You were going to join me on the tour of the mansion and discussion about the property."

"I apologize." I start to cross my arms over my chest, but Piper has pointed out that closing off my person drains me of presence and power. "After I got my uncle settled in, I needed fresh air." I reroute my hands to my hips. "And now"—I glance over my shoulder to gauge the sun's position—"look at where the time's gone." Two hours, I'd guess.

He sighs. "In our future dealings, am I to be stood up time and again?"

There does seem to be a pattern developing, and as I search for a better defense than simply the need for fresh air, I bump into two promising words. "Future dealings? You intend to purchase the Pickwick estate?"

"Intend? No. Interested? Yes."

It was silly to think a decision could be made today. We are talking *millions* of dollars. And many more to develop the estate into something environmentally friendly and income producing. I hate being made to feel stupid, especially when stupidity is doled out by my own hand. I should have been at that meeting.

"I'll send out my team to evaluate the property—survey and map the land, take soil samples, check water tables, address zoning issues, conduct feasibility studies."

He says it like it's no big deal, but it sounds like it could take a long time.

"Then," he says, "we go from there."

Why can't he just buy it and put an end to the circling and sniffing of the less environmentally friendly developers? "When can we expect your people?"

"I'll have to get back to you on that."

"You do know there are other interested parties?"

J.C. unhooks his sunglasses from the collar of his shirt and slides them on. "I'm taking it into account. However, I won't be pressured into something to which I'm not fully committed, especially when dealing with other people's money."

Commendable, providing a body isn't on *this* side of the matter. "Then all we can do is wait to hear from you."

"That's all," he drawls, once more letting in the South.

I step past him. "Well, just know that we can't wait forever. If you drag your feet, we'll have to go with someone else."

"Of course."

Not the response I was hoping for. "We'd best get you back to town."

I head for the kitchen's rear door but catch sight of Piper through the windows and veer right to avoid delaying our departure with small talk. As I lead J.C. around the side of the big house, he starts jangling.

Shortly we're back on Pickwick Pike, but as I relax into the silence, he says, "Tell me about your uncle."

Did he pick up on the dementia? Uncle Obe stumbled on a word or two and was a bit socially inappropriate with the J.C.–Jesus Christ digression, but I don't think anything was glaring. Fortunately. Though J.C. may be environmentally friendly and though he seemed to show genuine concern for my uncle, that doesn't mean he wouldn't see dementia as a ticking clock to be used to secure the property at a price below market value.

I cement my attention on the road. "What about him?"

"He became agitated when I started talking about the estate— couldn't wait to leave the room."

I tap the brakes to keep all four wheels on the road that curves above a steep ravine. "It's not easy for him to give up his family home. Of course, seein' as you're accustomed to a life of excess and have probably never lost anything of sentimental value, it might be difficult to appreciate his…feelings." I reluctantly finish the thought, knowing Piper would say I should not have said that.

Further evidencing the bridge against which I thoughtlessly struck a match, I feel J.C.'s gaze fall on me. "That's an assumption you have no right or insight to make."

Deep breath. "I apologize. Other than your reputation for being environmentally conscious, I know nothing about you or your past." Which is fair, considering he knows little about the real me—aside from my opossum-toting ways, lack of allegiance to fake nails, and off-again-on-again relationship with makeup.

He turns his head to survey the scenery. "We'll just put it down to sensitivity over your uncle's condition."

He does know about the dementia. Did Piper tell him? I don't see it. And since it stopped being a secret when Uncle Obe came out about his affliction last year, J.C. must have heard it from one of the locals. Hello, ticking clock.

"It must be hard." He angles toward me. "Standing helplessly by as all traces of the person you know are wiped away."

It is hard, and I'm only a niece. For that, I'm glad my uncle never married, since it seems that slowly losing a spouse to dementia can be nearly as difficult as suddenly losing a spouse. Some say more so, but I would argue. Yes, with dementia there's not only your own pain to deal with but that of your loved one as he slips into a shell of his former self, but there would be time to say good-bye.

"I'm sorry for what your family is going through."

"It's a cruel disease, especially when it happens to someone as kind-hearted as my uncle."

After a considering moment, he says, "He does seem like a good man."

Is that surprise in his voice?

In the next instant, he adds, almost to himself, "It makes one wonder if some sins of the father are still visited on generations of the children."

What's that about? Once we're on a straightaway, I look around. "Sins of the father?"

He looks out the window, shrugs. "I've heard some interesting stories about the Pickwicks."

He's done his homework, but I suppose that's to be expected. "And?"

"Your family has a—"

There goes his phone, tempting me to snatch it from him and chuck it out the window.

He consults the screen and smiles apologetically. "Excuse me, it's important."

Lord, how did we survive without cell phones? Yes, I'm talking to You, but only because You've got to be more disgusted than I am.

Shortly, J.C. is off the phone. "The Pickwick family has a reputation for the scandalous, beginning with your great-grandfather—"

Thank you, sire of my sire of my sire.

"—and the Calhoun land."

So he knows about that. Resenting the need to defend the Pickwicks' honor, I say, "You're referrin' to the tale that the land was ill-gotten by Gentry Pickwick."

"A rigged poker game."

"A hundred-year-old rumor." I reduce my speed as the pike opens up into the town of Pickwick.

"Then you don't believe there's truth to it. That it was put out there by bitter Calhouns."

Actually, if I had to go one way or the other, I'd probably side with the Calhouns. There may be no proof my great-granddaddy cheated, but there's proof he had other shady dealings, including the break with his business partner that made him grab his moneybag—and his partner's—and flee to the hills of North Carolina.

I consider telling J.C. about Uncle Obe's plan to make restitution to the Calhouns, but there's no need to raise concerns that the sale of the property will be anything other than smooth. After all, only a fool poisons the pond from which she's about to drink.

Making it through a yellow light, I glance at J.C. "Who am I to say—?"

The phone again! But this time it's mine. Not that I'll answer it, what with being behind the wheel and in the middle of a conversation. *Why not? A taste of his own medicine would do him good.*

I dig the phone from my pocket. "Excuse me, but this is *very* important." Of course, that might be more believable if I first consulted the screen. I flip open the phone. "Hello?"

"I believe that's a first!" a voice crackles in my ear as if I might lose reception. "Don't know that I've ever gotten through without first being sent to your voice mail."

"Daddy?" I say, too late remembering the man beside me. Well, that takes the wind out of my *very* important phone call.

"Just wanted you to know there's a change of plans for tonight."

Good. After the day I've had, I could do with a quiet night as opposed to sitting across the dining room table from my folks and my active niece and nephew. "All right. We'll have supper another night."

"No, we're still gettin' together, but we're going out."

"With Birdie and Miles?" Are we talking McDonald's?

Daddy snorts. "Bart and Trinity agreed to keep them another night. I don't understand it, but they seem to enjoy spending time with the young uns."

Hmm.

"Thought we'd try out that new place off the square, the one with the onion name."

"The Scallion?"

"Something like that. Anyway, we'll pick you up on the way there."

More unusual. However, as much as I don't care to eat out, I hate to disappoint my mother. "Don't trouble yourself. I'll meet you there."

"No trouble. Just wear something pretty—you know, fittin' for a fine restaurant."

Now *that's* trouble. Or would be if I had returned the dress borrowed from Maggie for the dedication. "What time?"

"Our reservation is for seven o'clock, so we'll swing by your place at six forty-five. Be ready, hear?"

"See you at six forty-five." I close my phone and toss it on the dashboard.

"Supper with your parents?"

I startle at the realization that I allowed J.C. to slip into the background. "Yes."

"That would be Bartholomew and Belinda Pickwick?"

I probably shouldn't be surprised he knows my folks' names. "Yes."

"I wouldn't mind meeting them."

Why? I nearly ask, but that would open a door best left shut since Daddy tends to talk himself into the ground—a weakness J. C. Dirk might exploit. "If you decide to invest in the Pickwick estate, I'm sure there will be plenty of opportunities to meet my folks."

He's quiet a long while, and when he turns to me, I catch a whiff of cologne. "So you don't believe the Calhouns were cheated in a card game?"

I should have known he would return to that. I give my tingling nose a rub. "Who am I to believe one way or the other? I wasn't there." With a sniff that makes me more grateful J.C. will soon be out of the vehicle, I put on my blinker to turn into the town square. "As I said, everything's legal, so if you're worried about Calhouns poppin' up to stake a claim, don't."

"You're sure about that?"

"I am." I draw the Jeep alongside the curb of the Pickwick Arms. "Here you are." And not a moment too soon. I sniff again to keep my nose from running.

"Coming down with a cold?"

Will he be offended if I speak the truth? Oh, why not? "No, colognes and perfumes irritate my sinuses, especially when they're strong, like what you're wearin'."

His eyebrows rise. "I apologize. I'll keep that in mind if we meet again."

He will? The only thing I want him to impress me with is his environmental stance. Of course, going by his "if we meet again," I may never know just how "green" J.C. is.

He reaches for the door handle. "Thank you for driving me around."

When he steps to the sidewalk, I have the feeling Dirk Developers is about to slip away. I lean across the seat. "So we'll hear from you soon?"

He peers back inside. "I'll be in touch."

When? And what is he doing between now and his return to Atlanta? "You said you're stayin' through tomorrow."

"I have a meeting in Asheville before I fly out, so I'll be leaving Pickwick early."

The good news is I won't have to reschedule the hotel's plant service to avoid further assassination of my image. The bad news is I have no idea how Asheville fits into his plans.

I tip my head to the side. "I assume your meeting has something to do with my family's property?"

"All part of the evaluation process."

What other parts are there? And why didn't I get myself to the meeting with Piper and him? Much as I'd like my involvement to be over, there's too much riding on it for me to take the easy way out. Thus when I return to the estate to swap out Axel's Jeep for my truck, I'll have to get the lowdown from Piper.

"Enjoy the remainder of your stay."

He reaches through the window. "Good-bye, Bridget."

I hate that I hesitate before slipping my hand into his. And there's the reason for the hesitation—skin on skin, even if it is only in the vicinity of palms and fingers. This thing that I don't want to be attraction bothers me more than I can say. It's too much like what I felt for Easton before he and I started dating. I haven't felt it with Boone or any of the others who have come sniffing around. And in spite of my intentions to reset my life, it feels like betrayal.

"Good-bye." I start to pull my hand free, but J.C. keeps hold of it. And smiles. "You ought to let your skin breathe more."

"Excuse me?"

"Freckles are a good look for you."

I wore makeup for the benefit of the image created for him, but I didn't expect him to notice. Maybe I'm not the only one feeling these flutterings. Though the possibility makes my pulse jump, I question whether I'm ready for something like this. Best not to encourage it.

I pull my hand free. "I don't believe I asked for your opinion on my freckles."

Something like confusion crosses his face, but then he chuckles and straightens from the Jeep.

Accelerating away from the hotel, I look in the rearview mirror and catch J.C.'s back as he enters the hotel. "Of all men, why him, Lord?" I slant my gaze heavenward. "Just so You know, I wasn't talkin' to You." *Oh yes, you were.* "No, I was…takin' Your name in vain. So don't be thinking You've found one of Your lost lambs. I'm *not* one of them." *Baa-aaa.*

"Not much to tell." Piper grimaces. "I expanded on the information you gave him in Atlanta and answered a few questions. Unfortunately, he's hard to read, so I can't say where he stands on the property." She sighs. "What he needs is competition."

I sit forward in the patio chair. "There are plenty of others interested in the property."

"They're not real competition."

Because of *my* standards. And J.C. knows all about them. "I shouldn't have come on so strongly about the importance of an environmentally friendly development."

"Probably not." Piper frowns. "You said Dirk is meeting with someone before leaving Asheville."

"Yes, but that's all I know." I look past her to Uncle Obe's garden. Its summer beauty is fading, but the deep oranges and golds of autumn are coming into their own. "I did consider setting Maggie on him, what with her undercover work experience."

Piper groans. "Don't remind me."

I'm surprised by the laughter that exits my mouth. "It all worked out, didn't it? Maggie got her DNA sample, found out who fathered Devyn, and she and Reece are together again. I call that a successful covert operation."

"She went about it wrong, and you know it." Piper sits on the opposite side of the wrought-iron table, her flippy red hair tucked behind her ears, blue eyes reproving.

"She was trying to protect Devyn." I defend my favorite cousin. Not that Piper hasn't grown on me, but a twelve-year absence from one's life does strain a relationship, especially if those in question don't much care for each other in the first place.

"Still," Piper says, "if she had—"

The kitchen screen door creaks, and Axel starts down the ramp he built to give Uncle Obe easier access to his garden. Good man. Piper had better deserve him.

"Am I interrupting?" His blue eyes, which have no business being so blue, smile.

"Not at all." I sit back. "We're just tryin' to figure out J. C. Dirk's game plan."

He brushes his mouth across Piper's, and I remember what it felt like to be loved that way. Is it possible to be loved that way again? Although I don't summon remembrance of J.C. holding my hand through the Jeep window, his smile, or his comment about my freckles, it rises all the same. And I feel warmer than the weather warrants.

"My guess," Axel says, "is that Dirk plans to make the most amount of money on the least amount invested."

Grateful for words that put me back on track, I hold up a finger. "But in an environmentally conscious way."

"That does seem to be where the money is nowadays."

True. And I wish it were more about the environment than making a buck off those who want to make a difference for future generations. (Honestly—organic jeans that cost five times what I pay for 501s!) Still, I'll take what I can get, even if it is J.C. with an eye on profit. And an unsettling ability to affect me.

I scoot my chair back. "I'm having supper with my folks, and I've been instructed to dress up."

Piper and Axel walk me through the house to the front door, where I pause. "Let me know how your interviews go tomorrow."

Piper nods. "You said you liked the woman who offered Uncle Obe a seat at the coffee shop?"

I shrug. "She seemed nice. But as I said, her personality is mousy." I raise a hand. "See you."

I hurry down the steps to where Axel parked my truck alongside the Jeep. "Hello, Ford," I croon as I turn the key in the ignition. I back out, shift into drive, and glance at Axel and Piper on the top step, his arm around her.

Feeling a pinch of jealousy, I loosen its grip by calling out the window, "Set a date!"

11

As sure as flies on butter, I've been had. I know it the moment the hostess halts at what should be a party-of-three table. And to further prove it, Tall-Dark-and-Handsome smiles from Daddy to Mama as he rises to greet us, then turns an even brighter smile on me. Yep, had. From my prettily pulled back hair to Maggie's girlie dress, Bridget Buchanan is all trussed up with no place to go. To make matters worse, our fourth wheel is wearing cologne.

I shoot a frown at the increasingly hefty Bartholomew Pickwick, who ought to know better than to set me up. I love my daddy, but I don't always like him. Mostly because *he* didn't like Easton…didn't believe Easton was good enough for me…refused to accept Easton even after the ring was on my finger. I touch it through my blouse. Though Daddy may be on the hunt for a husband worthy of *his* daughter, he's wasting his ammo.

As he continues feigning ignorance of my angst that began with our entrance into the restaurant when patrons set to whispering (she's wearing a dress *again*!), he thrusts a hand at the other man. "Glad you could join us, Caleb."

"I appreciate the invitation, sir." Their hands part and the man reaches to my mother. "You must be the lovely Belinda."

Mama gives an uncertain nod that speaks of her own surprise at his presence. "Why yes, I am." Perking up a little (she looks better than she did yesterday, though still tired), she drapes her hand in his.

And here comes the theatrical kiss to the back of her hand that makes her blush.

"And this is your daughter, Bridget."

I put my hand firmly in his and initiate the shake to let him know I don't go for hand kisses. That's when I catch another breath of cologne. It's not of the choke-me variety, but still…why can't men smell like men? "Bridget Buchanan."

I expect him to check my ring finger, but he doesn't. Of course, seeing as Daddy is behind this, my "suitor" is probably aware of my widow's status. Dark eyes peering into mine, he says, "As pretty as I've heard tell."

Don't let the dress fool you, mister. Your tune would change if you saw me in work jeans and dreads, fertilizer beneath my nails. "Thank you." I pull my hand free. "I don't believe I caught your last name."

"Merriman. Caleb Merriman the second."

Why does that sound familiar?

"Oh!" My mother's blond head bobs. "I remember your daddy. Why, the last time I saw…him…" Her gaze slides to her husband.

"Bygones be bygones." He grunts, then urges her into a chair.

Well, well. I start to lower beside my mother, but Daddy says, "That's where I'm sittin'. You take the seat beside Caleb so you two can get to know each other."

As sure as flies on butter…

Sitting between Caleb and him, it's awhile before I realize I'm holding my breath, and only then because Mama says, "Are you all right, dear? You've gone as red as a tomato." She reaches across Daddy and touches my forehead.

I let out my breath. "It's just a little warm in here."

"But you're—"

"She said she's fine." Daddy opens Mama's menu and places it in front of her. "Now let's see what fits your meal plan, Belinda."

If I was fine, I'm not anymore. I don't like that he monitors her fat and calorie intake, especially while ignoring his own. Yes, she's added extra pounds to her slight frame in the last five years, but she looks good, so why shouldn't she have what she likes from time to time?

"I think pasta, don't you, Mama?" I peruse the menu. "Somethin' with a nice thick cream sauce."

"Oh no," Daddy says. "What she wants is a low-fat marinara sauce."

I shake my head. "The house specialty is peppercorn chicken alfredo. Can't go wrong with alfredo, right, Mama?"

She stares at me across the table, as if for fear a glance her husband's way will find her swimming in red sauce, then presses her shoulders back. "You know how much I like cream sauces." She closes the menu, sandwiching Daddy's hand in it.

"But Belinda—"

"Oh, Daddy, if you want the marinara sauce, you go right ahead."

His frown lands on me with the weight of a slap. However, when Caleb sits forward to gain a better view of the unfolding scene, Daddy swallows whatever he meant to say. I'm liking my "suitor" better by the minute.

My daddy unsandwiches his hand and runs it through his silver hair that evidences he was once a very red redhead. "The alfredo sounds good to me too." He considers his wife. "We can split a plate."

I cup a hand between Daddy's ear and my mouth. "Split? Surely, you don't want Mr. Merriman to think you're cheap?"

I feel his startle. Though scandal is a trench coat he wears as well as other Pickwicks, he does like to maintain the long-lost appearance of wealth. "Actually," he says, "I've an appetite tonight. We'd best have two of that alfredo dish."

Shortly the server slips away, taking our meal orders with her as well as an order for a bottle of wine chosen by Caleb Merriman—some fancy something or other I'd gladly exchange for a beer if my father wouldn't be beside himself. I like the taste of beer, but only the taste, which is why I drink nonalcoholic.

Caleb turns to me. "Chicken primavera? I took you for a vegetarian."

What gives him the right to take me for anything?

"She was," Mama says, "but that was a while back. Missed your meat, didn't you, dear?"

Like I want to share my personal life with Daddy's replacement for Easton.

"And biscuits and pie crusts—all made with animal fat. Oh, and gravy. I make the *best*." Mama points at Caleb. "Let me tell you, tofu will never be to gravy what sausage is. I tried, for Bridget's sake, but substitutin' that wet-sponge stuff for sausage is plain wrong. That's not how the good Lord intended gravy to taste."

Though tempted to shut down this conversation, I determine to be civil. "As you may know, Mr. Merriman—"

"Caleb." His eyes smile—nice brown eyes, framed by long lashes.

"As you may know, it's hard to be a vegetarian in the South, especially when one's mama is as incredible a cook as mine. But I do stay away from red meat—well, mostly. And where free-range is available, that's what I buy." At a premium.

"Regardless, this girl is fit." Daddy gives me a rap on the back that makes me feel like a prize bull. "Not a sick bone in her body. Comes from good stock."

I swivel my head and hiss, "Daddy, I am not in—or *on*—the market for a husband, so please!" *What happened to civil?*

As Mama murmurs, "Oh my," and Daddy distances his gaze, Caleb clears his throat. "Actually…" Ridges rise across his neat brow. "I didn't join you for dinner to be party to matchmakin', Bridget. At this point, my interest lies solely in the Pickwick estate. When I approached your father about acquiring the property, he thought you could give me some insight."

That's the reason for this party of four? I'm relieved. But then, just because that's why Caleb is here doesn't mean Daddy doesn't have an ulterior motive.

I unroll my silverware and shake my napkin into my lap. "I'm glad that's straightened out." And that J.C. might have real competition. This time when I smile at Caleb, it's without effort. "Tell me about your interest in the estate."

He settles back. "I've done well for myself and, I'll have you know, my father didn't put me where I am. Nepotism?" He shakes his head, and his dark hair moves very little, as if full of gel. "No ma'am."

"Commendable." Daddy nods.

Caleb winks at him. "There's good money in latex, and now that I've sold my company, I'm set for life and ready for a change. As much as I like the pace of Asheville, I'm thinking about toning it down."

That surprises me. Yes, Asheville is larger than Pickwick, but other than the flocking of tourists to the Biltmore mansion, the city runs at a relatively sedate pace. Why— Hold it! Asheville!

As Caleb continues his monologue, I look at him anew. I'll bet he was the "important client" in the car with that real estate agent Wesley Trousdale. Ha! The man in the sunglasses revealed. Of course, if he's revealed, so might I be. Has he recognized me as the dreadlocked woman in the beat-up truck who chased them down? I tense, but this is different from J. C. Dirk. Not only does Caleb surely know about my scandalous family, but if Daddy's "bygones be bygones" is any indication of our past association, the Merrimans have been directly affected by our... ahem...shortcomings. So no scrambling to piece together a suitable image.

Caleb turns his attention to me. "That's why I'm considering buying your family's property for a private residence."

He doesn't want to turn it into a moneymaker? "Really?"

"Granted, the estate is a good deal bigger than what I had in mind when I decided to settle down—"

"Wants to settle down," Daddy murmurs to Mama, and I nearly elbow him.

"—but better too big than too small. That's the Merriman motto."

Good to know. "I assume you're interested in the mansion as well."

"I've seen pictures of it, and it's beautiful. Needs updating, but I can see myself living there and raising a family."

"Raisin' a family," Daddy rasps, causing Mama to "ooh" and me to struggle against kicking him under the table.

"What about the rest of the property?" I attempt to overwrite my folks' murmurings. "There's a lot of acreage."

Caleb shrugs. "From what I understand, it's not been doin' much but communing with nature all these years. I see no reason to change that."

Is this man after my tree-hugging heart? "What about the quarry?" I liked J.C.'s talk of setting it right. "You know it—"

Daddy's shoe connects with my ankle.

"Ow!" Snapping my head around, I sense the turning of other heads.

"You all right?" Daddy asks, all innocence.

And here I had the good grace not to kick *him*.

"Did somethin' bite you, Bridget?" Mama asks.

Apparently Caleb isn't supposed to know about that big ugly scar in the middle of the property. But not only is it wrong to try to hide it, nobody pays what's being asked for the estate without picking it over.

I turn to Caleb whose smooth face is lined with concern. "Nothin' to worry about. Now where were we? Oh, right, the quarry—"

"Do you know that man, Bridget?" Daddy interrupts.

Could he make it more obvious he's trying to hide something? I look to him, but the warning I stamp across my eyes goes unnoticed as he peers past me.

"He's payin' you a mite too much attention. Rude, I tell you. Probably a Yankee."

Whoever is looking at me, I'm sure it has more to do with my kick-induced yelp than anything that would give rise to my sire's rarely seen protective side.

Humoring him, I look over my shoulder. There *is* someone watching me. Sitting at a window table, J. C. Dirk raises a hand. Coincidence? I don't think so. He not only overheard my dinner plans but said he'd like to meet my folks.

"Who is he?"

Since the less Daddy knows about what's happening with the sale of the estate, the better, I search for a change of subject until it occurs to me this could be good. Just as J.C. needs a little competition, Caleb could do with some.

"That's J. C. Dirk of Dirk Developers out of Atlanta. I took him on a tour of the estate today. He's very interested." I hope.

I expect Daddy to be pleased at the possibility of two dogs wrangling over one bone, but uncertainty puffs his face. "I didn't realize we had any serious lookers." He glances at Caleb—an apologetic glance.

What's with that? Something to do with his matchmaking scheme? Might he be trying to throw me into the deal? I consider Caleb, but his face is in the blank range. "Based on his environmentally friendly reputation, I approached him about acquirin' the land."

Caleb clears his throat. "Your family ought to consider that you can't get more environmentally friendly than preserving the estate as a private residence."

"That is appealing." *Very* much, but Piper would warn me not to show my hand. I reach to the basket that has appeared on the table and pick out a breadstick. I take a bite and sigh when pockets of warm, yeasty air fill my mouth.

"Hello, Bridget."

Though the voice that speaks between Caleb and me cramps my enjoyment, I know this is an opportunity not to be shirked. "J.C.," I say, all friendly-like, "we were just discussin' you."

His gaze makes the rounds of the table. "Oh?"

I introduce him. Since Mama is the only one who seems pleased to meet him, batting her lashes and drawling, "Lovely to meet you," I almost feel sorry for him. Then she gasps. "Why, you could be mistaken for James Dean."

Mama *would* liken him to someone from her generation, an actor who stands out for me only because of the rebel he played in one of the few classic movies I've sat through with her. I can kind of see it, but Piper is nearer the mark with Simon Baker.

"Well"—Mama wrinkles her nose—"that is, if he wasn't long dead. Of course, he'd be pretty old if he were alive, wouldn't he? Meaning you couldn't possibly be him."

Did she get into chocolate? On the drive over, I thought I heard the crinkle of the foil wrappings that hug the Dove pieces she's so fond of. I didn't say anything since Daddy would come down on her, but I'll bet she was indulging.

"Your hair color is lighter." Mama slants her head to the side. "Or maybe not. I mean, James Dean's films were mostly black and white, weren't they? Or were they?" She looks to Daddy, who is frowning fiercely.

Time to step in. "J.C., I was just telling Caleb here—"

"So you're interested in our property, are you, Mr. Dirk?" Daddy says.

"I am, sir, though whether the estate is a good fit for my company has yet to be determined."

Daddy plucks a breadstick from the basket, takes a bite, and says around his chewing, "My advice is that you save your time and money." He points his breadstick at the man opposite him. "Caleb here is the son of an old family friend and is interested in acquirin' the property for a private residence."

Great. Even *I* know this is not how you play the competition against each other. What is Daddy doing? And if Caleb is the son of such a highly regarded friend that money should take a backseat—forbid!— why do I only vaguely know the friend by name?

J.C. looks more closely at the man to his left. "A private residence."

Caleb inclines his head. "I'm sure we'll come to terms."

"Yes, indeed," Daddy says. "And soon I imagine—"

"I appreciate your optimism, Caleb," I return to the conversation, "but the future of our family estate is a bit more complicated than *terms*. No decision has been made, and no decision will be made until my uncle who owns the property is satisfied with plans for the estate." There. Chew on *that*, Daddy.

J.C. leans down, so near I steel myself for an assault on my sinuses. "I'm pleased to know my trip to Pickwick wasn't for nothing."

Not even a whiff of cologne. And I feel a thrill in remembering he said he would keep in mind my aversion to the stuff. And another thrill at the realization he smells an awful lot like Easton.

He starts to pull back but pauses to finger my sleeve. "I have to say this is my favorite dress on you."

That unnerves me, at first because it seems a territorial thing to say in front of Caleb (I am *not* part of their competition), but then I realize it's the *only* dress J.C. has seen me wear, the first time being at the dedication. Is this his way of letting me know he's peeled away another layer of my image?

He pockets his hands and I hear the jangling. "It was nice meeting you." He looks to Daddy, Mama, and Caleb. "I'll let you get back to your meal."

A meal that drags, not only because of Daddy's embarrassing attempts to assure Caleb the property is as good as his but because of J.C.'s presence in the dining room. However, after Caleb settles the bill (much to Daddy's relief, I'm sure) and we rise to leave, I see two women have claimed J.C.'s table. When did he leave?

As we near the doors, I veer to the right. "I need to duck into the ladies' room."

Mama follows. "I'd best do the same."

"Belinda," Daddy calls, "have you got some antacids in your pocketbook?"

"I think." She turns back.

And that's how I find myself at Caleb Merriman's mercy when I return to the lobby.

12

"Where are my folks?"

Caleb unleans from the wall alongside the mahogany doors that lead to the parking lot. "Headed home."

"What?"

"Your father said he wasn't feeling well and asked your mother to take him home. That makes me your chauffeur."

Of course it does. I know what Daddy's indigestion looks like, and there was no evidence of it when we left the table. *This* is the reason he insisted on picking me up at home. "I've been set up," I say, not caring what Caleb thinks.

"I was thinking that myself, but that doesn't mean we can't make the best of it." He gives a grin that lends a mischievous air and makes me think of Easton. Might there be more to Caleb than tall, dark, and handsome? Of course, maybe he's just buttering me up now that competition for the Pickwick bone has commenced.

"Ladies first." He holds the door for me.

Despite a warming toward him—or maybe because of it—I'm tempted to refuse, but that would mean calling a cab. And so I tuck into his cow-appointed (what is it with men and leather?) sports car.

"Where to?" He slides in beside me.

I direct him away from the town square and down the lightly trafficked Main Street.

"Your father is quite a character," he says as he brakes at a light.

That's a nice way of putting it. "Yes, he is."

"I like him. And your mother seems a gentle soul."

An even nicer way of putting it. Mama may be scattered, overly in-dulgent with her children and grandchildren, easily railroaded by Daddy, and too worried about appearances, but she knows how to love. "Thank you."

"I suppose you're wondering why your father favors my interest in the estate, especially since you've probably never met my family."

Yet one more thing to recommend Caleb—no sneaking through the back door. With only the streetlights to part the darkness from the inte-rior of the car, I turn toward him. "That is a question I wouldn't mind having answered."

The light changes, and he follows another car through the intersec-tion. "Your father calling my father a family friend is…a truth stretcher." He chuckles. "What brought them together years ago was the textile mill."

I nearly groan.

"My father invested heavily in the business in hopes of getting it back to turning a profit." He glances at me. "What you may not know is that when it went under, it took our family's investment down with it."

I now understand my mother's flustered reaction to the Merriman name. "I'm sorry. It was a blow to a lot of people when the mill closed." Especially the workers who went without pay for a month based on Daddy's promise of future compensation. Thankfully, Uncle Obe re-cently made good on that promise, adding to years of accumulated in-terest that made his savings account stagger and moved him nearer the sale of his beloved home.

Caleb doesn't speak again until the traffic thins and Pickwick Pike lies ahead. "Don't think I take it personally." He smiles my way. "I'm simply trying to provide insight into what I believe happened tonight. You see, when I mentioned to my father that I was interested in the Pickwick estate, he insisted on putting me in touch with Bartholomew. Obviously, he views it as a means of gaining the property on more favorable terms—playing on your father's guilt over our loss."

At least Caleb is honest.

"And from his championing of my interest over that Dirk fellow, it seems to have worked. But I want you to know—"

"You're going to turn left, just past that old barn." I point ahead.

"Right. I just want you to know that though I'm very interested in your family's property, I'm not looking to steal it." He clicks on his blinker. "I'll pay what it's worth—providing I like it up close as well as I like it from a distance."

"I appreciate that." Not that anyone will be allowed to steal it.

Caleb slows his car and peers at the dirt road down which I'm asking him to take his shiny turbocharged toy. "Turn here? Really?"

"Really."

"All…right." He crosses the other lane and sucks air as his tires transition from pavement to rock-strewn dirt. Once his car's tail end is off the pike, he brakes and leans forward to consider my headlight-lit driveway. "How far is your house?"

"A quarter mile, give or take."

He slowly sits back. "You know, after such a filling meal, I could use a walk. What about you?"

In sneakers, but heels? Well, at least he's willing to walk me up the driveway. And I do have an alternative to these wretched shoes. "Sure, just let me get out of these high heels."

"Oh! I forgot about that."

"No problem. I'm a barefoot girl." I hook a finger in the back of each shoe and reach for the door handle. "Of course, your fancy loafers are bound to take a beating." I swing my legs out the car door.

"If you can go barefoot, so can I."

Shortly, his shoes and socks safely stowed in the car, pant legs rolled up, we start down the driveway bordered on either side by woods—the driveway Easton graded to ease the approach to the house, the woods he tramped and—

Stop it! Since Caleb cut the headlights, we have only bits of moonlight between the leafy canopy to guide us. However, it's enough so that, apparently, he doesn't feel obligated to offer his arm as Easton would have done. I'm good with that.

"So you own a nursery," he says as we reach the first bend in the driveway.

Then he recognizes me as the woman who chased down his real estate agent. "I do."

"Good business?"

"I like it, almost as much as I like designing and constructing crop mazes, which is what's runnin' me ragged right now."

His warm chuckle butts up against the nip of autumn, the official start of the new season only days away. "I remember now. You and your…what did they call it? The Great…"

"The Great Crop Circle Hoax."

"Right. I've never understood what possessed you to out yourself."

"I didn't make it so I could stand by all smug as a bunch of so-called experts in extraterrestrial phenomena proved they were anything but. I did it to keep the harvesters away from a mama deer that had birthed a crippled fawn. So, yes, when the area was overrun by the greater threat of lookie-loos, I put an end to the nonsense."

"As your father would say, commendable."

I nearly laugh with him, but Daddy did *not* call my rescue attempt commendable. He called it shameful—especially my "outing" of it.

I look across my shoulder and catch Caleb's eye. "Are you environmentally minded?" I ask.

"I am. Unfortunately, my stance on the environment is the quickest way to put a wall between my father and me. He says God gave man dominion over the earth and all its animals, and he doesn't see what all the hoopla is about."

Caleb gets better by the minute, even if he is overly concerned about his car. "Sounds like my daddy."

"Then we have something in common."

I could get to like Caleb.

We walk on a ways, not speaking again until my house, lit by a single energy-saving bulb outside the front door, comes into sight.

"Pretty secluded," Caleb says.

"I like it that way."

"You live alone?"

"I do now."

"Sorry, I forgot you're a widow." He touches my arm.

I stiffen as awareness passes through the material of my sleeve to my skin. That's twice tonight a man has invaded my personal space. First J.C., now Caleb, making me feel things I shouldn't—

Things a married *woman shouldn't feel. You're no longer Easton's wife.*

That makes me ache, but not with the weighted pain that once accompanied the simple act of breathing through the memories of the last days with the ever-optimistic Easton, the last hours before they lowered him into the ground, the painfully blurred days that followed when all I kept for company was a refrigerator full of casseroles from well-meaning Pickwickians.

"I understand it's been quite a few years since your husband passed away. A freak accident, wasn't it?"

Caleb's question sticks in my mind, my answer in my throat. I don't like to think about the accident. I reach to a dread, but they're long gone.

"That's what I heard," Caleb says.

I gather my breath. "I've been a widow for four years."

"Long enough?"

I falter, bare feet kicking up dust, and look at Caleb's darkened profile. "That's a strange thing to ask."

He turns his face toward me, but I can't make out his features. "I'm sorry. It's just…" He halts.

I turn. "What?"

"For all my talk that my interest is solely in the estate…" He blows out a breath. "That could change. I'm attracted to you, Bridget."

When did that happen? And why? I didn't encourage him.

"Bridget?"

I jump back at finding him standing over me, and he grabs my arm as if I need steadying. I don't. By the time I see what's coming, his mouth is on mine—off center, but he adjusts. And it feels almost good. As do his fingers in my hair. And his other hand on my back pressing me near and causing the ring between us to dig into my sternum.

What am I doing? Surely it's too early to be feeling things I was only supposed to feel with Easton. I wrench away, thrust my shoes into the space between us, and shake them. "Do that again, and I'll…well, I won't take kindly to it."

For a long moment, all that's between us is two feet, but another of his apologies soon fills it. "I'm sorry. I thought you were feeling what I was feeling."

Oh, I was, though oddly there seemed something more with J.C., and he was only holding my hand.

"Forgive me?"

I lower the shoes. "Providin' you don't try something like that again."

"What if I ask permission first?"

My mouth goes dry. At the end of my first date with Easton, we awkwardly stood on the front step of my folks' home, and he asked if it was all right to kiss me. I'd known then he was the one for me, having hated the pawing of suitors to whom I rarely gave a second chance. Might Caleb be the one too, though he did start with pawing? "I'll think about it."

He laughs. "Not too long, hmm? Should I walk you to your front door?"

"Better not. I have a Great Pyrenees staying with me, and the dark makes him all kinds of jumpy."

"Then I'll say good night now."

"Night, Caleb."

He turns, and I watch his shadow move down the dirt road. When I can no longer differentiate it from the other shadows, I head for the house.

"Ow! That! Hurt!"

I pivot. "You okay?"

He grunts out something like a curse. "Stepped on a rock. A sharp one."

Soft feet. "Are you bleedin'?"

"No. Limping."

He'll survive. "Drive carefully."

He mutters something and moves off again.

Soon, I enter my house, praise and pat the big dog that greets me, then scoop Reggie off the top of the hutch. "You and Errol not gettin' along, sweetums?"

Her beady eyes are shot with suffering.

"Now don't be like that." I pull her into my chest and look to where the ungainly dog that belongs to Uncle Obe's attorney, Artemis Bleeker, has settled on his haunches in the kitchen doorway. "You aren't givin' Reggie a hard time, are you?"

Errol gives a "who me?" twitch of his eyebrows.

Fortunately I know him well enough to be assured he would never hurt Reggie, but that doesn't mean he wouldn't engage in a little "chase the opossum."

"Come here, you big sweetheart." I pat my leg.

Letting his long foamy tongue hang, Errol trots over, his weight causing the hardwood floor to creak.

Reggie hisses and scampers onto my shoulder. She'd get used to Errol if Artemis would let me keep him permanently, but though the elderly attorney can't stand the dog, his wife notices her pet's absence from time to time. When that happens, Artemis has to collect Mrs. Bleeker's "big boy" from the person to whom he's farmed him out.

"How long you gonna stay this time, hmm?" I scratch behind his ears, and he pushes his head against my stomach. "I love you too." I say the words lightly, but they make me long to be able to say them to, and hear them from, a person. And *not* kin. This brings me back to the first kiss I've had since Easton was last on my lips.

"Caleb Merriman," I whisper. "Maybe." I touch the ring beneath my shirt, the earlier reminder of which shortened Caleb's kiss. "But probably not." Nothing to do with the ring. I will take it off. If not tomorrow, the next day.

Or the next. Or the week after. Or the month after. Or the year—

"Okay!" The strength of my voice jolts my companions. "Sorry." I meet Errol's big-eyed gaze, pat Reggie's stiff back, then pull the chain from under the dress and stare at my wedding ring as it unspins. It really is past time.

I return Reggie to the top of the hutch. Though Errol follows me to the bedroom I once shared with my husband, I slip inside and ease the door closed to avoid mashing his massive snout. I flick on the light that is used once a week when I come through with duster, vacuum, and furniture polish. I haven't slept in here for four years. Of course, that will change when I keep my word to have Miles and Birdie overnight. But one step at a time.

Unclasping the chain from around my neck, I cross to the dresser and open the wooden box that holds my meager selection of jewelry. For a moment, I stare through the ring's circular window to the box. Then, aching a little and a little more, I lower the ring alongside a leather bracelet that belonged to Easton.

As I start to close the lid, my gaze returns to the bracelet. I know the words hammered into the band, words by which Easton tried to lived: "I can do all things through Christ who strengthens me."

"All things except prevent what killed you."

That wasn't through Christ, Bridget. You know it. He shouldn't have done what he did.

I square my shoulders to argue with my inner voice, but then it adds, *And don't forget he did it for you.*

Never has the voice gone that far, and the shock of it leaves me with nothing to defend myself. Because Easton did do it for me. And because I'd rather God were to blame.

I drop the lid. The first tear falls before I make it to the guest room, the next as I toss back the covers and burrow into bed; then all tears break loose as I cry as I haven't allowed myself to do since the day after Easton's accident. No, I had reached deep inside, pulled up anger, and threw it at God where it belonged. Or so I told myself…

"Still"—I narrow my gaze at the darkness all around—"You could have saved him."

He was saved. Not your way, but by way of his Savior.

I pull the pillow over my head and press it to my ears—for all the good it does.

Easton is not suffering. And it's time you stopped.

"How?"

Get rid of the rest of your widow's weeds—the Band-Aid, sleeping in the guest room, the sour faith that hangs around your neck like a string of garlic, your fear of letting another man near.

I close my lids tight. "I'm trying."

I believe in you.

"Why?"

Silence. Not that I mind. I didn't come out on top, but the argument is over.

Though I don't expect to sleep much, I slowly relax into the mattress. Awhile later, I'm roused from something approaching sleep when Errol joins me on the bed, and I feel a little less alone. Later, Reggie settles into the tuck of my knees. Even less alone. I smooth her back. "You'll do," I murmur. "For now."

Because I do want out of these widow's weeds. I really do.

13

> *Ms. Piper Pickwick and Mr. Axel Smith*
> *request the honor of your presence*
> *when they stand before God, family, and friends*
> *to bind their lives together in holy matrimony*
> *Saturday, November 6 at 12:00 noon*
> *at the Pickwick Mansion*
> *1001 Pickwick Pike*
> *Pickwick, North Carolina*

Friday, October 1

Y ou outdid yourself, Bridget." Henry Martin winks, then resumes his side-to-side gum chewing.

I tuck his check in my back pocket and fold my arms over my chest. Standing shoulder to shoulder with the farmer on the balcony of his house overlooking his land, I concede that he's right. I did outdo myself. But then I had a lot to work with due to the longer-than-usual growing season that made the cornstalks shoot high. Henry's five-acre harvest maze, which will attract thousands of families in the thirty days between now and the end of October, is the largest maze I was commissioned to design and construct this year. He said he wanted something more out of the ordinary than usual—spooky for those who like a good chill but joyous in honor of God's blessing of this year's bountiful harvest. So I gave him The House on *Boo*-ntiful Lane.

From this vantage point, of which visitors will partake as they crest the hill and start down the dirt road to the parking area, the outline of the Victorian house cut into the cornfield is breathtaking. The less-intrepid visitors, mostly small children, have plenty of flagstone paths to follow among the topped cornstalks that make up the Victorian's courtyard. There they'll find stands of vibrant yellow and orange marigolds, a pumpkin patch, benches, and a small stage where Henry's granddaughters will enact puppet shows every half hour.

For those intent on goose bumps, shudders, and jolts, they have only to enter the "house" and explore its numerous rooms—especially at night—to get turned around and lost, since most paths either dead-end or wind back on themselves. Other than forcing a way between the dense cornstalks, there are only two means of exiting the maze: through the secret passageway in one of the "second-floor" rooms or the chimney that leads to a hay-chute slide.

"I'm glad you like it."

Henry chews some more, and I marvel at how smooth his earth-colored face is despite the sixty-some years he has to his name. "How's your uncle doin'? I keep meaning to stop by his place and sit a spell, but this festival eats up all my time."

Henry and Uncle Obe go way back. Though my uncle never exposed those who aided him in chucking the statue of Great-Granddaddy Pickwick in the lake, Henry was probably present. He was also what Easton called his "spiritual mentor," having befriended the young Christian when he first moved to Pickwick. And there's the root of the tension that sometimes rises between Henry and me. Hopefully, he'll leave Easton out of this day.

"All things considered Uncle Obe is doing well, especially now that Piper has hired a live-in caregiver." Not that Mary Folsom was my cousin's first choice, seeing as she has little caregiving experience, but once Uncle Obe locked on the woman who offered to share her table at the coffee shop, he made certain by argument and guile that the list of five candidates was narrowed to one.

Henry nods again. "That's good. How's he handling those experts snoopin' around his property?"

J.C.'s team that showed up a week ago, just four days after he returned to Atlanta. Piper was right; competition is good. For Caleb, too. Though I've been too busy to take around Daddy's choice of a suitor, Caleb has been back twice—once to tour the mansion and again to have Axel show him the acreage, including the quarry.

"He appears to be handling it fine, but you know it can't be easy on my uncle."

He shoots me a sideways look. "I have the whole family praying for him."

I recognize the bait as a door to Easton. Normally I wouldn't go through it, but I see Birdie and the tears my bitterness caused, hear my sister's angry words, remember my attraction for J.C., and feel Caleb's kiss and the emptiness in the guest bed that neither Reggie nor Errol can adequately fill.

I moisten my lips. "I'd feel better about those prayers for Uncle Obe if God had a better track record with answering them."

From beneath a gathering of silvered eyebrows, he stares at me with those soulful browner-than-brown eyes. "Nothing wrong with God's track record. He didn't answer your prayers for Easton the way you wanted Him to, but He answered."

I turn my hands up. "So why bother wearin' out my knees when He already has His mind made up?"

Henry sets a hand on my shoulder. "Because He wants to hear from you. Though His answer may not match up with yours, He wants to be your comfort."

I reach for my ring, but it's gone like my dreads. "Easton was my comfort."

"Yes, and when you accepted Jesus, God became your comfort. Know where He is? Standin' on the other side of that door you shut in His face, waiting for you to open up." Henry looks to my hand clutching a fistful of shirt. "I noticed you took off your ring. I'm hopin' that means your hand is on the knob and you're gonna turn it and ask God back into your life."

He's hoping big.

A few wrinkles appear on Henry's brow. "What's the Band-Aid for? Did you cut yourself?"

Time to change the subject. "I appreciate your concern, Henry, but you aren't in my shoes."

"Not anymore."

True. Though several times he's tried to tell me about his first wife, but I've bordered on rude to prevent him from drawing a parallel between our lives.

"Can I tell you about her? Won't take but a moment."

I sigh. "All right."

Momentarily resuming his side-to-side chewing, he looks out across his farm. "Long before that rascal daddy of yours met up with your mama, I lost my first wife after a year of marriage. It was hard, but I took comfort from the Lord. A couple years later, He gave me Lucy. And I love that woman—in the beginning, not as much, but soon enough more."

I feel a twinge of hope.

"Told you it wouldn't take but a moment."

That's it?

Henry checks his watch. "I'd best make sure the family has everything set up. When we throw open the gate in two hours, we gotta be ready for the crowds." Mud-flecked boots clomp on the badly-in-need-of-paint planks, and he steps back inside the house.

I'm as relieved by the change of subject as his optimism. Since he and several other farmers first hired me years ago to cut corn mazes to supplement their farm income, day-trippers have been coming from as far as Charlotte to experience the family-oriented fall celebration our area offers. And Henry's mazes are a favorite for all the extras he provides—hayrides, pumpkin patch, petting zoo, bonfires, plays, farm tours, and refreshments. And then there's the canned goods that showcase his wife's penchant for pickling just about anything that springs from the earth. "Therapy" she calls it, a way to relax after long days counseling troubled teens at the local high school.

Of course, there have been slim years when the crop yield is low or an early frost hits and there isn't much out of which to fashion a maze, but we've always pulled something together. And when that isn't enough to keep the farmers going, we turn to crop advertising, whereby my team transforms the leavings of sorry crops into company logos visible from the air—among them a Detroit carmaker, an airline, a chain of health-food stores, and a save-the-earth organization. Who would have guessed The Great Crop Circle Hoax would pave the way to today?

I follow Henry through his office, down the stairs, and into the kitchen, where Lucy is setting out Mason jars full of corn, green beans, and the like.

"Looks good, Mrs. Martin," I say as Henry kisses her proffered cheek in passing.

"Is good." She winks at me as she adjusts her Monet-print apron. "I put a jar of pickled green tomatoes in your truck—extra spicy."

"Thank you."

"Thank *you*." She jerks her head toward the screen door that bangs behind her husband. "That maze is a beauty. Are you coming back for opening night?"

"Count on it." But first I need to check on the progress of Bronson and Earla Biggs's maze that opens tomorrow night. I wave my way out the door, call a good-bye to Henry, then climb in my truck. Sure enough, a Mason jar is in the driver's seat. I pick it up. "Dinner." Well, that and a hunk of cheese and homemade bread.

I turn the key in the ignition. As has happened several times recently, it takes a couple of attempts before the engine revives. I'm going to have to get that checked.

The air from the heat vents cause the invitation I earlier tossed on the dashboard to scoot across the cracked vinyl, and I grab it and once more consider the fancy writing. Another wedding at the Pickwick mansion. I'm happy for Piper and Axel. And for Uncle Obe, who will see his efforts to join his niece and godson realized before the rest of him slips away. Unless his dementia accelerates…

I flick my gaze to the "great overhead," as Easton called it. "Surely You'll give him another month, won't You? Another year would be"—*a blessing*—"nice should Maggie and Reece and Devyn decide to become a real family, but at least another month. Please." I swallow. "Yes, that was a prayer. I'm trying." And that's all I can do.

I put the truck in gear and head out. When I reach the end of the dirt road, my cell phone rings. Poised as I am to pull onto the pike, I have no intention of answering; however, a glance at the screen shows it's the nursery. Business, then, and it would have to be important for Taggart or Allen to call me.

"Whatcha need?" I say.

"Nothin'."

Nothing? "That you, Tag?"

"Yep."

"I assume you have a good reason for interruptin' my drive?"

"You got a call."

"I do get them."

"From a man."

"I get those too."

"This one didn't want manure. He wanted to have dinner with you."

Oh. "Who?"

"Um…"

"Tag!" *Hold it. He's not your secretary. He's a man with a good work ethic, a deep sense of all things green, and a grudging willingness to answer the phone.* So who is it? It wouldn't be Boone, since I saw him earlier and he would have asked then. It wouldn't be J.C. looking to discuss the estate, since he's returned to Atlanta. So…

I remember Caleb's kiss. "Does the name Caleb Merriman ring a bell?"

"Hmm. I might have heard a tinkle."

It has to be him. "What did you tell him?"

"Said you were at the Martins' finishing up the maze."

Good thing it was Caleb who called and not J.C.

"He asked for your cell number, but since you don't like to give it out, I said I'd pass on his message and for him to call back in ten minutes so I can give him your answer."

I grab an old receipt and scrounge a stub of a pencil from the ashtray. "What's his number?"

"Don't know. I didn't have a pen handy."

Great. "When he calls back, tell him…" Not that I'll have dinner with him. After all, he's a "maybe," meaning baby steps are the best he'll get out of me. "Tell him if he wants to get together tonight, I'll be at the Martins' corn maze and we can grab a bite to eat there."

"Will do. Bye."

I flip the phone closed, pull onto the pike, and jump when the ringtone sounds again. "Mercy!" This one I'm definitely passing on— Oh, it's my mother. "Hi, Mama."

"Hello, dear. Do you have a minute?"

"I do. Everything all right?"

After a hesitation, she says, "I'm not feelin' up to myself—probably all this keepin' after Birdie and Miles. Goodness, they're a handful."

And I haven't been as much help as I should be. I've taken them to the park with Errol, to the movies, and even had them to my house for lunch, but I could help more.

"As for your father, he's on a golfin' and trapshooting kick, and he's rarely home before I wrestle the children into bed."

No surprise there.

"And I do mean wrestle. Bonnie has spoiled her little ones somethin' terrible." She laughs. "Takes after her mama."

I know what she wants me to offer, but— *Then step up to the plate and give back as she's given to you.* "How about I take them for a while?" Good thing I didn't agree to dinner with Caleb. "We'll go to the Martins' fall festival and…" *You promised.* "…I'll keep them overnight."

She gasps. "You'd do that for me?"

It pinches that my offer should come as a surprise. "I will, and I'm sorry I didn't offer sooner."

"Oh, fiddly-dee, you're offerin' now. That's what counts."

Nearing the Biggs's property, I lift my foot from the gas pedal. "I'll pick them up in a couple hours."

"Couple?" Her voice breaks on the word.

"Are you sure you're all right, Mama?"

I hear her draw a shaky breath. "Fine. I just wanted clarification."

No, she didn't. "Actually, how about I drop by in an hour?"

"Wonderful. I'll have them packed and waitin' at the door."

"See you then." This time before I close my phone, I turn it off. If I'm going to squeeze into one hour what requires two, I can't take any more interruptions.

This is fun. And I like the feel of the frequent smile stretched across my face, though it makes my facial muscles ache.

Once again, Miles goes from sight as he takes the path to the right. "Don't go too far," I call as Birdie dances around me.

"I won't!" Miles's voice floats back among the cornstalks over which dusk has prevailed, causing dark to run up the stalks and ride the softly waving tassels. "I think I found the way out."

Not yet he hasn't. Still, I don't correct him, knowing we'll double back soon enough.

"It's getting weal dark." Birdie reaches for my hand.

I close her small fingers within mine. "The darker the better."

"Why?" She looks at me with big eyes from which the coming night has stolen the color. Are they blue? No, brown. I think. I ought to know, especially since I'm determined to improve my aunting skills.

"The darker it gets, the harder the maze, and for those who like a bit of spookin'—"

"I don't like spookin'." Her feet drag. "Nobody's gonna spook us, wight?"

"That's right." And that's why I'm taking her brother and her through the maze before Henry opens the festival to the public. "No spookin'."

"Promise?"

"I promise." Meaning we'd better get a move on since it won't be long now. When we entered the maze twenty minutes ago, dozens of vehicles had staked out parking spaces in the cut field below Henry's house. By now there will be considerably more.

Birdie pulls her hand from mine, jumps in front of me, and raises her arms. "Carry me."

"Now, Birdie, I was carryin' you five minutes ago." And my back aches for it. "You can walk."

She shakes her curly blond head. "Carry me."

I nearly give in, but considering how demanding she and her brother were of my mother when I picked them up, I'm determined to work on their manners. I prop my hands on my hips. "What's the magic word?"

I may not know the exact color of her eyes, but there's no mistaking the spark in them. "Carry me."

"Birdie—"

"Carry me!"

I park my arms over my chest. "I didn't hear the magic word."

"Wrong way!" my nephew declares.

I peer over my shoulder. Yep, he doubled back and then some. "Would you like me to show you the way out?"

"No, I know where I'm going now."

Hmm. "The big kids are coming through soon. We'd better hurry." In that instant, the pole lights flicker on in the areas beyond the maze, lighting Miles just enough to put a face on his determination.

I turn back to Birdie. "Miles knows the way out. Let's follow him."

She takes a step toward him only to grab my sweater. "Carry me!"

"Say the magic word."

She drags on my sweater, and I brace my feet to keep my balance. She's stronger than she looks.

"Say 'please' and I'll pick you up."

"No!"

Miles hurries forward. "Come on, Birdie, I know the way to the slide."

She shakes her head.

"Oh, brother!" Miles whispers something in her ear.

I sense her hesitation, and then she releases me. "I'll say the magic word if *you* say the magic words. And they lived…"

Been here, done this—several times since their return to Pickwick. I clear my throat. "And they lived happily ever after." See, most things become tolerable with practice. I still don't agree with building up little girl hopes that grow into big girl heartaches, but I'll concede the battle if it gets us out of the maze before the hoard descends in their spooky finery. And from the sound of excited voices, they're just around the corner.

"Your turn, Birdie. What's the magic word?"

"I don't want up anymore." She drops her arms and runs around me. Shouting for her to wait, Miles follows.

I blow breath up my face. Well, I *could* be good at aunting given more time. And patience. And energy. And a halo.

Intent on getting Birdie and Miles home and down for the night, I start to follow but halt when remembrance catches up with me. Caleb is meeting me. In fact, he's probably waiting beyond the maze. Fortunately, I doubt he'll want to hang out at the festival, so maybe after a meeting over roasted corn I can excuse the twins and myself.

"Coming!" I call.

There's no response, and a minute later, I accept I'm a leading contender for the World's Worst Aunt award. And niece. I also let Uncle Obe get away from me at the dedication ceremony. "Miles! Birdie!"

No answer, and now that the maze is open to the public and the paths are filling, they aren't likely to hear me over the voices rising from the cornstalks. Did they find their way out? Did they take the hay-chute slide down the hill?

Ahead, I hear a squeal overlapped by another squeal. That was of delight, and I'm sure it came from my niece and nephew.

I run down the path that curves left, then the middle path that ends in the Victorian house's chimney. I peer down the dimly lit drop constructed of enormous sheets of thick landscaping plastic held in place by hay bales on either side of the six-foot-wide slide. As the visitors have yet to make it to the backside of the maze, I catch no movement other than the gentle sway of shadowy cornstalks.

I cup my hands around my mouth. "Miles! Birdie! Are you down there?"

Was that a giggle? Or the rustle of stalk on stalk?

"Come out now, hear?"

Still no answer. I know I have nothing to fear—that they're enjoying the chase—but that doesn't stop worry from prickling my back. They're only five. It's dark. And strangers are everywhere. Granted, they're mostly families, but I'm no fool. "I can find them," I say aloud. "They'll be safe. So safe I'll have a good reason to be mad."

I hear the giggle-rustle again.

"Not funny!" I shout, then drop to my bottom, push off, and slide down the skittery plastic. It's a fast ride, one I would normally enjoy, but my heart is pounding so hard it makes me dizzy. When I get my hands on—

If you get your hands on them.

"They're all right. They're just messin' with me."

I go sideways at the bottom of the slide, stagger to my feet, and listen for proof of Birdie and Miles. The only sounds are those of cornstalks talking to one another and the voices overhead.

"Birdie! Miles! Answer me right now!" I watch for movement on the path that winds uphill. Nothing. Maybe they are still in the maze. Without me.

I'm running again, all the while trying to speak into existence their safe return. And at some point, I start to pray—what, exactly, I don't know, but "God" and "Lord" resound around me as I stretch my legs beyond their normal reach. Finally I crest the hill. People are everywhere, moving among stands, chatting, laughing, and tossing back sweet sticky things, blissfully unaware that two children are missing. "Let them be here, Lord," I whisper as I sprint forward. "I won't be mad. I'll be a kinder, gentler aunt. Answer this one prayer. Please!"

Upon entering the throng, I pull breath to sound the alarm.

"I understand these rascals belong to you," someone says. Not anyone I'm expecting, but I'll take him.

14

I turn and there he stands. Hoping said "rascals" go by the names of Birdie and Miles, I look down. It's them, eyes bright with mischief, mouths strung with mirth. The bane of my exis—

Mustn't think like that. Must be grateful they're safe, that they were only messing with me, that I really didn't need to call on God.

Hello! You think He had no hand in returning them safe and sound? You merely spoke it into existence?

I don't want to think about it now. I drop to my knees and pull my niece and nephew into my arms. "You scared me bad. Don't ever, ever do that again."

"It was fun," Miles speaks right into my ear, making me wince. "We could see you, but you couldn't see us."

"We spooked you good," Birdie says into my shoulder.

I draw back. "That kind of spookin' is not nice. Your mama certainly wouldn't like it."

Miles shrugs. "She's not here."

"Yeah." Birdie's face rumples. "When's she coming back?"

Why did I mention Bonnie? My mother warned that Birdie has begun falling apart over her parents' absence, especially when tired.

She blinks, sniffs. "I miss her."

"Don't start crying." Miles furrows his brow. "Be a big girl."

She snaps her head around. "I'm not big. I'm little. So are you."

He puffs up. "Am not! Little is for babies, so if you don't wanna be called a baby, stop being one."

Now I'm in for it. As long as they're getting along and, thankfully, they more often do, I can handle them, but when they go at each other—

"How about some hot chocolate?"

J.C.'s suggestion surprises me, mostly because I forgot he was standing there. I look up at a figure fit with cargo pants and a light crew-neck sweater. Our eyes meet briefly before his stray down my crouched sneaker, jean, and T-shirt-clad self. When his gaze returns to my face, he's smiling as if pleased at having peeled back another layer of my image. But then, who wears a dress to a harvest festival?

Miles ducks out from beneath my arm and turns to J.C. "I want hot chocolate! A big one. With marshmallows."

I consider Birdie, who seems content to remain pressed against me, which is kind of nice. "Sound good to you?"

She works her bottom lip in and out. "I want whipped cream on mine."

Hopefully that's an option. "All right. Should I carry you?"

She snakes an arm around my neck. "Please."

The magic word! I nearly praise her, but something tells me that if I draw attention to it, she might think better of it next time. I stand and settle her on my hip.

Shortly, my niece and nephew sit at a picnic table across from J.C. and me. Intent on inhaling the whipped cream and marshmallows from the cups of hot chocolate that J.C. bought them, they ignore the roasted corn I bought them. Of course, my mother did feed them dinner before I picked them up.

I look at J.C. "How did you connect Birdie and Miles to me?"

Angled toward me with an elbow on the table and jaw on a fist, he says, "I overheard them trying to decide where next to hide from their aunt Bridge."

Then if he hadn't collared them, I would have called down a manhunt that might have ruined Henry's opening night. "Thank you for steppin' in." Gaze drawn to his light brown hair that the pole light over his shoulder turns almost blond, I have an urge to touch it—just to determine if he uses that gel stuff Caleb uses. "As you've probably guessed, I'm not the best at keeping track of others."

"It takes practice."

Does he have practice? Little ones of his own? Just because there's no wedding ring doesn't mean there aren't children. "I'm a bit shy in that department. My mother is the one keeping my niece and nephew while their parents are out of the country. I help when I can, but obviously not enough." Am I babbling? "So, I didn't know you were back in Pickwick."

He frowns. "I was told you were expecting me."

"What?"

"Here. Tonight."

"No, I wasn't."

His eyebrows rise. "You *were* expecting someone, though?"

"Yes." I look past Birdie and Miles who remain occupied with their steaming cups. "In fact, he's probably—"

"He's me."

"You?"

His mouth curves. "Earlier today, I called your nursery—"

He knows I own a nursery?

"—and spoke with someone named Taggart."

Then it wasn't Caleb who called.

"He said you wanted me to meet you here in lieu of dinner out."

I blink. "That's what I said."

J.C. lifts his head from his fist. "Who were you expecting? Merriman?"

I have no reason to feel guilty that Caleb remains interested in the estate. And it's good for J.C. to know the competition hasn't gone away. "I thought you were him. Unfortunately Tag is better versed with plants and irrigation than taking messages."

"I hope you're not too disappointed." He watches me as if to capture that disappointment.

I turn up a hand. "You surprised me is all."

He nods. "If I'd been given your cell number, we could have avoided the confusion."

"Tag knows I don't give my number out to just anybody."

J.C.'s head tilts. "Then Merriman is 'just anybody'?"

The question is loaded, but in a good way. He doesn't like competition, especially if it gets personal enough to squeeze him out. It seems J. C. Dirk has set his mind on buying the Pickwick estate, which means his team is giving a good report.

"I wouldn't say Caleb is 'just anybody,' being an old family friend. I just don't care to be in the middle of something, whether it's work or simply ponderin', and have my phone go off. Unlike you, I believe in quiet time."

His eyebrows go north. "You haven't heard my phone ring once since we met up."

First the cologne that remains absent, now the phone. Absent too or just—? "I'll bet you have it set to vibrate."

He laughs, a strong laugh that shows to the back of his teeth. "It's on vibration mode. However, when it went off awhile ago, I didn't even check."

Feeling Birdie and Miles's interest, I lean nearer J.C. "Let me guess. Not only can you now choose different ring tones to identify the caller, there are different vibrations."

He also leans in, and I catch the *sans*-cologne scent of him. It does something to me, and it appears the feeling is mutual since whatever he was going to say is left unsaid and his partly open mouth closes.

"Are you Aunt Bridge's happily ever after?"

J.C. pulls out of his lean. "Her happily ever after?" A teasing smile turns his mouth. "Why do you ask?"

I come out of my frozen state with a splutter. "Birdie—"

"Because her heart is happy tonight. Not weal happy, but happy."

"Yeah," Miles says. "Not constipated."

"Well!" I jump up so fast my knees knock the underside of the picnic table. "Time to go."

"I'm not done with my hot chocolate." Miles tips his cup to show it's half full.

"I'm done," Birdie says, though other than the absence of whipped cream, her drink is untouched.

"Let's get you home." I turn my back on J.C. and step over the bench.

"But I'm not done," Miles insists.

"Bring it with you." I don't relish a spill in my truck, but better that than further discussion about the state of my heart, especially if it takes us in the direction of M&M's. "And don't forget your corn."

"I'm not hungry."

"Me neither." Birdie tugs on my jeans. "Carry me."

Fine. "After you toss your cup and corn." I nod at where she left them.

Out comes her bottom lip. "I'm tired."

I'm tempted to clean up after her just to get away from J.C., but it's best to use the opportunity to teach about responsibility. "We clean up our own messes, Birdie. Now clean up yours and we can go."

The breath she exhales on the nippy night air shoots from her nostrils like steam from a cartoon bull. "You do it."

I glance from Miles, whose face is in his cup, to where J.C. stands beside the picnic table, appearing content to watch. But I'm *not* backing down. "No, Birdie."

More bullish steam, followed by pawing of the ground with a sparkly pink sneaker. I nearly drop my jaw when she grabs the cup and corn and turns into the path of a Darth Vader–clad festival-goer who stumbles to avoid her. Sloshing all the way, she stomps to a garbage bin. "There!" She stomps back. "Carry me."

I raise my eyebrows.

"Please!"

It worked! Not a nice "please," but I'll take it. I haul her onto my hip where she sits rigidly, as if it were my idea to carry her.

More tugging at my jeans. "I'm tired too."

I peer into Miles's upturned face. Surely he's not suggesting I also carry him? I'm hardly frail, but Birdie is one sturdy little girl and the walk to the parking area is mostly uphill. "Uh…"

"I'll give you a ride."

"You don't have to do that, J.C. I mean, why don't you hang out and enjoy the festival. Maybe try the maze."

He looks over his shoulder at the throng before the entrance. "Your creation, I understand."

He knows about my seasonal job, meaning he probably knows it got its start with The Great Crop Circle Hoax. So what else does he know about me? Does one shred of my Atlanta image remain?

"A piggyback ride?" Miles asks.

"Now, Miles…" I reach to him. "As big a boy as you are, I'm sure you can walk."

Still clutching his hot chocolate, he positions himself before J.C.

J.C. shrugs. "Piggyback it is."

Miles starts to set his hot chocolate on the table, hesitates, then grabs his corn and runs to the garbage bin. Sharp kid.

With Miles on J.C.'s back, we weave among the chattering crowd. Bit by bit, Birdie's rigidity recedes, and when we enter the parking area, she drops her head to my shoulder.

And there's my truck ahead. "I'm parked right over—" Oh. My truck. I'm not embarrassed by its dents and dings and dirt. It's my image—

What image? He knows you're an opossum-toting Pickwick, you're not much for fake nails or makeup, you muck it up at a nursery, and you're a pur-veyor of crop mazes. Face it, the suited-up, briefcase-toting Bridget Buchanan who wheedled her way into his meeting no longer exists.

Fine. But if he views it as weakness that will secure the estate at a price below market value, he'll be sorely disappointed. I take the last steps to my truck and turn to gauge his reaction. "This is it." I pat the fender with its shotgun spray of rust spots.

He halts three feet back and, as far as I can tell, doesn't react in any negative way.

I shift Birdie's weight, and she gives a murmur I hope means she'll be so far asleep when we get home I won't have to wrestle her into bed. "I appreciate you going out of your way to carry Miles."

"My pleasure, but it was hardly out of my way." He nods to the left. "I'm parked two cars down."

Miles sits higher on his back to peer past the gas-guzzling luxury SUV between our two vehicles. "Where?"

"The white Lexus."

"My dad drives one of those. But it doesn't look like yours."

I step toward them to confirm the car is something fast like Caleb drives, but it isn't. "Is that a hybrid crossover?"

"It is. Very fuel efficient."

Music to my ears.

"I'm considering purchasing one, so I decided to rent one on this trip."

Of course it's a rental. As busy as he is, he would have flown in from Atlanta.

"Can I ride with you?" Miles asks.

"No!" My sharp protest makes Birdie lift her sleep-weighted head. "Sorry." I pat her back down.

Miles leans over J.C.'s shoulder. "I'll bet Aunt Bridge's is on the way to wherever you're going."

"Not if he's staying at the Pickwick Arms," I interject.

"I am." J.C. holds my gaze. "But I don't mind Miles riding with me—providing *you* don't mind."

"I want to go with Mr. J.C.!" The whine in Miles's voice warns of worse to come.

And I'm too worn out to deal with it. "All right."

I secure the floppy, softly snoring Birdie in her booster seat and climb in the cab. The engine jumps to life with a single turn of the key. Hopefully, that means my truck's temperamental behavior has resolved itself.

With the Lexus on my tail, I exit the Martins' farm and head down Pickwick Pike. It's a short drive to my turnoff, and when I pull onto the gravel road, I expect J.C. to hesitate in committing his vehicle to the driveway as Caleb did. He doesn't.

Before long, I pull into the parking area in front of my dimly lit house. The Lexus draws alongside. As I unbuckle Birdie, J.C. exits his car, and I feel him rise at my back at about the time Errol sets to barking.

"Sounds like a big dog," J.C. says.

Is that wariness in his voice? Good. I'm sure J.C. is honorable, but it's best to be safe. "He's a Great Pyrenees."

Miles hops out of the Lexus. "Errol isn't Aunt Bridge's. She's baby-sitting him."

I ease Birdie into my arms and, as I turn, say low, "True, but I think he'll soon settle down here with me." Especially since the last time Artemis Bleeker availed himself of my baby-sitting services, it took his wife a week to notice the absence of her "big boy." Though Artemis has yet to verify the cause of his wife's memory problems, most everyone believes she's on the same path as my uncle. If so, the one bright spot for her is that her deterioration isn't marked by early onset. She had twenty more years of intact memories than my uncle.

"Does he bite?" J.C. asks Miles, and I have the sense he really wants to know. Is he afraid of big dogs? It hardly fits this confident man.

"Nah, he's like a puppy that got blown up big."

J.C. nods. "Would you like me to carry Birdie?"

Into the house where Easton and I grew as man and wife? Where no man other than kin has stepped since his death? Imagining J.C.'s feet on the same floorboards once tread by Easton, panic rises.

"Just to the door," J.C. clarifies.

"I've got her." I extend a hand. "Thank you for driving Miles home."

As his fingers close warmly around mine, my nephew tugs J.C.'s sleeve. "Come see Errol! And Reggie—she's an opossum."

He already knows about my unusual pet.

"Maybe another time."

My nephew thrusts his face up. "Why? I'm not tired anymore—all the way awake. See?" The whites of his eyes get big in the night.

"It's getting late, and I'm sure your aunt wants to put you to bed."

"Then you can read me a story—or tell me one." Miles jerks his head in my direction. "She doesn't have kids' books."

Makes me sound borderline abusive.

"Please, Mr. J.C."

Please again…

Still holding my hand, the man whom I'm responsible for bringing to Pickwick returns his gaze to mine. "It's up to your aunt."

"I promise I won't keep getting up for water, Aunt Bridge. I'll stay down and fall asleep like I do when Daddy tells me a story."

"Well?" J.C. prompts.

What harm, especially if it gets Miles down faster? And it is one more step in the right direction for you. "All right."

Miles whoops, and I'm sad for how much he misses his daddy. The emotional places inside him that need filling by a father figure certainly aren't being filled by his granddaddy.

I wag a finger. "A *short* story."

Miles bobs his head. "Short."

With Errol more vigorously heralding our approach, I lead the way across the stone path Easton laid for me weeks before his death…up the porch steps he replaced a month before his death…through the screen door he installed a year before his death…across the porch he repainted two years before his death…past the hammock he hung several years before his death…halt before the door he—

Yes, he did, but you *more recently replaced the weather stripping.* And I did it without perseverating on my loss. Why am I perseverating now? Does the answer lie in Caleb, who kissed me as Easton last kissed me? In J. C. Dirk, who disturbs me as Easton disturbed me when he first set his mind to pursuing the lone tree-hugging Pickwick?

As I slide the key into the lock, Errol's barking becomes a growl. He must sense someone unfamiliar is with me. Or if J.C. is wary of big dogs, maybe that's why Errol is frantic. A moment later, his big claws are scrabbling on the other side. Great. Just as the weather stripping fell to me, so will the refinishing.

"Behave," I say as Errol thrusts his face in the space that opens into him. "No jumpin'." And, hopefully, no piddling.

I push the door wider and flip the light switch, but as I carry Birdie inside with Miles on my heels, Errol pushes past. With my niece making waking sounds, I rasp, "Errol!"

The big dog halts before J.C. and gives a bark that rolls into another growl.

J.C. doesn't move, though his eyes meet mine. "Blown-up puppy?"

I see through his attempt at humor. He *is* wary of Errol. Not that he's shaking in his shoes, but discomfort comes off him like heat from pavement in summertime, and he's definitely avoiding eye contact with Errol.

"Are you afraid of dogs?" Miles asks. "Daddy says they can sense fear and it makes them suspicious."

"I prefer them small," J.C. says.

I shift Birdie's weight and step back onto the porch and touch Errol's head. "Come on, boy, it's okay. Let's go inside."

He looks up at me, back at J.C., at me again.

I nod. "Let's get a treat."

He gives a grunt, his tail a thump, and follows. I glance over my shoulder at J.C., who is about to enter the home that Easton— *Stop it!*

Fortunately, with J.C. keeping an eye on Errol, there's no need for me to force a smile. "Why don't you and Miles start on that story while I give Errol his treat?"

"Sure," J.C. says.

With repeated glances over his shoulder, Errol walks alongside me toward the kitchen.

"It's cold in here," Miles says.

It's that or too hot, depending on the season, since I always turn off the thermostat when I leave the house for the day. I refuse to waste energy to keep my furniture warm. As for Reggie and Errol, they have fur. "I'll turn on the heat." I slide the switch. "Just keep your jacket on until it warms up."

Miles gives a weary sigh. "She's a tree hugger. Hey, would you get Reggie? She's probably up there."

I feel bad that I didn't acknowledge my opossum atop the hutch, but my hands are full. On a good note, Reggie and Miles seem to have connected. Not once has she attempted to play possum in his presence. Now with Birdie… Reggie has never bitten anyone—well, other than me—but if my niece doesn't stop trying to outfit her in baby-doll clothes, she might make an exception.

Huffing with the effort to support Birdie, I enter the kitchen and hit the Play button on the answering machine. As I open the doggie canister, a time- and date-stamped voice sounds around the small room.

"Bridget, it's Caleb."

Again. Obviously, my father gave him my home number.

"I'll be in town tomorrow and thought we might have dinner."

At the prospect of wiggling out of another invitation, I draw a deep breath. But wait. Did J.C. hear Caleb's message? Probably. So not a bad thing to prove that competition is alive and well in Pickwick.

"Call me back, okay?"

I don't have much choice, do I? Oh, the lengths to which I must go.

15

Errol trots off with his treat. However, no sooner do I get the lid on the canister than he returns for more. "Oh no, a treat is a treat."

His ears lower only to perk at the sound of the toilet flushing. Guessing that was Miles and grateful I won't have to remind him to empty his too-small bladder that has led to "accidents" at Mama's house, I cross to the back door and pull it open. "Come on, Errol, I don't want any accidents from you either."

He goes reluctantly, and as he lumbers across the backyard, I close the door. When his business is finished, he'll let me know.

Birdie sighs heavily as I exit the kitchen, nearly masking the second flushing of the toilet. Miles again? Surely not. The last time he was here, he flushed three times during one trip to the bathroom. Under close questioning, he admitted he likes to watch the water "tornado." Thus, I instructed him on environmentally responsible toilet etiquette of one flush maximum per use. It sounds like the lesson didn't stick.

As I head down the hallway, my nephew flings open the bathroom door. When he sees me, he puts on the brakes. "Just two times, Aunt Bridge. Not three."

"That's an improvement, but—" I glance down the hallway to the light that pours from the guest room, where J.C. is waiting for Miles. Now is not the time to reinforce the lesson.

"I had to. I did a two! And I wasn't done. Mama says when that happens, you have to give a courtesy flush so you don't stink up the bathroom for the next person. It's rude if you don't, 'cause then they can't breathe."

I feel suddenly as warm as a sun-baked tomato. There is a man in my house who is surely amused by what he's hearing. "Okay. So why don't you go climb into bed and Mr. Dirk can tell you that story?"

My nephew frowns, doubtless surprised by my easy acceptance of his double flushing, then runs to the guest room. I follow, passing the bedroom I shared with Easton, where I *am* going to sleep tonight. Well, maybe. The sofa isn't all that uncomfortable, and when in doubt—

"Birdie can't sleep in here," Miles says as I enter the guest room.

I look from where he's settling in the middle of the bed, pillows piled behind him and Reggie making herself comfortable alongside his hip, to J.C., who sits in a chair pulled up to the bed, elbows on knees and hands clasped. The latter is grinning, no doubt a result of the toilet-flushing lesson.

Don't you dare get embarrassed over a conservation issue. I return my gaze to my nephew. "Of course Birdie can sleep in here. The bed's big enough—"

"She's a girl!"

I hesitate. The twins have separate rooms at home and at Mama's house, but their parents and mine have the luxury of more bedrooms than they need. My house is a modest two bedroom. If Birdie doesn't sleep in here, she'll have to—

"You're a girl too," Miles says. "She can sleep with you."

He's right, which means the sofa is not an option, which means I'll have to sleep in the bedroom I once shared with Easton, which means I won't be alone. I almost smile. Leave it to Miles to provide the solution.

"Good idea." I turn away. "Don't forget—a short story. Mr. J.C. needs to get back to his hotel."

As I step into the hallway, J.C. says, "I call this story 'The Seven Caves of the Seven Winds.'"

"Ooh," Miles breathes.

I enter the master bedroom, turn down the covers, and lower Birdie onto the mattress where Easton once slept. "That wasn't so hard." The words rush out on the breath I didn't realize I was holding. The hard part will be crawling in beside her. "No, it won't." I tuck her in, then walk to the other side. "It's just a bed." I fold the linens back in anticipation of J.C.'s departure.

"Then what happened?" Miles's voice drifts from the guest room as I return to the hallway.

"The winds met in the great valley beyond the caves, howlin' and circlin' one another—"

Ah! J.C.'s drawl has tipped its hand again.

"—around and around, faster and faster until they came to blows, and that's when an amazin' thing happened."

"What?"

"As they were dukin' it out, they began to mix and their strength multiplied."

"Like a tornado!"

"That's right."

"I like tornados. Then what happened?"

"The easterly wind, being the wisest of the seven winds, was the first to realize what their combined forces were capable of. With a twist and a heave and a mighty wrench, that old easterly wind broke away."

Who would have thought J.C. was good with kids?

A muffled *woof* sounds from the front of the house. If I don't quickly answer Errol's summons, he'll claw at that side of the door—more refinishing.

I hurry through the living room and throw open the door. Errol shoves his way inside, runs his tongue up my hand, and drops in a heap in the middle of the living room. I start to close the door, but one breath of the night air draws me outside. I hate that energy will be wasted but leave the door open. Not only will it allow J.C. to find me when he wraps up his story, but it ought to keep Errol's protective instincts in check.

Standing on the porch, staring through the screens at the star-pierced night sky, I wrap my arms around myself. If it weren't so cool and I didn't have a date with a certain bed, I'd stretch out in the hammock. I'll have to be content with sitting in it. That's where J.C. finds me when he makes it past Errol's growling ten minutes later.

"Trying to warm the great outdoors?" He steps outside, leaving the door open as if to assure the dog that followed him there he means no harm.

The porch light showing J.C.'s smile to be of the teasing sort, I say, "A waste, but I didn't think you'd be long."

"I made it as short a story as possible." He halts alongside the hammock.

I set it to swaying as I peer up at him. "'The Seven Caves of the Seven Winds'? You're good with kids."

The smile he aims across his shoulder increases. "Experience."

"Do you have children of your own?"

"Not yet."

"Nieces and nephews?"

He looks out into the night. "Yes, though my experience with children started with caring for my siblings while my mother struggled to put food on the table."

A voice from the past—mine—plays back the words I spoke during his first visit to Pickwick, when I accused him of being accustomed to a life of excess and concluded he'd never lost anything of sentimental value. He told me it was an assumption I had no right or insight to make.

I halt the hammock. "I'm sorry. I thought you came from money."

He continues to stare opposite me. "As your family came from money and lost it, my family came from poverty and made something of themselves, my brothers and I."

I recall the magazine article's mention of two brothers who also work for Dirk Developers, both having come on board some years after J.C. And there was something else. "But I read that you and your brothers inherited the company from your father."

"Our adopted father. And we did inherit it when he passed away, but at that time it was run out of a dilapidated warehouse in the worst part of town and was always one construction job away from bankruptcy. It took years of sacrifice, hard work, and long hours to make it what it is today."

"Is that why you aren't married?" The question pops out, and there's nothing I can do about it.

J.C. turns his head toward me again. "I've had opportunities, but never enough time to raise a family and give a wife and children the time my brothers and I didn't have with our parents. I don't want that, so I've waited."

"And your brothers?"

"The youngest is married. He and his wife have two boys and a girl. My middle brother says he's content to remain single. You met him in Atlanta."

"I did?"

His mouth lightens as if to smile again. "Parker's the one who escorted you into the middle of my meeting."

That was his brother? The scarred, spectacled man who materialized at my elbow? "I don't recall any brotherly resemblance. Must be a deep gene pool."

"I suppose." He goes silent a moment. "You're not what I expected, Bridget. You're different."

I laugh. "You aren't the first to notice. Suffice it to say, even my father is disappointed with how I turned out."

"Why?"

"I love nature, all those things that struggle up through the earth in search of the sun, the animals that are just trying to live day by day, the wind on my face, the rain on my skin." I shake my head. "I can't remember a time when those things didn't matter." I glance at J.C. "Of course, sometimes they get me into trouble."

"The Great Crop Circle Hoax."

"I figured you knew about that, but let me tell you it was for a good cause. I was trying to save a crippled fawn from the harvesters. Of course, you may not be able to relate to somethin' like that."

"What makes you think so?"

"What you said in Atlanta about there being good hunting in these parts."

He chuckles. "I'm no hunter, Bridget. I was pushin' your buttons."

I'm relieved. And I do so like that dropped *g* of his. "I was hoping that was the case. It's good to know you're not half as bad as you make yourself out to be."

"Neither are you."

"Oh?" Feeling strangely light, almost playful, I tilt my head farther back, the better to gauge his reaction. "Then you like the nursery-owner Bridget better than the briefcase-carrying Bridget?"

He holds my gaze across his shoulder, then turns to me. "Much better." He slides a hand up my jaw to my cheek.

In that moment, everything stops. No blink. No breath. No quiver. In the next moment, he drops his hand and steps back.

I blink. I breathe. I quiver.

He shoves his hands into his pockets. "You haven't asked why I wanted to have dinner with you."

Does it have anything to do with what just happened? Or is he changing the subject? I swallow. "All right. Why?"

The jangling starts up. "The reports coming in from my team are good, and my investors are interested in funding the venture."

Change of subject, then. What happened wasn't supposed to. And though he initiated it—or did he?—he regrets it. Good. I feel the same. "Great," I say, though the word *venture* sounds itchily moneygrubbing. "That is, if we're still talking an environmentally friendly development."

"We are. Barring any untoward findings, Dirk Developers will make an offer."

Though my insides remain tangled from the feel of J.C.'s hand on my face, hope goes to my toes.

"I understand Merriman is still interested."

Obviously his offer will be all the better for Caleb's interest. Now if Caleb would be so accommodating, we might have a bidding war. "He's still interested, so much that his own team is going over the estate."

"I've heard that too." His pockets quiet. "A large undertaking for someone who only wants it for a private residence."

I catch the doubt in his voice, and it worries me until I realize it was meant to be caught. The two men *are* in competition. "It's a lot of money. I'm sure Caleb just wants to know what he's getting for it."

A few moments later, J.C. says, "I'd like to discuss the plans for the estate further. Can we talk tomorrow over lunch?"

Another full day in the making, especially with the opening of Bronson and Earla Biggs' maze. But since J.C. is determined that I participate in the negotiations for the estate *and* he asked nicely this time, I'll make an early start of it. Miles and Birdie are not going to like getting up at dawn so I can get them to Mama's, but there's nothing for it. "Where would you like to meet?"

"My hotel has a nice restaurant."

It also has Boone.

"How about noon?"

I nod. "I'll be there."

"Good night."

As he crosses the porch, my conscience—or something like it—overcomes my relief at his leave-taking. "J.C.?"

Hand on the screen door, he looks around.

"Thank you for putting Miles down. I'm not very good with stories."

"All it takes is practice."

Of which he had plenty growing up. While Daddy was indulging my taste for environmental causes and exotic creatures, J.C. was raising his brothers. That's a lot to admire in a man, and though he sometimes goes against my grain, I do admire J.C. Not like I admired Easton, who saw good in those things on which I defaulted to bad...who spoke gently and lovingly—

The creak of the screen door returns me to the man who is here now. Shortly, his headlights swing onto the unpaved driveway. Then he's gone, leaving me to my lonesome. And the bed I will sleep in tonight.

I loiter on the porch before taking Errol up on his offer to escort me inside. While I check on Miles, Errol stretches his neck across the mattress to check on Reggie. Raising her head, my opossum issues a hiss that makes the big dog duck his head back.

"I suppose this means you're hanging out with Miles."

Reggie continues to glare at Errol. Yep, not only is she perturbed that I ignored her earlier but she wants nothing further to do with Errol. And considering Birdie is sharing my bed, Reggie won't be keen on joining me anyway.

After retrieving my flannels, I change in the bathroom and brush my teeth. As I run a washcloth over my face, I catch the bandage's reflection in the mirror.

Take it off.

But I'm sleeping in my bed tonight—*trying* to.

Good timing, then. But if you want to keep the grieving alive and feed into that big unending yawn, go ahead and cling to your sticky little piece of denial.

I drop the washcloth and peel off the bandage. "Done," I say, to which Errol gives a grunt.

I look to where he sits in the doorway and raise my hand. "See? Easy." Hard will be not giving in to the temptation to apply another bandage.

I flip off the hall light, then back on in case Miles or Birdie needs to see their way to the bathroom. It's harder to conserve energy with little ones.

Errol enters the master bedroom ahead of me and sniffs at Birdie before settling in the doorway.

I stare at the bed. I can do this. The mattress gives beneath me, feeling familiar and yet foreign. Something is missing, and I know who. However, his absence is not going to run me off. I won't let it, especially with Birdie here. I scoot nearer, turn on my side, and drape an arm over her like Easton draped an arm over me. It's not the same, but it's good.

With a murmur, Birdie turns and snuggles into my chest. Better than good. And in the hour before restless and sleepless become rest and sleep, I find myself thanking God that my niece is here at all. I lost her and Miles at the festival, and anyone could have found them, but it was J.C. Prayer answered, though the bitter Bridget defaulted to doubt.

"Thank You, God. Thank You."

16

Saturday, October 2

L ast night Reggie was perturbed with me; today it's Boone. I thought I made it through the lobby without detection, but no sooner did I lower into the chair opposite J.C. than my most persistent widow sniffer appeared at the restaurant entrance. I acknowledged Boone with a wave. He nodded and walked away but has returned twice.

"The butternut squash soup sounds good." I snap the menu closed.

J.C. looks up, his green eyes exceptionally bright in the sunlight that falls across our window table. "That's all?"

"It's a generous serving. Also, it comes with a bread basket and honey butter."

"I need something more substantial. Is the chicken potpie good?"

"Real good. It—"

His cell phone rings.

He looks at me. "I'm sorry, but I have to check." A moment later, he repockets the phone. "Chicken potpie it is."

My cell phone rings.

I look at him. "Sorry, but I need to see if it's my mother." When I dropped Birdie and Miles at her house this morning, she said she was doing better but was still slump-shouldered with fatigue. I dragged from my father a promise he would stay home and help with his grandchildren. Unfortunately he doesn't always keep his word.

I read the number and, with an apologetic grimace, flip open the phone. "Everything all right, Mama?"

"No," Daddy says. "I need you to watch the kids while I take your mama to the doctor."

I startle straight in my chair. "What's wrong?"

"Probably nothin' other than a woman's problem, but I want her checked out."

That's a first. Of course, Mama's health is more of a concern to him when it cuts into his recreational time.

"Though it's Saturday, her doctor agreed to meet us at his office and have a look. Can you be here in five minutes?"

"I'm coming now." I close my phone and push my chair back. "My father is taking my mother to her doctor and needs me to watch Birdie and Miles."

J.C. stands. "Nothing serious, I hope?"

"She's been under the weather lately. Probably a bug, but I'm glad she's finally seeing her doctor."

"I'll walk you out."

I nearly protest but Boone is back, and he's less likely to try to engage me if J.C. is at my side.

However, as we exit the restaurant, he steps forward. "I didn't know you were dining with us today, Bridget." He glances at J.C.

"I was, but a family…" Not *emergency*. My mother just needs her husband to do his part, and hopefully this visit to the doctor will bring him around. "…situation has come up."

"Can I help?"

"Thank you, but I can handle it. See you later." I continue past Boone, and J.C. follows me outside.

"I'll call you," I say as he walks me to my truck that looks especially shabby in daylight. Oh well.

"Perhaps we can have dinner instead."

I step off the curb and hurry around the tailgate to the driver's side. "I would, but I accepted an invitation from Caleb Merriman." Not only to learn where he stands on the estate but to see if that kiss of his had any long-reaching effects. No, I'm not buying into my father's matchmaking scheme, but when Caleb's cajoling voice and humor warmed me across the phone line this morning, I accepted that he's still something of a maybe. And since I've worked through the wedding band, the bandage, and the bed...

"Tomorrow, then." J.C. says, *his* voice far from cajoling, humor absent.

I turn to where he regards me from the opposite side of the truck, his lids weighted with what can only be disapproval. Though I didn't intentionally flaunt the competition, there you go. "You'll be in town awhile?"

"I've cleared my schedule to focus on the Pickwick project."

Then he'll be here a couple of days? A week? "Tomorrow it is." I pull open the driver's door. "I'll meet you at..." Not the hotel restaurant. I've had enough of Boone's Bridget-watching. I point across the square. "...the Grill 'n' Swill at twelve thirty."

"I'll be there."

I jump into the cab and flip the key in the ignition. "I'm comin', Mama." Maybe not. I try the key again, but it and the engine are no longer on speaking terms. And another try yields more unproductive chugging.

A tap on the passenger window turns my scowl from the dashboard to J.C. He raises his eyebrows and points to his chest.

I could run across the square to Maggie's auction house and ask her to drive me, but her regular Saturday auction will be in full swing, along with her gavel-wielding arm. I fling open the door and drop my feet to the asphalt.

"Thank you." I come around the front of the truck. "I knew something was up with my truck but didn't get around to havin' it checked. I apologize for the inconvenience."

"No inconvenience." J.C. heads for the white Lexus at the corner. "I did plan to spend the afternoon with you."

True, but talking property was what he had in mind, not chauffeuring.

He opens the passenger door, and I feel a fleeting touch at the small of my back as I slide in—as if he, a little late, thought better of stirring up whatever feelings made him touch my face last night.

We leave the town square behind, and he turns onto Main Street which becomes Pickwick Pike farther on. As always, the enormous billboard that advertises a single-family home development on Pickwick Lake jumps out at me. When old man Truman passed away, his children sold his land that bordered the west side of the lake, and now it burgeons with high-end homes so closely built neighbors can nearly reach out their windows to borrow sugar. I can't let that happen to Uncle Obe's land. Progress is inevitable, but it has to be responsible.

Take those office suites that look more like a village. The building was destined to be a monstrous mirrored thing, but when Easton found out, he and I drew up a petition that thousands of Pickwickians signed. In that case it worked, but not with Wal-Mart. The field where a fruit-and-vegetable stand once stood is now mostly asphalt and concrete block painted an ugly gray-blue color.

"The hotel manager—Boone, was it?" J.C. says.

My reflection in the glass comes into focus before my thoughts. I look around. "Boone?"

From behind his sunglasses, J.C. looks at me. "He obviously numbers among your admirers."

I sigh. "Yes, another widow sniff—" Oops. "So, are you likin' the gas mileage you get out of this fancy hybrid?"

"Widow sniff?"

Great. And since for the life of me I can't think of an acceptable alternative that could be mistaken for *widow sniff,* I'll have to lay it out there. "Widow sniffer."

His teeth flash in what I'd say is the most genuine smile I've seen from him, and it tempts me to snatch off his sunglasses so I can witness it all the way up to his eyes.

"I'm guessin' that means a man who is attracted to widows."

I can't help but like him better when he relaxes into his drawl, so I decide to ride out the conversation. "That's what I call them, whether it's the husband's life insurance they're after, they're lookin' to exploit a woman's vulnerability during her time of loss, or they merely rank high on the sympathy scale."

His smile begins to twitch. "Or they're anglin' to get their hands on a certain property."

I know what that's about—the same as last night when he mused aloud about Caleb hiring experts to evaluate a property that is to remain a private residence. My formal education may have ended with high school graduation and I may be more comfortable with dirt beneath my feet, but I'm not ignorant of the seed J.C. is sowing. However, neither am I offended, especially since competition can only help Uncle Obe's bottom line.

I figure my expression into the facial equivalent of a question mark. "You're sayin' I should read any interest you show me as purely mercenary?"

His smile stops its twitching.

"Well, I appreciate the warnin'."

After a moment, he says, "You're welcome."

I turn my gaze forward and am surprised to find we're already on Pickwick Pike, not far from my parents' home and a few miles from Uncle Obe's. "In about a mile, turn right at Mew Way." My folks' private driveway, *Mew* short for Bartholomew. Hold it! I look anew at J.C. "How did you know my folks live off Pickwick Pike?"

Did his jaw tighten, or was it like that already? "When I'm considering investing millions of dollars"—he flips on his turn signal—"I make it my business to know the logistics, not only with regards to the property but also the surrounding area."

Talk about thorough, but I suppose he would take into account the proximity of my folks' home. And I do remember Piper had one of those maps that showed their acreage, name and all.

J.C. turns the car onto Mew Way, which is in sorry need of a new layer of asphalt, what with weeds and grass poking through cracks. The driveway, a shorter version of the one on the Pickwick estate, rises and curves gently toward my childhood home that will come into sight any second now.

"So," J.C. draws out the word, "how do you distinguish between a widow sniffer and a man who is genuinely attracted to you?"

It's my turn to twitch, but not from a smile—rather, discomfort. How did we end up back here?

"That's assuming you don't label all men who show an interest in you 'widow sniffers.'"

"Of course not." My denial is knee-jerk, but it's all I have because, come to think of it, every man who has sought me out since Easton has been a widow sniffer.

"What about Merriman? Would you call him a widow sniffer?"

I remember his kiss. He can't be after Easton's life insurance money, since he seems to have plenty, and he doesn't strike me as someone who feels sympathy for a person he hardly knows, but because of his interest in the Pickwick estate and my involvement in its sale, he might be hoping to use me to his advantage. But that's none of J.C.'s business.

I cross my arms over my chest as he brakes before a scaled-down version of the Pickwick mansion and behind a car that is not Daddy's.

"Because there he is." J.C. inclines his head.

I look around, and as Daddy blusters off the bottom step, I see that Caleb—the owner of the car ahead—is on the veranda up top.

Have I been had again? I'll bet Daddy either eavesdropped on me telling Mama I was having lunch with J.C. or she let on (she did say J.C. seemed a fine specimen of a man). And under pretense of worrying over Mama, Daddy determined to interrupt my meeting by throwing Caleb at me. Sometimes I really do not like the man who fathered me.

I'm too mad to think straight enough to open the car door, and so Daddy opens it. He pokes his head in and glowers at J.C. "You again," he says, rude as all get out.

I could explain about my truck, but I'm in no mood. "J. C. Dirk,

Daddy, the *other* party interested in the property." I'm tempted to tell
J.C. to take us back to the restaurant, but Mama appears at the top of
the steps, a pink pocketbook swinging from her arm, makeup doing a
poor job of disguising her fatigue. This may have been a ruse on Daddy's
part, but Mama will see her doctor today.

"Excuse me, Daddy," I say as my mother gingerly descends the steps,
her little Malti-Poo dog tinkering alongside.

He steps back, and I swing my legs out.

"I suppose we'll talk tomorrow," J.C. says.

I peer over my shoulder at him. "Actually, providing you don't mind
a little down-home hospitality, we can talk here."

"Did I hear right?" Daddy huffs as I rise before him. "Did you invite that man into my home?"

"I did." I close the car door. "In between keepin' an eye on Birdie and
Miles, J.C. and I can finish what we started over lunch."

"But Caleb—"

"As I'm sure you know, I'm havin' dinner with him tonight." Behind
me, J.C.'s door opens and closes. "He and I can talk then. Now"—I kiss
the cheek Mama extends as she comes off the steps—"you'd better get to
the doctor."

Daddy clomps up the steps to where Caleb is watching.

"Hello, Mr. Dirk," Mama says as he comes around the car.

"Call me J.C."

She nods. "Welcome to our home."

"It's lovely."

True, though it needs a lot of TLC, most of which Daddy hasn't
delivered on despite his promises.

While J.C. shakes Mama's thin-boned hand, the Malti-Poo yips and strains to look up at the man who has hold of her beloved.

"Cute dog." He withdraws his hand, slips it into a pocket, and there's that jangling again.

Mama smiles, although normally she would beam—all the more reason for Daddy to get a move on. "I named her Itsy because she's so itsy-bitsy."

I look to where Daddy and Caleb are conversing in low voices and say, "J.C. prefers small dogs." Oops. I swoop my gaze to Mama, but she doesn't seem surprised by my insight. Miles probably told her about J.C.'s visit to my home last night and, going by Daddy's behavior, him too.

"If it's small dogs you like," Mama says, "you certainly wouldn't have wanted to be here when we had a pair of bull mastiffs years ago." She shifts her attention to me, and I suppress the impulse to rub away the dark smudges beneath her eyes. "I don't know if you remember them, you were so little."

"I do." Huge dogs, well over a hundred pounds each. I loved them like I love all animals but feared them too, the way they ran over whatever was in their path.

"Anyway"—she goes a little more limp—"I don't care that your daddy said they were the best guard dogs you could buy. If he'd had them properly trained, perhaps, but they were unpredictable. Why, we could have been sued when they chased a couple of boys who came onto the property and bit one of them on the face. Not long after, the male knocked over our little Bonnie and caused her to break her leg. And that's when I put my foot down and told Bartholomew to get rid of them."

"Is that right?" J.C.'s posture is the opposite of hers—all stifflike, as if he's remembering what made him wary of big dogs.

Time for Mama to go. "Daddy!" I scoop up Itsy for fear she'll get tangled in Mama's legs and unbalance her. "You'd best get Mama to the doctor."

He leans nearer Caleb, chuckles at something, and tromps down the steps again.

As Itsy settles against my chest, I touch Mama's shoulder. "I'm glad you're getting checked out."

"I'm fine." She pats my hand, then her little dog. "Your daddy's makin' this tired of mine more than it is." Her smile is wan. "I appreciate you watchin' the young uns. They're eating lunch now, but if you can get them down for a nap—Lord knows, they hardly ever go down for me—it would make the afternoon less busy."

"I'll do my best." But if J.C. wants to weave another of his "Seven Caves of the Seven Winds" stories, I'll take *his* best.

Daddy cups his wife's elbow. "We'll be back soon." He gives J.C. a meaningful glare.

I look beyond him to where Caleb is descending. "And Caleb?"

"I told him he could stay, but he's got business to attend to."

Good. Juggling J.C. and the twins is one thing, adding Caleb to the mix, quite another. Hopefully, the twins will give me time to settle in before—

"It's Mr. J.C.!" Miles shouts.

I guess not. As Daddy urges Mama toward their car, J.C. waves at my nephew, who has come out onto the veranda.

"Aunt Bridge," Birdie pulls up behind her brother, "come read the new book Grandma got me. It's a happily…ever…after story."

Right. "Coming!"

Or I was. Suddenly, Caleb is in front of me, and before I realize what he intends, he kisses my cheek. "I know," he whispers as Itsy squirms between us, "I should have asked permission, but…" With a smile and a glance at J.C., he says, "I'll pick you up at your house at six o'clock. Wear something that looks good in candlelight."

Seeing as we already confirmed the time and dress code, that was for J.C.'s sake.

"I'll do my best to get Bridget home on time," J.C. says smoothly.

Doubtless, he's letting the competition know there *is* competition, and he's as familiar with where I live as Caleb. And in J.C.'s case, his claim *is* backed up by Miles's excitement at seeing him again.

With a slightly slipped smile, Caleb says, "You do that," and looks to me. "Tonight."

Goodness, if a body didn't know the bone these two are wrestling over is the Pickwick estate, she might think I'm the most eligible woman in North Carolina. I blink at the realization that the seed J.C. sowed took hold—that Caleb's interest in me is tied to the acquisition of the property. But is he just another widow sniffer? Or might he still be a maybe?

He steps past me. As he opens his car door, he finds my gaze, smiles a smile that would earn him the front cover of a magazine, and winks.

Yeah, maybe.

17

I step onto the porch overlooking a deep Carolina wood through which a creek runs wet and cool all year excepting the hottest summer months. And there on the back lawn that would be scrubby if I didn't keep it groomed for Mama, J.C. and Miles are running plays with a child's football, which looks tiny in J.C.'s hands. As for the energy that seems to churn within him, it's being put to good use as he gives my nephew a workout. Hopefully, it will pay off at nap time.

I ought to have put Miles down shortly after I entered the house behind the others, but he begged J.C. to throw a ball with him, buttering his toast on both sides by reminding me his daddy isn't here and his granddaddy is too busy for him. I relented, mostly because Miles is in need of male attention but also because it got J.C. out of the house.

Though I'm at Mama and Daddy's fairly often, I feel out of place in the home Daddy managed to hold on to through the thin times when his investment schemes went belly up. Inside, the need for TLC is less evident, since Mama works hard to keep it bright and in good repair, but the aged house is out of date—lots of lace, lacquer, and gold this 'n' that.

After watching J.C. take it all in, gaze moving up the walls of the foyer, tracing gilt mirrors, sliding over thick-waisted pillars better suited to supporting a roof than framing a formal living room, I found myself on the verge of apologizing for the bold extravagance. Instead, I excused Birdie and myself and headed upstairs.

After closing Itsy in Mama and Daddy's bedroom to save her from my niece's attempts to dress her in baby-doll clothes, I tackled the task of putting Birdie down. This was easier done than expected, Birdie drifting to sleep after a single reading of her "happily ever after" story.

"Catch, Aunt Bridge!"

A widening of my eyes sharpens Miles's blurred figure a moment before I focus on the flying football. I easily catch it, my love of the outdoors extending to sports.

"See," Miles smiles, "I told you she could catch—almost as good as my dad."

That's debatable, and I think that not to brag but to prove a child's education ought to extend to the great outdoors. Claude de Feuilles may be highly intelligent, but it's obvious his parents' love of knowledge took precedence over time spent in the pursuit of the increasingly endangered outdoor play of children. I'm encouraged that J. C. Dirk appears to be at home outside as well as inside a shiny office tower. Maybe more so.

"Join us?" He looks decidedly un-Atlanta with his mussed hair, tieless shirt, rolled sleeves, and bare feet.

Since the image meant to impress him has been dismantled—excepting my dread-to-silky hair, thank goodness—I step from the porch.

"All time quarterback!" Miles pokes his chest. "You and Mr. J.C. against each other."

I falter. I don't want J.C. chasing after me, literally or otherwise.

"I'm game," he says. "Two-hand touch."

Though I know it's backyard football terminology, I don't like the sound of that.

"You're defense, Aunt Bridge."

"O…kay." With the toes of one shoe, I peel off the heel of the other and, shortly, cross the lawn in bare feet.

J.C. smiles, a true smile as verified by the absence of his sunglasses, extending the warm expression to his eyes. "Let's do it."

Over the next fifteen minutes, marked by whoops, laughter, and fairly benign laying on of hands, J.C. and I catch Miles's throws and attempt to reach the agreed-upon goal between oak trees on the far side of the lawn. With two touchdowns to my name, two to J.C.'s, we take up positions for the tiebreaker.

On offense, I run toward the goal, looking over my shoulder for Miles's throw and J.C.'s whereabouts. He's too near, unlike the football that arcs high toward me. However, I pull off a fingertip catch and carry the ball into my chest. I pump my legs hard to evade J.C.'s reach, but he's nearer than before, so near I can hear him breathing as he forces me to zig and zag toward the nearest oak.

A hand brushes my upper arm, but just one. It has to be two. Another brush, then a hand lands in the middle of my back, the other on my shoulder.

"Oh!" I cry as the tree rises before me. A moment later, I collapse against the gnarly trunk, as does J.C.—rather against *me*. Feeling heat fly beneath my skin, I twist around and the football falls from my hand.

"Sorry." J.C. pulls back maybe six inches, a hand on the trunk on either side of me. "You're a hard one to catch."

Though reason tells me momentum is responsible for what feels like intimacy, it also points out there is no excuse for us to remain so close—unless he's trying to catch his breath. I know I'm trying to catch mine. In fact, I seem to have lost it altogether. Our bodies are no longer touching, but I feel him. And for some reason, it doesn't bother me that he's practically smothering my personal space.

"So"—he peers into my face—"let the tie stand? No winner, no loser?"

I pick out the gold flecks in his green eyes only to wonder if I imagined them. Perhaps even the color, his pupils have grown so large. I swallow, an unladylike gulp that, had I not already tarnished my image, would do it for me lickety-split. "I can live with a tie." Was that my voice? And what's he doing looking at my mouth? He'd better ask permission first, is all I can say. *And if he does?*

His gaze returns to mine, and I see the question in his eyes. Was it there last night when he touched my face? I don't know what possesses me, but I lean forward.

"Whatcha guys doin'?" Miles asks from far away. Or so it seems until J.C. drops back and I find my nephew beside me, the football under his arm.

His mouth transforms into an open-mouthed grin. "Aunt Bridge and Mr. J.C. sittin' in a tree, k-i-s-s-i-n-g. First comes love, then comes marriage—"

"Miles!"

"—then comes baby in a baby carriage."

Avoiding J.C.'s gaze, I push off the tree. "Nap time, buddy."

The grin evaporates. "Do I have to, Mr. J.C.?"

"That was the agreement. Also, your aunt and I need to talk business."

With a grumble, Miles turns toward the house.

Keeping my gaze averted, I walk wide around J.C. He about kissed me. And I made it easy for him. I can't believe he's really interested in me—

Bingo! He did warn me on the drive over that any interest he showed should be considered purely mercenary.

Actually, that was your *conclusion—and sarcastic at that.*

True, but that doesn't mean this isn't his answer to Caleb—as in, what's good for the goose is good for the gander. Or something like that. And I don't like it. J.C. and I need to talk. Caleb too. If either of them thinks he's going to the head of the property-acquiring line by courting me, he has another think coming.

Thirty minutes later, I'm in a bit of a better place when I hear J.C.'s tread on the stairs. When he offered to put Miles down with another story of the "Seven Caves of the Seven Winds," I was so perturbed I nearly turned him down, but that would have been cutting off my nose to spite my face. Too, it gave me time to make lunch and put Mama's recycling bins in order that Daddy always puts out of order. The man simply can't be bothered to do his part to ensure his grandchildren and their grandchildren inherit a world worth living in.

"I hope you like Spanish omelets," I say as J.C. enters the kitchen.

"I do."

As he settles at the glass-topped table, I slip a slice of my creation on each of the plates I set out. "Orange juice okay?" I nod at his filled glass.

"Sure."

I return the cast-iron skillet to the stove top, seat myself opposite J.C., and raise my fork. As I zero in on the beautifully turned omelet (I'm something of a cook, if I say so myself), I realize something is missing that is always at this table whether I like it or not. I glance at J.C., who is watching me, but is he waiting? And how's it going to look if I jump in and eat without saying grace? I suppose I could—

He lifts his fork and cuts into the omelet.

Problem solved.

"This is good."

"Thanks to Mama. She pretty much let me grow in the direction to which I was inclined, but she did push me to learn to cook." In fact, those are some of my best memories. She longed for me to be a Southern belle befitting my "lineage," but after the cotillion-skunk incident, she settled for a tomboy who could whip up a batch of tasty.

"So no cotillion or fancy coming-out balls for Bridget Pickwick?"

Did I think that out loud? I'm sure I didn't. I suppose it just follows that my nature-loving self wouldn't go in for the stereotypical Southern-girl things. "No cotillion. No debutante ball."

"But plenty of tree hugging."

I look sharply at him; however, the light in his eyes isn't derogatory. Nor is his smile, which reminds me of a certain tree and a certain leaning toward something I shouldn't have. "That's right."

He slides another forkful in his mouth, and I watch his lips close around it and remember—

I look to my omelet.

A few bites later, J.C. says, "About the estate—"

"Can we clear the air first?"

"What air is that?"

"The stuff that was floatin' around when we were up against the tree outside."

He smiles another smile that goes straight to the center of me. "Yes?"

Why is my heart thudding? It's not as if I'm not used to speaking my mind. It's second nature. Maybe first. I clear my throat. "You nearly kissed me—"

"You nearly let me."

I feel another blush coming on. "That's neither here nor there."

"Isn't it?"

I lower my fork. "I just want you to know I'm not up for that kind of sport."

"What kind is that?"

Is he baiting me? "You asked earlier how I determine the difference between a widow sniffer and a man who is genuinely interested in me."

"And you didn't answer." He leans back, looking so relaxed I almost wish he'd start jangling. "However, something tells me you think I was sniffing."

"Weren't you?"

He looks ceiling-ward as if replaying the scene.

I wish he wouldn't do that. It sets my own film rolling. And for some reason, it's not only in high definition, it's scented. Why I should smell the grass, dust, and sweat of J.C. now when I don't recall smelling any such thing when he was inches from me, I can't say.

"I suppose there was some sniffing goin' on." He looks back at me.

Only *some*? Then a part of him really wanted to kiss me?

"Chalk it up to business instinct, something I've struggled with since I stepped back into my faith a year ago."

Meaning he also turned from God? Why? And what brought him back?

"As I said the last time I was in town, I have a hard time being a what-you-see-is-what-you-get person, especially when I perceive the competition is playing dirty. Or, in this case, sniffing around. It tends to bring out the worst in me. That and my...past."

The vulnerability that peeks through his face is gone in an instant.

Obviously, behind that big-city facade lurks someone who has more to say than he's saying.

Amid the awkward silence, we return to our omelets. "I appreciate your honesty, J.C. However, just because you're doing *some* sniffing doesn't mean Caleb is."

"I could be wrong, and if I am, I apologize. But what I do know is that Merriman has ties to a firm looking to plant an industrial park outside of Asheville."

That gives me pause. J.C. has been checking on his competition. Piper did the same, but she didn't find anything like this. If it's true, it could be coincidence only. I slowly chew through egg, tomato, and green peppers. "You know that for certain?"

J.C. nods. "That brings us back to the question of how you spot a widow sniffer."

I guide another bite of omelet toward my mouth. "Now what kind of fool would I be to reveal my means of sniffin' out a sniffer?" I laugh to lighten the mood, but he stares at me. "All right, you got me. I tend to see y'all as widow sniffers."

J.C. pushes his plate forward and rests his forearms on the table. "You must have loved your husband very much."

My heart flickers, but the weight I anticipate to descend on it is blessedly—did I think *blessedly*?—lighter than expected. "I did."

"How many years has it been?"

"Four." Disgusted with the wimp in my throat, I sit straighter. "Easton's been gone—" Here I go again, refusing to acknowledge the finality of his death, as Bonnie so painfully pointed out. "My husband died four years ago." There, I did it. Out loud. On my own.

"And you still feel the loss deeply."

Is he giving me a talking-to the same as Bonnie? "You think I shouldn't?"

His shrug is slight. "Though four years seems a long time to be in mourning, some people take longer to heal than others. Of course, there are those who simply find it easier to live in the past. They refuse to move on and miss out on life—God's plans for them, if you will."

Maybe he *is* giving me a talking-to.

"They play dead. Like your opossum."

Not *my* opossum. But Reggie tries, bless her heart. In the next instant, I draw a sharp breath, belatedly struck by the irony to which J.C. is alluding—a woman who pronounces every man who threatens her widowhood a widow sniffer keeping a pet that, in the face of danger, closes down.

I cross my arms over my chest. "Which one do you think I am? Someone who takes a long while to heal or one who finds it easier to live in the past?"

He considers me. "I don't know you well enough to be certain, so it's not for me to say."

"All right then, which are you?"

He blinks. "What makes you think I'm one or the other?"

"You said your past tends to bring out the worst in you."

He inclines his head. "So I did."

"Then?"

With a smile that seems directed at himself, he says, "I'd say I'm missing out on life, letting seemingly unfinished business get in the way of the present. You?"

Seemingly unfinished business. In my case, regret over something I wish could be undone. And disillusionment with God denying me the ability to undo it. "The same, I suppose, but I'm making progress. After all, though I did suspect Caleb was a widow sniffer, I gave him the benefit of the doubt."

"Do I also get the benefit of the doubt?"

I don't look away. "You admitted to being guilty of sniffin'."

"Some."

That little word makes me so jumpy, my fork nearly gets loose. I set it down.

"It's true the business side of me longs to beat Caleb at his own game, but I am interested in you in a personal sense, Bridget."

Feeling my skin warm, I snort. "I may come from a prominent, albeit scandalous, Southern family, but you can't tell me I'm what you're accustomed to. I clean up fairly well, is all."

"You're one surprise after another. I like that." He lowers his gaze to his arms on the table and is gone a long moment. "You're not the typical Pickwick."

He's dug into our family's history. But that's just it—*history*. Yes, my daddy falls into the "typical" category, as do two of my expatriate uncles and my used car–salesman cousin Luc (to an extent); however, despite a here-and-there peculiarity, the rest of us are doing just fine.

I push the remains of my omelet aside. "You mean *stereo*typical Pickwick."

"True."

I really ought to be more annoyed. "Well, in case you haven't heard, firsthand knowledge is more credible than tittle-tattle."

He looks down again and draws a breath. "Actually, Bridget—"

"I woke up."

I look around, and Birdie's in the doorway, a book dragging from her hand. "Why, Birdie, that wasn't a long nap." I push my chair back.

"I need another happily...ever...after."

Me too. I scoop up my niece, and she drops her head onto my shoulder. "As soon as I get her back down"—I look at J.C.—"we'll talk about your plans for the property." Which is what we *should* have been doing all along.

"I'll clean up here."

"Thank you."

As Birdie and I near the stairs, the house phone rings. "Don't worry about that," I call. "The answering machine will get it."

When Birdie drops off again, I return to the kitchen, where J.C. is at the sink.

"All done." Wiping his hands on a towel, he turns to me.

"I appreciate—" I falter at the sight of Mama's cast-iron skillet overturned on another towel. "Tell me you didn't..." There are beads of water on the black iron surface. "You did."

"What?"

I point at the skillet. "You washed it."

"Yes?" He frowns harder. And then stops. "It appears I've forgotten the importance a Southern woman places in a skillet that's... What do you call it? 'Well seasoned,' isn't it?"

*Was*n't it? I turn the skillet over and whimper when I see that, instead of being wiped clean, layers of seasoning are scoured away. And there, in the bottom of the sink, is the steel wool pad that did it in—with the help of J.C.'s energy-infused elbow grease.

"I'm sorry."

I draw a deep breath. "I know. You were just trying to help." Poor Mama. What will become of her gravy? And fried chicken? And breaded okra? Wait! She gave me the skillet's twin when Easton and I married. Much as I hate to lose it, I'll gladly give it up to keep her from becoming anxious—and Daddy from grumbling over his supper not tasting right.

"You'll want to listen to the message." J.C. nods at the answering machine. "It's from your father."

Probably complaining about how long it's taking the doctor to see Mama. I set the skillet on the counter and hit the playback button. How am I going to swap skillets without alerting Mama?

"Bridget? You there? No?" He grunts. *"Probably outside. Just want you to know we won't be home anytime soon. Though I see no reason to get all het up, the doctor insists on admitting your mama to the hospital in Asheville for testin'."*

My breath seizes up.

"Typical doctor junk. You just know they get a kickback on every test they order. Well, we'll see you when we see you. Probably late." With a click, he's gone.

Tests…Mama's fatigue…the circles under her eyes… What if Daddy's wrong? What if she really is sick? It could be cancer. Or something worse. *Is* there anything worse? Besides death?

"Oh, God," I breathe, and I mean it. *You aren't going to just stand by this time, are You?*

"Bridget?"

I can't go through it again. Please don't make me go through it again.

A hand on my arm startles me, and I turn and come chest to chest with J.C.

With a sharp breath, he releases me and steps back. "Are you all right?"

"Yes. Fine."

"If you'd like, I can give you and the kids a lift to the hospital."

That's right, I have no way of getting there. Actually, I do. "Thank you, but I'd best wait to hear from Daddy. And he's probably right, that it's nothin'. But if I do need to go into Asheville, I can borrow a car from him." Surely he won't begrudge me one of his garaged classics, the sale of which would go a long way to keeping Mama and him from being financially strapped all the time.

"I should probably go, then."

I nod. "I'm sorry we didn't get to discuss the property."

"We can discuss it tomorrow at the Grill 'n' Swill."

I shake my head. "Until I know what's happenin' with my mother, we'd best not plan on that." Goodness, if I'm not canceling on Caleb, I'm canceling on J.C. How did life get so worrisome?

"I understand."

A minute later, I close the door behind him and rest my forehead against it. "Okay, God, I need You to make this better, to make Mama well. You wouldn't do it for Easton, but please do it for her. Amen."

18

Sunday, October 3

I'm going in. I can. Not will—can. Now. I draw a solid breath and, with Birdie and Miles in tow, enter. The lobby of Church on the Square opens up wide as I cross the threshold. For a moment, I feel as if I'm being swallowed, but then I hear, "Bridget! Oh my goodness, Bridget!"

I turn to the side, and there's Maggie, the elegant length of her advancing past the others who make their way to the sanctuary. A moment later, my red-headed cousin is upon me, the mint of her recently brushed teeth fanning my face. And it's okay. Her smile is that big and eyes that bright, it's okay if she stomps all over my personal space. Providing she doesn't make a habit of it.

"Hey, Birdie and Miles," her daughter says, having followed her mother. When Devyn grins up at me from her petite height, I notice the gap between her front teeth is closing. Bit by bit, the sweet little duckling is growing out her swan's wings. "Welcome back, Aunt Bridge."

Welcome back... Though I'm sending out feelers in an effort to reconnect with God, I wouldn't go that far. "Would you mind takin' the kids to their Sunday school class?"

"Sure." Devyn waves a hand. "Come on, you two. I saw Miss Elaine with a plate of oatmeal cookies. You don't want to miss out."

Without a backward glance, my niece and nephew follow.

Maggie hugs me. "I'm so glad you're here."

Is she thinking of making a habit of this touchy-feely stuff? Not that it doesn't feel good…

She pulls back. "I sure didn't see this comin'."

"Mama asked me to bring Birdie and Miles and…I could hardly refuse her."

Her lush mouth turns down. "Is she not feelin' well again?"

I tell her about yesterday's events and the half-dozen calls from Daddy informing me that this, that, and the other test came back negative.

"Praise the Lord." Maggie's pretty brow smoothes.

"I'm tryin'." I'll save further praise for when His answer is different from Easton's answer. "I'm just…a little scared, what with Mama havin' to stay overnight for further testing." That, of course, meant I had to cancel dinner with a rather curt Caleb, which annoyed Daddy when I refused to ask Bart and Trinity to watch Birdie and Miles.

"That's understandable." Maggie nods.

"So, any more news from Aunt Adele?" *My* aunt, her mother.

"She extended her stay again—says Daddy's been real good to her and she's taken a shine to Mexico." She frowns. "Makes me wonder if she might not be coming home at all."

That could be a good thing. My aunt has always been a difficult woman, but life without her husband all these years made her doubly so.

Maggie looks around the emptying lobby. "We'd better go in."

I peer into the sanctuary where, the last time I was here, I set my hand on the casket and asked God, "Why?" It got grittier, as Maggie can attest. I don't remember exactly what I said when I ran out of church that day, but I pointed at God up there who didn't care about me down here and told Him and His Son to leave me be.

Maggie tugs me forward. "You'll sit with the family, won't you?"

My feet drag as we near the wide-open doors. "There can't possibly be room for another body in that little pew." Which is true, but mostly I'm thinking it would be better for me to wait in the lobby until the kids' Sunday school class lets out.

"Ergo, we traded it for a bigger pew," Maggie says.

Ergo? Since I understand she's given up her quest to be taken more seriously by increasing her vocabulary with highfalutin words, that one must be a throwback.

"Since our family is growing, now that Bart and Trinity are married," she continues, "Piper and Axel are soon to be, and I—" She chuckles. "We'll see."

I believe we will. In fact, there's Reece ahead, briefly meeting my gaze before settling on Maggie.

"Anyway," she says at the moment I realize we've crossed into the sanctuary, "we've taken over one of the big center pews. Didn't your mother tell you? She started sittin' with us too."

I look down. I know life, not death, is at the end of the aisle; however, I'm afraid if I look too closely, I'll remember too vividly the casket I last saw there. And it will feel as if it's there now. What am I doing here?

"Hello, Bridget."

What is *he* doing here? Oh, wait—Daddy. One-quarter relieved by the distraction, three-quarters annoyed by my father's interference, I glower at Caleb.

"What?" He splays his hands.

"I'm Maggie Pickwick." My unruffled cousin sticks out a hand. "A cousin. And you are?"

"Caleb Merriman." As he accepts her handshake, I catch a gleam of appreciation in his eyes before they dip to Maggie's left hand. No ring yet, but Devyn confided that when Reece took her mom and her to a mall in Asheville and they went their separate ways, she saw him across the walkway looking into a jewelry store window.

Get a move on, Reece. Not because I'm worried Maggie will snatch this "maybe" out from under my nose, but because I want to see my cousin and her daughter happy. And for Uncle Obe to see them happy while he still can.

Maggie slides her hand out of Caleb's. "You're the other interested party."

"That's right. I'm considering buying the Pickwick estate for a private residence."

"That's what I hear. And I'd love to hear more, but the service is about to begin."

"Mind if I join you?" Caleb turns his *secondhand* appreciation on me.

I'm tempted to discourage him, but when I catch sight of J.C. past his shoulder, I have no choice but to agree, though it appears the competition is, as yet, unaware of our presence.

"Sure," I say, then to Maggie, "lead the way." And she does, past J.C., whose attention remains on the church bulletin.

Despite the length of the pew our family has claimed, there isn't much room left when I slide into it after Maggie and ahead of Caleb.

"Good to see you here, Bridget," a voice says. I know who it belongs to, and when I turn my head, first taking in the earthen fingers that curl over my shoulder, I'm grateful to see Henry and Lucy in the pew behind.

"Yes" is all I can say, and he smiles big.

As I seat myself, my sister-in-law's voice soars above the chatter. "Gol!"

I peer past Piper and Axel, beyond Uncle Obe who is conversing with the woman beside him—his caregiver, Mary—and on to Trinity, who is staring at me.

"Am I seein' things?" She pokes Bart beside her. "Tell me if that ain't your sister Bridget what just slipped into our pew—*at* church, I might add."

Talk a little louder, won't you? Caleb surely heard and quite possibly J.C., but those in the back row might be feeling left out.

My brother meets my gaze as I lower to the bench. "Why, it *is* her." He taps Uncle Obe on the knee. "Bridget's here."

My uncle raises his head and says something too low for me to catch over the other voices; however, I see my name on his lips and his smile is for me, the reach of which I haven't seen in so long it makes my walk down the aisle worthwhile. Then he shifts his gaze toward the ceiling and moves his lips in what has to be prayer.

"It would seem you're not much for organized religion," Caleb says.

I shift around to face him where he sits on the end of the pew. "God and I…" *No need to go into specifics.* "Well, it's been awhile since I felt comfortable attending services." Not that I feel comfortable now. "What about you?"

He opens his mouth, but it's Devyn's voice that sounds between us.

"I got the twins settled." She slips past our knees, and I scoot nearer Caleb to make room for her between her mother and me. "The oatmeal cookies are a hit."

"Thank you, Dev." As I return my attention to Caleb, the music starts, causing conversations to hush and the congregation to rise.

Caleb stands with me. "Since we couldn't get together last night"— he takes my hand—"I thought we could have lunch."

I stare at my fingers. Compared to his, they appear more tan than they are, even my ring finger without its bandage. One of us spends quite a bit of time outdoors, the other not enough. I gently tug, but he holds on.

"What do you say?"

The voices around us rising in song, I put my mouth near his ear. "Let's talk after service." He releases me, and I catch sight of J.C. on the other side of the aisle, several pews back. He meets my gaze.

I have no reason to be bothered by his witness to what appears to be intimacy between Caleb and me. And I'm not. Well, maybe a little, but that's because of J.C.'s kiss.

He didn't kiss you.

True, but for some reason, I feel his almost-kiss more deeply than Caleb's actual kiss. But what am I doing thinking such thoughts? I snatch up the hymnal, open it at random, and set my eyes to words penned in the eighteen hundreds.

"Wrong song," Devyn whispers. "Page 232."

I flip ahead but don't join in the voices that praise God. Everything is moving too fast. I'm here, and that's enough for now—maybe too much. Even the sermon that follows pretty much goes over my head, since it doesn't apply to me. All I can think is that if God really wanted me here today, the sermon would be relevant to Bridget Pickwick

Buchanan. After all, how many times did Easton go on about sermons that seemed tailor-made for him?

In fact, on one occasion, I pointed out that perhaps they seemed that way because he was looking for a fit. He frowned, then said, "You're right, but that's just good stewardship of God's Word—taking it in and letting it conform itself to one's own circumstances. Not letting any of it go to waste."

His words had been lofty, and still are, seeing as there seems no way this particular topic can conform to my life and struggles—raising up a child in the way he should go so when he is grown he won't turn from it. I'd like to have children to "raise up," but that doesn't seem likely to happen anytime soon, even though two men who say they're attracted to me are nearby.

I glance at Caleb. He's nodded off, though not in any way obvious. He still sits erect—no telltale leaning or snoring—but his lids are closed. Despite his claim to wanting the Pickwick estate as a private residence where he can raise a family, maybe children don't figure into his near future either. Maybe he does want it for an industrial park. Or maybe J.C. is dabbling in deceit to eliminate the competition.

So how do I discover the truth? Though I best like the idea of the property remaining a private residence, even if the scarred land of the quarry is left to mend itself, I'd take whatever ecologically sound development J.C. has in mind over an industrial park.

I consider Caleb again. I could ask him, but if J.C. is right, then he's a proven liar and I can't believe anything he says.

I peer over my shoulder. J.C. is *not* sleeping but appears to be following Pastor Stanky's sermon. Surely *he* could show me proof of Caleb's intentions, seeing as he professes to have uncovered them.

His gaze shifts to me, making my breath back up, and he raises his eyebrows in silent question.

I turn away. Ten minutes later, my reintroduction to church comes to a close. And if I wouldn't have to climb over Caleb, I'd be the first one down the aisle.

"Lunch?" Caleb asks as he takes his sweet time exiting the pew.

I'm tempted to put him off, but it is getting to be past rude. "Sure," I say as we walk side by side up the aisle, "but I am keeping my niece and nephew, so—"

"Oh. Right. Look, let's do it another day. I know how seriously you take your responsibilities."

No, he doesn't, but since I prefer to postpone our get-together, so be it. "Yes, I do."

"I'll call you."

We exchange the sanctuary for the lobby, and he leaves me behind. I step aside to await my family, who are moving at a trickle—well, not Maggie and Reece or Trinity and Bart. They're not moving at all where they stand outside the family pew, engaged in what appears to be a lively conversation.

Devyn crosses the threshold, tells me she'll collect Birdie and Miles, and hurries away.

"Bridget." Uncle Obe appears, an arm hooked with Mary's, which surprises me, since he doesn't care to be coddled. "I can't tell you how good it does my heart to see you here." He sets a hand on my arm. "All through service I prayed your comin' back to God would be fulfilling and you would resume the blessed habit of w-worshipin' with fellow believers."

My smile feels tight. "I suppose this is a good start."

"Your mother has also been in my prayers."

Then Daddy must have called him. "Thank you." I turn my attention to the woman at his side. "It's good to see you again. Mary, isn't it?"

"Marie," Uncle Obe corrects despite Mary's nod.

Beginning to blush, she pats his hand on her arm. "Your uncle has taken to c-calling me Marie."

"Because you are a Marie," he says.

She nips her bottom lip. "It's nice to see you again, Bridget."

Piper appears. "I'm glad you're still here. I just spoke with J. C. Dirk. He wants to meet with the family to discuss the acquisition of the estate."

Moving right along, with or without me. Not that I have the right to be offended, since he has tried to discuss his plans with me. "When?"

"Today, two o'clock, at the mansion."

I sigh. "I'll be there, along with Birdie and Miles." I had hoped to drive in to Asheville to see Mama, even though Daddy discouraged a visit, since I would have to bring the kids and "Really, your mama needs a break from those two." True, but more, I think, Daddy is looking for a break, though hardly well deserved. However, in his defense, he has stayed by Mama's side, going so far as to cancel a tee time that was "not easy to arrange in the first place, let me tell you."

Tomorrow, then, I'll go see Mama if she's still in the hospital.

"Uncle Obe, Mary"—Piper turns her attention to them—"while Axel's gettin' the Jeep, I'll let Maggie and Bart know about the meeting. Be right back."

"We'll be here," my uncle says as she hurries away.

"I want another cookie."

I look down to find Birdie looking up. "I don't have any—"

"Devyn does." Miles points at his second cousin, who does indeed hold a Ziploc stuffed with two cookies. "I want another one too."

Since they've already indulged, they don't need more sugar. "Maybe after lunch. *If* you eat well."

Birdie's big, beseeching eyes turn small and smoldering. "I want mine now."

"Later," I say firmly.

She stomps, causing churchgoers to frown. "Now!"

"Now," Miles echoes. "I'm hungry."

More eyes turn to us, and I resent how often it falls to the Pickwicks to provide entertainment for those with nothing better to do than tune in to our show. Though I try to act as if I'm not bothered by the attention, I don't care for it, especially when it's negative.

I look Miles in the eye. "If you're hungry, what you need is food, not sugar."

He thrusts his jaw forward, then whips around and strains for the Ziploc.

As Devyn stumbles back, she tosses me a wide-eyed question.

I answer it by reaching past my nephew and relieving her of the bag. With a grateful smile, she hurries back into the sanctuary to join her mother.

"That's enough, Miles."

He jumps, and his fingertips brush the bottom of the bag. A glance around confirms we're the cause of much murmuring. Is that J.C. at the entrance?

"I want my cookie." Birdie drops to the floor and starts kicking her heels like the three-year-old she isn't. As for Miles, he continues to jump for the bag.

I want this mess over—to be out of the spotlight and on my way home. Maybe this isn't a battle worth fighting, after all. Maybe for the sake of sanity I ought to—

"Don't forget what…er…the guy at the podium said," Uncle Obe whispers.

What? Oh, Pastor Stanky and his message about raising children and the importance of not giving in to the temptation of easy fixes that will lead to long-term behavioral problems. But these aren't my kids, so it isn't my place to instill values.

Whose place is it? Your mother's? She's in the hospital. Your daddy's? He passed on the privilege. Bonnie and Claude's? They aren't here. You *are and you agreed to help. As for wanting today's sermon to apply to your situation? Here you go.*

Too bad I didn't stay tuned in to the pastor's words. Of course, common sense tells me what's needed—that I stand firm. "It's time to leave, Miles."

As he jumps again, I hear a telltale jangling. I start to look behind, but this time when my nephew comes down, the weight of his sturdy little body lands on my foot. I yelp, the bag slips, and it's all I can do not to grab my foot and hop around the lobby.

"Miles!" I snap as he scrambles for the bag. However, it's not his hand that whisks it from the floor but a broad and long-fingered one.

Miles glares at J.C. where he straightens beside me, but he doesn't jump at him. Oh no, he has too much respect for the man. Though I've tried to earn that respect by being firm with my sister's kids and teaching them manners, they still think they can manipulate me as they do their grandmother. And here's J.C. coming to my rescue as if to confirm I'm incapable of such respect.

"Need help?"

I look up only to have my resentment sputter—a little—at the realization J.C. isn't completely bulldozing me. "No, thank you." I take the bag and feel a tingle where our fingers meet. Unfortunately Miles starts jumping again…threatening my feet…testing my patience…and then Birdie joins in.

J.C. leans near enough that his shoulder bumps mine, his breath warms my ear, and I feel another tingle. "You sure I can't help?"

"Gimme!" Birdie whines.

Once more I consult our audience. Though it's diminishing as rumbling bellies urge the congregation outside, the die-hard gossips want to see how this plays out. I meet J.C.'s gaze. "What do I do?"

"Time-out."

I've seen Bonnie use that discipline at the mansion. But what about in public? "Here?"

"It's just for a few minutes," he says low, disturbing me with that breath of his. "Remove them from the situation and their audience, and they'll likely settle down."

Worth a try. "Time-out."

My declaration ends the jumping, but as I silently congratulate myself, Miles says, "No!"

"Now what?" I murmur out the side of my mouth.

"A good paddlin', is what." The strength of Uncle Obe's voice startles me. "Worked for my brothers and me when we got out of l-l-line with our daddy."

Not a good example—at least, where the other three Pickwick boys are concerned.

Miles glowers at his great-uncle. "Mama and Daddy don't believe in paddling."

"No paddling," Birdie chimes in.

"May I?" J.C. asks. At my nod, he bends down, puts a hand on Birdie's shoulder and one on Miles's. "Your aunt Bridget has told you it's time-out. Do you want to walk to that bench over there"—he juts his chin—"like the big girl I know you are, Birdie?"

Some of her scowl slips.

"And the big boy I know you are, Miles—especially as demonstrated by that powerful throwin' arm of yours?"

My nephew smiles.

"Or would you prefer that your aunt carry you?"

Carry them? Have them fighting me all the way? Making more of a scene?

"I can walk," Miles says. "I got powerful legs too, you know."

"Me too," Birdie says, and the two of them run to the bench where they plop down and look to J.C. for approval.

He gives a nod and straightens.

I sigh. "I'm relieved they chose to walk there on their own. The thought of carrying them kicking and screaming…"

"You can't let embarrassment dictate discipline or you'll be hostage to them," J.C. says. "Also, remember that nearly everyone staring at you has been or will be in the same situation." His grin is one-sided. "Of course, time-out doesn't always work. Sometimes you just have to let them melt down."

"Well, thank you."

"We appreciate your help," Uncle Obe says. "Uh, what was your name?"

J.C. turns to him. "J. C. Dirk, sir."

My uncle nods. "Like Jesus Christ, but…not Jesus Christ."

J.C.'s hesitation is barely perceptible. "That's right."

Uncle Obe taps his temple. "I'll try to remember."

Mary touches his hand. "Piper's waving at us. Time to go."

"I should go too," J.C. says. "But I'll see you at the estate in a few hours?"

I glance at my niece and nephew, who sit on the bench with elbows on knees and chins in hands. "I'll be there."

J.C. starts to move away, but I catch his arm. "And I'm sorry that circumstances bein' as they were, we didn't have the opportunity to discuss the estate before today."

"I understand. How's your mother?"

It's nice of him to ask. "The doctors are still running tests. Hopefully, we'll know soon what's goin' on."

He nods. "Let me know if there's anything I can do to help."

I realize my hand is still on his arm and pull it back. "Thank you. I just might." Though what could he do? I wonder as he walks away. All I need from J.C. is an ecologically sound plan and a fair market offer for the estate.

Are you sure that's all you need?

19

S he's had a calming influence on him." Piper peeks around me to
where our uncle is sitting on a sofa beside his caregiver, head tilted
toward her as if what she's saying is of importance. "He hasn't asked
about Daisy and Antonio for weeks."

"That's good—unless it means he's forgotten them." I grimace. "But
considerin' their lack of response to reconciliation, it's probably for the
best."

Piper sighs. "All I know is that woman is a godsend. She may not be
the nurse we were hopin' for—Uncle Obe made sure of that—but she
seems what he needs."

I'm happy for him. "How are the weddin' plans coming along?"

Scooting a hank of short red hair behind an ear, Piper grins. "Fine,
since we're keeping it simple by holding the wedding here and having
Martha cater the reception like she did for Bart and Trinity." In the next
instant, she leans to the side to peer past me. "Look who's here."

I turn. Having traded his church wear for dark jeans and a white ox-
ford shirt, J.C. strides from beneath the arched doorway and turns up his
mouth when I catch his eye. Insides going all funny, I look to Maggie at
his side. Despite my cousin's excess height in heels that cause her to top
J.C. by a bit, they're a good-looking couple. Fortunately Reece has already staked his claim to Maggie—

Fortunately? You're not thinking of staking a claim yourself, are you?
No! *Could've fooled me with those suddenly moist palms of yours.*

Pressing them to my thighs, I growl at the voice in my head. Not that it takes the threat seriously.

"You all right?" Piper says.

"Yes." I scan the library, pausing on Maggie's brother and his wife, who sit at the back of the room on an old tufted bench that lost its tuft ages ago. Two feet separate Luc and Tiffany, though from the look of them, it's only for lack of a longer bench. Jaw jutted, Luc leans forward with his hands clasped between his knees. Chin up, Tiffany sits straight with her hands in her lap and legs crossed, the upper foot bouncing in time with what appears to be indignation.

I consider her other foot anchored to the floor by a four-inch heel. Going by Tiffany's taste for high-end shoes, my guess is that until yesterday the only home those shoes had ever known was a box with fancy gold lettering. I almost feel sorry for Luc, who foots (ha!) the bill for his wife's expensive tastes—*almost* since his own spending habits contribute to keeping him in the red. Doubtless, he hopes the sale of the estate will translate into a nice inheritance when...

I look at Uncle Obe. He's doing better, so hopefully "when" won't come for a long while.

"Well," Piper says, reminding me she's still at my side, "I believe we're all here."

Except Birdie and Miles—thankfully. Wide-eyed from their second cookie after lunch, they lay awake at nap time; however, on the drive over, they conked out and barely stirred when Axel and I carried them to an upstairs bedroom.

"That's assuming your father isn't coming," Piper says.

Daddy's still at the hospital. Though I wish it were a testament to his love for Mama so I could forgive the many ills I often find myself pinning to him like badges of shame, more than likely he wasn't informed of the meeting. Certainly not by me.

"We'd better find a seat," I say. Not that they're in short supply in the large library that features floor-to-ceiling bookshelves, the upper half of which requires a rolling ladder to access the leather-bound books.

I settle on the sofa that is also occupied by Trinity and Bart, who cuddle at the opposite end, and catty-corner to the sofa Uncle Obe and Mary occupy. Considering the bookshelves, I pick out the growing number of gaps, evidence their former occupants have been sacrificed to keep the money flowing at the Pickwick estate.

I pause at a large hole in the Charles Dickens section. Only a few books remain there, a first edition *Bleak House* and a three-volume set of *Oliver Twist* having most recently departed. According to Maggie, the books should command upwards of four thousand dollars at next week's auction. Their disappearance saddens me, as does the disappearance of many of the antiques that once defined this big old house.

"Hey there."

I look around to find Maggie's daughter has claimed the threadbare cushion beside me. "Devyn Divine!" I lift an arm.

The recently promoted "teenager" hesitates, something I'm trying to get used to, but ducks beneath my arm and hugs my side. "Don't be sad." She tilts her head back to meet my gaze.

"It feels like the Pickwick roots are being sheared straight off."

"I was feelin' that way too, but Unc-Unc reminded me—I don't re-member the Bible verse, but it was Matthew. Anyway, it's the one about storing up treasures in heaven and not on earth where they'll come to nothin'. You know, rot and theft."

It is Matthew, specifically 6:20. I know this since it was among

Easton's guiding verses. In fact, it's one of the things that first drew me to him since neither did I seek a lavish lifestyle.

I give Devyn a smile. "That is a good verse."

"Plus"—she puts her mouth near my ear—"*we* have good news. The best!"

If "the best" for her still means acquiring a father, then Reece has proposed to Maggie. "Oh?"

Devyn smiles.

"All right, all," my newly engaged cousin calls from the far end of the room where she stands before Uncle Obe's immense desk. "Mr. Dirk is here to discuss his proposal for the estate."

She steps aside, and J.C. takes her place. "I'll keep it brief. As you know, Dirk Developers—"

"Stop that!" Trinity swats at Bart's hand on her stomach, seemingly oblivious to the reason for our family gathering.

With a muffled groan, I return my attention to J.C. in hopes he'll ignore the interruption. However, his gaze has settled on my brother and sister-in-law.

"Ba-art!" Trinity swats again, tempting me to lunge past Devyn and snatch his splayed hand from her...stomach.

"Oh," goes Piper, straightening where she leans against a wall of books alongside Axel.

"Oh my," goes Maggie, her steps slowing as she nears the sofa where Uncle Obe and Mary have been joined by Reece.

"That's great!" goes Devyn, scooting down the sofa to place her own hand on Trinity's stomach.

"Oops," goes my sister-in-law, giggling, shoulders wiggling. "I think you done let the cat out of the bag, Bart."

He grins. "Then we might as well give it a name." He clears his throat. "Baby Pickwick is gonna make us a mommy and daddy come May."

There seems a lot of breath holding going on, evidence other members of our family are uncertain about my brother and his wife becoming parents. But I know something they may not. Bart and Trinity are really good with Birdie and Miles.

"And it's a boy," my brother continues.

They know already? But she can't be that far along.

"It's just a feelin'," Trinity says, "but since we both feel it, chances are this little one is gonna wear blue."

"That's mighty fine news." Uncle Obe looks to the woman beside him. "Don't you think, Marie?"

She nods.

With my brother's gaze awaiting mine, as if he's anxious for my agreement, I'm thankful Daddy isn't here. "It *is* good news. I'm excited for you and Trinity."

Relief melts into his smile.

"You'll be an auntie again," Trinity says. "Doesn't that just goose your bumps! And hey, since you never had kids and in case you don't ever— you know, what with you bein' a confirmed widow and all—"

I feel myself tighten like a screw in a hole that's in danger of being stripped of its threads.

"—you can always borrow our little one. Or two. Maybe three." She tosses her hands up. "Who knows?"

The room suddenly pressurized, doubtless from all that breath holding, I long to walk out, and more so when a glance at J.C. confirms he's watching me. However, I can't fault my sister-in-law for putting a name on these past four years. After all, I have lived as a "confirmed" widow. Well, until that kiss. And the almost-kiss. And this longing to live in the present so my future doesn't remain buried with Easton.

I sigh. Trinity, for all her running at the mouth, knows a thing or two. I turn to her and see wariness in her eyes, the first sign she's clued in to the silence.

"You're right." I nod. "Who really knows?" I look to J.C. "I believe we're ready to hear your plans for the estate."

He shifts his gaze to the other end of the sofa. "First allow me to offer my congratulations. I'm sure you'll make fine parents."

"Here, here!" Uncle Obe raises an imaginary glass.

The rest of us murmur congratulations, restoring Trinity to her glowing self.

J.C. clears his throat. "As you know, Dirk Developers—"

"Since we're all gathered here," Luc says, "I might as well share my news too."

I throw J.C. a look of apology before peering over the back of the sofa at my cousin who has risen from the bench.

"In order to finance the spending sprees my wife so enjoys, I'm expanding my car business. Which takes money, Mr. Dirk, so you'd best not be lookin' to steal our family's land."

Oh, to be a mouse with a hidey-hole nearby…

J.C.'s face darkens. "I assure you, Mr. Pickwick, *I* am not in the landstealing business."

I look to Maggie. We both look to Piper, who meets our frowns with one of her own, evidencing she also caught J.C.'s emphasis that I interpret to mean *Luc* is in the land-stealing business. Of course, J.C. knows the land belongs to Uncle Obe. Our cousin's interest in it is merely a result of the inheritance our uncle has promised each of us. Meaning J.C. believes Luc is taking advantage of Uncle Obe's generosity?

"Well now, Luc," Uncle Obe says, "I'm proud of you for plannin' for the future, but why don't we let our guest get on with his…uh…talk."

"I just want to be sure he and I understand each other. Do we, Mr. Dirk?"

As J.C. stares at Luc, Uncle Obe eases up off the sofa, shaking his head at Mary when she reaches to assist him. "If you sit down now, Luc," our gaunt and suddenly tight-faced uncle says, "I might not cut you out of the will."

Luc's upper lip draws back. "Cut me—?"

"Sit down." Uncle Obe points to the bench where Tiffany has gone still to the tip of her formerly bouncing shoe.

Luc drops to the bench.

I feel bad for Mary, whose hands are clasped white tight in her lap. However, once Uncle Obe resettles beside her and gives her hands a pat, she sets them free. Though it's true the Pickwicks can be overwhelming, especially in concentrated doses, I wish the woman had more of a spine.

"Now that we're done with family announcements," Uncle Obe says, "let's return to the business at hand."

If Maggie and Reece had planned to announce their engagement today, it's definitely on hold.

"Thank you, Mr. Pickwick." J.C. widens his stance. "First, let me assure you all that the reports coming in indicate the estate's asking price is commensurate with its market value. However, there is a problem. The quarry."

Of course.

"As Dirk Developers is an environmentally minded company, leaving the land to struggle in its reclamation of the quarry over thousands of years is not an option. Any responsible development, whether it's for single-family homes, a wilderness retreat, a golf course, or an industrial park"—he meets my gaze—"has to take into account the scarred land at the center of the property. The cost of reclaiming it to make the estate whole and, therefore, financially viable, is high."

The sound of the front door slamming puts an exclamation mark on that last word, causing us to look to the doorway that will soon frame the person who didn't ring the bell. I have a bad feeling about our late arrival, even before I hear the huffing and puffing that proves I have every reason to feel this way.

"Bridget!" Daddy calls.

It could be worse. Had he arrived earlier, he would have been present for the announcement of Trinity's pregnancy, and his response might have made J.C. rethink his interest in becoming involved in our family in any way.

"Where are you, Bridget?"

I'm on my feet when he enters the library. "What are you doin' here, Daddy? You're supposed to be with—"

"She's sleepin' off the latest test, so I ran home for a shower and a change of clothes. And do you know what I found?" He halts before me. "Rather, what I did *not* find? My favorite classic car. Gone!"

It is not his favorite, which is why I chose it over the others.

"And where do I find it? Here! And who's the culprit? My own daughter, who I brought up better than to take a man's prized possession for a joyride."

Deep breath. "My truck broke down, Daddy, which is why I had to ask J.C. to give me a ride to your house yesterday so I could watch Birdie and Miles while you took Mama to the doctor."

Daddy growls at J.C., "*You* again!"

J.C. smiles, and I don't doubt that some of that smile is born of amusement. Leave it to us Pickwicks to turn his meeting into a joke.

"Sit down, Bartholomew," Uncle Obe says, "you've interrupted our meeting long enough."

"Meeting?" Daddy shifts his regard to his brother, then around the library, eyes widening as he takes in the other family members.

"J. C. Dirk has called us together to, uh…" My uncle flips a finger through the air as if paging through a book. "…you know, t-talk about his plans for the estate."

Daddy harrumphs. "Surely you're not seriously considerin' selling to this big city slicker when we have Caleb Merriman in our pocket?"

Uncle Obe frowns. "I am. Now if you want to stay, sit. If not, you'd best get back to…" His eyes trip back and forth, as if scanning for my mother's name. "…your wife."

Daddy lowers to my place on the sofa, all the while grumbling about the insult of not being invited to the meeting. Though tempted to remind him that this is not where he ought to be, I want J.C. on his way before he witnesses more of our dysfunction.

Hoping Mama is fast asleep, none the wiser for having been abandoned, I wedge myself between Daddy's hip and Devyn, who has settled beside Trinity.

J.C. clears his throat. "I'll get to the point. We believe the Pickwick estate has the potential to be developed into an environmentally responsible destination golf resort."

I was hoping for better, but in a world where profit comes first, something like a wilderness retreat comes last.

"To that end, we're drawing up plans for a world-class eighteen-hole golf course. Our vision is for the mansion to serve as the clubhouse and administrative center"—he holds up a hand as if expecting protest (he's getting to know me)—"however, in the interest of historical preservation, only minor changes will be made."

I still can't say I like it, but if I have to, I can live with it.

"Phooey!" This from Daddy.

J.C. flicks his gaze over him. "The development will include a hundred-room timber lodge, restaurant, and fitness center."

I squirm.

"But we'll push past the boundaries of a typical golf resort and incorporate the feel of a wilderness retreat."

I perk up, only to unperk. The *feel*?

"We're looking at walking and horseback riding trails, an equestrian center, and converting the quarry into a fishing lake bordered by private cabins where guests looking for peace and quiet can find it."

"Phooey, I tell you!"

J.C.'s jaw shifts. "Within the next week, Dirk Developers will submit an asking-price offer, along with preliminary plans."

Daddy heaves himself to the edge of the sofa. "I ask you, why would my family sell to you when Merriman is willing to buy the property for use as a private residence?"

J.C.'s nostrils flare. "Are you sure about Mr. Merriman's intentions, Mr. Pickwick?"

Daddy hesitates. "He's a man of his word. And even if he decides to develop the property, why wouldn't we let the two of you start a biddin' war and put more money in our pockets?"

Uncle Obe's pockets!

J.C. pushes his hands into *his* pockets and starts jangling. "The price *Obadiah* Pickwick has set for the property is workable; a bidding war is not. Dirk Developers' full-price offer is a take-it-or-leave-it proposition."

Daddy harrumphs. "Sounds like a bluff." He looks to his brother. "I'd call him on it, Obe. That is, unless you do as I wisely advise and sell to Caleb Merriman who, I assure you, is sincere in his desire to acquire the estate as a private residence."

My uncle glowers at his brother, smiles lightly at Mary, then tips his head back to consider the ceiling.

"If my uncle were to accept your offer, Mr. Dirk," Piper takes a step away from the shelves, "what's the timetable we're talking about?"

"Best-case scenario, development will begin in one year. Worst case, two years, since one or more of hundreds of things could gum up the process, whether on our end or the local government."

She nods. "And durin' that time, the mansion sits empty?"

I know where she's going. I shift my attention to Uncle Obe, whose gaze is still stuck on the ceiling.

"We believe it's an ideal base of operations before and during development," J.C. says, "the lower rooms serving as offices, the upper rooms as lodging."

Piper stands taller. "It sounds like an efficient use of space. However, I believe the family will agree that your offer on the property would be more desirable if it allowed Uncle Obe to remain in his home until the development is well underway."

Good for you, Piper.

"Well, I don't agree!" Daddy scowls. "Clearly, Merriman's offer is the best."

Her smile is patient. "Though Mr. Merriman has expressed interest in the property, *supposedly* as a private residence, he has yet to make an offer."

Daddy backhands the air, his sturdy fingers coming within an inch of my nose. "Oh, he'll make an offer. You can bet your fancy education on that, Piper *Wick*."

My cousin blinks at yet another dig at her attempt to disassociate herself from her family when she fled Pickwick at the age of eighteen and shortened her last name. Though it didn't sit well with me when I heard about it, I understand her motivation—especially when Daddy acts like this.

"As for my brother continuin' on here," he says, "you know better than most, Piper, he isn't much longer for this place."

A strangely musical gasp goes around the room. I could just pinch my father.

"That's enough!" Mary, the spineless one, jumps up and points at Daddy. "You…parasite!"

We all look from her to Daddy to Uncle Obe, whose gaze has finally come down off the ceiling, wearing a smile, no less.

My red-faced father heaves upright.

I check on J.C., who is staring, jaw slightly agape, jangling absent.

"Young lady"—Daddy pokes the space between them—"need I remind you that you are here in the capacity of caregiver to my ailin' brother? This is a *family* discussion, and if you can't keep your yap shut—"

"Bartholomew!" Uncle Obe's voice is strong; then he's on his feet alongside Mary. "You will not speak to my daughter in that manner."

Another collective gasp, then silence so complete the sound of a pin dropping would have little on a gnat similarly afflicted. Beneath our startled regard, Mary Folsom colors and her rigidly held arms sink to her sides.

Daddy heaves a sigh. "Well, there you have it. You are officially off your rocker, Obe."

"No, he isn't." Reclaiming her presence, Mary turns to face Uncle Obe. "When did you know?"

Despite the gauntness of his face, the angles soften, and he lays a hand on her cheek. "I wasn't sure the day in the coffee shop, seein' as Bridget hurried me away, but when you came for the…talk about the j-job, I knew you were my Daisy Marie."

That's his daughter's middle name? I stare at her. Marie…Mary…? As I noted the first day I saw her, she has a Catherine Zeta-Jones look, and if she's to be believed, it comes from her Hispanic mother's side. *Is* she to be believed?

"Hogwash," Daddy trumpets.

She looks around. "If you want proof, I have my birth certificate… Uncle Bartholomew."

Daddy startles so hard he jiggles, but then his glower is back. "If what you say is true, that's the most underhanded thing I ever heard— hiding your identity to spy on our family…size us up…maybe even work a swindle…dabble in a little vengeance."

"I want you to leave, Bartholomew," Uncle Obe says. "Now."

J.C. clears his throat. "I won't keep you any longer."

I pry my eyes from my newly discovered cousin and apply them to the man who is battening down his briefcase. Keep *us*? More like we're keeping him, in all our scandalous glory. How is it that I, who am not easily embarrassed, should feel every shade of that emotion at him witnessing our assorted dysfunctions in one sitting? If ever J. C. Dirk was a maybe, he is no more. I'm just glad that kiss didn't happen, because…

It would hurt more?

As he draws near on his way out, he meets my gaze and his mouth turns wry. *That's* how it could hurt. I don't want a wry smile. I want a real smile. But J.C. has to be thanking his lucky stars that, for all he had to endure, he's been warned.

He won't be touching me again, not even with a ten-foot pole.

20

Monday, October 4

Mary Folsom is Daisy Marie Marshall, Marshall her adoptive father's name, Folsom her married name. According to Piper, who spent time with her and Uncle Obe after I hurried Birdie and Miles home following J.C.'s departure yesterday, our cousin is divorced from a physically abusive husband. However, when she decided to get to know her father on her own terms, she used her married name to conceal her identity. It worked, though Piper says only because she allowed Uncle Obe's ancient attorney, Artemis Bleeker, to oversee the applicants' background checks. The man really needs to retire.

I feel bad that I scooted off after giving Mary…Marie…or is it Daisy…a cursory "welcome to the family," but I needed the outdoors to clear my head, especially when Daddy demanded the keys to his car. Not that he left me stranded. He loaned me his boat of a car—as in maybe ten miles to the gallon. Things should have gotten better from there, but after a half hour at the park, my niece and nephew were downright bored. So I called Trinity last night, and she picked up Birdie and Miles this morning. Her enthusiasm over "mothering practice" was a bit annoying, but still I could have hugged her for reworking her schedule so I can tend to my nursery and visit Mama this afternoon.

As I pick off the fingers of my old gardening gloves, I turn my wrist to check the time. "Not bad for four hours' work." I tuck the gloves into my right rear pocket and step back to survey the rows of weeded, fertilized, and repotted plants.

"Lookin' good!" Taggart calls.

I consider the lanky, scruff-faced man who looks older than his almost-fifty years. From the top step of the trailer that serves as our office, he gives a thumbs-up.

"Has the mulch come in?" I start across the yard toward him.

"Allen's unloading it now."

"What's the status on the pumpkins?"

"Ted promised a truckload first of next week." He grins. "I squeezed a fifteen percent discount out of him to make up for the delay."

I would have asked for twenty. "Sounds good. I'm goin' in to Asheville to visit my mother. Will you keep an eye on the office?"

"Sure thing."

"I'll take your truck, if you don't mind." Actually, it's the nursery's truck, as is the one Allen drives, but for as hard as these men work, I do my best to take care of them.

"Fine with me."

"If you need to run errands, you can take my daddy's Oldsmobile."

He nods. "Did they figure out what's wrong with your truck?"

"All three hundred dollars' worth. It'll be ready Wednesday." As I near the steps, the sound of a vehicle entering the parking lot gives me a boost. Though it was busy this morning, it's been dead for the past hour. This time of year that's to be expected, which is why the unexpected is so welcome—providing I'm not up to my elbows in something. Thinking customer, I glance over my shoulder.

It's J.C., not a customer.

Yet. If Dirk Developers buys the Pickwick estate, they'll need plants and trees and fertilizer. Trying to focus on that rather than the discomfort over yesterday's three-ring circus and my disappointment over his plans for a golf resort, I tell Taggart, "I'll handle this."

A moment later, the trailer's screen door bumps closed, and J.C. halts near enough to confirm he hasn't gone back to his stinky cologne. And I can't help but note he looks good in a black jacket over a white open-collared shirt and worn denims.

"I was hoping to find you here."

Refusing to be self-conscious about my appearance, I turn my hands up. "Hope granted." You work at a nursery, you're gonna get dirt under your nails. "What can I do for you?"

His hand brushes my cheek, but before I can sputter my surprise, he turns his smudged fingers toward me.

And you're gonna get dirt on your face. "Occupational hazard," I say, trying to lighten the lingering feel of his touch. "How can I help you?"

"First, accept my apology; second, my invitation to lunch."

Goodness, by now he and Caleb should have given up on cozying with me over a meal. But here stands J.C., and last night Caleb left an invitation for dinner on my answering machine. I should call him back, since a private residence, even without a reclaimed quarry, seems preferable to a golf resort. That is, providing Caleb isn't trying to obtain the property under false pretenses as J.C. would have me believe.

I cross my arms over my chest. "Unless you're apologizing about your resort and making good on that apology by rethinkin' it, I don't need to hear it." Yes, as Piper pointed out, investors expect a return on their investments and J.C.'s investors are no different, but if he were Easton—

He's not. And even Easton couldn't change the course set by the Pick-
wicks years ago and cemented by your uncle's determination to do right. One
way or another, the estate has to be converted to cash.

"My apology is for cutting out on you yesterday," J.C. says. "I knew
you wouldn't be thrilled with the plans for a resort, and I intended to talk
to you afterward to alleviate your concerns, but…"

His slow smile crawls the wall of my resentment. While I want to be
mad at him for not buying the estate for a wildlife preserve or some other
beneficent purpose, I recall him in the library, looking out of place as one
eyebrow-raising scene after another shook out like so much dirty laun-
dry. Though I try not to smile, I feel my mouth curve. "But suddenly you
found yourself on the set of *The Good, the Bad, and the Pickwicks.*"

He chuckles. "I did wonder if I was being had."

"You wouldn't be the first. But in defense of my family, what you saw
is not the norm. We're usually better behaved—well, some."

"I'll take your word for it. Lunch?"

I sigh. "You won't be surprised to know I have plans, but I could do
an early dinner. Fiveish?"

He shakes his head. "I'm going to Asheville this afternoon. I'm not
sure I'll be back by then."

"What's in Asheville?"

"Business."

I raise my eyebrows, but all he says is, "How about a late dinner?"

Here we go again. "Sorry, but Trinity is dropping Birdie and Miles
at my house around seven, and I'll have them all day tomorrow, so that
won't work either—" My plans catch up to my brain. "Hold it! The reason I can't have lunch with you is that I'm visiting my mother at the hos-

pital around one. If we drove to Asheville together, not only will one less car on the road save gas and put one less ding in the environment, but it'll be a good use of time since you can *try* to alleviate my concerns about your golf course during the drive."

He starts to frown.

I return the favor. "Or was that all talk?"

He looks momentarily away, and I get a whiff of the discomfort that came off him yesterday when he was a lone Dirk among Pickwicks. "No." He looks back at me. "But if I drop you at the hospital, it could be as late as six before I pick you up."

I shrug. "I like my mama. We'll find some way to while away the hours."

"All right."

"And maybe we could do a drive-through on the way out of town. I'm starved."

His eyebrows jerk. "*You* eat fast food?"

"I prefer slow food—even make my own bread—but sometimes a body's gotta have a good ol' greasy burger." I tip my head to the side. "What about you? Do you ever give in? Or is it fine dining all the way?"

He smiles again. "Sonic and I go way back."

I'm surprised, and yet not. As I've seen time and again, J. C. Dirk has more layers than first supposed. "It would seem we're both more than we appear to be."

He checks his watch. "When can you leave?"

"Give me ten minutes to clean up." Motioning for him to follow, I take the steps two at a time; however, when I enter through the trailer's rickety screen door, I find myself fighting my own discomfort. My office with its cluttered desk, cracked vinyl chairs, and stained indoor-outdoor carpeting is a far cry from the one J.C. is accustomed to. And then there's Reggie curled up on the desk. I whip around to tell J.C. I'll meet him at his car, but he's right behind me.

Oh well. "There's water in the fridge if you're thirsty." I point to the cubicle that contains a dozen stainless-steel bottles of water I purify myself so my employees and I can do our part in keeping plastic bottles out of landfills.

"I'm fine."

"I'll be right back." I indicate the chairs before my desk, behind which sits Taggart, glasses down his nose as he examines the nursery's bank statement, having exchanged his gardener's hat for a bookkeeper's hat. What would I do without him?

"Well, if it isn't Reggie," J.C. says as I scoot into the bathroom. Then, "J. C. Dirk. And you are?"

"Name's Taggart."

I close the door and step to the mirror over the sink, relieved to find I don't look half as bad as expected. Still, I wish I kept a change of clothes here. I shouldn't care how the man who wants to commercialize the Pickwick estate perceives me, but I do.

"A waste of time." I unwind the rubber band from my ponytail and rake fingers through my soft blond hair to which I've finally become accustomed. "J. C. Dirk is not part of your world." I narrow my eyes at my reflection. "Never has been, never will be."

21

T ell me about your husband."

I stop dragging at the milkshake that remains reluctant to inch up the straw though we left Sonic ten minutes ago.

"Easton, right?"

I lower the milkshake to my lap alongside the cheeseburger I was hungry for a moment ago. Is Trinity's comment that I'm a "confirmed widow" behind J.C.'s request? Is it curiosity that makes him ask?

"That's right—Easton. But shouldn't you be trying to sell me on your plans for the estate?"

"True."

Only curiosity, then. The open places in me start to close, and I feel relief at the protection they offer—but also a flutter of resentment that they're trying to keep me in the past where I don't care to stay.

"I apologize." J.C. merges onto the highway. "That's too personal—at this point."

What point is that? And what other points lie ahead? "What do you mean?"

He balls his burger's wrapper and drops it in the paper bag. "Though the…meeting with your family made me think twice about crossing the line between business and personal, I'm attracted to you, Bridget."

Still?

"I'm hoping it's mutual."

The almost-kiss. I sigh. "Just as you question Caleb's interest in me, I'd be a fool not to question your continued interest in me, especially seein' as my family made you think twice *and* you admitted to being a widow sniffer."

"Some."

I shrug. "I don't care to be a knuckle on the bone you and Caleb are wrestlin' over—you know, the part that's the first to get chewed up. So if you really want to know me on a more personal level, let's start with J. C. Dirk. You said your past tends to bring out the worst in you. What past is that?"

His jaw tenses. "I do want to talk to you about that, but it would probably be best if we hold off on the personal side of things until negotiations for the estate are closed."

Is his past really that bad? Might he have experienced greater loss than I have? Though the stubborn in me doesn't want to share if he won't, I remember Bonnie's warning about carrying my loss to the grave. "All right, I'll go first. What do you want to know about my husband?"

J.C. reaches for his bottled water, and his Adam's apple slides twice before he returns his drink to the cup holder. "Why Easton?"

Talk about personal. "We met shortly after he moved to Pickwick and opened the nursery. He understood who I was, even when I wasn't sure myself." I nip my bottom lip. "We wanted the same things—a good but simple life that respected the environment. Of course, we had our differences, especially in matters of faith. He was a Christian and I wasn't sure about God. But Easton didn't push, and eventually I wanted what he had." For awhile…

"You loved him."

"As I'd never loved. I was sure we'd grow old together. You know"—I settle on J.C.'s profile—"so bent and feeble we'd get to hold even tighter to one another."

After a brief laying on of eyes, he nods.

"It didn't work out that way. Do you want to know how he died?"

"If you want to share."

Strangely, I do. And J.C.'s eyes being turned forward—that he can't look pity at me—makes it easier. "I suppose my brother, Bart, put it best when he said Easton 'up and died.' Of course, I about purpled his arm the first time he said it." My hand remembers, curling into a fist. "Bad timing."

Peripherally, I see J.C.'s head turn toward me.

"Hunting season was coming on, and I was banging around the kitchen one morning, gripin' about the owner of the neighboring property who allowed family and friends to hunt his land. If that wasn't bad enough, the bow hunters—his teenage nephews—liked to use an old deer stand our neighbor claimed was on his property, which the tree probably was as a sapling but I was pretty sure had grown partly onto our land over the years.

"Since I'd caught the teens using it to take down a buck on our property the year before, I told Easton I had a mind to chainsaw it. When I said I could get away with it since the stand was rotting and could be declared an attractive nuisance if our neighbor tried to bring charges against me, Easton said the Christian thing to do was talk to him. I reminded him I'd done that when the buck was killed on our property, and he reminded me there was more yelling than talkin' going on."

I peer out the window at the blur of trees, many of which autumn has turned sunshine yellow, blazing orange, and brilliant red. "I said I would pray hard that sometime in the next twenty-four hours, the old deer stand made its last stand." I pull my bottom lip between my teeth. "I did that sometimes when Easton riled me—poked at his beliefs though I was also saved. He—"

J.C.'s cell rings. He ignores it. "Go on."

I almost wish he'd take the call to give me time to consider how far I'm letting him in. "Easton knew I meant to take care of the problem, so he did it for me, though I didn't know it until I came out of the shower and heard the chainsaw. I hurried and got dressed so I could help him, but when I got there…" My throat feels full. "…he was on the ground, the stand in pieces, the chainsaw biting up the dirt."

Catching the tightening of J.C.'s face, likely due to the horror he thinks I witnessed, I shake my head. "The chainsaw didn't get him. It was the rotting wood that had been my justification for taking the matter into my own hands. Still, Easton seemed all right, if shaken up. He told me he'd only started with his chainsaw when the stand collapsed—said it was a good thing it was him and not a bunch of boys, since they might have broken their necks. Though he said God would do any healing that needed to be done, I insisted on taking him to an emergency clinic. The doctor said everything looked fine but recommended an MRI. Easton refused, but since I was driving…" I replenish my breath. "He hated the hospital, seein' as he lost his mother as a child when she went in for a routine surgery and died from complications."

"So you drove him to Asheville."

I nod. "We argued until he passed out a couple miles from the hospital. He came to as he was being wheeled into the emergency room and insisted prayer and rest were all he needed. I begged him to let the doctor take a look, and he got mad. In the exam room, he pushed the nurse aside, got up, and walked out. 'God will heal me,' he said when I went after him." I close my hand around the burger to absorb its fading heat. "Easton collapsed outside and died from a ruptured spleen."

Sensing a sob in my chest, I push past it. "Everyone called it a freak accident, even our neighbor, though he swore it wasn't rotting wood that did Easton in but trespassing. He said Easton cut the stand out from under him." I shake my head. "Regardless, he was dead, and God and I haven't been on the best of terms since."

The car fills with silence so full it seems it might spill out into the rest of the world. And then J.C.'s hand is on mine. "I'm sorry."

His warmth is real, not fading, and I don't understand what makes me turn my palm up into his, but I close my eyes and draw his heat to the cold places my husband left behind—places I thought only Easton could warm. I turn my face to J.C. "Thank you."

His hand tightens on mine.

I breathe in, breathe out. Then, as light as I can manage, I say, "Seein' as the skeletons in my closet are feeling exposed, how about you give them a little company?"

His grip tightens further, though I sense more from tension than an attempt to comfort.

I squeeze back. "Tell me about your bleached bones."

He returns his hand to the steering wheel. It appears he does so to pass an eighteen-wheeler on the steep grade, but when we shift back into the right lane, my hand remains alone in my lap.

"Your turn."

He nods. "A while back, you accused me of being accustomed to a life of excess—assumed I'd never lost anything of great sentimental value."

"I shouldn't have. I'm sorry."

"I grew up in real poverty, Bridget, not the kind that loosely determines who's eligible for welfare. The kind where it isn't holes in shoes you're worried about but having shoes at all. Growing up, the other kids called my brothers and me the 'grubs.'" His mouth tightens. "It didn't have to be that bad, but my father wouldn't take what he called handouts. But neither was he willing to take a regular job. Our mother brought in the little income we had, working two and three jobs to keep us all under one roof and with as close to three meals a day as possible. We'd come home from school, and our father would be at the kitchen table where we'd left him, books all around. Usually he hadn't eaten, so we had to scrape together a meal for him."

"Did he drink?"

"Sometimes, but that wasn't the problem. Bitterness and revenge were what ruined him."

His cell rings again. I sense hesitation as he considers the small screen, as if—as I did—he's rethinking how far to let *me* into his personal life. But he returns the phone to the console.

"You said revenge ruined your father."

He glances at me. "Those books were about the legal system, on which he was educating himself in hopes of righting a wrong our family had been dealt years earlier."

"What wrong?"

"Something was taken from us."

"Stolen?"

"That's what he believed. And since he couldn't afford an attorney or law school, he chased the dream of restoring our family's fortunes with a library card."

"Did he succeed?"

"Since we only had one car that was barely reliable enough to get our mother to work, he walked to the library. One day, on the way home, he was hit by a truck."

I catch my breath. "I'm sorry."

"Witnesses said he was too busy reading to watch where he was going and that he stepped off the curb into traffic. He wasn't killed instantly, and for a while we had hope, but he had too much internal bleeding."

"I'm sorry."

J.C. nods. "Before he died, he passed the torch to me."

"What torch?"

"As he'd promised his dying father he would get back what was stolen from us, he asked the same of me."

Then the wrong was an old one.

He looks at me. "And I'm still trying to get it back, Bridget."

"What is it?"

"We'll get to that." He returns his attention to the road. "A year later, in hopes of a better life, our mother moved us out of the South to Oregon where her brother lived."

"That's why I only catch your drawl once in a while."

"Though we were young enough for the change of environment to alter our speech, peer pressure had a more immediate effect. We were out of place, and our classmates mocked us, called us rednecks." His hands flex on the steering wheel. "It took them awhile to draw a connection between cause and effect—their taunting, my fists."

"How many times were you suspended?"

His mouth curls. "I lost count."

"So life wasn't any better in Oregon?"

"Not for a long while, but it started improving when I was in my teens and got involved in sports. That's when our mother reconnected with an old friend and moved us to Atlanta, where her friend had a business. They married a month later. It didn't sit well with us, but Cameron Dirk proved to be a good man, if not a good businessman. He adopted us and gave us his name. You see, our mother thought that if we cut out our father's name, we could lay down the torch…move on…heal…"

"But you still wanted justice."

"I started my quest in college and continued it after I stepped in to help with our adopted father's failing business. Nearly all my spare time was spent on the same path my father traveled, reading up on the legal system in search of a way to lay claim to what had been taken from us." He smiles grimly. "I was so obsessed with keeping my promise that women weren't much more than an afterthought."

That explains why he's unmarried.

"In the end, I couldn't find any legal recourse, no way for the courts to restore it to us."

I'm about bursting to know what *it* is. "But you said you're still trying to get it back."

"I am, but not by way of the law."

I blink. "You're trying to steal it?"

His laugh is short. "I'll get it back, but in such a way there's no question as to whom it belongs. Everything on the up and up."

"I don't understand."

His cell phone rings again, and on the second ring, he sweeps it from the console. "It's my assistant again. She wouldn't persist if it wasn't important."

"Then take the call."

Within moments his conversation with the woman turns grave, and he sits straighter. "Other than that, he's all right?" He sighs. "Anyone else hurt?"

An accident at one of his developments?

"Good. What time did it happen? All right." J.C. thrums the hand gripping the steering wheel—in lieu of jangling? "Get me on an early-morning flight, and let Burns know I'm coming." He listens. "Thank you, but I'll call Dunn. Right. Let me know."

J.C. ends the call. "There's been an accident at a convention center our company is renovating in Alabama."

"What happened?"

"An interior stairway that was recently replaced for safety reasons collapsed on some workers." He shakes his head. "It's a miracle no one was killed."

"But someone was hurt."

"My brother."

I catch my breath. "The one who escorted me into your meeting in Atlanta?"

"No, that was Parker. Our younger brother, Dunn, was at the site. Fortunately he only suffered a broken arm and a couple of cracked ribs, and the other two men have minor cuts and bruises."

"Thank God." The gratitude exits my mouth as automatically as it did when Easton was at my side, and part of me wants to take it back.

After all, there was nothing to thank God for when it was my husband who fell victim to an accident. And yet the other part of me thanks Him again that other wives and families don't have to suffer as I did. I don't understand it. Maybe I never will.

"We're fortunate. If you'll excuse me, I need to call Dunn."

"Of course." I can't help but listen in on his conversation, and though it's one sided, it's obvious Dunn is fine. When J.C. ends the call, we're entering Asheville and only minutes from the hospital.

"We'll finish our talk on the drive back to Pickwick," he says as I motion for him to take the next right. "Maybe even get around to discussing your concerns over the resort." A smile lightens his mouth.

I look out the window at the colorful street fronts of various shops, most I've never set foot in, including a chain coffee shop. Here a Starbucks, there a Starbucks, everywhere a Starbucks. Well, not everywhere, but they are a bit like rabbits. I sigh but perk up at the sight of one of my favorite restaurants: Mellow Mushroom. What I wouldn't give to trade in my grown-cold burger for one of their salads, maybe the capri with its layers of tomatoes, fresh mozzarella—

I deflate again when I see the huge sign on a corner office: Trousdale and Associates, a Premier Real Estate Agency. As in Wesley Trousdale, Caleb's gum-flinging agent. If I never see that woman again…

A couple minutes later, I point. "Turn there."

Shortly, J.C. brakes in front of the hospital entrance. "Would you like me to walk you in?"

I would, but if Daddy is here, he might say something to J.C. I would regret. "Thank you, no. Are you headin' to your business meeting now?"

He consults the dashboard clock. "It doesn't start for another hour,

so I'll make some calls and see if I can get to the bottom of the accident."
His brow furrows. "It doesn't speak well for a developer to have new construction collapsing."

"I understand." I reach for the door handle.

"Bridget?" His hand touches my shoulder.

A thrill runs through me, and I turn back.

"I appreciate what you shared. It helps to know you better."

I chuckle. "Are you sure you still want to?"

"Yes." His gaze drifts to my mouth. "I do."

Here we are again, in the vicinity of an almost-kiss. What happened to holding off on the personal side of things until after the sale of the estate?

J.C.'s hand moves from my shoulder to my jaw. Fingers graze my neck, and he leans in and there's nothing "almost" about this kiss. It's all there, gentle at first, then deeper as I press nearer…angle my head… breathe in his salty scent…

He pulls back, and it's a moment before I orient myself. That shouldn't have happened, but I liked it. Maybe too much. It felt good to feel things I haven't felt in a long time, things I didn't know I was capable of experiencing beyond Easton. But there it is—with J. C. Dirk, whose invasion of my personal space hardly registers.

He clears his throat. "As I said, I want to know you better."

I hate that I have to ask, especially after his kiss. "Even if Caleb buys the estate?"

J.C. stares at me, then past me. "Even then, but he won't. When we head back to Pickwick, I should be able to show you proof of his plans for an industrial park."

Is that what his meeting is about?

"I'll try and wrap up the meeting early so I can take care of a few things in Pickwick before I leave tomorrow morning. If you'll give me your cell number"—he retrieves his phone—"I'll call you when I'm close to being done."

I recite the digits few have access to, and he enters them into his phone.

"Thank you for the ride." Still tingly from our kiss, I drop my burger and shake into the Sonic bag and take it with me as I step onto the sidewalk.

As J.C. pulls from the curb, I toss my garbage into a trash receptacle, then turn to face the doors that grant entrance to the place where Easton breathed his last. Fortunately this isn't my first time here since that day, so it shouldn't be that hard to enter. Hard was when we had a scare with Uncle Obe a year and a half ago, and it took a half hour of pacing back and forth in front of these same doors before I called on anger to push me through.

And I can do it again. I touch my lips. I most certainly can.

22

Standing outside Mama's hospital room, one hand on the door, I brush my lips with the other to remove traces of J.C.'s kiss. Then I roll my eyes. A body would think I wore lipstick.

When I open the door, my father is sitting alongside Mama where she's up on pillows, eyes closed. His presence isn't what makes me falter. It's his face. I've seen it bluster red before, but I don't remember seeing it sorrowful red, complete with matching eyes and tear-tracked cheeks.

I gasp. "Mama?"

He blinks. "Shh, she's restin'."

Then she's… Yes, her chest is rising and falling.

"Birdie and Miles?" He peers warily to the sides of me.

I step inside and ease the door closed. "They're spendin' the day with Trinity," I whisper. "What's wrong, Daddy?"

His face brightens further, this time with what I'm sure is embarrassment. "Nothin'. Those fancy doctors still don't know what's wrong." He releases Mama's hand and sits back. "What are you doing here?"

"Visiting, like you."

"I'm not visiting; I'm…vigilin'."

I don't think that's a word, but I'll give it to him. "Were you cryin'?"

"Me?" He snorts, the sound of his congestion confirming my suspicion. My seemingly self-centered father is worried for his wife. That makes me feel good. "Don't be reading anything into this cold." He pulls a handkerchief from his jacket and dabs at his nose. "That time of year, you know."

In that moment, he's nearly huggable.

"You taking good care of my car?"

"Yes sir."

"Not puttin' any dings in the doors or letting Birdie and Miles eat in it?"

"No sir."

"Good. Of course, you are putting needless miles on her drivin' all the way in from Pickwick."

Needless? "Actually, I drove in with J.C."

His jaw drops. "*Him* again?"

"He was coming anyway, so I hitched a ride."

Daddy presses his lips so hard they whiten.

"Bridget?" my mother says softly. "You're here." She reaches to me, and I hurry forward to clasp her hand.

"I would have come sooner, but—"

"I know. Are Birdie and Miles doin' all right?"

I nod. "They miss you. How about you, Mama? How are you doing?"

"I'm bored. And tired of all these tests. You know what I think? I'm just old."

I shake my head. "You're fifty-five. That's not old."

"I feel it."

With a grunt, Daddy stands. "I'll let you two visit. I need coffee."

When we're alone, Mama says, "Was your daddy cryin'?"

I refuse to cover for him, especially since it will do her good to know he's worried. "He won't admit it, but he was definitely crying."

Smiling lightly, she nods at the chair. "Come sit by me."

I settle in, and her gaze roves my face, and a frown collects between her eyebrows. "Oh my, you've been kissed."

I jerk. "What?"

"Don't *what* me. I always knew when you went at it with some boy, especially when you were a teenager and your lips were unaccustomed to all that smoochin'."

Heat stings my cheeks. "Mama!"

"Just look at them—all swollen up." She shakes her head. "You've been out of practice too long. Was he a good kisser, that J.C.?"

Then she heard me tell Daddy I drove in with him, meaning my lips probably aren't all that swollen. She was looking for it, is all. Though I don't care to talk about what happened between J.C. and me, her face is bright against the backdrop of a hospital bed. And I want it to stay that way.

"He's a very good kisser, but best we not say anything to Daddy, hmm?"

"I understand."

"So when will they let you come home?"

"Maybe tomorrow. Depends on the results of the colonoscopy they did awhile ago."

I stiffen. "Why are they checkin' your intestines?"

"They're kind of hush-mouthed, but I heard your daddy in the hall with the doctor. He said they're lookin' for signs of something called… celiac?"

What is that?

"And colon cancer."

That takes my breath away. No wonder Daddy was crying.

"It's just a test." She pats my hand. "No need to get all het up about it."

I nod. "What can I do for you?"

She raises her eyebrows. "Bridget darlin', the one thing I'd ask of you, I don't think you'd give me."

I frown. "Of course I can—anything."

"Even prayer?"

I blink.

"I know that's what Easton asked of you, and for all that, God didn't answer the way you wanted Him to. And His answer may be the same for me, but still I take comfort in knowing our prayers are heard and touch the heart of God."

So give her some comfort. You did it for Uncle Obe the day the statue was dedicated. And you've started adding prayers to your attempts to speak into existence. Same thing, just open your mouth. "Of course I'll pray for you."

Mama beams so bright it's hard to believe she's in the hospital. "Thank you."

"Okay…so…" I close my eyes, bow my head and, after two false starts, say, "Dear Lord, thank You for hearing the prayers of one who has had a hard time believin' in You these past years. You know why. I'm trying to get back to You, and it's slow, but if You'll just heal Mama, I'll—"

"Bridget."

I look up.

She shakes her head. "This isn't about testing God…putting conditions on your faith. It's about comfort. That's all I ask."

I draw a deep breath, close my eyes. "In Jesus' name, I ask You to give Mama comfort, and if it's in Your will, go all the way and heal her of whatever is workin' against her body, especially if it's cancer. Though I have a hard time understanding how Your will to heal can be different from ours—"

My cell phone vibrates, then rings. J.C.? Surely he can't be finished with his meeting. Probably hasn't even started it.

"—I'll try to trust that Your plan is without error as Easton promised me. Be with my mama and daddy, give them comfort and strength. And I'd like some too."

"Yes," Mama whispers. "And ask Him to help your daddy with his patience. He's been hard on the nurses."

I'll bet. "And please help Daddy to be patient with Mama's caregivers. Amen."

"Amen." She opens her eyes. "That means more to me than I can say."

"I'm glad I could do it." I am. "Excuse me, but I need to check to see if that was J.C. He's my ride home."

"Certainly."

The call is from Caleb, and his message points straight to Daddy, who surely called him the minute he left the room. He wants to have dinner with me and is happy to relieve J.C. of driving me home. He suggests dinner around five when he's done meeting with his real estate agent, who's putting together an offer for the estate. Wesley did warn we'd have future dealings.

Uncertain as to whether or not to call him back—I'll just have to turn him down again—I pocket the phone.

"How are things goin' with those rascals of ours?"

I tell her about my adventures with Miles and Birdie, leaving out anything that might make her feel guilty about not being with them, then transition to talk of her garden club, her work on the Pickwick Beautification Committee, and her ideas for another family Christmas at Uncle Obe's. An hour passes without word from Daddy, then another, during which Mama struggles to stay awake, though I encourage her to rest.

Finally she says, "I should get some sleep."

I kiss her forehead. "Sweet dreams, Mama."

She closes her lids. "I'm glad you're being kissed again," she murmurs. "So very glad, Bridget."

"Me too," I whisper and stay at her side until Daddy reappears a half hour later.

"Did he call?" are the first words out of his mouth.

I frown. "He did."

"And?"

"Mama and I were in the middle of somethin' so I let him go to voice mail."

"And you haven't called him back?"

"No." I rise and move toward the door. "Let's talk outside."

He follows me into the corridor and holds up a hand. "Trust me in this. Caleb Merriman is the one we ought to go with."

I grit my teeth. "There isn't any 'we' in this, whether you're talkin' the estate or trying to marry me off."

He glowers. "I'm only looking out for our best interests."

"Nor is there any 'our' in this. The estate is Uncle Obe's to dispose of as he chooses, and I am my own to dispose of as I choose." Though that last didn't come out right, he gets the gist. I touch his arm. "Please, stop pushing."

To my surprise, his fleshy chin quivers, and he squeezes my hand with such ferocity one might think he's drowning.

"Daddy?"

Even a passing nurse falters at the sight, her soft-soled shoes losing their rhythm.

I look closer at my father. "Are you all right?"

His face starts to crumple, but he looks down, heaves a breath, then looks up. "You know your mother and I have only ever wanted the best for you." More crumpling and again he averts his face.

First crying, now this. Softening toward him, I put an arm around his shoulders. The first words of comfort to come to me are ones that reassure him Mama will be fine, but I stop myself from saying so. We don't know she'll be fine, at least not in the way we want her to be fine. Only God knows. So I hug Daddy. "We'll get through this."

He shakes his big head against my shoulder. "I don't know if I can— not if something happens to Belinda. They were checking her for cancer. Cancer!"

Again I squelch the impulse to offer reassurance. "I'll be here for you, Daddy."

He gives a shallow laugh. "Like I was there for you when Easton died? Excuse me if that doesn't make me feel better."

I stare at his profile, hardly able to believe what I'm hearing. Is his regret real? In my darkest times, especially during those first weeks following the funeral, anger at Daddy was what often got me up off the floor and spoonfuls of cold funeral casseroles down my throat. I imagined his satisfaction over my husband's death…his relief that Easton was finally out of the way. And he made no attempt to convince me otherwise. Not that I would have let him.

So you don't know. Open your fists and let it go, Bridget. I have an overwhelming urge to listen to that voice, but— *Or you'll take it to the grave. And so will he.*

I ease back and wait for him to raise his head. When he looks up, his eyes are veined and wet. "You remember, Daddy? I wouldn't let anyone in. Not even Mama for the longest time."

"Still, I should have tried."

I wish he had. "It probably wouldn't have changed much. I was hurt and mad at everyone, especially God."

"Humph!" He feigns a nose scratch so he can drag a hand beneath his right eye; another nose scratch so he can clear his left eye. "I'll be mad at Him too if He takes your mother from me."

I'm a little surprised, since you have to believe in someone to be mad at them, don't you? If I had to guess where Daddy stands with God, I'd say he doesn't. The only times he attends church are when Mama drags him along for Christmas Eve and Easter services, and he makes it clear it is not where he wants to be. Of course, as Easton once pointed out, a person's faith cannot be measured by church attendance.

"Well," my father says, "hopefully all those prayers she's asking me to pray for her are reaching His ears."

"You've been praying?" My disbelief pops out before I can think better of it.

He pulls away and clears his throat. "Part of the marriage vows." He reaches for the doorknob. "I'd best get back to your mother. Have a good day."

And I'm dismissed. I check my watch. Unless I hear from J.C., it could be a couple more hours before I leave Asheville.

Daddy starts to close the door behind him, then sticks his head through the gap. "Did you listen to Caleb's message?"

"I did."

"And you'll take him up on his offer of dinner and a drive home?"

Trying to recapture the compassion I felt minutes ago, I set my teeth. "I'm still thinkin' about it."

His brow trenches. "Better think quick. He won't keep asking."

"I wish he wouldn't."

His face tightens and I steel myself, but in the next instant, he nearly hangs his head. "Please, Bridget, call him. If not for me, then for your mama."

I don't see what Caleb Merriman has to do with her, but I suppose it can't hurt. "All right, I'll call, but that's all I'm promising."

"Thank you." He closes the door.

I return the looks of hospital personnel and visitors who stroll past as I debate what to do with the time. What decides me is the cart pushed past that is stacked with picked-over meal trays. The foodstuffs are unappetizing, and yet that doesn't stop my appetite from kicking in—an appetite that would have been satisfied had I eaten my burger. Time dilemma solved.

I consider the hospital cafeteria, but the possibility of cancer hangs heavy in the air here, and I long to shed its weight. With the beauty of Asheville outside and Mellow Mushroom within a mile or so, I opt for a walk. As the autumn sunshine warms away my worry, I point myself down Biltmore Avenue and salivate at the prospect of a Brutus salad—kalamata olives, roasted red peppers, feta cheese. Or maybe their Greek salad. Of course, the portabella mushrooms are something else, stuffed with artichoke hearts, sun-dried tomatoes, mozzarella, garlic butter—

Garlic. No, wouldn't want to leave J.C. gasping for fresh air on the drive back, especially if he's of a mind to kiss me again. I shouldn't want it, especially if I'm not ready for it, but maybe I am. Maybe it's time to take a chance—with J.C., of all people. Daddy will be so disappointed.

As my worn sneakers eat up the sidewalk and cars zip past, their exhaust fumes make me scrunch my nose, and I pull up the missed call and let my phone do the dialing. Three rings later, I'm sent to Caleb's voice mail. I tell him I'm returning his call and end the call. "I tried. Mellow Mushroom, here I come."

I nearly make it there, but when I come to that awful sign again: Trousdale and Associates, a Premier Real Estate Agency, I recall that's where Caleb is—or was. Might he still be?

My stomach growls, and I keep walking. After all, Daddy can't fault me that all I got for my effort to return Caleb's call was his voice mail. *You could try a little harder.* I consider the real estate office across the street but veto my conscience. *You could invite him to join you for a bite to eat—get it out of the way and Daddy off your back.* Yeah, and have to deal with that Wesley woman again. *You could ask about his connection with industrial park developers.* Right.

I jaywalk between cars heading in opposite directions—both of which honk—and hop onto the sidewalk in front of the real estate office. As I approach the door with its fancy lettering, I scope out Wesley's little empire through the big windows. The place is impressive, the dark brown couches and armchairs at the front endowed with the plush look of money that contrasts nicely with taupe and tan walls.

A young woman, whose willowy figure is topped by a graceful neck and angled head that causes her dark hair to drape her face, staffs the receptionist's desk, which looks more like a table with spindly legs. I'll bet she pulls in the men, even if they don't think they're in the market for real estate.

As I set a hand to the door, I look to the glass-partitioned offices that allow one to view the agents and clients within. I pause. No need to go in unless Caleb is here. One after another, I dismiss the occupants of each office, and then my gaze falls on Wesley's office, obvious not only because of the size but her presence. She nods and smiles across the desk at a man whose back is to me, whose light brown hair—not dark—is lightened further by the overhead lights.

It can't be. I put my face nearer the door. After all, there's no reason I should know him from the back. Wesley's client just reminds me of him.

I sip air as I continue to stare at the man's back. And then he raises an arm and gestures in that expressive, excessive-energy way that first caught my attention when I crashed his Atlanta meeting.

23

The receptionist rises from her desk, a question furrowing her brow as she stares my way.

I force an apologetic smile, shake my head, and hurry past the windows. At the short brick wall between the real estate office and a stationery store, I press my back against it. I have to think this through, whatever "this" is. Unless I am imagining things. After all, J.C. can't be the only man with light brown hair who gestures like that. However, the car parked at the curb *is* identical to his rental car.

What does this mean? That Caleb and J.C. have the same real estate agent? Is that ethical? It couldn't be. So the day the gum landed on my windshield, Caleb wasn't the "very important person" in the car looking to maintain his anonymity. It was J.C. He's the one who saw my indignation through those impenetrable sunglasses. And yet, what are the chances that of all the developers in the country, the man I hand-picked to buy the estate was already looking to acquire it? That's pretty unbelievable.

What's going on? Why didn't J.C. tell me he was already interested? Why didn't he mention it that day on Pickwick Pike? He had to have recognized me although I still had my dreads. Or maybe not. No, he did, though not at first. I recall standing in his conference room and correcting his assumption that I was a real estate agent. When I told him my full name, Bridget *Pickwick* Buchanan, surprise widened his eyes, and he looked from my empty left ring finger to each side of my face. I'd thought my undreaded hair had been victimized by the Atlanta humidity, but that wasn't it. That was when he realized I was the one who forced Wesley Trousdale to stop her car. She must have told him who I was.

A groan slips from me, causing a middle-aged, dual-ponytailed man to look around as he treks past.

"I'm fine," I say, and he continues to the curb.

So J.C. knew from that moment on…amused himself with the glaring contrast between the barefooted woman who hopped out of a pickup truck and the one who crashed his meeting wearing high heels and bearing a briefcase. And he's been laughing ever since, probably straight through our kiss.

I pull a hand down my face. Despite the looks I receive from a hand-holding couple, I start to scoot down the brick wall. I don't care what they think. *I* need to think, to figure out what's missing.

"I'll let you know as soon as I hear anything," says a voice that drips sickly sweet honey.

I look to where Wesley Trousdale exits the real estate office with J.C., who is carrying a briefcase.

I should have kept walking, but it's too late. I have only enough time to straighten from the wall and clear my face of confusion before J.C.'s jangling ceases.

"Bridget," he says.

"Bridget Pickwick?" Wesley puts her hands on her hips. "Goodness, it is you. And don't you look different from the last time we met? In fact, if J.C. hadn't said anything, I don't know I would have recognized you without that poufy dress, not to mention…uh, what are they called? Dreadlocks?"

I square my shoulders. "I clean up well, as I'm sure Mr. Dirk can attest."

She presses her lips inward as if to contain laughter. "Well, you are wearing shoes today. That's something. So, what brings you to Asheville?"

I look at J.C. "Mr. Dirk gave me a ride in so I could visit my mother in the hospital."

Wesley tut-tuts. "Why didn't you say, J.C.? I had no idea you and Bridget had gotten friendly and all."

He shifts his regard to his rental car. "Are you ready to head back, Bridget?"

Wesley's presence saves me from acting juvenile and being forced to call on Daddy, who would call on Caleb to take me home. Considering J.C.'s deception, that might not be so bad, but there are a few things I need to say to this man. Too, he has the missing piece of the puzzle.

"I'm more than ready." I cross to the car, Mellow Mushroom reduced to a distant stomach rumble.

"I'll be in touch," J.C. tells Wesley; then the car twitters as the locks are released. I reach for the handle, but he gets there ahead of me, and I jerk back when his hand brushes mine.

I glare at him as he holds the door for me, continue to glare as he walks around the car, lowers into the driver's seat, and sets his briefcase onto the backseat. And I keep it up as we head out of Asheville.

"How's your mother?"

Oh no, if we're going to talk, it will not be touchy-feely stuff, especially about my mother. And cancer. "How is your conscience?"

His jaw shifts, and I can't help but be satisfied with his discomfort.

I pick his sunglasses from the console. "All this time, I thought it was Caleb with Wesley that day on the pike, but it was you." I hold out the sunglasses. "Need these? It's not as bright as it was last July, but they're still good for hidin' behind."

He gives me a sidelong glance. "No, thank you."

As he accelerates on the on ramp to merge with highway traffic, I return the glasses to the console. "You must have thought it funny when the woman whose phone calls you refused to return—"

"I thought you were a real estate agent."

"Right. Anyway, out of the blue and dressed down to her formerly bare feet, Bridget Pickwick Buchanan shows up at your office beggin' to sell you on something you were already sold on—something I'll bet you had a firsthand look at that day." I sigh. "Yeah, funny."

He glances at me. "I didn't recognize you until you said you were a Pickwick."

Then I guessed right. Wesley told him who the barefooted, truck-driving woman was. "Don't you think it all a bit of a coincidence? No." I hold up a hand. "Too *much* of a coincidence." I swing my body toward him. "Caleb may have a secret agenda, but so do you. What else aren't you telling me?"

He stares at the road, and his tension rubs so hard against mine it's all I can do not to raise a hand to it. "That bad, hmm?"

"Could be."

As much as I long for him to be straight with me, I almost wish for a lie. Because if it is that bad, I shouldn't have liked his kiss so much. "Tell me."

"All right."

I steel myself, but then…nothing. As I'm about to press him, he flips the turn signal and takes a nondescript, roughly paved exit.

"Where are we going?"

"To talk."

"We are talkin'."

He slows the car. "What you want to know not only requires your full attention but mine." He stops the car on the shoulder of the exit and turns to me. "I should have told you sooner."

"What?"

He pulls out his wallet and opens it to his Georgia driver's license. "This."

I stare at the small picture that can't have been taken long ago, the resemblance is so strong, then read through the personal data of Jesse E. Dirk. *Jesse?* I wouldn't have guessed, but then I'm accustomed to J.C.

I shake my head. "I don't know what—" I return to the license. Jesse *E.,* not Jesse C. "What does *E* stand for?"

"Emerson. My mother's maiden name."

I turn up my hands. "Why J.C.?"

"That's what I started going by when my brothers and I took our stepfather's name. It was my way of staying connected to my father and not forgetting what I'd promised him—to get back what was lost." He tosses the wallet on the dashboard. When he faces me again, I see something in his eyes I'm not going to like.

"The *C* is for Calhoun, Bridget."

But that's the name of the family Uncle Obe believes was cheated—

I think I must stop breathing, I get so tight in the throat and full in the chest, but air rushes in when the name drops neatly into the hole left by the missing piece. J.C.'s interest in the estate isn't an outlandish co-incidence. The only coincidence is he's the eco-friendly developer I landed on when he stared out at me from the magazine cover. So much explained. There was the drive to the Atlanta airport—

"Bridget?"

—when J.C. cornered me about the center piece of the property, and I'd had to acknowledge the quarry. At the statue dedication, I'd seen Wesley wave at someone and minutes later discovered J.C. was in town. When I'd taken him on a tour of the estate, he'd insisted on seeing the chewed-up piece of land, asked about the old Calhoun homestead, and broodingly walked around the huge hole in the ground. He knew the way to my folks' home and stiffened up when Mama talked about the dogs that had chased some boys and bitten one of them on the face…

"You were the boys our bull mastiffs went after." The reason he's wary of big dogs. "It was you and…" I recall the scarred man who walked me into the conference room. "Parker."

"Yes. That day at your parents' house when you accused me of relying on gossip rather than firsthand knowledge of your family, I was going to tell you I was a Calhoun, but Birdie came downstairs."

I return to that day. As we sat at the kitchen table, he admitted to being guilty of "some sniffing" due to Caleb's "sniffing," told me his past tended to bring out the worst in him, said he let seemingly unfinished business get in the way of the present. *Was* he trying to tell me? Or was it just part of his plan—reel me in with personal confidences to make me think he was interested in me beyond his acquisition of the estate, thereby forcing Caleb out of the picture?

I don't want to believe it, but that would be like playing dead, which I do not care to be better at than Reggie. If J.C. wasn't laughing at me before, my acceptance that he had no other chance to come clean would give him cause for a laughfest.

"Well, seein' as that was your only opportunity to let me in on your little secret, I suppose I'll have to pardon you for the deception."

His nostrils flare at my sarcasm. "The time was never right after that; then it seemed too late—that I'd waited too long and it would be best if my Calhoun roots were revealed when the sale of the estate was finalized so you and I wouldn't go where we are now."

Now being this moment when the evidence points to him being a widow sniffer all along. And of the worst sort—after monetary gain.

"The way your father reacted yesterday to the news your uncle's caregiver is Obadiah's daughter was further confirmation I'd made the right decision."

Another scene to replay, this one with Daddy up in arms as he accused Daisy of being underhanded, spying on our family, and seeking vengeance. J.C. left soon thereafter, looking as uncomfortable as if *he* were under attack. He was.

"If he knew I was a Calhoun, he wouldn't view the revelation in any better light than he did when he learned the woman who has been calling herself Mary is his niece."

"And it would provide ammunition in his push for Caleb to acquire the property. Isn't that right?"

"Yes."

If only I'd known this before his kiss. "That sounds like a bad thing for Jesse Calhoun, who is carrying the torch his father passed to him— to not only take back his family's land but repay the Pickwicks in kind by taking their land."

"Buying, not taking, Bridget." His mouth is flat. "Though I do admit to feeling satisfaction at the prospect—in the beginning."

"Only the beginning? What about now?" Before he can answer, I laugh, a creaky bitter thing. "I suppose you can't really answer that since you've been found out and the prospect is"—I shrug—"not much of a prospect."

He stares at me. "You're saying you'll oppose our offer on the estate even if we are the only ecologically responsible choice?"

"You're saying after all this I should believe Caleb's the con? No." I shake my head, hating the rising ache I feel at allowing myself to believe his kiss was real. "You used me when you learned the property wouldn't necessarily go to the highest bidder."

"That's how it started, I've already admitted it, but that's not how it ended. And you have to know that after you opened up about Easton, I was prepared to chance answering your question about what was taken from my family."

That *was* the direction he was heading before he got the call about his brother. Or was it? Maybe it would have been a lie had there been time to speak it. "I don't know that. Now if you don't mind, I'd like to get home." I look out the passenger window at the kudzu strangling the trees. If deception were a plant, it would surely be that tangle of life-sucking ivy that relentlessly grows with leaps and bounds.

When J.C. finally returns the car to the highway, I settle in to watch the mile markers pass.

"Let's discuss your concerns about the golf resort."

I look around. "At the moment, they're hardly relevant."

"They might seem more relevant if you pull out the folder that's in the top of my briefcase." He nods over his shoulder. "Proof that Merriman is in partnership with investors looking to build an industrial park."

Call me stubborn, but I don't care. After all, it's probably just more kudzu. "No, thank you."

A muscle in J.C.'s jaw ticks, and I wonder how men do that. Easton's jaw did the same when he was tightly wound, but that little spasm was always telling—as in, "Lord, give me patience."

"All right," J.C. says, "but it's a long drive, so let's discuss the resort."

I cross my arms over my chest. "I don't like it." *And don't you sound like little girl Bridget when Mama tried to get you into a ruffled, poppy-bedecked dress?*

"I know you'd prefer that the estate remain in its natural state, which would be possible with private ownership if the land wasn't so commercially desirable that it commands an exorbitant price. However, whoever buys it either has to be incredibly wealthy with a desire to root himself in Pickwick—"

Of which he does not believe Caleb capable.

"—or have the ability to develop the estate so it promises the kind of profit that attracts investors."

I feel his gaze but don't give it back.

"Well-designed golf courses draw locals and tourists. In this case, a golf course will anchor the development, serving as a hedge against what could be a passing fad if the property were developed strictly as a nature retreat or wilderness resort."

I believe the surge of environmental consciousness and the desire to get back to nature won't fade, and yet my beliefs—happily ever after, for instance—have been toppled before.

"I'm sorry you don't like the plan, and I understand your objections, spoken and unspoken, but I have a responsibility to be straight with my investors. They aren't coming on board without the golf course."

Wishing the day away—Mama's sickness that may or may not be cancer and Jesse Emerson Calhoun Dirk's revelation that seems like a cancer—I close my eyes. I feel like a baggy old balloon blown nearly to breaking point. I feel betrayed, used, resentful. And oh so hurt. If only I hadn't let myself be ready...

I look at J.C. "I imagine it did your sense of justice good to see the family you believe stole from yours forced to sell their heritage."

His nod surprises me, and that it's the kind of nod a person on death row might give when told it's time to go to the chair. "Yes, there was a sense of triumph. In the beginning."

Then he's no longer gloating? Why? Because he's come to know us? To know me? To care? Remembering his kiss that felt so good and seemed so real, my insides soften; however, that way lies vulnerability, all the more terrible and painful if J.C. is playing me. And he probably is. More than likely, this is simply Plan B.

"Well," I say, "now we know why you're having as much trouble getting back to God as I am, don't we?"

He doesn't answer, and this time the silence that settles stays settled, during which I pick apart and regret every encounter we've had. He was laughing at us. At me. But at least I can be grateful my discovery saved my family from giving him the last laugh.

J.C. won't be buying the Pickwick estate—not if I can help it.

Finally he pulls into the nursery; the parking lot is empty save for Daddy's car and Allen's truck.

The second J.C. brakes in front of the trailer, I'm out of the car. I start to slam the door but pull it back open. Neither will I have the last laugh, but I will have the very last word. I bend down and meet his gaze.

"I have news for you, Jesse Emerson Calhoun. Though my family is far from perfect, we're only *related* to Gentry Pickwick. In fact, had you been honest about your interest in the estate, you would have been told that upon the sale of the property, my uncle intends to compensate the Calhoun heirs for what he also believes was stolen from them—to do it while he can still savor the peace of righting the wrong."

My satisfaction multiplies when something like alarm jumps in his eyes.

"You said revenge ruined your father. Maybe it ruined you too." I raise my eyebrows. "Jesse Calhoun." I pull back, toss the door closed, and bound up the steps.

Without a backward glance, I step into the trailer and turn my attention to my beady-eyed critter perched on the corner of my desk. As I tuck her beneath my chin, I hear the crunch of J.C.'s tires.

"Hey, Reggie." I stroke her from head to little bit of tail. "Your mama's had a rough day." But surely not as rough as *my* mama's day. Tears tingle my nose. "How about we go home and snuggle down, just you and me—" I sigh. "And Birdie and Miles."

"She's dead."

In light of my phone conversation with Piper about Mama's condition, the little-voice-trying-to-be-a-big-voice takes my breath, but one look at my nephew who has come to stand in front of me, and I know exactly who "she" is. Great.

"Yep." He shakes his head. "Dead again."

I cover the mouthpiece. "I'll be right there." And I'd better be or Birdie will take full advantage of Reggie's attempt to escape the unthinkable.

"Birdie has the bonnet on her," Miles warns, then turns away.

Poor Reggie. "I need to go, Piper. Do you mind letting Maggie know what's goin' on?"

"I'll call her. Just know I'll be praying for the situation with J. C. Dirk."

"Jesse Calhoun."

She sighs across the phone line. "I'll be praying for Aunt Belinda too."

"I appreciate that."

"Talk to you later, Bridget."

As I hurry past Miles into the room I once shared with Easton, I shove J.C. to the back of my thoughts. And there lies Reggie, as still as stone in the middle of the bed, outfitted in a ruffled bonnet too big for her head and bloomers that wouldn't stand a chance if she hadn't lost most of her tail.

Birdie looks up from where she's trying to fit one of my opossum's arms into the sleeve of a miniature dress, squeaks, and whips the pink thing behind her back.

"Oh, Birdie," I say, to which Reggie opens an eye. Not your usual playing possum, but she tries. A moment later, she's moving fast across the mattress. I scoop her up, bloomers and all. "You know Reggie doesn't like baby-doll clothes." I pat her. "I've told you that."

Birdie sinks onto her bottom and frowns up at me from beneath long lashes. "I want my mama."

I want my mother too—out of the hospital and in good health. And not so she can take Birdie and Miles off my hands.

As I round the bed, Reggie begins to scrabble out of my hands, but I stroke her into semirelaxation as I lower to the mattress beside Birdie. "She's coming home soon. Remember what she said when you talked with her on the phone awhile ago?"

"Just four more weeks, Birdie," Miles says from the doorway. He seems so brave standing there, but consciously brave. I feel for how hard he's trying to be a big brother to his twin even though he misses his parents just as much, as evidenced by the tremor in his voice when he spoke with my sister awhile ago. "And they're bringing us presents, one for every week they're gone."

Birdie drops the doll dress, lifts her left hand, and tucks her thumb into her palm. "Four"—she tucks the other thumb—"plus four. That's eight. Eight presents."

"Each." Miles smiles.

She considers this, and I remove the bonnet from Reggie and ease off the bloomers.

"Okay." Birdie sighs. "But I still want Mama."

"It won't be much longer." I lower Reggie to the floor. As she scurries away, I look to Birdie. "Ready to tuck in?"

My niece jabs a finger to the middle of her forehead. "I need a kiss wight here like Mama does."

"I can do that." I lift her finger and put a kiss right…there.

"Me too," Miles says.

I barely disguise my surprise. "All right. I'll be in shortly to see you down for the night."

He starts to turn away but comes back around. "Your bed is really big."

Am I reading this right? "It is. Too big for just Birdie and me. In fact, I'm sure we'd sleep better if we had you in here with us."

His brow furrows. "I could protect you since Errol had to go home."

Unfortunately it's true. Well, unfortunately for me since I'm overly fond of that dog. But fortunately for Artemis's wife, who was having a good enough day to remember her big boy and want to see him. "That would be nice, Miles."

He turns. "I'll get my pillow."

"And brush your teeth," I call over the thump of his bare feet.

"Tell him to go potty," Birdie says. "I don't want him to wee on me."

"And go potty!"

"I will!"

Still, I'll slip a doubled towel under the fitted sheet to be on the safe side. I hold out my arms to Birdie. "Let's get you ready for bed." When she props up my chin with her curly blond head, I feel myself lighten. I'll get past J.C. Of course I will.

"I want Snow White tonight."

"Okay."

She peers up at me as I carry her toward the bathroom. "You're getting better at happily ever after."

So says a five-year old who has no idea that the crown-wearing prince carrying a torch for a princess and riding around on a horse might really be a sunglass-wearing guy carrying a torch for revenge and riding around in a hybrid. Not that I expected a happily ever after with J.C., did I?

A half hour later, I stare at the darkly shadowed ceiling from where

I lay between my softly snoring niece and nephew. Restless again, though this time for reasons other than Easton's absence.

Answering the tug inside me that I suspect is what's keeping me awake, I close my eyes and whisper, "Lord, I'm asking You again to heal Mama like You didn't heal Easton. Though it will be hard if You don't answer as I ache for You to do, I'll do my best to accept what comes. But I am hopin' You want Mama's healing as much as I do. Please, Lord."

I feel another tug.

"And I need to move on. I need Your help, 'cause otherwise Bonnie could be right about me taking my grievin' to the grave. And after what happened with J.C., I'm tempted to do just that. However, I don't want to be like his daddy, carrying such a burden until the end, or like J.C. takin' joy in others' misery. I want...I need to heal." I sigh. "Help me."

24

Monday, October 11

Prayer answered. Not the way I wanted it, but closer than it could have been. Thank You up there, God. Mama doesn't have cancer, but she does have something called celiac disease. Providing she sticks to a gluten-free diet, the doctor says her intestines should heal and she can expect to live a long, healthy life. If she can stick to it.

In this case, it's good Daddy has an eye on her diet, since Mama loves her grains. In the week since her release from the hospital, my father has been more attentive to her needs than I can remember him being. In fact, he's decided to sell one of his classic cars—the one *I* supposedly put a ding in—so he can update her kitchen and take her on an Alaskan cruise like she's always wanted. I just hope the possibility of losing Mama stays with him.

"Okay, kiddos"—I look from Birdie to Miles, who have polished off their grilled cheese sandwiches—"go outside and play while I finish cleaning up here; then we'll get on home."

I'm pleased when they bring their dirty plates to me before running out the back door.

"I wish you could stay longer," Mama says as the screen door bangs behind her grandchildren.

"I know, but we've been here two hours, and you need your rest." I return her cast-iron skillet—the one that was mine before it was hers again—to the cabinet, wipe my hands on a dishtowel, and slip into the chair beside hers. "How was your salad?"

She considers the remains. "Tasty. Of course, it would have been better with croutons—you know, those Texas toast ones?" She sighs. "But I suppose I'll get used to all this deprivation."

I check my watch. "Daddy should be home any minute." It's nice that I can say that with confidence. "Do you want to lie down while I finish up here?"

She nods, and I reach to her, but she waves me away. "I'm not an invalid, dear."

Awhile later, as I'm drying her salad plate, my cell rings. I set the plate in the cupboard, check on Birdie and Miles through the kitchen window, and take the call. "What's up?"

"Bad news," Piper says. "The offer we received from Dirk Construction? Withdrawn."

My breath catches. "What?"

"Withdrawn."

Then it's over, though I'd thought it had only just begun when Wesley Trousdale submitted the offer the day after J.C. left Pickwick—a full-price offer that included the provision that Uncle Obe could remain in his home without cost for a minimum of one year. "Did they say why?"

"No, though I'm thinking, as you probably are, that it has everything to do with the revelation."

That's what we—Piper, Maggie, and I—call the bolt from the blue that scorched the earth between J.C. and me. Piper's fiancé, Axel, and Maggie's boyfriend-turned-fiancé, Reece, know about it as well, but that's all. There seemed no reason to muddy the water further, though Piper suggested Uncle Obe be told since one of the reasons for selling the estate is to make restitution to the wronged Calhouns. I saw her point, but Maggie had her own point—Uncle Obe needs to focus on his relationship with his daughter, not on a vendetta born a hundred years ago.

"It makes sense. J.C.'s withdrawal of the offer has everything to do with his Calhoun roots," I say. "I'd just like to know if he pulled out because he saw the error of his ways or because it caused him to reevaluate the purchase of the estate and realize it isn't a good investment after all—that he was letting his emotions run roughshod over business sense."

"I'd like to think the first," Piper says, "but we may never know."

True, because it appears that J.C. is entirely out of our lives. I feel a pang I wish I didn't. "So that leaves us with Caleb Merriman. Well, when he finally gets around to submitting an offer." Piper notified him that Dirk Construction had offered on the property, and he'd told her his own offer would be forthcoming, but so far nothing.

"Unfortunately, the only other serious offer we have is for a large single-family home development," Piper says.

"That horrible thing? Not only will most of the homes be slammed up against one another on one-sixth acre lots, but there was nothing ecologically friendly in the proposal—a sketchy proposal, I might add."

"And the offer is far below market value."

Half—nowhere near enough to do what Uncle Obe wants to do. I sigh. "Hopefully, Caleb will come through with a decent offer."

"*And* he'll keep the estate as a private residence."

It's good to know I'm not the only one concerned about that. Piper was appalled at the possibility of the estate becoming an industrial park.

Unfortunately I have no proof one way or the other, and it's my fault. J.C. offered and, from atop my high horse, I refused. Of course, without the interest of Dirk Developers, it doesn't matter, since Caleb may be the only viable buyer.

"All we can do is wait and see," I say.

"And pray."

That solution seems to come naturally to her, like it did to Easton, as if the moment trouble strikes, it's the first place to turn. Will it ever come naturally to me? I can't see it, but I suppose unnatural is better than not at all. "I should do that more often."

"You're doin' just fine," Piper says.

Based on yesterday's church attendance? *Two* Sundays in a row? I have my doubts. "Thank you. Let me know if you hear anything from Caleb."

"I will."

As I end the call, Daddy enters the kitchen. "That Piper you were talkin' to?"

When did he get home? And how much of my conversation did he catch? "I didn't hear you come in."

"Just a minute ago." He smiles and, from behind his back, produces long-stemmed red roses. "I bought these for your mama. They don't smell much, but they're a good sight prettier than the perfumy ones they had."

I nod, pleased he thought of it on his own. "I'm sure Mama will love them."

"Is she nappin'?"

"She went down a little while ago."

"Rest'll do her good."

I look out the window at where Miles is swinging from a tree limb and Birdie is chasing Mama's little dog round and round. I forgot Itsy was out there. Hoping to avert whatever fate awaits her in the dog apparel department, I head for the back door. "The kids and I are heading out. Trinity's expecting them in a half hour." Trinity, who continues to be my saving grace since I stepped up to the plate with my niece and nephew.

"I worry about that Trinity. You know, her bein' attentive enough with my grandchildren."

Lord, I could use help with patience. A hand on the doorknob, I glance out the window to verify Itsy is staying ahead of Birdie. "Number one, Daddy, I believe your daughter-in-law has proven she is responsible with Miles and Birdie. Number two, she is going to be the mother of another of your grandchildren. Number three, I couldn't do what I'm doin' without her."

Though nursery business has slowed with the season, I still need to be there. Thankfully Trinity once more rearranged her schedule so she can keep the kids in the afternoons, freeing me up to take care of business.

Daddy shrugs. "You might be right. She does seem to be pulling her weight."

That wasn't exactly where I was going, but all right. "I'll see you tomorrow."

"Oh, expect to hear from Caleb soon."

I look over my shoulder. "About?"

"The estate."

"Do you think he's ready to make an offer?"

He smiles, and for a moment there's a glint in his eyes like light reflecting off gears in motion. "I can pretty much guarantee it."

Is he up to something? "How's that?"

"Well…"

As he ruminates, a yelp sounds from the backyard, and I wince at the sight of Birdie holding Itsy tight to her chest, the little dog's head where her rear end ought to be. "Gotta go!" For Itsy's sake, not mine, 'cause that glint worries me.

Now he sneaks up on me. Now that he's washed his hands of Pickwick. And me. Until Piper's call, I'd done just fine turning away thoughts of J.C. that got too personal for comfort—like the sorrow I'd felt for the poverty he and his family suffered…their loss…remembrance of his hand on mine…the kiss I hadn't wanted to end…and the thought that maybe, just maybe—

"Fool." I direct my hose at the next thirsty shrub. "It was all about sniffin'."

In the beginning.

"So he said."

You, of all people, know how hard it is to let go. You clung to Easton long after he was gone. J.C. clung to a promise made to his father. And look, he let it go.

"Hey there!"

I whip around, causing the stream of water to fall short of Maggie by inches—fortunately, since she's wearing a designer-looking woolen skirt and fabric-covered high heels.

"Sorry." She makes a face. "I didn't mean to startle you."

I sweep the hose to the side. "It's all right. I was just thinkin'."

"Deeply." Her bottomless legs close the distance between us. "I called to you three times."

"Er, your shoes." I point at them, the lower edges of which are picking up hose-dampened earth.

She looks down. "Oh no."

I close the valve to the nozzle, drop the hose, and cross to her in my muddied sneakers. "What are you doin' here?" My gorgeous red-headed cousin is not a gardener. In fact, I can count on one finger the number of times she's come by the nursery expressly for the purpose of beautifying her home with greenery.

"Piper asked me to stop by. She's tried calling you several times."

I frown. "Something wrong? Oh! Uncle Obe—?"

"He's fine. In fact, I just came from one of the most lucid conversations I've had with him in a while—well, with him and his daughter."

"I'm glad she's doin' him good."

"Seems to be. She's nice," Maggie says.

"And his son?"

"Daisy believes she can get him out here to meet Uncle Obe, but obviously he's not as keen on knowing his father as she is."

"What about her mother?" Uncle Obe's one and only love.

"Apparently, she supported Daisy's desire to meet her father, but Anita is happily married and doesn't want to open old wounds any further."

"It probably is for the best." I swipe at the hairs on my brow that have come loose from my ponytail. "What does Piper want to talk to me about?"

She raises her eyebrows. "Caleb Merriman. Though his real estate agent called this morning to tell us he would be sending over an offer today, this afternoon he called and said it might be another day or two."

I pick off my cotton gloves and tuck them into my waistband. "In the big scheme of things, what's another couple of days?"

"Well, what with the timing, Piper wonders if Caleb got wind that Dirk Developers pulled out of the running. She's worried that if he knows, he'll offer less."

I shake my head. "How would Caleb—?" My day rewinds with a blur, lands on my visit with Mama, fast-forwards through my phone conversation with Piper, and slows upon Daddy's appearance in the kitchen. How much of the conversation did he overhear? Something tells me too much—the glint in his eyes. *Oh, Daddy.*

"What is it?"

I blink at Maggie. "The kids and I had lunch with Mama today."

She ducks her head back, clearly confused by what seems a change of topic. "How is she doin'?"

"Better. But Daddy got home before we left, and I'm afraid he may have overheard a phone conversation I had with Piper about J.C.'s withdrawal of his offer."

She whistles long and low. "Oh."

Her tone is clear, and I can't take offense. She knows my daddy well enough, so she has good cause to believe he's our leak.

"Why would he do that?" Maggie turns her hands up, then has the grace to add, "That is, if he *did* run to Caleb?"

You did, didn't you, Daddy?

She takes two steps away and comes back. "The more Uncle Obe gets for the estate, the better off his heirs, right?"

I draw a tired breath. "Caleb's family invested in the textile mill before it went under. Maybe it's Daddy's way of makin' restitution for the money they lost." The moment I say it, I cringe. Since when has my father taken responsibility for his financial failings? He certainly didn't want his brother Obe making restitution to those our family has wronged.

Maggie's frown deepens, and I know she's thinking the same thing. So I dig deeper. "He's been encouragin' me to return Caleb's interest. If he did tell him about the withdrawal of the offer, and I admit it's not a stretch, it may have been in hopes of securing a husband for me—one better suited to what he believes I need."

"It may be more than that."

I don't have to dig much deeper to know what *more* is. I don't want to believe it, but it's true that Daddy has always had an appetite for the biggest piece of the pie. If he's angling for a backhander…a kickback…a bribe…

My cousin sighs. "I suppose we'll never know for certain, but my guess is that Caleb's offer will be substantially less than if he'd submitted it this afternoon."

This is turning out to be one peach of a day. "I'm sorry, Maggie." The apology is weak-kneed, but I don't know what else to say. I do, however, know what to do. Unfortunately since Trinity will soon be dropping off Birdie and Miles, my confrontation with Daddy will have to wait.

Maggie gives her shoulders a shake as if to dislodge a load of worry. "Gotta go. Devyn and I are being fitted for our bridesmaids' dresses in half an hour."

I gasp and look down my grubby self. Though I was supposed to stop at the wedding boutique after Trinity picked up the kids, I headed straight for the nursery. See, I told Piper she'd regret asking me to be in her wedding—my way of giving her an easy out since it was probably a sense of obligation that made her ask.

"Let me guess; you missed your fitting."

"Yep."

"An act of passive aggression?"

"No, I—" I snort. "Come on—*me*? Passive aggressive?"

She grins. "Good point. So why don't you come with Devyn and me? I'll bet the seamstress can squeeze you in."

"Yeah, but can she squeeze in Birdie and Miles? Trinity will be dropping them at my house shortly, and something tells me that boredom and racks of satin and lace are a bad combination."

"Gotcha." Maggie gives my arm a squeeze. "I'd better get goin'."

So had I. I don't want to repay Trinity's kindness with inconsideration.

Maggie turns and comes back around with a big old smile on her face. "Speaking of weddings, expect another invitation in the next day or two."

Then she and Reece have set a date. I'm happy for them, and for Devyn. "Congratulations. Count on me being there." Just as I'll be there for Piper and Axel, all gussied up in some impossible dress— Oh no!

Maggie's laughter is proof my face is speaking my thoughts. "Nothing fancy for Reece and me. Just a simple ceremony with Devyn as my bridesmaid. You can wear whatever you like."

I breathe easier. "I appreciate that."

She turns and waves over her shoulder. "See ya."

Fifteen minutes later, Reggie and I jostle down my dirt-packed driveway in my once-more-faithful truck. Sure enough, parked in front of my house is a VW Beetle painted to resemble Cinderella's pumpkin coach, with Cinderella Sanitation Inc. painted on the side. And there's my sister-in-law hurrying off the porch as I park alongside her car.

"You got one too!" She waves something as she hurries across the yard, Miles and Birdie following like a couple of chicks.

I retrieve Reggie, climb out of the truck, and slam the door. "What is it?"

"I know what it is," Birdie calls, her little shoes crunching through the fall leaves beginning to dry out. "It's a happily ever after."

Another Little Golden Book? Great.

"Birdie's right." Trinity halts before me. "The kids wanted to get your mail out of the box—"

"Can I hold Reggie?" Miles reaches for my opossum.

At my hesitation, he glances at his sister and says quietly, "Poor Birdie can't find her baby-doll clothes." He winks.

I wink back and ease Reggie into his arms.

"Anyway," Trinity says, her voice its usual breathless self, "we got your mail, and look-it here what was in it."

In her hand isn't a book but a cream-colored envelope with Maggie's return address. The wedding invitation.

"Bart and I got ours today too." Trinity shudders. "Don't you just love happily ever afters?"

I'm tempted to say there's no such thing, but Birdie is following her brother toward the porch, and she's still too near for me to remind Trinity of my husband's death and tell her about J.C.—

J.C.? What's he doing serving as an example alongside Easton? Why, he was barely a maybe. Or was he?

"Don't you love 'em?" Trinity asks again, nodding as if to show me how it's done.

"I…"

When she leans in and up from her two-inch deficit, her breath carries the scent of cinnamon. "Of course," she whispers, "if there's one thing us grownups know, it's that there's only one true happily ever after, and that's with Jesus. Just ask Scarlett O'Hara."

A fictional character. And was she even a believer?

"Yep, only one true happily ever after." Trinity points her chin at the sky. "And not until we get up there." There's a smile in her eyes bettered only by the one on her mouth. "Not that we shouldn't try to get a taste of it here on earth—you know, so we have somethin' real good to compare it to."

She's right. As I stare at her, I feel a rush of gratitude that my brother found and kept her despite the initial opposition from Daddy and me. "Off" she may be, but in a good way. "You, my sister, are wise."

Surprise opens up her face, and I feel it open up mine. I just called her *sister.*

She wrinkles her nose. "Gol, wise?"

That's what surprised her—more than me calling her *sister*? "Yes, you are."

"Nah, it's my gran who's wise, but maybe when I'm old and prickly like her." She waves at the twins. "I'll see you tomorrow, sweetness one and sweetness two."

"Bye-bye," Birdie calls back, which is followed by Miles's "See ya, Aunt Trinity."

Trinity putters her pumpkin coach down the driveway, and I watch until she goes from sight. And still I stand there as her words play in my mind: *"There's only one true happily ever after, and that's with Jesus. Not that we shouldn't try to get a taste of it here on earth."*

I wish her words didn't bring J.C. to mind, but they do. In turn, J.C. brings an ache to a place inside me where he doesn't belong. Am I a mess, or what?

25

> *Maggie Pickwick, Reece Thorpe,*
> *and Devyn Pickwick*
> *invite you to share their joy*
> *when they become a family joined together*
> *by holy matrimony*
> *Saturday, November 20*
> *at 2:00 in the afternoon*
> *The Old Dock at Pickwick Lake*
> *Pickwick, North Carolina*
> *P.S. Dress Warmly*

Friday, October 15

Two weddings in one month. When the Pickwicks rain, they pour. I look from Maggie's invitation on my refrigerator to Piper's peeking out from behind it, both secured by the only magnet I could rustle up. I'm happy for my cousins, because Trinity is right—a body needs a taste of happily ever after, even though "happily" doesn't last "ever after" down here. So is it okay to go back for seconds? And what does it say about the depth of one's first love if one *wants* to go back for seconds?

I've been round and round this for days. Round it with myself.

Round it with God (yes, I'm speaking to Him fairly regularly). And round it with Maggie and Piper, who seem to think I asked them to butt into my personal life. Of course, I probably shouldn't have told them about my confrontation with Bonnie at Trinity and Bart's wedding—a weak moment over chips and salsa yesterday at a new Mexican restaurant. Since I rarely indulge in processed, fried tortilla chips, the stuff must have gone to my head.

Maggie agreed with Bonnie about my widow's weeds, and I pointed out that I'd shed my dreads, put my ring away, let my finger tan, and was sleeping in my marriage bed again. Then Piper had to put in her two cents by saying there was one last weed that needed to be pulled—my fear of allowing another man into my life. And I said it wasn't worth the possible pain of losing another man I might come to love. All she'd said was "Better the possibility of pain than the certainty of pain in living a long, lonely life." She may be right.

"Ready to go!" Miles appears in the kitchen doorway dressed in the cutest little jeans I ever saw—worn in all the right places, a little raggedly here and there. Of course, they probably cost two or three times what a new-looking pair of jeans would cost.

"Great," I say. "And Birdie?"

"Me too!" She steps alongside her brother.

Those are also cute jeans—pink piping along the pockets and pink plaid patches on the knees. Unfortunately much of that pink will be going bye-bye. We're heading to the mansion, Miles and Birdie having surprised me with their enthusiasm over my suggestion we spend the morning working in Uncle Obe's garden.

I warned them we would be pulling weeds, getting our hands dirty, and coming into contact with earthworms. Birdie's response: "Can I cut one in half to see if it really grows into two?" My response: "No." She was still game, but for how long?

One hour. That's how long she makes it before she wrenches her last weed, plops onto her rear, and thrusts a fist above her dirt-streaked forehead. "As God is my witness—oh wait!" She scrambles to her feet and raises her fist again. "As God is my witness, I will never be hungry again."

I stare at my niece. What in the world? Miles snickers, and I look sharply at him. "What's she doin'?"

He sticks his nose into the crook of his elbow and drags his arm back, leaving a trail of "ugh" down his sleeve. "Pretending to be that Tara girl in *Gone with the Wind.*"

"Scarlett!" Birdie glares at him. "Her name's Scarlett, and she's not a girl. She's a weal woman."

Okay, so now I know where the quote came from. What I don't know is where this Scarlett thing came from. "Did you see the movie?"

Birdie nods. "At Aunt Trinity's yesterday. She made us popcorn."

There we go—the dots connected, from Birdie's performance back to Trinity's suggestion that I confirm with Scarlett O'Hara that true happiness is only found in Jesus. Somehow, I don't think Bonnie will be pleased her five-year-old has graduated from fairy tales to old movies.

"Except for the fighting and the soldiers, it was boring," Miles says with another wipe of his nose.

"No, it wasn't!"

"Yes, it was. It was a stupid girl movie."

Birdie kicks dirt at her brother.

He jumps up. "What'd you do that for?"

" 'Cause you're wong! Scarlett didn't get her happily ever after, but she got strong."

Miles's mouth pinches. "Frankly, my dear, I don't give—"

"Okay!" I shoot upright, separating them by placing my hands on their shoulders. "How about some iced tea? Or lemonade? Miss Daisy said she'd make up a pitcher."

They grumble at each other as I guide them along the winding path and up the ramp to the kitchen. No sooner do I settle them at the island counter opposite each other than Piper appears.

"This just in." She holds up a white envelope, and I know what it is.

I finish pouring glasses of lemonade for Birdie and Miles, remind them to behave, then cross to where my cousin stands before the pantry flipping through the papers.

"Oh, Lord," she breathes. "Would you look at that?"

I growl when I see the dollar amount. The string of numbers is certainly long enough; however, the first number following the dollar sign is nearly half what it should be. And I know what happened—what Maggie feared.

I step back from Caleb Merriman's joke of an offer. "Would you keep the kids for me? I need to drive over to my parents' and talk to Daddy."

"But he's here."

"What?"

"Arrived a half hour ago and said he needed to speak with his brother in private."

"Where?"

"Uncle Obe's room."

I don't know what that means, but it fits. "Birdie? Miles?"

Their baleful eyes, which have surely been inflicting silent wounds on each other, turn to me. "I need to talk with Uncle Obe. Miss Piper will keep an eye on you, all right?"

They go back to glaring over their lemonades.

I turn right out of the kitchen and a few moments later stand before Uncle Obe's bedroom. The door is closed, and I can't help but put an ear to it.

"Now I don't rightly know what he'll offer," Daddy's voice is muffled through the door, "but it has to be as clear to you as it is to me that preservin' the estate as a private residence is best for all. And Caleb Merriman is prepared to do just that."

I shouldn't eavesdrop.

"So he says," Uncle Obe's rickety words struggle through the wood, making me wonder if he knows or suspects what J.C. tried to convince me of. "Now that J.C., him I kind of like."

"As I told you, Obe, Dirk Developers has withdrawn their offer."

Does Daddy's eavesdropping on me justify my eavesdropping on him?

"And need I remind you that their proposal was to turn the estate into a golf resort? Humph! So they're no longer a consideration, meaning we have only two legitimate offers on the table. The offer from the single-family home developer and the one from Caleb Merriman—well, when he makes an offer, which I'm sure will be soon."

"I don't like one and I don't trust the other." Uncle Obe's voice rises. "And you know why I don't trust Merriman? Because of your ch-ch-championing of him."

"Championin'?"

"Now, Bartholomew, I'm not so far gone I don't remember your feelings about Caleb's daddy for the inflated interest rate he charged on the...money you took from him to keep the mill afloat. Why, if I hadn't negotiated a settlement, you'd have lost your house and more."

I hang my head. Always Uncle Obe to the rescue, chipping away at his inheritance to keep his brothers' heads above water and out from behind bars.

"Regardless," Daddy says, "Merriman's is the best offer you're goin' to get, and I say you take it before it walks away like the offer from Dirk Developers."

A long silence, then, "I've half a mind to put in a call to J.C. to see if we can't come to terms."

Another long silence, during which I imagine Daddy building up a head of steam. And that's when I open the door—for fear his desperation will cause him to fling Uncle Obe's "half a mind" back at him.

I step into the sunshine-lit room and settle my gaze on Daddy, who stands over the armchair in which Uncle Obe reclines. "Is this a secret meeting or can anyone join?"

Daddy turns, his face red in some places, purple in others. "Your uncle and I are engaged in a discussion that does not involve you, Bridget."

"But it does involve me, since I'm fairly certain it's based on a conversation I had with Piper at the beginning of the week—one it appears you listened in on."

Daddy's eyes nearly come out of their folds, they get so big. "I...well...couldn't help but hear...and you...eavesdroppin'...respect your elders..."

I stand taller. "I know two wrongs don't make a right, so before we commit another wrong, there's something Uncle Obe ought to know."

Daddy's mouth twitches. "All's said that needs to be said."

"There's more. You told him Dirk Developers walked away from their offer, but did you tell him why?" Not that he might have arrived at the conclusion, and not that I'm certain of it myself, but biased as I am by my time with J.C., I'm less inclined to believe he pulled out simply because he decided the property was a bad investment.

"I have no idea what you're talkin' about. Now why don't we let my brother get his rest?"

As Daddy moves toward me, flapping a hand as if I'm a sheep to his shepherd, I look to Uncle Obe, whose eyes on me are little more than dashes between narrowed lids.

"The Calhouns," I say, and Daddy gurgles as he halts between us. "J. C. Dirk is a Calhoun."

The dashes snap to O's. "That young man who was here with you awhile back?"

I cross my arms over my chest. "Yes."

Uncle Obe settles deeper into his chair. "Right here, under our…" He taps his nose.

"Not by coincidence either, I wager." Daddy trundles back around. "By design, Obe—to exact revenge on our family for swindlin' his great-granddaddy out of his land. Not true, of course. Anyone with half a brain knows that poker game was played fair and square."

He knows Uncle Obe believes the poker game was rigged and that he intends to make restitution to the Calhouns. Thus, I'm inclined to believe the "half-brained" comment was intentional. I grind my teeth. I've never understood why black widow spiders eat their mates, but if it were their daddies…

Uncle Obe merely smiles. "No, Bartholomew, I don't know that, and neither do you. What I know is our great-granddaddy was a… What'd you call it? A swindler. And the Calhouns were as likely a target as the others." As Daddy blinks, my uncle slants his head to the side and gives me a smile. "So this J.C. was lookin' to restore his family's property."

"That's right. Before his father passed, he promised him he would get it back—but not tit for tat, Uncle Obe. By buying it."

"How do you know this?" Daddy demands. "And why did you keep it to yourself?"

"J.C. told me." I push my hands into my pockets. "I didn't say anything because we didn't part on the best of terms. I was mad at him for deceiving—"

"He most certainly did, the scoundrel."

Uncle Obe raises a hand. "Bartholomew, let her finish. What happened, Bridget?"

"I told him our family is far removed from Gentry Pickwick"—though times like this I'm not sure I should include Daddy in that generalization—"and that the reason you're selling the estate now is because of the high cost of making restitution to his family and that you wanted it done before…"

Uncle Obe slowly lowers his lids, then slowly opens them. "You told him right."

"I also suggested revenge might have ruined him as he said it had ruined his father. Though he put in his offer the next day, I'm thinkin' that once what I said settled in, he saw the truth of it."

"And withdrew the offer," Uncle Obe murmurs.

"Hallelujah to that," Daddy says. "Though I do think you're givin' the man too much credit for decency. More'n likely, it was a business decision—he decided the estate wasn't a good investment after all."

I considered the same thing myself, so I can't be too upset with him.

"I remember the Calhoun boys." Uncle Obe stares past my shoulder, as if at a movie screen on which the memory is playing back. "Dirt poor but proud those young uns were. Had a bit of the wild in them, always runnin' around and getting into trouble. Their mama worked all the time, and their daddy... Well, he was around. One day he was sittin' at the counter of Martha's place, looking scrawny as a cat caught in the rain, nothing but a cup of c-c-coffee in front of him. Martha tried to give him a bowl of stew on the house, but her only thanks was that he didn't throw it back at her."

Uncle Obe stares hard at that place over my shoulder. "I knew his family was struggling, same as his daddy and his daddy before, so I took the..." He pats the arm of his chair. "...this thing beside him and offered him a job."

"And he spat on your shoes," Daddy says. "I was there, Obe, and you were supposed to be havin' lunch with me, not dispensing handouts to ungrateful slackers."

Uncle Obe's gaze flies to Daddy, and there is such anger in his eyes that my own seems little more than an appetizer. "Do you recall why you were there, Bartholomew?"

"Not rightly, I don't."

"You needed another loan, though we shouldn't call it a 'loan,' should we?"

Gripping my hands before me, I silently beg my father to blush to prove he isn't more closely related to great-granddaddy, and he does. Still, he splutters, "Regardless, those Calhouns were bad news."

"No, b-broken, is what they were. Like we all are, though some more noticeably than others. But now we Pickwicks have a chance to make things right, and we will."

"What's that supposed to mean?" Daddy is obviously as suspect as I am that Uncle Obe's plans have changed.

"Excuse me," someone says, and I look over my shoulder at Uncle Obe's daughter where she stands in the doorway, a glass in one hand, the fingers of the other closed over something. "It's time for my…er, for…" She sets her jaw. "It's time for my father to take his medicine."

Good for you, cousin.

She steps forward, and the sun slanting through the room lights on her dark hair, drawing out the auburn tint that evidences the red passed on to her by Uncle Obe.

Daddy shifts his weight, and I know he's eager for Daisy to exit so he can get to the bottom of his brother's meaning.

However, after Uncle Obe washes down his medicine, he says, "Won't you stay, Daisy Marie? We're nearly done here."

She looks from Daddy to me. I nod, and her face lightens as she positions herself alongside her father.

"So, Bartholomew?" Uncle Obe prompts.

"How, exactly, do you intend to set things right with the Calhouns?"

Uncle Obe seems to disappear from the room, but eventually he says, "I need to think on it."

Daddy huffs. "But you will sell to Caleb Merriman?"

"I don't know that, though I'll give his offer a look-see when it comes through."

"It came through a little while ago," I say. "But it's not going to work."

"Whyever not?"

"Because the offer is for sixty percent of the asking price, Daddy."

If I didn't witness the depth of my father's startle, I don't know I'd believe his surprise. Then he didn't tell Caleb that Dirk Developers withdrew their offer?

"Sixty percent!" He scratches out the words. "That's all he offered? Why that—"

"Go home, Bartholomew." Uncle Obe reaches for his daughter's hand. "Take care of that sweet wife of yours, and let me handle this."

My daddy's mouth twitches, but he raises a hand and swipes a good-bye.

"I'll walk you to your car," I say.

"Bridget?" Uncle Obe calls as I follow my father.

"Yes?"

Once Daddy is gone from sight, he says, "Anything goin' on between you and this J.C.?"

A lie tempts me, nearly justified as it is by Daisy's watchful gaze, but I say, "Not anymore."

He nods. "Come see me before you and the kids leave. I might have somethin' you can do to help me."

"Something to do with J.C.?"

"Maybe."

I start to protest but say, "I'll drop by before we leave."

I catch my father as he slides into his car and lay a hand on the door to prevent him from closing it. "Did you tell Caleb what you overheard of my conversation with Piper?"

His face puckers with distaste and denial, self-righteous in its intensity.

"Daddy, the truth."

He remains puffed up awhile longer, then sags. "I told him. But I did it for you. I thought he'd make you a good husband, give you the life you deserve, a life like Bonnie's."

Heard that before. Too bad he doesn't understand me well enough to know that would not be a good fit.

"Now," he continues, "I'm not so sure. Can you believe he offered only sixty percent?"

"A lack of real competition will do that. Was there any money involved in helping Caleb secure the estate?"

He stares at the emblem at the center of the steering wheel.

"Daddy?"

"All right, there was to be a little somethin' in it for me for brokerin' the deal."

My shoulders drop. "How much?"

"A hundred thousand dollars."

"A *little* something!"

"But I'm tellin' you, it was with the understanding that I help him obtain the property, not steal it. Sixty percent! Don't know how I'd sleep at night knowin' I had a cheat for a son-in-law."

He doesn't have to worry about that. "Daddy, do you know anything about his plans to turn the estate into an industrial park?"

"'Course not. He said he wanted it as a private residence, and the possibility of you being lady of the manor made the apple that much shinier."

I sigh. "For you and Eve both."

"What?"

"Nothin'." I touch his shoulder. "I appreciate your being straight with me. Tell Mama I'll bring Birdie and Miles by tomorrow."

He pulls the door closed.

Hoping my niece and nephew have reconciled and Uncle Obe won't ask of me something I can't do, I slowly climb the steps of the mansion. Unfortunately when I return to my uncle's room, he is at a complete loss as to what he wanted my help with. Or maybe fortunately.

26

Monday, October 18

This time I told Caleb yes. Not because I mean yes but because J.C. hasn't returned Piper's or Uncle Obe's phone calls. Because if there is going to be a counter to Caleb's insulting offer, there's something the Pickwicks need to know. And it's up to me to determine if the man who tried to bribe my father is slippery in other ways. Unfortunately I believe J.C. is right, and if I'm not stood up—

"I'm pleased you agreed to join me for dinner," a voice stirs my hair, and as I look around, a kiss lands on my cheek.

Be still, my livid heart. I meet the gaze of the man over my shoulder. "Caleb."

Grin as bowed as a quarter moon, he pulls out the chair catty-corner to mine. "Of course, I can't help but hope this will also be a celebratory dinner."

I'm tempted to play dumb, especially in lieu of an apology for him being twenty minutes late, but I'm not sixteen anymore. "Actually, the reason I accepted your dinner invitation was to discuss your offer on the estate."

"Wonderful! Not that I'm not up for enjoying the company of such a lovely lady and"—he lays a hand over mine—"getting to know her better."

Just in case the possibility exists he still needs to exploit my influence with Uncle Obe as he tried to exploit Daddy's influence with me? More than ever, I lean toward the belief he wants the estate for an industrial park, and I resent that I'm here, especially since I could be home with Birdie and Miles. However, they're spending the night with Mama and Daddy, my father having insisted on it though Trinity and Bart were willing as usual. Feeling a pang of loneliness at the prospect of having no one to share the big bed with tonight, I close my eyes.

"What can I get you to drink?"

I open my eyes on the server who has sidled into the space between Caleb and me.

He smiles at her. "I have the feeling we're going to need a wine list."

"No." I pull my hand from beneath his and wrap it around my perspiring glass of ice water. "I'll stick with this."

"Are you sure?"

I incline my head. "Although if I were to order something from the bar, it would be a beer." This time, Daddy's not here.

Caleb blinks, as I intended him to.

Yes, I'm once more dressed up, the restaurant he suggested having called for it, but I still prefer the taste of beer over wine. "Of the nonalcoholic sort."

He ducks his head back. "Nonalcoholic?"

"It's the taste I like, not the dizziness or false feelin' of happiness."

He waves the server away, clasps his hands on the table, and leans forward. "But we're not talking false feeling. Not if you're here to tell me what I hope you are."

Here goes the bluff I've been practicing since I took his call this morning. "I have to disappoint you, Caleb. You see, I don't believe we have anything to celebrate."

Full-fledged frown. "What are you talking about?"

I take a sip of water. "You haven't been straight about your plans for the estate."

I watch him closely for signs of guilt and surprise, but there's nothing to be seen in his eyes or his facial muscles. "Of course I've been straight. I'm looking forward to calling the Pickwick mansion my home."

He seems sincere. Might I be wrong? Did J.C. lie? *Don't let your bluff down.* "Caleb"—I hold his gaze—"I know about your plans to build an industrial park."

This time there is something in his eyes, but it's so fleeting I can't say it's incriminating. "You think I want to turn your heritage into an industrial park? Where'd you come up with that idea?"

I'm starting to feel gullible. "J. C. Dirk told me."

Caleb snorts. "My competition—a man who wanted the estate probably more than I do."

Want*ed*. Not that I need further evidence he knows J.C. withdrew his offer. "True. And for that reason, he brought me written proof." I didn't see it, but that's my fault.

Again, something crosses Caleb's eyes, but after it flits out, it flits back in. With a sigh, he reclines in his chair. "All right, so Dirk dug up my association with investors who are scouting for an industrial-park site." He inclines his head. "It's true."

Still I cling to the frail, barely visible thread of hope tied to both ends of me—that despite the look of things, it's coincidental Caleb is looking for an industrial-park site at the same time he's trying to buy a private residence.

"And, yes, the Pickwick estate is ideal for our purpose."

Good-bye, hope. I sit straighter. "Then you lied."

His gaze slides left, and I follow it to the server, who does an about-face when he once more waves her away. "Let's just say I didn't elaborate on my plans for the estate."

I lean forward. "Now would be a good time."

"Is your family still interested in selling to me?"

I wish I could say no, but J.C. is out of the picture. "Not at the price offered."

He starts to smile. "I'm negotiable—never said I wasn't."

Obviously, he's been practicing at bluffing longer than I have. "So elaborate."

"I do want the mansion for a private residence. It's beautiful, has historic value, and is in decent shape. As I've already said, I can see myself raising a family there."

Just because he can *see* himself doesn't mean he plans to.

"As for the bulk of the property, it is ideal for the development of an industrial park, and it's possible that pieces will be broken off and developed as such."

And there's the truth cloaked in the word *possible*—his way of throwing me a bone. But I would be a fool if I tried to gnaw on it. My nails dig into my palms, throat muscles tighten, nostrils widen. "And manufacturing comes to Pickwick Pike," I say with a hard edge of resentment.

Caleb's lids flicker. "I understand your misgivings, Bridget."

No, he doesn't.

"However, environmental concerns aside, your family needs the money."

Only because the Calhoun heirs have a sizable restitution coming to them. If not for Uncle Obe's determination to see our wrongs righted, time would be on our side, which would allow him to remain undisturbed in his home while he's lucid enough to be comforted by its familiarity. But the estate needs to be liquidated, and all because of that middle piece of land.

I back up my thoughts, the wheels of which reverse over Caleb's words, then shift back into drive. The whole idea to sell the estate in its entirety was based on an assumption. But the assumption may have been wrong. I push my chair back and stand.

Caleb jumps up. "Bridget?"

"I don't believe we'll be in touch."

Irritation distorts his attractive face. "As I said, I'm negotiable."

"Even so, I think I speak for my uncle when I say you'll have to look elsewhere for your industrial park site. Good-bye." I catch the unhinging of his jaw as I turn away. Striding past the other tables, the hem of my skirt flapping at my knees, I put all my hope in having happened on the solution.

Piper thinks it might just fly, but Uncle Obe… It was not a good day for him, according to his daughter and evidenced by his inability to understand the solution I tried to lay out for him. Just when I thought he was tuning in, he tuned out on J. C. Dirk and Caleb Merriman, becoming agitated when I reminded him they were the ones who wanted to buy the estate. He didn't like that one bit, and Daisy had eased him to his feet to help him to his bedroom. He called her by her mother's name as she led him from the library, and he went on and on about selling the estate "over my dead body."

I had hurt for him. And prayed for him when Piper started to cry. For some reason, talking to God for others comes easier than talking to Him for myself. When I mentioned that to my cousin, interrupting the awkward silence that followed my prayer, she said it seemed to her I was a lot further along in my faith than some people.

I don't know about that, but what I do know as I lie here in the dark is what I keep coming back to. J.C. didn't lie. He may be guilty of widow sniffing (some) and his investigation into Caleb's interest in the estate may have been self-serving, but he was telling the truth. As wary as I am of reading too much into what happened between us, I feel it, especially as loneliness reaches out to me from all corners of the bed.

I turn from my back to my side and press a hand to the empty place beside me. It's not so bad. Even the temptation to sleep in the guest room wasn't too hard to resist. And I suppose I have Birdie and Miles to thank for easing me into this. There's still emptiness, but the murkiness has cleared enough that I can see to the bottom of it.

"Thank You, Lord." My voice slides into the night. "Thank You for letting me have my 'happily,' even if not for ever after. Thank You for allowing me to brush my fingertips against Yours, though I know it's my whole hand You're lookin' to hold. And my heart too. Speakin' of hearts…" I sigh. "I think I mislaid a piece of mine in the vicinity of Jesse Calhoun Dirk. Just a little piece, but I'd like it back—that is, if he has no use for it. *Does* he have a use for it?"

I flip to my back again and try to make out the ceiling. "I was too hard on him, said things I shouldn't have. If what was between us was real, and it seemed like it, I've messed up. But I'd like to try and fix it. And I could use some help." I close my eyes. "That's it. For now. So amen."

27

Friday, October 29

This time J.C. is expecting me, though that doesn't necessarily mean getting in to see him will be easier than it was the first time. In fact, my advance warning in the form of a phone call might make it harder if he's set against meeting with me.

Surprisingly, his assistant wasn't as curt as when I last tried to see him. She asked my reason for wanting to meet with him, and when I told her it was regarding the Pickwick estate, she started to place me on hold. Guessing I was about to be put through to J.C., I told her to tell him I would be in Atlanta around noon on Friday and would see him then. I'd hung up and, since no one called back, assumed it was a done deal.

Now as I cross the lobby, noting the business types awaiting their appointments, the same young woman I slipped past months ago looks up from behind the reception desk. She doesn't seem surprised, so she probably knows to expect me. A good sign—unless she has a security guard waiting in the wings. Or she doesn't recognize me.

Far more comfortable this time in a new pair of 501s, a lace-edged cotton top beneath a smart denim jacket, and carrying a courier bag, I halt before the desk. "Bridget Pickwick Buchanan. I'm here to see Mr. Dirk. He's expecting me."

"Actually, his brother Parker Dirk is expecting you."

Not a done deal. I'm a little relieved, a lot disappointed. Still, it's not as if the bulk of what I'm here to do can't be done with J.C.'s brother. As for the rest? If J.C. doesn't want to see me, it's probably for the best. And if I tell myself that enough, maybe I'll believe it.

"If you'll take a seat, I'll let him know you're here."

Five minutes later, the man who fell victim to our bull mastiffs as a boy enters the lobby. "It's good to see you again, Mrs. Buchanan." He advances on me with an outthrust hand and a seemingly genuine smile that makes his eyes behind his glasses crinkle at the corners.

I stand and slide a hand into his. "And you, Mr. Dirk."

He releases me. "I'm sorry my brother couldn't meet with you."

Couldn't or *wouldn't*?

"Hopefully, I'll do."

Though I want to ask why J.C. pushed me on to him, I say, "You'll do fine. How is your brother doin'—I mean, the one who had the stairway collapse out from under him?"

"Dunn. He and the others have recovered and are back at work."

"Glad to hear it."

He glances around the lobby. "I imagine that whatever you'd like to discuss requires privacy."

"I'd appreciate it."

Shortly, he motions me into a chair before a somewhat unkempt desk and settles his slender form behind it. "May I call you Bridget?"

"Certainly. Parker?"

He nods and clasps his hands amid papers scattered across a blotter. "What can I do for you?"

I glance at the scar above his right eyebrow. "You know the story of the poker game between the Pickwicks and the Calhouns."

"Too well. I had hoped that when J.C. returned from North Carolina this last time, we could finally put it to rest."

Meaning Parker was against his brother's quest?

He opens a hand toward me. "But here you are."

"Yes, but I also want to put it to rest. Or, at least, try. It's up to you and your brothers to decide if it's enough."

His forehead creases, causing the crescent-shaped scar to kink. "If what's enough?"

I open the courier bag and pull out a large envelope. "Did J.C. tell you that, for some time now, my uncle has been set on makin' restitution to your family for the loss of your property?"

His head rocks slowly. "He did, but you do realize we have no proof the poker game was rigged. That it could as easily be our great-grandfather's bitterness that set the rumor in motion."

"My uncle is convinced otherwise; the only proof he requires is of his troubled conscience. Thus, he wants to make amends before his dementia is too far along for him to enjoy peace of mind." I pass the envelope to Parker. "As I'm sure you know, the estate has increased considerably in value over the years. Though there are other wrongs my uncle has righted by sellin' off properties and family heirlooms, the wrong done to your family requires a larger outlay than he can access. Since it was believed the Calhoun heirs would be more receptive to monetary compensation than the restoration of their land, the estate was listed for sale in its entirety in the belief it would command the greatest dollar amount." I point to the envelope. "Inside is a proposal that will not only give my uncle peace but allow him to remain in his home for the duration of his illness."

Parker Dirk glances at the envelope.

"Outside of the acreage my uncle has set aside for my inheritance, the Pickwick estate will be divided into four pieces—the original Calhoun acreage, the acreage to the north, and the acreage to the south."

He frowns. "You said four pieces."

"The fourth piece—the smallest—will be cut off from the southernmost acreage, which is the land on which the big house sits. My uncle will retain ownership and continue to reside there. As for the other three pieces, the Calhoun land will be deeded back to your family, who will be given first right of refusal on the other pieces, which will be priced at significantly less than the whole. Since the fourth piece will consist of only twenty-five acres to allow my uncle to maintain his privacy, those three pieces should be enough to build your golf resort if Dirk Developers is still interested. If not"—I shrug—"we'll sell elsewhere, and your family can do with your land as you please." I turn my hands up. "That's it."

Parker sits back. "What of Merriman?"

Of course his brother told him about Caleb. "My uncle has rejected his offer, since it appears Mr. Merriman's primary interest in the estate is as an industrial park. A golf resort is one thing"—I shake my head—"an industrial park, another."

"Good call."

"Regarding the wrong done your family and the hardship generations of Calhouns have endured, I am here to formally apologize on behalf of the Pickwicks."

Parker smiles with what could be sorrow. "Thank you, Bridget."

That's it, then. If the Calhoun heirs decide to add to their property and take up their original plans, they'll be in contact. If not, the land will be sold to another party. I stand. "If you have any questions, my cousin Piper will be happy to answer them."

"Actually, I do have a question, but one only you can answer."

The intensity of his gaze and tilt of his head give me pause. "Yes?"

"Is there something between you and my brother?"

Though my insides jump, I keep my features as immovable as possible. After all, Uncle Obe asked the same thing. "Why?"

"Because I know him, and it would take a stronger longing than that of justice to cause him to abandon the responsibility our father put on him. Even our mother, when she was dying, couldn't completely bring my brother around to letting go of the past."

My center clinches at the news their mother has passed away.

"To his credit, J.C. made an effort, but then your family's estate came up for sale and all that effort was put on hold." Parker spreads his hands. "So I'm asking you what I asked him—what took him longer to deny than it should have. Are the two of you involved?"

I stare at this man whose handsome-enough face resembles his brother's more than I thought the first time I stood before him. "I'm not sure why I feel inclined to answer a question like that, but there did seem to be something between us. However, seein' as J.C. isn't here, I think you can understand why it probably isn't worth discussin'."

"No, I can't. Though I know I shouldn't interfere, I think you and Jesse ought to sit down and talk this out."

Jesse. I can't help but like the sound of J.C.'s given name, nor silently note it better fits the man who kissed me than the man who deceived me. "Unfortunately, I don't think your brother is interested."

He smiles with his teeth, going up a notch on the attractive scale.

I frown. "What?"

"You said, 'unfortunately.'"

"A figure of speech." I turn away. "Now I need to get to the airport." In and out, just like the last time, though this truly is the last time.

I hear the sigh of Parker Dirk's chair as he rises. "I'll see you out."

I step from the office ahead of him, but he draws alongside and I allow him to navigate the hallways. Which is why I don't notice we're going the long way around until something comes into sight that we didn't pass on the way to his office—the conference room where I first *knowingly* encountered J.C. And there he is again, leaning over a portfolio, assistant to his left, two women and a man to his right.

Something weak and wanting unfurls within me, and I ache all the way to my fingers that splay off my jeans, as if to take hold of something.

"I know," Parker says near my ear. "I shouldn't interfere."

I look into his face and only then realize I've halted.

"I thought if he saw you…" He shrugs.

So it's not that J.C. *couldn't* meet with me. He *wouldn't* meet with me. It's good to know for certain. "I believe I can find my own way out." I look one last time at J.C., and in that instant he looks around. And my heart drums. And chill bumps rise on my skin despite the heat rushing beneath it.

"Well, he's seen me," I mutter and turn on my heel. "Good-bye, Parker." Grateful I'm not strapped into heels, I head back the way he led me.

I don't care to have J.C. chase after me like a tights-wearing fairy tale prince clutching at a glass slipper and spouting "happily ever afters." And yet I'm disappointed when I make it to the lobby uninterrupted, into the elevator, and outside onto the sidewalk where late October whispers coolly across my face. Starting to shiver, I wait for an opening in the foot traffic, then hurry out of the building's shadow to the curb where the sunshine tipping past the noon hour warms me.

"Mission accomplished." I scan the slow-moving vehicles caught in the congestion of lunch hour. Though it's four hours until my flight leaves, providing plenty of time to get a bite to eat in the city, I decide to head to the airport. Doubtless, the food won't be as appetizing, but neither is my appetite what it should be considering all I've eaten today is a container of Greek yogurt.

I catch sight of a taxicab and throw a hand up, but as the driver nears, I see his backseat is packed with passengers. Another cab's not far behind. It isn't occupied; however, the driver stares straight ahead as he passes.

"I can give you a ride," says a voice to my right.

I swing around, and his unabbreviated name forms on my lips and carries past them on a sharply hopeful breath. "Jesse."

From beneath the light brown hair on his brow, his eyebrows rise. But his mouth doesn't. "If you prefer."

Now I'm really warm. What's wrong with me? I'm not supposed to be pleased that he came after me. But I am. Still, as I hold his green gaze, I waver between pride that will get me nowhere I want to go and gratitude that will allow me to close this chapter of my life.

"I do prefer Jesse. And, yes, I would appreciate a ride."

"To the airport."

I nod.

A very slight smile. "This feels familiar." He pulls his cell phone from inside his jacket. "I'll call for a car."

He makes the call, and as we stand at the curb waiting, I try not to inhale too deeply of exhaust fumes that are too overwhelming for me to determine whether or not J.C. has gone back to his cologne-wearing ways.

"Did your brother tell you why I'm here?" I finally ask.

"He briefed me when he pulled me out of my meeting."

"You didn't want to see me."

He looks down. "No."

Since that's what I already concluded, it shouldn't hurt.

"I'm afraid Parker thinks he knows better than I do."

"Does he?"

J.C. slides his hands into his pockets. Above the hum and chortle and growl of traffic, the thumps and clicks and scrapes of footfalls behind and to the sides, I catch the jangle of change. "The last time Parker thought he knew better, he took it on himself to supply me with a date to our company Christmas party—a friend of a friend several times removed. It took months to convince the woman I was not flattered by her constant calls and numerous visits to my office."

Then J.C. is as afflicted by good-intentioned kin as I am, though I'd bet my pinkies and little toes Daddy is more of a terror.

"While Parker is determined to remain a bachelor, he seems to think I won't be complete until I settle down."

"And you don't want to?" I don't mean to speak that as a question, but though I catch myself before my voice rises at the end, it comes out that way. And the jangling ceases, only its sudden absence recalling its presence.

J.C. looks past me. "Here's the car." To my surprise, he opens the front passenger door and gestures me inside. Guessing that means he doesn't plan on accompanying me to the airport, I'm once more disappointed. However, a few moments later, the driver steps aside and J.C. takes his place behind the wheel. And he's not wearing cologne.

As he negotiates the traffic sludge, he says, "Let me ask you something."

The depth of his voice warns this isn't just some little *something.* "All right?"

"Did it matter whether it was my brother you met with or me?"

I consider my thumbnail that tempts me to nibble, but I won't. "Not to do what the family sent me to do."

"Then returning the Calhoun land and formally apologizing aren't your only reasons for coming?"

I draw a steadying breath. "I wanted to talk to you about what happened between us before I found out what the *C* stood for."

He cuts a sideways look at me. "Why?"

"I want the truth—to know if it was real. For you." Because, otherwise, I don't dare let it be real for me.

"Yes, I told you it was real. It had nothing to do with your family's land."

Once more, my thumbnail looks mighty tasty. "It did in the beginning when you decided that two—Caleb and you—could play the game."

"True, but let's go back to the very beginning when a dreadlocked, barefooted woman driving a beat-up truck and wearing an impossibly stiff dress practically ran my real estate agent off the road—all over a piece of gum."

Is he making fun of me? I sit straighter. "Had the gum Wesley tossed out her window landed any place other than my windshield, some poor creature could have choked to death."

J.C.'s mouth curves, but he continues to direct his gaze forward as we enter the freeway. "There was something about you I liked, Bridget, but when Wesley told me you were a Pickwick, that was the end of it. Then you showed up here without the dreadlocks and looking like a professional. Again, I was attracted to you—until you identified yourself as a Pickwick and I realized you were the one out on the pike." He looks at me. "I wanted the property, not complications."

"So much for what we want."

He maneuvers the car into another lane. "I knew I was crossing a line I shouldn't when I saw what Merriman was doing to secure the estate."

"Courtin' me."

"Yes, and since I'd already crossed one line, I eventually reasoned it couldn't hurt to cross another."

"What was the first line you crossed?"

"My mother was always after me to let go of the past—said that if I didn't, the quest to reclaim the Calhoun land would ruin me as it had my father. My response was always that I would try. Then a couple of years ago, she got sick. Before she died, she asked me to try harder and get back to God, and I told her I would, though I was never certain I'd gotten to Him in the first place. A month after we buried her, I started attending church and began making the necessary changes to lead the life I thought I owed her."

He glances at the airport exit sign and flicks his turn signal. "But then I got word your uncle was putting the Pickwick estate up for sale, and all those years of resenting your family for making our lives so hard came back to me. That was the first line—going after the Calhoun land as well as the property of those who had taken it from us. I wanted the Pickwicks to know that the trailer trash they'd made of my family had risen above them, so I bent myself toward that end, but with every Pickwick I met, I found myself questioning what I was doing. None of you was as I'd imagined all those years. Well"—his smile is light—"there is your cousin Luc and your father."

I can't fault him for that.

"I was most uncertain about my plans when I was with you. It was as if I'd played a bad joke on myself—reeling in a Pickwick only to find the hook was in *my* mouth. Knowing I was the one who put it there only made it worse, but still I put off what I knew God was calling me to do. And then you found me out. Strangely, I still felt somewhat justified with what I'd done, which is why I offered on the estate."

"Why did you withdraw your offer?"

After a long moment, he says, "I couldn't stop thinking about what you said—your uncle wanting to make restitution to our family all along. I realized I was the one visiting the sins of the father on the children." He looks my way. "You said the quest for taking back my family's property may have ruined me as it ruined my father. There was too much truth in that, and it seemed the best way to get out from under the Calhoun curse was to walk away."

After a long pause, he says, "Do you know how hard it is to be right with God when you aren't right with people? When you can't forgive as you should? When you're holding the past tighter than it's holding you? When you think you're better at being God than God Himself?"

I don't believe he expects me to answer, but when I don't, the silence stretches. "I know," I say. "I haven't been right with God since He took…" No, He didn't *take*, though like Uncle Obe I believe my great-grandfather *did* take. "Well, not since He didn't answer Easton's prayers for healing. And like you, I've been holding on to the past beyond the time I should have let it go."

"What about forgiveness?"

"That's why I'm here, not only to return your family's land and offer to sell the other pieces should you decide to build your golf resort, but to ask for your family's forgiveness, for yours, and to extend mine to you, Jesse."

He draws a long, slow breath. "I don't need an apology. Our differences are in the past where they should have been left long ago. But I do thank you for accepting my apology." He peers past me. "Which airline?"

Oh. I hold myself in as I tell him, and he doesn't resume our conversation.

"Here you are." He eases the car into the drop-off lane.

That's it? Pride makes me reach for the door handle, but determination makes me turn to J.C. "I didn't think I was ready for anything with you to be real, but"—I try to smile—"it was real for me too, Jesse."

He looks momentarily away. "I'm sorry about that."

Not what I was hoping to hear. "Why?"

He starts to say something but shakes his head.

Then what was real for him was only real for that moment in time? Ah, there's the little piece of my heart I mislaid. And this is "the end"— no Little Golden Book riding off into the sunset for me. I open the door.

His hand on my arm stops me from stepping out, and I look around. "Nearly everything significant I've done in my life was to get me to where I've been these past months, and it was the wrong place. Do you understand, Bridget? I have a ways to go to get where I should have been all this time."

From playing the role in which his father cast him to being simply Jesse. "I understand. I have a ways to go too. I was just thinking maybe we could get there together." I lean in and press my mouth to his. "Bye, Jesse."

He loosens his hold on my arm, and I step onto the sidewalk, then lean down to peer at him. "As soon as the estate is legally divided, Piper will be in touch. If you decide to purchase the other two pieces, she'll take care of you."

He nods.

I close the door and don't look back. After all, I have a lot to look forward to now that I'm walking lighter with the shedding of the last of my widow's weeds. Jesse Calhoun may not be the one on whom to reset my heart, but that doesn't mean I'll grow old alone. Still...

28

Saturday, November 6

At least the dress isn't poufy, and it certainly isn't stand-alone stiff like the one I wore to Bart and Trinity's wedding. And I do like the color, a soft green about the shade of the underside of a dogwood leaf. It's also a nice length, and the bodice fits decent enough—

I did it again, drifted away from this beautiful day beneath which Piper and Axel are speaking their wedding vows.

I return my attention to where they stand three feet away at the front of the gazebo, Piper pixie-pretty in a simple white gown with elbow-length sleeves and touches of lace.

"...for better, for worse," my cousin speaks back to her dashing Axel, "for richer, for poorer, in sickness and in health, to love and to cherish, till death do us part..."

When Axel earlier spoke those vows, I first drifted away, but not to turn morose over my parting from Easton. Rather, to thank God I didn't feel those words like a thousand aches as I had four months ago at my brother's wedding. I've truly put off my widow's weeds, and even Bonnie, who returned from the Ukraine yesterday and whose lap was covered in Birdie when last I glanced over my shoulder, noticed. And took credit for it. I'm good with that. Now if I could just put off my longing for the man who has a long way to go—without me.

"I give you this ring," Axel says, "as an eternal symbol of my love and commitment to you." As he slides it onto Piper's finger, I look down at my own against the pale green skirt and lift it at the wrist. My ring finger is now tanned beyond recognition.

Maggie gives my arm a bump from where she stands beside me in a matching dress. I frown, and she nods over her shoulder.

My gaze falls first on Uncle Obe, where he went to sit between Piper's mother and Daisy after giving away the bride. The wedding is an even smaller affair than Bart and Trinity's, so it requires little effort to pick out the newcomer in our midst.

Oh, Lord, he came.

I stare at him where he stands behind the rows of chairs, looking stiffly out of place. Daisy said he would come, but he didn't. And yet, here he is, albeit late.

"By the power vested in me by the state of North Carolina—"

I share a smile with Maggie and Devyn.

"—I now pronounce you husband and wife. You may kiss the bride."

And do they kiss—so long, I wonder if Maggie might want to cover Devyn's eyes. When the kiss ends, the minister presents them as Mr. and Mrs. Smith, just like, once upon a time, he presented Easton and me as Mr. and Mrs. Buchanan.

But I refuse to allow the memory to hurt me. I have no right—and no longer any reason—to reduce it to pain. For too short a time, I had something beautiful, and for too long a time, I made it ugly with anger, resentment, and fear. *Better to have never loved at all than to have loved and lost* is how I've been living, turning Tennyson's words on their head.

Though I don't know when, or even *if*, I'll get my faith around God being my happily ever after, I do know it does no good to turn my back on Him when I don't get my way (honorable and right as my way may seem). He was meant to be first in my life, but in bestowing that place on Easton and blaming God for my loss, I set myself up for four long, lonely years of widow's weeds. Whether or not I'll get another chance at the kind of love that leads to marriage vows, I have no idea, but if I do, I hope my heart will hold fast to what it's learned.

I come back to applause and turn with Maggie and Devyn as the newly married couple step from beneath the gazebo and start down the aisle. The guests are on their feet, and as we near the front row, I step to the side and touch my uncle's shoulder. "He's here, Uncle Obe," I say, loud enough for Daisy to hear. "Antonio's here."

The smile he wears for Piper and Axel slips into blankness, out of which confusion rises. "Who?"

"Your son, Daddy," Daisy says.

He blinks. "An-Antonio?"

"Yes, he is."

As I hurry to catch up with Maggie and Devyn, I congratulate myself on the relative ease with which I do so. Of course, it helps that the heels I'm wearing are of a sensible height—well, as heels go.

The reception that follows is different from Bart and Trinity's in that I don't feel suffocated. And neither do I feel the need to escape, though even if I wanted to steal away with Birdie and Miles for a "happily ever after" reading in the library, I doubt they'd be willing accomplices. Nor would Bonnie or Claude let me. They've been glued to their children since their return. In fact, Claude even budged from my parents' back porch this morning to join Miles and me in a game of touch football. Admittedly he was all thumbs—make that *toes*—but he tried.

"So…" A cake-faced Birdie in tow, Bonnie sidles up to me where I lean against a Bradford pear tree that still sports a scattering of brilliant leaves. "…another cousin."

I've been keeping an eye on him too, and so far things appear to be going well—with help from Daisy, who sits between her brother and father at a table on the edge of the gathering. "Antonio," I say.

"Pretty good-looking if you discount the nose—hawkish, don't you think?"

"Like Uncle Obe's."

"I'm tired." Birdie reaches to her mother. "Pick me up."

"Magic word," I say. Oops. It's no longer my place.

Birdie sighs. "Please."

"Why, isn't that polite." Raising her eyebrows at me, Bonnie lifts her daughter and kisses her forehead. Once Birdie settles on her shoulder, my sister returns her attention to Uncle Obe. "I'm happy his prayers were answered."

They certainly were. As were my prayers for their reconciliation. *Thank You, Lord.*

Bonnie sighs. "His dementia is getting bad, isn't it?"

"Good days, bad days, though the bad ones are on the rise."

"Sad. But at least Mama's lookin' good." She points her chin at where our parents lean toward each other over a small table.

"She's doin' well with her diet. More, I think, Daddy's doing well with her."

"He needed the scare."

God turning bad into good.

"You look well too, Bridget—better than I've seen you in years."

"Her heart's not constipated anymore." Birdie peers at her mother from beneath her lashes. "And I taught her how to say happily…ever… after weal good."

"Did you?" Bonnie fights a smile. "Hmm." Her gaze slides to me. "It sounds like you fixed your aunt Bridge right up."

"She's gonna miss us."

My sister looks doubtful, but I nod. "I hope you'll get out this way more often, Birdie. I'll be sore lonely without you."

"I know." She closes her eyes.

"Speaking of lonely…" Bonnie whispers. "Who's this J.C. character with whom you were sitting in a tree, k-i-s-s-i-n-g?"

Miles has been talking, but now is not the time to tell the story, though maybe when Bonnie and her family return for Maggie's wedding at the end of the month. "He's not here anymore."

"Okay?"

I shrug. "He might come back, but I don't know." My nose tingles. "What I do know is…I'd like him to come back."

She beams. "Then you really are ready."

"I'm gettin' there, and I have you to thank for putting me on the hook when I made Birdie cry."

She wrinkles her pert nose. "That's what little sisters are for."

I open my eyes wide. "Really? And what are big sisters for?"

She pats her daughter's back. "Being great aunts."

I hug her over Birdie, and I know everything will work out. One way or another.

He did *not* do that. Oh yes, he did—flew right past me, though it's not as if I'm slowpoking it on Pickwick Pike. Doesn't the fool know how dangerous these curves can be?

I glare at the back of his head, though little is visible beyond the headrest. He—or *she,* if she likes very short hair—needs a talking-to. And I just might do it, bridesmaid dress and all, if I didn't have to put the pedal to the metal to overtake him. Even if Ford were up to the task, it isn't worth the risk to life and limb.

"Go on, then," I mutter as the car disappears around a curve ahead. "And consider yourself lucky."

But that's not the last I see of the car. When I hit the straightaway a minute later, there it is, straddling the two lanes, brake lights lit. What is he doing? Trying to pull what I pulled on that Wesley woman and…

"Jesse." As I brake twenty feet back from the car, the driver's door swings open, and a man steps out. I'd know him anywhere, even with the sunglasses he removes as he walks toward me, even without the jangling.

The autumn breeze goes in one window and out the other, freeing more of my hair from the soft upsweep Maggie pinned this morning.

J.C. sets his forearms on the ledge beneath my rolled-down window and looks from my face to the soft green dress. "Reverse déjà vu." His gaze returns to my face with a smile.

I drop my hands from the big steering wheel. "Why?"

"To ask if you still want to get there with me—where we both need to go."

I doubt I could ever count the number of hairs that stand up all over my body. "Really?"

"Really."

"Even though I'm a Pickwick to your Calhoun?"

His face turns serious. "I made it matter, but it doesn't. What matters is you, Bridget. I want to know you beyond the mess I made of us." He reaches through and gently tugs at one of many loose hanks of hair.

I moisten my lips. "What about the estate?"

He inclines his head. "Your proposal is good, and we want to go forward with the purchase. But that's separate from what's between us."

My heart has the thuds again. "All right—as long as you don't turn it into an industrial park."

"I think you'll approve."

When his hand grazes my jaw, I turn my mouth into it and say against his palm, "I'm glad you came, Jesse."

"I hoped you would be." He pulls his hand back, and when he opens the door, his gaze goes to my feet. "Barefoot too."

I wiggle my toes. "Wonderfully so." Then I slide into his arms, and we kiss right there on Pickwick Pike. And it feels…right.

When J.C. lifts his head, I know my out-of-practice lips will evidence where he's been. Not that I care. "It wasn't coincidence that you found me on the pike, was it?"

"No, I stopped by the nursery, and Taggart told me about your cousin's wedding. I sat in the car for two hours, waiting for your truck to pull out of the estate."

"I didn't see you."

"Obviously, I had plenty of time to get creative about how to approach you."

"Reenactment."

He grins. "More like redo."

I laugh. "So how are we goin' to do this, you living in Atlanta and me here?"

"That's where Parker comes in. I'm taking time off to get where I need to be, and I thought I'd do it here."

Where I am. "And when you get where you need to be?"

"If where I need to be and want to be are the same, there will be commuting involved. Of course, it will help that I'll have a development to oversee right here in Pickwick. And that could take years."

Years… I settle my head beneath his chin and listen to his heart beat near mine. So *this* is what happens *after* ever after. "I like you, Jesse Emerson Dirk. I really like you—maybe more than like you."

"I feel the same." He holds me tighter, and I can't imagine being anywhere but here.

"Gol!"

Well, not *here,* in the middle of Pickwick Pike. And certainly not in front of my brother and sister-in-law.

J.C. and I turn to face the car that has pulled up behind my truck, and I wince as Bart grins at me from behind the windshield and Trinity pops her head out the window.

"Look-it there, your sister has herself a beau, Bart. Can you believe it? 'Bout time." She waves. "Don't let us interrupt."

J.C. looks down at me. "I think we'd better. Dinner?"

I nod. "This time I won't cancel."

"Promise?"

I lift my hands, lay my ringless, bandage-less fingers on either side of his face, and touch my lips to his. "Promise."

First comes love, then comes marriage,
then comes baby in a baby carriage!

Please join us on Friday, April 22 at 6:00 p.m.
to celebrate the blessed arrival
of Trinity and Bart Pickwick's
bouncing baby boy at the home
of Bridget Pickwick Buchanan
1 Little Pickwick Pike
Pickwick, North Carolina

Mr. & Mrs. Bartholomew Pickwick
request the honor of your presence
at the marriage of their daughter
Bridget Pickwick Buchanan
to
Jesse Emerson Dirk
Saturday, the tenth day of September
at two o'clock in the afternoon
The Pickwick Mansion
1001 Pickwick Pike
Pickwick, North Carolina

Readers Guide

1. Due to the death of her husband, Bridget has a problem with reading aloud the conclusion to all good, romantically minded fairy tales: "And they lived happily ever after." Are there words or memories or activities from which you distance yourself in order to avoid dealing with pain? What action might you take to air the pain and move on?

2. Bridget's sister believes grief is contagious. What do you think? Do you believe Bonnie did the right thing in confronting Bridget and demanding she rid herself of her widow's weeds?

3. Bridget is environmentally conscious, as evidenced by the steps she takes to lessen her impact on the environment and her reaction to others who litter and waste. What steps have you taken to be a good steward of God's creation?

4. In this third and final book in the Southern Discomfort series, readers continue to witness the path of dementia as Uncle Obe's memory and ability to care for himself further deteriorate. How have his experiences and those of his caretakers impacted your understanding of this painfully debilitating disease?

5. Why do you think Uncle Obe is able to recite Scripture "without stumbling" and yet struggles with the names of everyday items?

6. When Uncle Obe asks Bridget to pray for him, she grudgingly agrees despite her attempt to keep God on the other side of the door. Have you ever been asked to pray for someone though you didn't feel moved to do so? Did you pray? If so, how did it feel?

7. For a while, Bridget is the primary caregiver of her niece and nephew. In accepting this responsibility, she also has to accept the task of disciplining the children. Have you had to be a stand-in parent? How did you deal with the issue of discipline?

8. Bridget's assumption that J.C. inherited his wealth is based mostly on appearances. When have your assumptions about others proven wrong? On what did you base those assumptions? How could you have better acquainted yourself with the person?

9. Bridget's mother takes ill, causing Bridget to confront God and ask if He intends to take her mother from her as He took her husband. Though Bridget finds herself in a narrow place on the journey back to faith, she resists the temptation to jump off and instead draws nearer to God. Have you ever found yourself in such a narrow place? Were you able to stay the course? If so, what was God's answer, and how did you deal with it? If not, where are you now in your relationship with God?

10. When J.C. belatedly reveals his deception, the rift that opens between Bridget and him has the potential to destroy their feelings for each other. What situation have you been in that you believe would have benefitted from the truth being revealed earlier? How might it have turned out better?

What does it take to truly make amends?

Public relations consultant Piper Wick wants to persuade Uncle Obadiah not to change his will and humiliate the entire family. Her tenuous relationship with Congressman Grant Spangler depends on it! But her uncle's rugged, blue-eyed gardner has her thinking instead about what it means to make amend—and to forgive.

She's changed, but can she make him see it?

Maggie Pickwick is a lifetime away from her days as head cheerleader and the mistakes she made in high school. Twelve years later, this single mom has traded pompoms for an aucioneer's gavel, popularity for peace and quiet, and strives to be a good example for her daughter, Devyn. She's keeping it together just fine, too—until an old flame moves back to her little North Carolina town.

Read an excerpt at www.WaterBrookMultnomah.com

Girls you can relate to

Maizy Grace Stewart needs a second job to Help pay bills as she seeks her dream job as an investigative journalist. But Steeple Side only hires committed Christians. Can she fake her way, or will British hottie, Jack Prentiss, her managing editor, prove her a fraud?

Kate Meadows is a successful San Francisco artist looking for a nice, solid Christian man. When two handsome bachelors enter her orbit, she has to decide what she's willing to change—and who exactly is she trying to please?

Harriet Bisset used to be a rebel. Join Harri on the spiritual journey of a preacher's kid turned rebel turned legalistic Christian who discovers the joy of trusting in God's security—and having fun along the way.